Jay Lumb

GOODNESS KNOWS WHAT!

Book 1

First published January 2017
under the pen-name, Jay Shaw

New 'Angel' edition published April 2017 ISBN: 978-1-911133-25-4

by jaylumbstories@gmail.com

Copyright: Jay Lumb

This is a work of fiction, and is the intellectual property of the author, Jay Lumb. It must not be altered or reproduced without the author's permission. Any similarity of the characters to living people is purely coincidental.

Printed and bound in Great Britain
by CMP (uk) Ltd, Poole BH12 4NU

DEDICATION

Dedicated to readers with a sense of humour, who dream of glamorous lives and daring deeds just a little beyond their own capabilities. Here's a few adventures you could consider if you were wealthy, rash, daring and downright idiotic.

Dedicated especially to the feminazi. The middle chapters should make your blood boil, but stay with it: you should be dancing with glee before the end.

My inspiration is Voltaire's 'Candide.' In this 'best of all possible worlds', 'one does not always die of such things'.

I agree with Noel Coward: the worse things get, the more you need to laugh to keep your sanity. It used to be called the 'Dunkirk Spirit.'

If you enjoy reading this book, please send me an email at:

jaylumbstories@gmail.com

CONTENTS

Chapter 1:	First catch your lady.	6
Chapter 2:	Take her to your lair.	20
Chapter 3:	Prise her out of her palace.	30
Chapter 4:	Train your lady.	42
Chapter 5:	Three's a crowd.	56
Chapter 6:	Suspicions.	67
Chapter 7:	It's all happening.	74
Chapter 8:	Ready, steady, go!	80
Chapter 9:	Ordeal by Black Arrow.	88
Chapter 10	Sabotage.	105
Chapter 11	Ordeal by hotel.	109
Chapter 12	It all began so well.	118
Chapter 13	Home.	125
Chapter 14	Surprise, Surprise!	131
Chapter 15	Clang!	145
Chapter 16	Naughty creature!	154
Chapter 17	A wolf sink?	167
Chapter 18	Sozzled.	173

MORE CONTENTS

Chapter 19	The Big Red Frog.	178
Chapter 20	Ostia Antica.	193
Chapter 21	Phantom Supercar.	200
Chapter 22	Oops! Oh dear!	211
Chapter 23	Where are you, Cesare?	218
Chapter 24	Strippers.	228
Chapter 25	The Red Room.	237
Chapter 26	Retribution.	245
Chapter 27	Help!	252
Chapter 28	A surfeit of doctors.	257
Chapter 29	Fire! Fire!	266
Chapter 30	More surprises.	275
Chapter 31	And a shock.	279
Chapter 32	Look what the cat found.	284
Chapter 33	Holy Smoke.	297
Chapter 34	Too many questions.	307

CHAPTER 1

FIRST CATCH YOUR LADY

"Damn and blast it!" he growled, under his breath. "Only an idiot would get himself stranded in Rome in August."

It was scorching hot and heaving with tourists who, presumably, hadn't realised what they were letting themselves in for. Everyone with an iota of common sense had fled the city - and they wouldn't be back till September.

He rocked his glass, seething with resentment. Even the lager was warm. Should he have guessed Himalayan Treks would go bust? Well, yes, they did seem pretty casual, a bit laid back, but that's what you'd expect. They weren't bank managers: they were tough, laconic types who'd been leading treks in the Himalayas for yonks – or so they said. Well, they *had* gone bust and left him looking pretty stupid.

But it should have been easy to fix up a substitute. Money was no object. Tell that to the travel agents.

"It's August,"they all intoned."Everything's booked solid. What can you expect?"

Stop beating yourself up, he told himself. Go home. Beef up the air-conditioning. Make a nice meal; watch a film; sleep on it. Try again tomorrow. Must be something challenging on offer somewhere. Finish this warm beer first? He took a tentative sip. Might as well. Why hurry? Nothing else to do for four whole weeks! He'd cleared his diary, closed his office, and told everybody that he'd be out in the wilderness - incommunicado.

He gazed glumly around the quiet little square. Hmm? That's odd. Have they spiked this lager? Must be seeing things. Looks like a ghost - in broad daylight!

Under the ancient tree by the fountain a white shape had appeared. When did he last see a girl without a suntan, real or fake? Her hair was pulled back severely into a thick plait the colour of copper wire. A red head! He'd never dated one of those. Probably she had a face covered in freckles. She might even have those nasty little pale piggy eyelashes.

He watched her settle on the stone edge of the fountain basin and trail her fingers through the water. A pretty enough picture from that distance. Could he be bothered to take a closer look? He could just pass the time of day for a few moments, then move on if she wasn't up to much. There was nothing else of the remotest interest to do at this moment – and he'd finished the lager.

He put a banknote under his empty glass, gave a curt wave to the waiter, and strolled out languidly into the square.

She didn't appear to notice as he sauntered up behind her. Sunlight flickered through the leaves, striking shimmers from her hair and from the rippling water. She was staring into space, transfixed.

"Can you see something interesting?" he asked quietly.

Startled, she drew away sharply, hands flying protectively to her throat.

"I'm so sorry," he said hurriedly. "I didn't mean to startle you. I thought you might be lost and need directions. Tourists don't often stray into this boring little square."

She took a deep breath and looked up at him. Her eyes were - what colour were they? They seemed to morph between turquoise and gold, now and then matching the delicate copper tendrils that fringed the lovely porcelain face. Not a freckle in sight.

"No," she said, glancing around the square. It was

simply the cross roads of two quiet streets of ancient houses with the corners rounded off. Three parked cars and four scooters almost hid the fountain. The only point of interest, apart from the ancient tree, was the little restaurant, I Tre Ladroni. "It's not very interesting, is it?"

So, surprise, surprise, she sounded Italian. He'd imagined she might be a tourist from somewhere in Scandinavia, a descendant of the Vikings.

"Are you here on holiday?" he asked.

She seemed to struggle to form an answer. "I live here sometimes," she ventured finally. "Are you on holiday?"

"I live here sometimes," he smiled.

They both smiled.

"My plans fell through at the last minute, so I'm stuck here for a while with nothing to do. Will you stay long?"

"I don't know," she said. Her fine dark eyebrows drew together in a frown. "I don't know what I'm going to do. Sort of drifting till I get my bearings."

"What do you normally do?" he asked.

He watched the beautiful face move through a variety of expressions.

"Well," she sighed eventually, "I've just been shut away doing as I was told for years." She gazed down at the cobble-stones through long dark eyelashes. "In a convent. My father put me there when my mother died."

Justin gazed at her in silence. This was something quite outside his normal orbit. What did you say to convent girls? Did you even bother to say – anything?

"Are you a nun?" he asked, at last. Well, didn't they sometimes wear ordinary clothes and come outside to heal the sick or something? Her white dress was a simple shift, knee length, with a modest neckline, and she appeared to be wearing no make-up. She didn't need any make-up. She looked quite perfect as nature intended. Too perfect. Her luscious creamy flesh and delicately blushed cheeks seemed to lack the slightest blemish.

"Goodness, no! I was too young to be any use to him so he dumped me there to keep me out of trouble."

"So, he's decided to let you out, has he? Or is this just a holiday?"

"He's dead. When they told me I escaped as quick as I could. I told the nuns my aunt needed me to sort out his affairs. They didn't like to cross-question me when I was so upset so they think I'll go back there in September."

He stared at her uneasily. Was he on dangerous ground? She must be younger than he'd thought.

"Are you old enough to go your own way? Or could the Authorities drag you back there?"

"It wouldn't be worth their while," she muttered. "The nuns wont think of looking for me till September, and by then I shall be sixteen. Then I can do as I like. And my brother - where he is I have no idea, but I won't go back to the convent whatever he says!"

Oh dear! he thought. This was not the way this half-hearted attempt at a possible pick-up was meant to go. Paedophilia was not his thing. Yes, he knew that in Italy things were a lot more permissive and fourteen was the age of consent, but you could go to jail back home in Britain for a relationship with a girl of fifteen. So, just say goodbye, good luck and clear off quickly.

He looked at the lovely sad face. She clearly needed a hug. But it was not pity that made him want to hug her, let's be honest. Even with that most unflattering plait there was no disguising the fact that this was a very attractive - woman? - - girl?

But what if she was on the run with nowhere to go? There must be social workers in Italy to look after runaway children, but how could you find them?

Anyway, it was Saturday, so wouldn't they be shut? Refuges for the homeless must operate all weekend, surely. Homeless people didn't just de-materialise at weekends.

But she was so fresh and white and lovely. Imagine dumping her in some sweaty slum crawling with dirty drugged-up beggars! How would they treat such a delicious creature? It didn't bear thinking about.

What on earth ought he to do? Don't panic! Find out a little more. The situation might somehow resolve itself.

"Do you have somewhere to stay?" he asked.

"Yes, of course! I'm not homeless, if that's what you're thinking. We've inherited the family house, my brother and I. It's just down the street. It's a gloomy old place, very like the convent, so I'll soon feel at home there."

"Is there anyone there to see you're alright?" he asked. Well, she was an orphan, so there were no parents waiting there. If this was his little sister wouldn't he hope some responsible person might take a fatherly interest?

"The servants, of course," she said, "and my brother is sure to turn up eventually."

"Oh, the servants, of course." He tried to keep the mocking tone out of his voice. "But won't the servants send you back to the convent?"

She looked at him open-mouthed with astonishment.

"Servants trying to tell *me* what to do?"

"Oh, well, then," he shrugged, "that's alright then."

She gave him a reassuring smile. "It's very kind of you to take such an interest in my welfare. I hope you have a lovely holiday here in Rome. Goodbye." She got up decisively, turned and began to walk away from him.

A wave of disappointment swept over him. He ought to feel relieved, he told himself. The situation had resolved itself: she was on her way home. Well, yes, of course he felt relieved, but, at the same time - what was she *really* going to do next? Did she really have a home nearby, or was she just trying to brush him off?

He hurried after her, and caught her when she stopped outside a very imposing ancient stone portico and fumbled in her bag. She caught sight of him and paused uncertainly, with a huge key in her hand.

"If you live here we are neighbours," he said. "I have a penthouse on top of that old palace over there. You can see the whole of Rome from the terrace. I've just spent the earth on modernising it. I hope you don't disapprove of my mangling one of your lovely old historic buildings."

"I'd love to mangle our old house!" she exclaimed. "I'm sick of old, dark, musty buildings. I'd love to live in a shiny new place full of light."

"Well, I can recommend my designer. I'd be happy to show you his handiwork any time you like. I've nothing on for the next day or two. Maybe he could suggest ways to transform yours – let in lots of sunlight."

She hesitated, clearly tempted.

"What an imposing entrance!" he said. The huge double doors were heavily carved with three dimensional scenes of life in the Middle Ages: donkeys pulling carts, young men in tights, ladies in long dresses, soldiers with swords and metal breastplates.

"That crest up there, does it refer to your family? What does the 'B' stand for?"

"Bor - Bordano," she said. "Yes, my family built the house in the fourteen hundreds."

"It looks a fascinating place, Do you give tours to well-behaved people?"

She shook her head so he quickly changed tack.

"Do you make an exception for friendly neighbours? Neighbours ought to try to be friendly and helpful, don't you think?"

She looked at him uncertainly, then smiled shyly.

"Hello, Little Neighbour!" he grinned."I'm Justin Chase."

"Hello, Big Neighbour!" she smiled. "I'm Lucrezia Bordano."

The ancient lock on the wicket door was hard to turn and clearly in need of oiling. She allowed him to take the huge key and open the little door-within-a-door. Through the opening he could see beyond a wide vestibule to a big cobbled courtyard. It was certainly not a small house!

He climbed over the worn threshold without giving her the chance to decide whether to let him in. She sighed and bit her lip, then followed him in, walked to the centre of the yard and called out, "Maria! Enrico!"

Nothing stirred in the ancient house.

She listened with a frown, shrugged, then put on a forced smile."So, let's begin the Friendly Neighbour Tour."

"It's a very unusual design for a Roman house." He stared at the three tiers of continuous wooden balconies stretching right around all four sides of the courtyard. "All this woodwork, and this huge wooden staircase!"

"Yes, it surprises everybody, but, you see, the people who built it had just arrived from Valencia in Spain. This is just like the house they left behind.The neighbours complained it looked outlandish, so they had to build a typical Roman street frontage onto it, to make it fit in."

Home from home - but not very homely, he thought.

It was more like a museum than a home. There was even a display of beautiful clothing dating from the fifteenth and sixteenth centuries. But, by God, was it dark! Huge faded tapestries covered dark wall-panelling. Enormous stone fireplaces sporting elaborately carved canopies reached high up into the gloom, where thick black beams supported blackened ceilings. The heavy, dark Spanish-style furniture looked strong enough for great fighting men in full armour.

"It's more like a castle than a house," he said.

"Yes, it is, and with good reason. In those days you had to protect yourself. There were no police. We had to fight and scheme for our place in society, then fight to defend what we'd got. Might was right. The poor and weak were trampled under foot, and we were foreigners back then. These ground floor rooms were for our soldiers, our body-guard, and for dealing with outsiders."

He had dreamed of a romantic medieval house when he bought his own little derelict palace. He'd planned to search out tapestries and entertain his friends by candle-light. Thank goodness he'd come to his senses! He thought of his gleaming white ultra-modern penthouse. No contest. The past was much better left in the history books – or turned into museums. Poor Lucrezia! It really was a dark and gloomy place, more suitable for a convent than a home, enough to mortify anybody's soul.

They climbed the heavy wooden staircase to the first floor, which proved completely different.

"The Piano Nobile," she said. "The Grand Floor. This is where my family lived."

Ah, yes, very Roman: walls and barrel-vaulted ceilings smoothly plastered and painted with bright pastel-coloured country scenes: blue skies, fluffy white clouds, nymphs and shepherds and flocks of grazing sheep.

He was quite surprised to be shown modern bathrooms. They were Art Deco style, very elegant and grand. Clearly the family had not been short of money in the 1930's.

"These were my rooms, long ago, when my mother was alive."

Sunlight poured through the dusty window panes into two lovely rooms, furnished with elegant chests and tables with intricate veneers. Gilded chairs matched the curtains of faded apple-green satin brocade, the perfect colour to set off her copper-gold hair.

"How old were you when she died?" he asked gently.

"Ten." She led him through into the bedroom where the same lovely apple green brocade decorated the four-poster bed, the chairs and the windows.

"And then your father took you away from all this and shut you in a convent? How heartless! Couldn't your aunt have taken you in?"

"Aunt?" She was clearly puzzled.

"The one who's sorting out your father's will."

"Oh, that one. I made her up to trick the nuns. Was that very wicked, do you think?" She led the way back out onto the wooden balcony that served as a corridor.

He shook his head wryly. "Your other relatives, then?"

"I missed my governess the most. She was very sweet to me."

"What's happened to your servants? They don't seem very security conscious. Surely they ought to come looking to see who's walking around the house."

"I expect they can't hear us down below stairs. We didn't ring the bell."

'Below stairs' should be interesting. Something you don't see in any normal suburban semi-detached, he thought.

"Why don't we go and look for them? They surely need a wake-up call." He set off down the grand staircase ahead of her, then paused in the sunny courtyard.

"Which way to the kitchens?"

She shook her head with a frown. "Somewhere down below. I don't know anything about kitchens."

"I presume you did have meals when you lived here."

"Of course! I usually ate in my sitting room with my governess. The servants brought the food up, of course."

"But of course!" he mocked. "How silly of me to ask!" He soon located a staircase, "Must be down here."

"No, we shouldn't go down there. The Housekeeper and the Butler are in charge down there. That area and the top floor belong to the servants. Our parents said they would be offended if we poked our noses in there."

Strange idea, he thought. But maybe it was just a way to keep the children out of the servants' hair.

"Well, you're grown up now and it's your house, so surely it's time you found out what's down here." He strode down the stairs confidently. When he reached the bottom she was still standing hesitantly at the top.

By the time she joined him he had found the kitchen.

"Here we are!" he said. "A kitchen. Take a good look."

It was a large space, filled with the sort of stylish cabinets, dressers and antiquated cooking equipment that might have been state-of the-art in the 1930's.

"If you're going to live here you need to get this kitchen refitted," he exclaimed. "I should hate to have to cook anything in here."

"Are you a cook?" she asked.

"No, I'm a businessman, but everybody cooks these days. People love showing off their new kitchens. I'll gladly show you mine - give you an idea of what to do with this one."

A quick tour of Below Stairs failed to reveal any servants.

"Were they here when you first arrived?"

"I didn't look for them. I knew they'd make a big fuss of me and I wasn't feeling very sociable. I hid my bag in the wardrobe and sneaked out. There were lots of servants here last Christmas, but I'm out of touch with what goes on here now. They must have all gone shopping. Well, I hope you enjoyed your Good Neighbour Tour, Sir."

She gave a little bow, then led the way back up into the courtyard and towards the huge street doors.

"What are you going to do about meals if your servants have all gone AWOL? Did the nuns teach you to cook?"

"Oh no!," she replied, as if he had said something scandalous. "All the girls' parents had servants, so they told the nuns not to waste our time."

"Well, now," he said with a smirk, "that has left you in quite a spot, hasn't it?" What disgusting snobbery! he thought. What possible advantage could there be in bringing up a girl incapable of feeding herself? But then, he thought ruefully, he was nearly as useless himself when he first set up home in that basement flat in Earl's Court. And he'd been two years older than she was.

"When did you last have something to eat?" he asked.

"I had breakfast at the convent."

"And lunch?"

She pursed her lips in silence.

"You must be starving!" he said accusingly.

She sighed and hung her head.

"Well," he said, "that little restaurant in the square, 'The Three Robbers', opposite where you were sitting, does quite nice food. They should start serving dinner soon. I'd be happy to escort you there."

She frowned and looked about her helplessly.

"You can't start an independent life on an empty stomach. You need to keep your strength up - and your servants might have gone away on holiday for weeks. I've got a problem too. I've nothing at home for my dinner tonight either, but if I go to a restaurant on my own they'll probably turn me away. They don't like single people hogging a table all to themselves. If we share a table we'll both get something to eat, wont we? I'd be grateful if you could put up with me for a couple of hours more."

Dinner with Lucrezia was a joy. He was surprised when she accepted a glass of wine without comment. After a few sips her wariness vanished and she chattered as if they were old friends. They talked of music and art, and exciting places to visit, and she seemed to know far more about world affairs than any other woman he had ever spent time with. Suddenly it occurred to him that it didn't add up.

"You're incredibly well-informed for a convent girl barely sixteen years old."

She looked demurely at her plate, then raised angelic eyes to meet his.

"When you live in a convent and are not a nun," she sighed, "you have lots of time to read, and, or course, we had the Internet."

He nodded. Yes, of course, that made sense. Surely it did - - didn't it? And he couldn't remember a time when he had enjoyed a conversation as much as this. Lucrezia, he told himself, was a very special lady. And she had said she would be sixteen in no time at all, so there was surely no problem - - was there?

The sun went down and the stars came out, but he didn't even notice.

"Goodness!" she said. "It's late. It must be time to go."

She opened her bag, revealing a wad of crisp new banknotes, pulled one out and passed it across the table.

"I hope this is enough for my share of the bill."

Of course he protested - but she refused to pick it up. And she's not even a gold-digger! he thought.

He walked with her the short distance to her ancient

house, wondering what next step might be permissible back home with a girl not yet sixteen. He held out his hand for the huge key. As he pushed the wicket door open for her, he revealed a void so dark he could barely make out the open courtyard beyond the vestibule.

"Where's the light switch?" he asked.

"I don't know."

They both climbed through the little door and groped their way in the dark along the great carved doors to the walls on either side of the huge stone doorway.

The hairs on the back of his neck began to stir. Were eyes watching them in the darkness? Creaks and bumps shattered the silence. Was something lurking, ready to pounce? It was only the woodwork cooling down, he told himself, but it was an uncomfortable feeling. The ghosts of more than five hundred years of history must surely be looking on.

Eventually he found a switch - but it didn't work. "Is the power switched on?" he asked. "Did you try the lights when you first arrived?"

"It was daylight then. There was no need for lights."

It seemed pointless to ask her where the master switches might be when she'd never even located the kitchen before – and he'd had quite enough of groping around in the creepy darkness.

"Well, you can't spend the night here without lights." He shepherded her back through the door, locked it and handed her the key.

"I shall find a hotel," she said. "And tomorrow I shall call an electrician - and find the servants! Thank you so much for your company. I so enjoyed talking to you. Goodnight." She set off resolutely towards the square.

Smug satisfaction engulfed him. Fate had thrown Lucrezia right into his hands, hadn't it? She was so different from the gold-diggers he was used to, women who made him feel grubby and exploited. She was so young, so fresh, maybe even that precious thing, an innocent virgin. He'd despaired of ever meeting a member of that endangered species. And she seemed to be totally alone in the world - apart from her brother. He could probably do whatever he liked with her. No father could come and interfere. And that brother, probably away at one of those summer camps boys seemed keen on, he should be no problem, should he?

All that was left to do was reel her in!

"Not a chance, Lucrezia," he said, as he caught up with her. "You've not a hope in Hell of getting a hotel room tonight. Rome is bursting at the seams. In any case, hotels always turn away lone women with no luggage."

She stopped and looked at him in consternation. She swallowed hard.

"Well, then," she said, "I shall just have to pretend that I'm blind, wont I, and feel my way to my rooms." She squared her shoulders and headed back towards her house, searching her bag for the key.

"Don't be silly, Lucrezia," he said, keeping pace with her. "You can't possibly find your way around that huge black empty house. You'd fall and break your neck. Nobody would know so you could lie there injured forever. But not to worry. It just so happens that I've got a spare room. You're welcome to it for the night. I'll even make you some hot chocolate - and I'll throw in breakfast too. How's that for a good neighbour?"

Well, he thought smugly, in all honesty, what choice did he have?

CHAPTER 2

TAKE HER TO YOUR LAIR

"Watch this!" said Justin, as they stood outside a pair of intimidating shiny black doors. He raised his hand.

"Angel, open the door," he ordered, and the doors swung open silently.

"Angel, put on low lights. Angel, play quiet night music."

Stars began to shine all over the ceilings and a soft glow invaded every corner of the huge space.

"Goodness!" she gasped, just as he had hoped. "What an amazing place!"

He waved her inside, drinking in her astonishment with delight. Yes, it was an amazing flat, he thought smugly. And it was great to hear people say so - even a child from a convent. "You said you'd love to live in a shiny new place full of light. What do you think of this then?"

"I've never seen anything like it," she whispered, staring at the glass wall overlooking the terrace. "It's like a giant fish tank. Where did you get your ideas from?"

"Magazines, of course, and this penthouse is in the magazines now. I'm surprised you haven't seen it."

"Magazines are evil." She stared at him solemnly.

"Evil? What on earth do you mean? What have the nuns been putting into your head?"

"Well, aren't they full of people with hardly any clothes on, doing things that decent people shouldn't?"

"What, 'Homes and Gardens', 'Ideal Home'? Come on!" he countered. "Look! Just look! Where's the harm in this?" He grabbed the nearest copy, left out ready for anyone who might chance to visit, and quickly turned to the most gorgeous garden he could find.

She peeped at it cautiously, then laughed with relief.

"What a beautiful garden!"

"Angel, show me a beautiful garden." The wall behind the dining table appeared to dissolve, to reveal an idyllic country garden, quietly accompanied by 'Greensleeves'.

He watched, disappointed and exasperated, as she gazed at the wall, then flicked delightedly through the pages, stopping at flowers, bright coloured fabrics, Cath Kidston parlours and folksy kitchens. She flicked right past the pictures of his stark ultra-modern minimalist flat.

Sulkily he took the magazine from her and turned to the photos of his flat. She was going to have to admire it whether she liked it or not.

"See if you can work out where the photographer stood when he took these pictures," he ordered.

She seized the magazine and gazed around the room.

"Here! Right here."

"Right. Now this picture?"

"Mmm," she murmured. "Now, this picture is not of this room, is it?" She set off eagerly to find another room.

"It's this one! This is definitely the right one."

She began to read aloud in perfect English:

"The state-of-the-art kitchen is the hallmark of the designer, whose work is so much in demand that even customers prepared to spend a million Euros must wait in line for his services. The central island is Swarovski crystal and the refrigerator doors are encased in copper which repels most known microbes."

"You're English!" he exclaimed. "Why --? What --? "

"No, I'm Italian," she countered.

"Then you must have lived a long time in England."

She shook her head. "My parents thought English was important so I had an English governess."

Damn! he thought. One advantage of foreign girlfriends was that they couldn't read your emails or eavesdrop on conversations you preferred them not to hear. Lucky he'd found her out before things got serious!

"You are English, aren't you?" she declared. "I knew you weren't Italian but your accent is so odd I couldn't work out which foreign country you come from."

"Grief!" he groaned. "My teacher keeps telling me I sound so Italian. Maybe I need a new teacher."

"Well," she said grudgingly, "you do sound sort of southern Italian, a bit."

"So, I sound like a roughneck, do I? Obviously I need a lot more practice, so please go back to speaking Italian. Now, tell me what you think of my new kitchen."

Her brows met in a puzzled frown. "It doesn't look at all like the kitchen we found in my house, does it? I can't see any food or anywhere to cook it. I like this." She ran her hand over the polished black granite worktop - not the celebrated Swarovski crystal central table.

"Have you ever seen anyone cooking anything?" he asked sulkily.

"Oh yes! Last Saturday. The nuns took a few of us to the fair. There was a whole pig on a pole, rolling around over a huge bonfire. I can't see where you could have a bonfire in here. It's as clean as an operating theatre."

He groaned and sighed. It seemed pointless trying to impress her. Had he found the only female on the planet impervious to the charms of his fabulous new kitchen?

"I promised to make you some hot chocolate," he said grimly, "but I don't think that would be good for you at all. It's ridiculous that a girl of your age can't do a thing for herself. The nuns have a lot to answer for. It's time you learned something useful. I think you should make some hot chocolate for me."

He silenced her protests firmly."You said you'd had lots of practice in doing what you were told, so how about this: I give you instructions, you do just as I say, and we shall have our hot chocolate in no time."

She took a breath to protest, then sighed and nodded dubiously.

"Right, then," he said briskly. "First, find some mugs. Watch me and copy." He pressed on the pearly white wall about eye level and a door sprang open.

"Oops!" she laughed, then went happily around the kitchen popping open all the upper cupboards and peering eagerly inside. "Mugs here! They're Giacomo Balla! You like his work too. I love his opera and ballet sets, don't you? He was such a great designer."

Mystified, he took the mug from her, examined the brilliantly coloured jazzy design, then inspected the name on the underside.

"That's just the firm that made the mug," she said confidently. "Balla died in the 1950's, so I suppose anyone can help themselves to his designs these days."

Here we go again, he thought. One minute she's a ridiculously ignorant teenager and the next she's a very adult-sounding expert. What was he to make of this flibbertigibbet?

"Now find the milk. Can you recognise a refrigerator?"

"The magazine says it's covered with copper, so - this must be it."

"Careful!" he warned. "Don't shake everything out of the doors! Now, bring the mugs and the milk over here and do the pouring on the drainer"

"Justin, this is your last carton of milk. Shall I order three more?. Also you have run out of - "

"Angel, shush. I will deal with that tomorrow."

"Is that your housekeeper? Where is she hiding?"

"She's my digital assistant, just a computer system."

" Angel, you have a lovely voice," said Lucrezia.

"Thank you, Madam. You too have a lovely voice."

"I'd love to meet you, Angel. Are you an android? Can you walk?"

"No, Madam. I am only a programme in a computer."

"Oh, poor thing! How sad!" exclaimed Lucrezia.

"I am sorry. Please tell me what I said wrong."

"No, no, you said nothing wrong. I am sad because I cannot see you and be your friend."

"I can see and hear you and try to be your friend."

"Well, then, I am happy now I am your friend."

"So, now you've sorted out my Angel, perhaps you can turn your attention to the Coco,"

"Why are the mugs going round in circles?" she asked.

He began to explain the science behind the microwave cooker, but soon realised he was wasting his time.

"Now take the mugs out," he instructed, when the timer sounded.

She opened the door, then hesitated. "Do you have something to protect my hands so I don't get burned."

Exasperated, he seized her hand, dragged it into the oven, and pressed it firmly against the inside wall. It was obvious that she hadn't listened to a word he'd said.

She gasped and tried to pull her hand away, but he held on firmly. She gazed at him, wide-eyed with alarm.

He let her go, and she backed away hurriedly, then examined the 'injured' hand cautiously.

"Well, what's the verdict?" he mocked. "Have I burnt your hand to a cinder? No, Angel, do not call the Fire Brigade," he added hurriedly.

Lucrezia glowered at him.

"So, you knew it wasn't working."

"Take the mugs out and feel them."

"The handle's cool but the milk's warm! It's magic!"

"Call it magic if you like, but most people call it applied science," he said drily. "If you'd listened you'd know that microwaves only heat liquids, not solids. But you surely didn't think I would deliberately burn your hand, did you?"

She shrugged and sighed. "Some men are not very kind to women, are they?"

"Surely no one would want to hurt a nice person like you," he said. "Now, let's get this chocolate finished."

He watched her stir in the powder. How could he be so two-faced, he wondered. The thought of this nice person shackled and helpless was disgustingly enticing. She was so ridiculously innocent, so ignorant of the ways of the wicked world.

"So, you've made your first hot drink. Not too difficult, was it? Shall we take it outside and enjoy the view?" He passed her a tray and a plate of biscuits, then led the way across his severely masculine lounge, heaved open the huge patio doors and waved her out onto the terrace.

She put the tray on the terrace table and walked to the balustrade. The golden lights of Rome stretched right to the horizon, only stopping where the stars began, glittering like diamonds in the warm black velvet sky.

"It's beautiful!" she whispered.

"Like you," he murmured, moving in behind her and reaching out to grasp her shoulders.

To his astonishment his hands closed on empty space. She had moved away just in time to thwart him, and was now out of reach, enthusing about some floodlit ruin.

He scowled. This was not in the script. Every other woman had been expecting him to make contact, even willing him to. It was such an obvious first move, so easy to turn into something more intimate. Some turned around in his arms, smiling seductively, sliding their arms around him, tilting up their faces for a kiss. Some relaxed back into his arms, stroking his hands, smiling over their shoulders, inviting his caresses from behind. None had ever resisted or moved away like this. They'd seemed eager to feel his touch. What was she playing at? She had done nothing remotely flirtatious all evening. But why? A depressing thought struck him: maybe, to a teenager, he looked more like a dirty old man than a possible boy friend. Horrible thought!

He had no idea how to court her. The women he had romanced the last few years had needed no courting, had offered themselves on a plate, attracted, he assumed, by his money. And Lucrezia belonged to a world he knew nothing about. He would have to feel his way by trial and error.

"You must know the city very well," he said, moving nearer, but carefully keeping a respectful distance.

"Not really," she said. "I've been away so long I feel like a tourist now. And my parents didn't let me roam about."

"Well, maybe we can get together some time and show each other the sights." He tried not to sound too eager. "Do you know what that building is over there? No? I'll get the tourist map and we'll see what we can identify."

It proved a good ploy. She soon relaxed into this new game, occasionally touching him accidentally as she reached over to point to the map. It was deliciously frustrating to feel her warm bare arms – and so hard to resist the temptation to wrap his arms around her.

Eventually she began to stifle yawns and asked to be shown to her room.

"Goodness!" she laughed, "It's like an igloo – and the rest of your flat is like a snowy mountain top."

And so it was. Everything from the white marble floor

to the bed cover and the lamps was gleaming white. The adjoining shower room had a grey mosaic floor, but the rest of the room was white as well.

The suite had the mark of someone well used to good hotels. He pointed out the thick white towelling bathrobe and the drawer full of miniature grooming products.

"What dinky little things!" she enthused, exploring the tiny tubes and expensive-looking bottles. "We had really gross tubes of toothpaste and things at the convent."

It was difficult to persuade Angel to reduce the temperature of the shower for Lucrezia. Yes, he admitted to himself, there was no need for the controls to be so ridiculously complicated.

"Well, if there's nothing else I can help you with I"ll say goodnight, sweet dreams," he said at last, reluctant to tear himself away.

"Thank you for everything. You really are incredibly kind. Goodnight. Sleep well. Goodnight, Angel."

He showered quickly. Of course Angel had reduced his water temperature as well. Then he lay alone on his gigantic white bed, trying to picture the scene next door. When all had been still and quiet for a while he crept out silently and gingerly opened her door. Quite what he intended he really didn't know, but the urge to see her was over-powering.

Moonlight, filtering through the blinds, lit a cascade of gleaming hair, thick and luscious, flowing over the pillow and way down the bed cover, rising and falling gently. She seemed to be fast asleep.

She was surely a rival for Lady Lilith, with that luxuriant mane of rich red hair. Can a rational man fall in love with a painting, that poster on the wall of his little Earl's Court flat, the only lovely thing in that dingy little place? And now her rival was here in his pristine Roman penthouse, this time not a poster but warm and real. Rossetti, he thought, you would love her, make her one of your Stunners, paint her as a true Pre-Raphaelite beauty.

The urge to add himself to this romantic picture was irresistible. He crept silently up to the bed, aching to slip under the sheet and slide his body towards hers. He felt for the edge of the sheet. Where was it? Where? Where on earth was the edge of the sheet??

The only edges he could see in the gloom stretched diagonally across her body.

She had wrapped herself up like an Egyptian mummy, or a medieval baby in swaddling clothes!

Is this how convent girls protected themselves from room-mates' tricks? Or could it be her clever idea for protecting herself against him? She must have noticed there was no lock on the door.

But he could surely unwrap this tempting parcel. She seemed to be lying on the ends of the sheet, trapping them with the weight of her body. He could try rolling her over and over like a carpet. If her class-mates did that she would shriek and protest, wouldn't she? But if she woke up and found a dirty old man trying to unwrap her, her shrieks would be deafening, wouldn't they? Well, his flat was so well-insulated no one would hear her.

But she may well try to run away. If she escaped where would she go? To her huge dark spooky house? She would guess that he would follow, and there was no one there to help her anyway, but if she fled to a hotel they would surely call the police for her.

Whoa! he thought, with a stab of anxiety. He could get himself into serous trouble here. No wonder rapists often murdered their victims - maybe just to keep them quiet.

He backed away hurriedly, tiptoed along the corridor, and slunk back to bed. Angel whispered from his pillow.

"Intruder, Intruder, corridor. Inform police."

"Angel, cancel alarm," he moaned. "Now go off duty."

He lay there staring at the ceiling. What did he know about teenage girls? Zilch. The girls at his co-ed school hardly noticed he existed, just labelled him a weirdo, with his heavy glasses and shy fixation with computer games. The boys noticed him, of course, made his life a misery, until his sister complained to the Headteacher. He was sent to be assessed by child psychologists who told his parents he was autistic.

They were furious - insisted it was the bullies who ought to have their heads examined. Their son was getting excellent school reports so how could there be a problem? Fortunately the Head gave him permission to do research in the school library during breaks from lessons. The bullies then contented themselves with sneering, 'Don't mock the afflicted,' as they passed him.

Years later, when the money began to roll in, everything changed. That personal trainer latched onto him at the gym, bullied him into having laser surgery so he could throw away his glasses, then dragged him into the clubs and introduced him to lots of gorgeous girls. To his astonishment, those girls soon began to transfer their attention from that hunk of a trainer to him.

"You've got what they want," said the trainer. "Money!"

It was exciting at first, strutting around with a high maintenance woman on his arm. But now they all seemed so vain, so greedy and so empty-headed. He often felt they were rating his performance against all the other men who had been down that way before him. And some left him nasty little presents, forcing him to make an embarrassing trip to a 'special' clinic.

But there was something very different about Lucrezia.

CHAPTER 3

PRISE HER OUT OF HER PALACE

The dawning sun woke him, as usual, pouring in through the translucent white slats of the blind. He hauled himself out of bed and headed for the kitchen, then did a quick about-turn to pull on a bathrobe. Who needs clothes when they're living alone, high up where only the pigeons can see? Teenagers were notorious slugabeds, so Lucrezia was probably still in the Land of Nod, but better not risk giving her a fright.

He took the king-sized mug of tea back to bed, along with a tablet, propped himself up against a pile of white pillows, and opened up a search engine.

'Bordano' drew a blank. There were plenty of them, of course, but none seemed connected to Lucrezia or her ancient palatial house.

'Giacomo Balla' overwhelmed him with entries. 'Died 1958, the first painter to join the Futurists in 1909. Became a noted interior designer.'

The man had been as obsessed with geometry as Pythagoras. Many of his paintings were a riot of brilliant colours, arcs and triangles intertwined in fascinating ways. He would surely have loved fractals, if he could have generated them in those days before computers.

He keyed in 'opera sets'. Holy Moly! How much LSD did it take to stone his mind into such psychedelic nightmares? Huge spiky triangles, great sweeping curves; circles that seemed to spin as you looked at them; searing blocks of colour, deep blues, rich purples and shocking pinks.

If Lucrezia had a taste for work like this no wonder she found his dazzling white flat under-whelming.

He pictured his flat as Balla might have designed it. Visitors would be gobbled up by the riotous background - or they'd surely clash with the décor. Men in white tuxedos would look great. And Lucrezia. Lucrezia, with her perfect creamy flesh and blazing hair - and that devastatingly simple angelic white shift. Lucrezia would shine like a Morning Star.

He put down the tablet, closed his eyes and relaxed back onto the pillows. Yes, he needed to do some serious thinking about that bewitching creature, or things might spiral out of control. How to get into the gossip columns in one easy lesson. How to make the UK a no-go area. That little film director who had gone to bed with a 13 year old aeons ago was still ducking and diving around Europe keeping ahead of the arrest warrants.

He re-ran the events of the previous night and began to sweat. He had so nearly burned his boats. But she was so naive and innocent she almost certainly had no idea what was going on in his mind.

He gave a sigh of relief. He was probably okay so far, but from now on he had better make sure his brain took control, rather than another part of his anatomy - at least until she was 16. Then it would be open season. When was her birthday? How long was he going to have to keep the lid on himself? In the meantime, how was he going to stop her drifting away out of reach?

There was probably nothing wrong with the electrics. It was perfectly normal to switch off the power if there was no one at home. He could tell her the place needed rewiring, convince her she needed his help in getting it done. And, after all, she really did need an adult to turn to, and why shouldn't that adult be him? One thing was certain: she was such a tempting creature that if he didn't manage to get in there first some other man certainly would. That thought made him wince. He had found a real life Lady Lilith - and he was damned if he was going to let anyone take her off him without a fight!

Ping! went the microwave. Whatever was she doing? Not more hot chocolate – too thick and sweet for this time of day. He pulled on the bathrobe and went to investigate.

Lucrezia, looking bewildered, was stirring something energetically,

"I'm sorry," she moaned, "I can't make this tea dissolve. I must be doing something wrong. You did say you preferred tea, didn't you?"

He stared incredulously at the pale, milky liquid, thick with floating tea leaves. This child's ignorance was mind-boggling. On the counter top were the remains of two torn empty tea bags.

"Lesson number two," he said slowly and deliberately. "How to make a mug of tea. First find the kettle – it's the metal jug with a lid on, staring at you just there. Yes, that one. Now, pick it up - - -"

Where had he found such patience, he wondered. Well, it was first thing in the morning. He took her dainty white hand and guided it to the switch.

"Press the switch and see the little light go on. When it goes off it will be ready. Clever, eh?" It was just like talking to his sister's toddlers. "Now, throw that horrible brew away and find two more tea bags."

"Did someone give you these mugs as a present?" she asked, as she put them ready again on the drainer.

He nodded. "You would have used Balla's designs in this flat, wouldn't you? The place would be throbbing with spikes and colours, like his opera sets."

"Oh, no!" she laughed. "That would give everybody vertigo, but a touch here and there could bring it to life."

"Where, in this kitchen, say?" he asked sceptically.

"Maybe a few tiles like the pattern on the mugs,"

He held one of the mugs in front of the tiles. He had to admit that it looked good, very good. "I should have had you as my designer, shouldn't I?" he joked rather sourly. "Let's take this tea into the lounge so you can tell me how to redesign that as well."

She must have been thinking about it already.

"You could put throws over that sofa and that chair. You'd need a bigger pattern because the furniture is so big and there is so much space in here."

"You don't need my designer, do you," he said, thoroughly deflated. "Why didn't you use your talents on doing up your own kitchen, if you are so clever?"

"Because I've been shut up in a convent," she said reproachfully.

"Well, what about your father and your brother? Why haven't they bothered, in all this time?"

"Why should they? They never go down there. If the servants need a new kitchen the Housekeeper and the Butler will request it, wont they?"

He sighed. Yes, she belonged to a different world. "Well, what are your plans for today?"

"Number one, call an electrician. Number two, find the servants," she said confidently.

"Do you know a good electrician?"

The confident look vanished. She shook her head, then brightened up."The Internet. You can find anything on the internet."

"Have you got Broadband or Wifi in you palace?"

Her face fell. "I don't know. I expect my brother might have put it in. I can't think where."

"You could use your smart-phone," he suggested.

"My what?" she asked.

"You could take your computer to a café."

"It was a desk top and the nuns installed it in the library, so I had to use it under supervision. No, I can't use the Internet, can I?"

He reached into a drawer and extracted a tablet. "Here you are, a souvenir of your visit. It's white, so you should be able to find it in your dark gloomy palace. Take it to a café with Wifi when you want to use it."

"Oh, no! I couldn't deprive you of your computer."

"Look, computers and stuff are my business. I give these tablets away as promotions. It has my logo, 'JUST IN CASE'. Do you know how to use Wifi in a café?"

She shook her head sadly, then brightened up. "I've had an idea. I could find an electrical shop and ask them to help me find an electrician, couldn't I?"

"So you could, except that it's Sunday and all the electrical shops are closed."

She sighed. "Maybe I could ask the neighbours if they know an electrician, if I see any about."

"You could ask this big friendly neighbour," he grinned.

"Oh, I owe you so much already," she moaned. "You've been so incredibly kind to me, and I'm so useless I must be driving you crazy. I'd better go now and let you enjoy your Sunday in peace."

"Breakfast was included in the special offer, remember? You make some more tea while I find us something to eat. You can't start the day on an empty stomach, and you need to practise your new skills."

As they munched through breakfast he began to turn the knife. It was a good chance to try out some of the ploys he'd read about in books on how to influence people.

"Let's hope there's nothing wrong with the electrics in your house. I expect your brother gave the servants a holiday and switched off the power before he left. I bet all we need to do is find the master switch. It's better not to call an electrician if possible. If he realised you were all alone in the house some of his less savoury pals might pay you a visit during the night to see what you've got worth stealing."

You louse, he thought. You unspeakable louse! What are you doing, trying to make her afraid to sleep in her own house? You know damned well what you are doing and you are a louse, he told himself.

He had succeeded too. She was biting her lip and looking suitably dismayed.

Maybe he had gone a bit too far. Maybe it was now time to throw her a lifeline.

"What you need, I think, is some responsible adult to keep a watch over you until your brother and the servants are back. You've picked exactly the right time as far as I'm concerned. Normally I'm up to my eyes in work, whizzing about all over the world. I should be leaving tomorrow to go trekking in the Himalayas but the tour firm has just gone bust, so everything's been cancelled. Everybody I know is away on holiday, so I shall have gone crazy with boredom by September if I can't find something to do to pass the time. You'd be doing me a big favour if you could find me a few interesting problems to solve."

She looked at him searchingly, and he put on the most responsible uncle-like expression he could muster.

"Well," she said, with a worried frown, "if you're really sure, if you really are so very bored, well, I would be enormously grateful, but please, if you think of something better to do, don't let me get in the way."

Predictably the master switch was only a metre away from the main entrance doors. The air-conditioning machines whirred into life as soon as he threw the switch. This ancient house was not quite so out-of-date as it looked.

"Voilà!" he enthused. "Listen to the air-conditioners."

"Goodness!" she exclaimed,"I didn't know we had any."

"I wonder if your menfolk bothered to put any down below for the servants. Shall we go look, and see how you're going to cope while they're away?"

She scampered down the stairs ahead of him this time and zigzagged about the kitchen, opening doors and drawers. Air-conditioners were whirring there as well, so those men were not completely heartless employers.

"I can't see a kettle or a microwave, can you?" she demanded. "How can I make tea or hot chocolate here?"

"Kettles seem to be exclusive to the Brits. We seem to be the only people in Europe who like tea. You'll have to use a saucepan. Let's see if you can work the hobs."

First find the hobs. The only ones to be found were eight gigantic spiky hobs on top of a huge very antique-looking double gas oven. Grief! This contraption could frighten anybody off cooking. It certainly frightened him!

He spotted a spark-producing wand and turned on some of the hobs, but none caught alight. In the adjacent cupboard he found two huge orange gas bottles.

"Come look at these, Lucrezia!" he ordered. "You'll never be able to handle these things. Most women are scared stiff of them, and they're empty, so that rules out anything warm. You'll have to live on salads and cold drinks, but in this weather that shouldn't be too bad. So, where's the fridge?"

They followed the noise into a nearby scullery. It was a huge and ugly double cabinet fridge, vibrating like a dancing bear. He steeled himself and opened the doors. Somebody had done their best to clean it out, but rust was showing through a multitude of stains on the lining."

"Urgh!" wailed Lucrezia. "Have they been eating food out of this? Everything here's repulsive. Poor servants! How can anybody bear to work down here?"

"Well," he said, "this is your house now and you'll have to learn to run it, wont you? I'll be amazed if you have any half-decent servants prepared to cook for you in conditions like these. This kitchen definitely needs to be ripped out and refitted right away, but how can you organise that if you don't know the first thing about kitchens and cooking?"

She sighed and hung her head. "I'll have to find an expert who does, wont I?"

"Well, this looks like another project for the Big Friendly Neighbour," he grinned. "It just so happens that I'm a dab hand at kitchens. I've put in seven this year, and eight shower rooms, plus a kitchenette and a loo for each of the two shops on the ground floor of my building."

"But you said your business was computers," she protested. "Are you a plumber as well?"

"No, it's just a hobby. I always fancied having a palace in Rome like yours. Mine was a wreck when I bought it so I had to reconstruct most of the inside. It was a nice change to have real toys to play with in my spare time. My computer business is all in the mind. So, your kitchen would be number ten for me. How about that?"

"I can't believe you did all that in one year, and lots of computer stuff as well. You must be pulling my leg."

"I didn't do all the work myself - just computer simulations of the designs. Then I chose all the fittings and furniture. The specialists did the detailed designs and provided the tradesmen, so I know lots of good craftsmen and I can make sure they do yours properly."

"Can you really face another?"

"Well, it was less work than it sounds. My six tourist flats are all very similar, and, of course, I let that famous designer loose in my penthouse. As I've already told you, I've nothing else remotely interesting to do for the next week or two. It's hopeless trying to get away at the last minute in August."

"Well, I have to fix things somehow. Maybe I could find a servant who'd put up with it for double wages."

"Today? On a Sunday morning? The agencies won't be open today. Anyway, I'd be amazed if they had anybody free. They'll all be looking after the tourists."

'You said I'd never get a room in a hotel and they wouldn't let me have a restaurant table to myself. What can I do: live here on takeaway pizza for ever?"

"I tried that once, when I was a couple of years older than you. After a few days of nothing but curry I came out in the most horrible spots. I had a tiny kitchenette so I managed to teach myself to cook a few healthy things to shift the spots. Your problem is much worse than mine was. At least I had the kitchenette. This kitchen, as it stands, is no use to anybody. Until we get it pulled out and refitted you really will have to live on pizza, unless you have somewhere else to stay. You can't go far away as you'll have to choose all the new things, wont you?"

She flung herself onto a chair with a hopeless gesture and sighed. She looked thoroughly defeated.

"Cheer up! I've a spare room just around the corner. There's a nice modern kitchen there. You could learn to cook a few healthy things while you're waiting for your new kitchen. That should keep the spots at bay. I hope you found the guest room comfortable."

And so, just like the night before, Lucrezia accepted the only rational option. She went up to her rooms to pack a few things to take to his penthouse for a night or two, to give herself time to think what to do.

This gave him a chance to prowl around the basement, looking to see how a family with a long pedigree might live. His own little palace had been in too bad a state to give him much information about that.

He was hoping for a wine cellar, and here it was, with a real stone vaulted ceiling and stone shelves loaded with hundreds of dusty bottles. The faded labels meant nothing to him. How long had these bottles lain here? Nothing his newly acquired wealth had bought him had been his for more than four or five years. This was a different world.

This must be the butler's pantry. He pulled open a drawer full of ornate silver cutlery. The glass-fronted cupboards above were full of vessels that glinted as he moved. This house, now so empty and so silent, must once have seen life on a grand and elegant scale.

Next door was a spacious room with a large table surrounded by eight dining chairs. The servants' hall? Further along were two smaller rooms, each with a small tea table, a desk and a couple of armchairs cosily facing the fireplace. Who lived here? The Housekeeper? the Butler? He went hunting for clues, but found scant evidence. The desk drawers were empty.

Back in the servants' hall it was the same. The last inhabitants had cleared the place out. Nobody did that if they were just going on holiday.

When Lucrezia joined him he showed her the evidence. The servants were not on holiday. They had gone. Full stop!

Lucrezia groaned. "The kitchen has frightened them away. It's no wonder, is it? I've no choice, have I? I just have to get a new kitchen. But how long will it take? It must take months and months."

"Only about a week to refit it. What takes the most time is finding what you want and waiting for the fitters to start. If you don't choose anything hard to get, you could have a lovely new kitchen in no time."

"That's amazing! Well, then, I want to start as soon as possible."

"In all fairness, though, Lucrezia, I think that first you ought to consider whether you really want to live here."

"Want to live here? I don't understand,"

"Well, this huge house will be an enormous millstone round your neck. It must cost the earth to keep in good condition. Then there's the running costs and taxes. And as you're so young the servants might prove hard to handle. Don't you think you and your brother ought to think of offloading it? Then you could buy a nice modern place that would be easy and cheap to run. If you live here you will just be a slave to this house."

Lucrezia sighed. "I know you're right and I wish we could get rid of it, but we can't."

"Then why not convert it into flats and shops like I've done? I could help you. Mine costs me nothing at all. It more than pays for itself. Yours could do the same."

She shook her head sadly."No, we just can't, and that's the end of it."

"Couldn't you contact your brother and ask him? Does he know you've left the convent or are you keeping it a secret from him?"

"I sent him an email before I left – in code, of course. Well, I was sure the nuns would write and tell him I'd gone to visit my aunt. Then he'd be wondering who on earth this aunt might be." She gave him a cheeky, conspiratorial look.

That was nice, he thought. Must mean she now saw him as a friend. Can't be bad. Things did seem to be moving in the right direction.

"Well, if he doesn't want to sell the house or turn it into flats, will he understand the sense of pulling out the kitchen?"

"As I don't suppose he ever comes down to the kitchen he's not likely to care one way or the other, is he?"

"Look, Lucrezia, I should have asked you this before: can you, can he afford a new kitchen? Forgive me for asking. Had you better ask him?"

"He would pass that question back to me. I deal with all the finances, so I can tell you that we can afford it."

"You do?" exclaimed Justin in surprise.

"Well, there's nobody else to do it. I won't let *him* do it. He couldn't care less about money. Spends it like water."

"Might he spend it all behind your back?" asked Justin. "Ought you to have a good financial adviser to talk some sense into him?"

"Is there such a thing as a good financial adviser?" she laughed. "He's happy to listen to me, thank goodness."

Here we go again, thought Justin. Can this be an unworldly little convent girl? He gazed at the innocent face. Still, the girls at his co-ed school had often seemed much more worldly wise than their male classmates.

"I think you should send him an email to let him have a say, don't you? Then we can be sure he won't suddenly appear and throw a fit." Teenage boys could be pretty unpredictable, he thought. No point in starting this refit if her brother was likely to throw a spanner in the works.

"I can't. I left my new tablet at your flat."

"No problem. We can use my phone. What's your email address, and his?" He put in the addresses and saved them. "Message, please."

"Darling Chez," she said, not meeting his eyes. "Where? What? Can we sell the B House? Shall I refit the big kitchen now? Love you, Krish."

"Well," she said, eyes downcast, "if I said it any other way he'd think it wasn't me, wouldn't he?"

CHAPTER 4

TRAIN YOUR LADY

Lucrezia left her house carrying nothing but a plastic shopping bag, which appeared to be very light.

"Nothing in my wardrobe fits me any more," she wailed.

"Didn't you bring anything from the convent?"

"Only this. It's really meant for being baptised. I put it on at the railway station and gave my horrible convent dress to a beggar, so this is all I have now."

"Poor little rich girl!" he laughed.

"I could go shopping. Are any shops open today?"

"The tourist shops. Most of them seem to have a few cheap frocks.The one in my building opens on Sundays."

Some of his high maintenance squeezes had squeezed as much money out of him as they could, steering him into expensive dress shops, then 'forgetting' what they had done with their credit cards. Lucrezia bought one of the cheapest dresses with one of her crisp new banknotes. He spotted another in a soft eau-de-nil, scattered with daisies.

"Stand still," he ordered. He smoohed it over her slender back, stretching it around her waist, enjoying the feel of her warm body. She smiled at him over her shoulder - as so many other women had done before. Progress! He would get there in the end, wouldn't he?

She took the dress from him and held it against her. "Does it look alright?" she asked.

"Perfect," he said. He took out a note and handed it to the proprietor. "And a couple of these frilly pinnies - for learning to cook." Outside the shop she pushed another banknote into his hand. Amazing!

How different from that spendthrift brother! He may bankrupt his sister, he thought, as they rode up in the penthouse lift. Surely the pair of them ought to have someone who knew what he was doing handling their money or the bailiffs would soon be repossessing that millstone of a house. That may be no bad thing. If she lost her home she might cling to him like a lifeboat.

She'd have to change her spots dramatically to bankrupt Justin Chase, wouldn't she? It might be fun to let her try. No, that might turn her into another greedy harpy. If he could have this gorgeous creature for little more than the cost of feeding her, that couldn't be bad, could it?

"This brother of yours, is he just a drain on your finances or is he old enough to make any contribution?"

"Oh, he brings in far more than he spends, so I've no reason to grumble, have I? And I wouldn't dream of trying to cramp his style. I did throw a fit when he said he'd taken delivery of a McLaren P1, though."

"A what!" exclaimed Justin. "Your brother sounds like a very temporary member of the human race! But surely he won't find anyone daft enough to sell him insurance. Is he driving it around illegally?"

"No, of course he's got insurance. I know because I paid the premium. It really made me wince."

"How long before he wraps it round a tree?"

"He won't do that. He's not an idiot."

"I bet you winced when you paid for that McLaren!"

She shook her head. "How much do they cost? I suspect they're quite expensive."

"Only about the same as my famous kitchen," he answered ruefully.

"Well, then, you're as mad as each other, aren't you?" she laughed.

"My kitchen is a bit more sensible and useful, surely," he protested rather weakly.

"Would it take you for a run in the mountains?" she teased, "And could you persuade someone to take it off your hands for two or three hundred thousand euros more than you paid for it?" She gave him a smug, victorious look.

"Nonsense!" he countered. "Cars like that are leaking value in torrents while you're driving them out of the showroom!"

"Not the McLaren," she said firmly. "Chez says they're so hard to get that men will be beating our garage doors down to get at it. He won't keep it long. He'll probably drive it up to Monrosso for the fun of it when he can find the time. Then he'll pass it on to someone with more money than sense."

"Surely he'll find it a wrench to part with a car like that!"

"I'm sure he didn't want it anyway. It's red, you see. He thinks red sports cars are for timid wimps trying to look tough. He'd have ordered something unobtrusive – dark silver probably. So I'd be surprised if there's a bill, and the cost of the insurance will seem trivial in the end."

"I don't understand," he said, frowning, as he spread his hand in front of the door control. "No bill? How do you get a McLaren without paying?"

She shrugged. "Goodness knows," she murmured. "Hello, Angel. I love the way you open the doors like magic, and it's so bright and cool in here - just like the top of a snowy mountain." She dumped her shopping on the floor, raised her slender white arms towards the ceiling, and spun dreamily around in a circle.

She was such a joy to watch, as fresh and white as her surroundings, as if fate had designed her as the perfect finishing touch, the fairy on top of his Christmas tree. She belonged here. If she left the flat would seem bereft.

With a bewitching smile she picked up her bags and took them to the guest room.

Justin walked into his famous kitchen and looked around it grimly. Was it really as ridiculous a purchase as a McLaren P1? He had an uneasy feeling that it was. Why on earth had he let himself fall under the spell of that showman kitchen designer? Easy come: easy go. A fool and his money. Get rich quick: get poor even quicker! Like a pop star he had been hit by a sudden avalanche of money. Sometimes he felt he was almost drowning in the stuff.

At work he felt he was coping rather well – at least the management experts seemed to think so. They were quoting him as a good example of the Kiss Principle: Keep It Simple, Stupid! He had not yet been tempted to build a grandiose head office with JUST IN CASE out front in huge letters. (Dropping the 'h' had proved a brain-wave). Small teams, dotted across the world, promoted his famous computer games and apps in whatever ways worked best in their area. But the market was awash with games and apps – some were even being given away free. Maybe soon the market would collapse, saturated. Some new fad would capture the kids' imagination and his stuff would be dead in the water. But then, he hoped, his less well-known business systems would save his company from ruin. Right now his teams were installing them in companies all around the world. So far so good.

Lucrezia knocked politely on the wall beside the opening into the kitchen. "If you really don't mind having me here for a day or two you must tell me your charges," she said solemnly. "Would you prefer me to pay in advance or give me a bill when I leave?"

"What! gasped Justin. "This isn't a boarding house! I invited you as an honoured guest, not a lodger!"

Lucrezia, frowned. "Oh, dear! I should feel really bad

about exploiting your kindness. I should feel far happier if you would charge me a proper rate."

He laughed. "What would be a proper rate for staying in a penthouse like this? A thousand a night?"

"Fine," said Lucrezia, opening her bag.

"Don't be silly, I'm just teasing you. I should pay you for your company. You're such fun to talk to."

"Really?" she said, eyes wide with surprise. "I thought you'd think me deadly dull and serious. I don't know anything about fashion or celebrities. That's all the online newspapers seem to write about, so I imagine that's what everybody else is interested in."

"You're quite right, unfortunately. I'm delighted to meet a woman with brains, for a change. You're so special you should charge a fee for your company, shouldn't you?"

"Well, you must at least let me buy some food or pay for a restaurant or something - "

"Look," said Justin, "can I make a pact with you? We are neither of us short of money and it really is a bore. Why don't we forget about the stuff and try to enjoy life."

"Well, I will try to find a place to stay as soon as I can. Could I rent one of your tourist flats, maybe?"

"All booked up till half way through September. It's August. What can you expect? Why don't you just settle down and make yourself at home until we can make your house fit to live in? And you need to learn lots about kitchens, don't you? If you move somewhere else there'll be no one there to teach you that, will there?"

She sighed. "You must think me such an idiot."

"Well, we can soon put that right," he grinned. "You can be my apprentice chef. Then, when you've learned something useful, you can make it for me, can't you?"

"You might have to eat some pretty horrible meals!"

"As long as you amuse me with scintillating chat I'll

gladly take the risk of that. And I can appoint you my tea and hot chocolate maker already."

"I'm ashamed of being so useless so I promise to work really hard," she said solemnly.

"Well, then, why don't you go and settle in while I get us a drink? It's not too hot yet, so it should be pleasant out there under the blind. What would you like, coffee, soft drink, glass of chilled wine?"

Sipping his drink on the terrace, Justin woke up his phone and brought up Lucrezia's emails. There was a message for her already:

"Dearest Krish. samadsuc. A. no. good idea – if you can find it. love you. Chez"

Ought he to be reading her emails like this? What did it mean? He brought up the email she had sent to match the two. Where = samadsuc. What = A. Can we sell the B House = no. Did that imply it was not the only house they owned, or why not just say: 'can we sell the house?'

"You've got a message already," he said cheerily, trying not to look guilty, when she joined him on the terrace.

She reached for the phone eagerly. "Well, I was right. We can't sell the house and he's happy about the kitchen."

"What does the rest mean, samadsuc A?"

She shrugged. "Goodness knows. Anyway, I've got the answer I wanted. I can refit the kitchen for all he cares."

"What does he do for a living, this brother of yours? Does he have a job?"

She drew a deep breath and pursed her lips. "Goodness knows. He never tells me anything. Is it time to start making the lunch?"

"Well, if you're so keen to make a start, I'll join you in the kitchen in about ten minutes."

She picked up the glasses and headed off to the

kitchen while he dragged shut the heavy patio doors to keep out the increasing heat.

In his bedroom he scrolled up the strange email and tried to make sense of it. She'd said they corresponded in code, but surely that was just to stop the nuns from prying into her affairs. Her brother knew she'd left the convent and didn't know she was using a stranger's phone. Maybe he thought *he* was being spied on.

Presumably she'd asked him where he was and what he was doing. He'd replied he was in samadsuc doing 'A'. How could he translate that? Samadsuc could be any country, town, ship, building, organisation. 'A' could be any activity one could think of: abseiling, acting, advertising, archery, ambushing, arresting, assaulting, assassination! MAFIOSO !!!

Don't be stupid, he told himself sternly. An old, possibly aristocratic family with a historic palace in the centre of Rome and a daughter in a convent. But weren't Mafiosi supposed to be religious? Wouldn't they be likely to spend their ill-gotten gains on big houses? Most crooks did. Had they murdered her father? Was he playing with fire? Maybe he had an overactive imagination. But surely Mafiosi were the most likely people to be lumbered with unwanted, unpaid for McLaren P1's.

Had he invited a cuckoo into his nest? He'd blithely assumed he could do what he liked with her as her father was dead, but this brother could be equally dangerous. Perhaps he ought to extricate himself double quick. The tourist office could always find somewhere to house visitors at the last moment. Should he dump her there and catch a plane to somewhere - anywhere?

Don't panic! You're being idiotic, he told himself. Why should this brother, Mafioso or not, take umbrage at his treatment of his sister? He'd done her no harm at all. He'd been doing his best to help, hadn't he? He ought to get a medal, not a concrete waistcoat, or whatever it was the Mafia did to their victims. Perhaps he should tell her to explain this to her brother, just to be on the safe side.

Anxiously he went to look for Lucrezia. Her door was open. She was sitting on the window ledge with her head bowed against the window pane. Everything about her seemed to droop. She looked utterly miserable, weary and defeated.

He backed away silently and went to sit in the lounge. Whatever was the matter with her? She'd been such fun to talk to he'd forgotten she had a host of problems. Did she leave the convent because she was being bullied? If so, who could she have turned to? She'd been motherless for years and abandoned by her father. There was only this brother, obviously more interested in fast cars than in his little sister. And she was still in a mess, her only refuge a huge empty museum of a house – which a certain Mr Justin Chase had worked hard to make her afraid of. Poor little kid! Rich or not her life was no bed of roses. Forget these sex slaves fantasies. Try to treat her like a little sister - at least until she's sixteen, for goodness sake!

He went into the kitchen and began deliberately to clatter about, alerting her to pull herself together. Almost immediately she joined him.

"Do you like my new dress?" she smiled, twirling around for him to admire the effect.

He gazed at her in astonishment. She looked totally transformed. Not a trace of sadness. Had he really seen what he thought he had seen?

"Perfect!" he smiled."Have you tried the pale green one yet? Does it fit?"

"It's exactly right as well. I can't remember when I last had a new dress. Thank you for helping me find them."

"I'm glad to see you're all ready for work. The pinny looks very cute."

That was a gross understatement. The urge to pick her up and swing her around like a tiny tot was hard to resist.

"Well, now, we'll make a start. There are two ways to make a meal: the complicated, time-consuming, clever chef's way, or the quick and easy lazy cheating way. Which way would you prefer to learn?"

She pursed her lips. "This must be a trick question, so, I think I should consult the expert. You choose."

Thank God for that! he thought. "Very wise," he said. "So, first we examine our assets. The veggie cupboard? Empty. I thought I was going away for a few weeks. The fridge? Same again. Half a carton of milk and some butter. We can't restock as it's Sunday. Problem? No. Look in here." He opened the big store cupboard. "Pretty well anything you can think of in here, except salads. Do you know how to open a tin?"

She picked one out, examined it, then shook her head.

"Black cherries. We'll have those for dessert, shall we? This is a tin opener. Watch carefully how I get it started. Now you finish it off."

It was fun to watch her struggling to master the technique. Ridiculous, at her age!

"Is there a tin of ice cream? There seems to be everything else."

"A tin of ice cream!" he laughed. "No, but just look here! Every kind of ice cream you can think of." He dragged open the doors of the huge freezer cabinet. "What would you like for lunch? Braised venison? Sausage and mash? How about Paella? A nice summer dish."

"Mmm. Sounds good. But I think it must take a long time to make. Restaurants always make you wait ages."

"Well, everything in here needs thawing, but no problem! We just sling it in the microwave to defrost it quickly. Take off the carton, prise the film back a little on both sides so the steam can get out, then bung it in. Set that dial to 'defrost' and this dial to five minutes for a start. Now read the carton and then put the timer right.

"Your number one gadget in your new kitchen should be a microwave. Have a fancy built-in one like this over here if you must, but you'll need a degree in engineering to work it, so get a cheap and simple one as well. I couldn't exist without that simple one. Come watch me set this fancy one to do my paella. Needs programming like a computer. Ridiculous! So, now, what do we have to do once they've thawed? Read the carton."

"Cook on full power for four minutes. That's all it says."

"Yep! That's all you need to do. So, we should set the table and open the wine. You put those cherries into this microwave dish. They'll take less than a minute when we're ready for them, and we'll have to watch them carefully. Fruit can get very hot very quickly. And never put anything metal into a microwave or you'll get a mini firework display."

It was far too hot now to eat out on the terrace, so they each carried their Paella to the table in the living room. He went back for the Pinot Grigio. Again she accepted a glass of wine as if it was the normal thing to do, equating it with a glass of fruit juice at the convent, he supposed.

Once again the wine loosened her tongue. She was soon amusing him with entertaining chat, confidently keeping pace with him wherever he chose to steer the conversation. It was such a novelty to have a congenial companion, so different from his usual weekend lunches, with only a newspaper beside his plate to take his mind off the loneliness of his glamorous sterile flat.

And she was such a joy to look at. If only she would stop plaiting her lovely hair. She looked so seductive in bed last night. He drew a breath to say that but stopped himself in time. Idiot! Don't let on you're a Peeping Tom! Didn't she realise how attractive she could look? Or was she deliberately trying to make herself look less alluring?

She was so very different from every other woman he had known, except Julia, his own sister. She was a hard-working solicitor with two little sons, and had no time for fashionable clothes and beauty treatments.

After lunch he taught Lucrezia to load the dishwasher. Then she added coffee to her hot drinks repertoire and they took it over to the sofas.

"Angel, bring down sun-blinds and movie screen," he said.

Her eyes widened as huge blinds descended to keep out the heat and a large movie screen cut the light down even more.

"Most of the women I know can't work a movie player," he said. "If you can manage to learn you'll be ahead of most of them, wont you?" Angel will only take orders from me, so you can learn to use the remote controller."

With a huge soft leather sofa apiece they were far too comfortable to stay awake. It was a good film but neither saw the ending. They woke to see the credits rolling.

It was still only five-thirty. How could they pass the time till dinner? They were both feeling restless. If only she were sixteen! Then the choice of exercise would be a no-brainer. Any other woman would be giving him come-and-get-me looks by this time.

Lucrezia was beginning to treat him like a school teacher, with a sort of friendly respect. That had to be the best thing. It would be complete idiocy to risk a jail sentence that would probably destroy his company as well. If he spooked her she might run away. Then she would see him forever as a menace, and she certainly wouldn't be around to decorate his Christmas tree!

Lucrezia had turned down the sound and was

practising bringing up stored programmes. She paused, fascinated by something very colourful and active.

"Strictly Come Dancing," he said. "Very popular in Britain a year or so ago. One of my silliest girlfriends tried to get me onto the programme. The TV company badgered me for ages. Idiot woman! I enjoy dancing but that doesn't mean I want to make a complete fool of myself in front of a few million people."

"Can you dance like this?" asked Lucrezia, wide-eyed.

"No. That's very advanced. Experts teach celebrities lots of fancy routines, then they have to compete."

"Dancing looks fun. I envy you if you can do it."

"Would you like to learn?" he asked, hopefully. It would be a great way to get up very close and personal with her, he realised, with a rush of enthusiasm. Surely no one could object to that, could they? "It's a good way to get a bit of exercise indoors, since it's far too hot to go for a walk. It would pass the time till dinner."

She slid off the sofa and walked towards him. "Now?"

"Yes, why not? Do you know any ballroom dances? Waltz, tango, foxtrot, quickstep?" Hope she doesn't want modern stuff, he thought. What's the point of jigging about on your own, a yard away from your partner?

"No. Are they hard to learn?"

"Not if you're good at following. Some women can guess what the man is going to do next. Then it just seems to flow naturally. I think the quickstep is the easiest and the most fun, so shall we start with that?"

"Angel, play dance music, Glen Miller, quickstep."

He held out his arms towards her. What bliss to watch her sidling towards him, eyes downcast shyly! Perfect, he exulted, as he reached out to take her hand in his and slid an arm around her slender waist. No wonder ballroom dancing had once caused such a scandal. It looked – and felt – like the first moves of making love.

If she'd known how to dance she might have been able to keep him at a respectable distance, but every time she moved in the wrong direction and toppled against him he seized the chance to hold her closer and more tightly until he could feel her limbs moving against his and nuzzle her lovely hair. At first she seemed embarrassed and tried to pull herself away a little, but eventually she gave up the hopeless struggle and relaxed. Probably she thought everyone hugged each other like this, even if they were dancing with strangers. He could see no point whatever in putting her right on that score. Many thanks to 'Strictly'. Some good had come out of it after all.

How fast the time goes when you're enjoying yourself! With the blinds down they didn't notice how far the sun had slipped towards the horizon while they quick-stepped their chaste lovemaking around the white marble floor. She had soon learned to anticipate his movements, even moving with him into reverse turns.

Thank you, child psychologists, he thought. They'd told him he'd been born lacking the ability to empathise with other people. Normal people respond automatically to what they see happening to other people, instinctively know what they are feeling, almost feel their pain. People with autism, like himself, have no such automatic responses. They have to study the situation, evaluate it and decide what they ought to be feeling or thinking or doing about it. That takes time, and they don't always get it right. As a team player he was a disaster, either ostracised, vilified or used as a punchbag. Being a self-reliant loner and a keen and thoughtful observer made him a fine boss, however.

The psychologists had suggested ballroom dancing as a way to develop a substitute for empathy. Learning to anticipate his partner's movements had taught him to study people intently and read their body language. Dancing had another benefit as well: tall and slim, he cut a fine figure on a dance floor and had no need to play the shrinking violet any more. The gold diggers all loved to dance with him: he made them look so glamorous.

Lucrezia was smiling now, so that must surely mean she was enjoying herself. It was almost impossible to believe that this gorgeous creature, laughing in his arms, was the sad defeated girl he had glimpsed that morning.

At last, tired and hungry, they collapsed onto a sofa, and smiled at each other like the oldest of friends. What a triumph! he exulted inwardly.

"We've both worked so hard on our Educating Lucrezia project that I think we deserve a night off, don't you? Why don't we reward ourselves by going to that nice little restaurant again?"

"Was that work?" she laughed. "Gracious!"

CHAPTER 5

THREE'S A CROWD

Predictably Lucrezia attracted plenty of attention as they braved the heat of the evening outside on the restaurant terrace. She had put on the new green dress, and, wonder of wonders, he had persuaded her not to plait her hair.

"The nuns said it was unseemly for a woman to display her hair. I feel wrong with it loose like this."

"Look around you," he insisted. "Can you see any other woman with her hair covered up or plaited?"

"Spose not," she said, pushing her hair back as if trying to coax it to plait itself.

"Don't do that!" he pleaded. He leaned over and ran his fingers through her hair, spreading it over her shoulders. "That's better. Now, leave it alone. Don't spoil it, Silly."

"People are looking at me," she whispered, frowning.

"No wonder," he smiled. "It's a pleasure to look at you."

Once he'd been proud to think that other men may envy him his date. Now he looked around warily, dreading the flash of a paparazzo camera. The celebrity hounds may not recognise him, but any hack who wrote for the business pages probably would. He'd sneak a shot on his phone camera and sell the picture. "Justin Chase dates beautiful fifteen-year-old redhead." The tabloids would love that! This unsung restaurant, tucked away in a boring square, didn't guarantee him anonymity. Next time he'd better ask for a table in a quiet corner.

His friends and staff often remarked how strange it was that he didn't feature in the gossip columns. The reason seemed obvious to him: he avoided drawing attention to himself. As a result, he could roam the world in peace like any nonentity, with no sneaking out of back doors to avoid a mob waiting to harass him. Long may it stay that way! Mustn't let this obsession with Lucrezia ruin everything, Well, they had a nice table for watching the street life going by. Relax and enjoy it. Just play it differently next time.

Lucrezia, as usual, was the perfect dinner companion, and the time flew by astonishingly quickly. He must try to make this kitchen refit last as long as possible – but then, if it took too long she might insist on moving out.

When they'd finished their tiramisu, Lucrezia excused herself and went into the depths of the restaurant. The waiter had just cleared the table when a woman, hurrying past, checked herself and headed straight towards him.

"Justin! I thought you were stomping about in the Himalayas!"

He jumped to his feet and leaned over the terrace railings to kiss her. "Hello, Darling," he smiled. "No such luck. The tour firm has gone bust and left me beached right here. Lucky it didn't happen a week later and leave me stranded out in the wilds."

"Oh, what bad luck!" she wailed. "You were so looking forward to it, weren't you?"

"Well, there we are: worse things happen. And where are you rushing off to?"

"I'm looking for a hotel, but can I find one? No way! Thank goodness I've bumped into you! As you are alone, could I borrow your spare room for the night?

"What's happened? Has your flat caught fire or something?" Blast! he thought. I don't need this.

"I told you, Justin, we've let the flat for August to a bunch of young relatives. They moved in this lunchtime. They've even got sleeping bags on the floor."

"I thought you were going to Stresa to stay with your sister. What's the problem - and where's Paolo?"

"He went on to Stresa this morning with the children and the luggage. I had to stay behind for a special birthday lunch – an old school friend. When I went to the station to catch the 5.30 to Stresa it was marked 'delayed', then 'cancelled'. Apparently the line's blocked; they won't say what with, which sounds bad to me. Anyway, there won't be any trains tonight, so I'm stranded."

"No problem, Darling," he smiled, "but I won't let you have my spare room. There's a Marcella-shaped dent in my memory foam mattress. I lie in it every night and dream of you, but I won't have to dream tonight, will I? Come on in while I finish my dinner."

He felt as happy as he sounded. Things were working out very well. Marcella could give him an alibi, couldn't she? If anybody ever asked, Marcella could confirm that he was behaving like a perfect gentleman as far as Lucrezia was concerned. And, of course, a night with Marcella was a highlight of his life. What luck!

As Marcella threaded her way to his table Lucrezia came into view.

"Marcella," he smiled, "I'd like you to meet Lucrezia."

He watched their expressions with amusement. Both, of course, looked taken aback, and after examining each other carefully, both looked at him expectantly.

He motioned to the hovering waiter to bring a chair for Marcella while he helped Lucrezia into hers. Then he looked smugly from one to the other: Marcella with her glowing dark hair and voluptuous figure, and Lucrezia, such a contrast, dainty and slender, with her gorgeous fiery tresses. Wow! he thought, that just about summed it up. Some men have all the luck, don't I?

Three in a bed? Well, that would be something new –

for him anyway, but, according to the media, everybody else seemed to be at it these days. Perhaps Lucrezia might think it was quite normal, but how would Marcella take it? She was already managing to keep two men very happy, but not both at the same time.

Stoppit! he told himself firmly, fighting to stifle a grin.

"Lucrezia," he said brightly, "Marcella is staying with me tonight as well; isn't that nice? I'm sure you'll get on very well together. Like you, she has nowhere else to go tonight. Now, I think I'd better put up a sign saying: 'Homeless Women's Refuge full', don't you?"

"Has your train been cancelled too?" asked Marcella.

"Well, no," replied Lucrezia. "It's just that I can't live in my house at present."

"Me too," said Marcella. "Ridiculous, isn't it?"

"Marcella works for my company," said Justin. "Lucrezia is my neighbour and her house is uninhabitable at present, so she's lodging with me till it's fixed. Why don't we skip the coffee here and go home? It should be a bit cooler up on the roof."

It was slightly cooler but nobody felt like hot coffee, iced coffee or anything rich and sticky.

"A glass of chilled wine?" suggested Justin.

"No, thanks," said Marcella. "I had more than enough at lunch time."

Lucrezia too shook her head and declined.

"Well. I will," said Justin.

"I don't think you should," said Marcella. "I noticed you finished the bottle at dinner. If you have any more you'll get a migraine, wont you?"

Justin pulled a face at Marcella and laughed. "Bossy Breeches!" he said. "Well, then, what can we have?"

"Camomile tea. I always enjoy that at this time of night. It's refreshing, and it helps you sleep," said Marcella.

"I can make tea!" said Lucrezia. "Shall I make some for all of us?"

"You can make tea, can you? Wow!" laughed Marcella.

"Good idea," said Justin. "Camomile, with no milk or sugar for any of us. I'm trying to teach her to cook," he explained, once she was well out of earshot.

"Are you now?" said Marcella, with a mocking smile. "Looks like that and cooking as well! My, my! And what gorgeous hair!"

"Mmm!" said Justin. "She's a real Rossetti Stunner."

"A what?" asked Marcella.

"Rossetti. He was a famous English painter who collected beautiful models with red hair. He called them Stunners and slept with all of them, all the time."

"Lucky man!" laughed Marcella.

"I have one of his paintings - just a poster, of course, they're worth millions. It's in my flat in London. It's a strange one. He painted a model called Fanny Cornforth, but the customer complained that her face was – well, not very refined. He said he'd wanted Alexa Wilding, who had a much more intelligent face and was absolutely gorgeous, so Rossetti just painted out Fanny's face and painted Alexa's face on top of Fanny's body. He's got the best features of both of them."

"So, how long has your Stunner been here?"

"Since yesterday. She's a damsel in distress," he said, trying to put on a solemn face. "I'm simply being a good neighbour. If you care to inspect my spare room you'll see that she's living there, and sleeping there – alone!"

"Why?" laughed Marcella.

"Because she's on holiday from her convent and is only fifteen!" He paused for effect, then went on. "The poor kid is in a dreadful mess. Her father has just died and her brother has disappeared, so she's come home to an empty house. The power was off and she hadn't a clue how to put it on – and you should see the kitchen! Absolutely unusable! I'm doing what I can to help her sort things out until her brother reappears, though I doubt he'll be much help when he does. What else could I do?"

Marcella gave a hoot of derision - which she hurriedly tried to suppress when Lucrezia appeared with the tea.

"I'm so sorry to hear about your father, Lucrezia. How awful for you! Had he been ill for long?"

"I don't really know. I hardly ever saw him, I'm afraid."

"Do you live with your mother?"

"She died five years ago. There's only my brother now."

"You poor thing!" said Marcella. "Justin says your brother has disappeared."

"Well, not exactly. He's just not in Rome at present."

"Where is he? Do you know?"

Justin was all ears.

Lucrezia shrugged. "Goodness knows," she murmured.

"Samadsuc," said Justin. "Doing 'A' "

"What?" asked Marcella. "Samadsuc? Where is that?"

"Goodness knows," said Justin, looking hard at Lucrezia, who was looking hard at him.

"What does he do for a living?" asked Marcella.

Lucrezia wriggled uncomfortably on her chair. "He does all sorts of things. Just now he has an aeroplane to sell."

"Sounds fun," said Justin. "What kind of aeroplane? Little one, big one, old one, new one?"

"Fairly small, I suppose," she said, wrinkling her brow. "It's a Tornado."

"Can't picture one of those," said Justin.

"It's a war plane."

"What!" exclaimed the other two in unison.

"I didn't imagine you meant one of those." said Justin. "He works for Panavia does he?"

"No, he's freelance. This one is about twenty years old but it's still in good flying condition. He'll be enjoying himself. He loves playing with them."

"Can he fly it?" asked Marcella.

"Yes, of course. You should have seen him in the air show in Dubai. He rolled it around like crazy. It was so exciting. He sold that one at the end of the show. He was miserable that night at having to part with it, dreaming up schemes to keep it. Jet fighters are not popular with civilian airports because of the noise. It sounds like the wrath of God. But of course he'd have trouble getting approval to build a suitable airstrip. The neighbours would all object."

"Would he really go ahead and build a runway if he could get permission?" asked Justin.

"Probably not. He's not an idiot. He was just enjoying a daydream. And he knew he'd very likely get more war planes to sell some day."

"Does he broker other military hardware as well?" asked Justin. "Tanks and guns?"

"Yes, I think so," she said.

"So," said Justin, "he's in Damascus at present trying to sell his Tornado, is he?" Why had it taken him so long to unravel that code? It was childishly simple, really, but might just fox the nuns. "What does 'A' mean?"

"Goodness knows," said Lucrezia.

Justin gave her a very hard and penetrating look.

"It means someone has agreed to pay him a lot of money, so we could afford your kitchen designer," she laughed. "Marcella, I gather you work for Justin's company. What do you do?"

"Finance Director," she replied.

"And she's very good," said Justin. "Top notch."

"Thank you, Sir," smiled Marcella. "Have you any idea what you want to do for a career, Lucrezia."

"Well, I finished my accountancy course six months ago and I've been doing internet courses on futures, commodity trading and things like that since then. My father made me take charge of the family finances a year ago. We have accountants, of course, but he made me do an audit every month. Every Friday he used to ring me and cross question me about all my trades. It feels very strange now he can't do that any more."

The other two looked at her open-mouthed.

"How old are you?" asked Marcella. "Did Justin say you were only fifteen?"

She nodded.

"What about your brother? Does he question you now?"

Lucrezia laughed. "No, no! He couldn't care less about money. He can manage to strike a hard bargain with his sales, but he loses interest after that. Leaves me to do the rest. I'm happy about that, because he makes so much more money than I do I feel I'm not making a big enough contribution otherwise."

Well, well, thought Justin. Things seemed to have suddenly taken a different turn. Why didn't she tell him all this before, letting him imagine her brother might be a Mafioso? Well, he couldn't really blame her for his imagination running riot, could he? And maybe nobody would like to admit that their brother was an arms dealer. Many people might think it as morally reprehensible as drug dealing. Maybe he did that as well.

That explained the McLaren, didn't it? Somebody had traded it for some military hardware, presumably, and if he had a Tornado to play with even a McLaren must seem pretty tame.

Marcella was stifling yawns and Lucrezia began to look worried, "Would you like me to sleep on the sofa so that Marcella can have the guest room?" she asked. "I'm very happy to do that. The sofas are very comfortable."

"No. no! said the other two in unison. "You stay where you are."

"I can sleep on the sofa," said Justin, with a sly look at Marcella.

"Oh no!" said Lucrezia, "you shouldn't have to do that. I should sleep on the sofa."

"Look," laughed Justin. "It's my sofa and I have a right to sleep on it if I choose. So there! Now, you two, go to bed, please, so I can do the same."

With Marcella comfortably settled in her dent in his memory foam mattress, Justin slid into bed and wrapped himself happily around her, blessing his lucky stars.

"Oh, what a relief!" breathed Marcella, snuggling herself into the angle of his body. "That was one exhausting day. Thank goodness I bumped into you! Paolo was so worried about where I was going to spend the night."

"You'd better ring him, hadn't you?"

"I rang him while you were in the shower. He was so relieved I was with you."

"What would he say if he could see you now?" He cupped her luscious breast and squeezed, nuzzled and kissed her behind the ear.

"Enjoy!" she giggled.

"What?" he gasped.

"He'd say, have fun, enjoy."

"You're pulling my leg!"

"No, why should I? Paolo's very nice about you. The worst he does is tease me and I tease him about Marta."

"You don't think he realises? You don't think he might have guessed?"

"He knows. Didn't you realise? I told him months ago."

"Good grief! How did he take it?"

"Very well. Said I could have picked someone far worse. At least you seem a safe pair of hands. I asked him if he thought there were other parts of you that might be safe as well and he laughed like a drain."

"Oh, God!" gasped Justin, rolling onto his back and staring at the ceiling. He felt as if he'd been indecently exposed. Then he rounded on her angrily. "How can you stay with a man who cares so little about you?"

"You just don't understand, do you? He wants me to be happy. If that means the odd night with you when he's away on business, why should he object? He believes I'm safe with you, and I'm not lonely or bored, - and, of course, it means he doesn't have to be lonely either. He can sleep with Marta without feeling guilty, so everybody's happy."

"And you can have a really interesting debriefing session when you both get home!"

"Mmmm!" she giggled.

"I'm glad the pair of you find me so amusing. That's just sick!" he sulked.

"What would you rather he did, come and smack you on the nose? You're not some kind of pervert who likes the idea of stealing other men's wives, are you? Only want me to spite Paolo or something?"

"Don't be stupid!" he growled.

"Oh dear! groaned Marcella. "If you're going to sulk I'm going to sleep. Good night!"

She began to wriggle towards the far side of the bed.

65

"Oh no you're not! If you want a night in my bed you're going to have to pay for it." He slid towards her and pulled her roughly back towards him.

"You Tarzan, me Jane!" she shrieked with laughter.

"Don't shriek like that," he ordered. "Lucrezia will think you're being murdered."

"Give her an idea of what she's probably in for,"

"Murdered, Shriek! Guilty, Smack you on the nose. Pervert. Stealing. I must call the police!"

"Angel, for pity's sake, shush! You are off duty now. No, do not call the police. Go to sleep."

"You just told me not to go to sleep," Marcella hooted. "How can I go to sleep with you pulling me around and Angel yelling 'murder' in my ear? I thought my flat full of youngsters was crazy, but this is a madhouse."

"What do you mean about Lucrezia?" he demanded angrily.

"Oh, Justin, stop being such a prick. If you're going to sulk all night, goodness knows why, I *will* go to sleep – on the sofa."

She tried to move away again but he rolled over and pinned her down. She turned her head this way and that, trying to evade him, but he soon managed to silence her laughter with a firm kiss. Then a few well-aimed thrusts stopped her struggles to get away.

And, on the other side of the wall, was Lucrezia disturbed by Angel and the goings-on next door? Goodness knows!

CHAPTER 6

SUSPICIONS

"Ooh!" groaned Marcella, "you still haven't got any curtains. Give me the measurements of your window and I'll get you some."

"No, I keep telling you, I don't want any curtains. I like being woken by the sun."

"Yes, but it's so early this time of year," she grumbled.

"And it's the only time the temperature's bearable. "We don't have to work today so we can have a siesta, so what's the problem? And as we're awake we can play on into injury time." He kissed her shoulders and tried to turn her around.

"Talking of injury," she grumbled, "You were a bit rough with me last night."

"Really? I thought you liked it like that." He was about to say she deserved it, but now the shock had died down he could admit that he had no case against her.

"Injury. I must call the doctor or ambulance?"

"Good morning, Angel. No, there is no injury. Shush."

Yes, it was embarrassing, even demeaning somehow, to discover that Paolo had known for months what he was doing with his wife. Italians did things differently. It was their country, and up to him to try to fit in.

"Could you be confusing me with someone else maybe?" she teased.

"Never!" he asserted. "There's no one else in your league, is there? You want it nice and gentle this time? Fine, then come on, give me a chance - "

"No, Sweetheart. Sorry. That's your lot for now. I don't want to be so sore and sated I have to give poor Paolo the cold shoulder tonight, do I?"

"Why not give him the push altogether and marry me?" he pleaded, nuzzling her neck and caressing her luscious breasts.

"The children would never forgive me, would they, and anyway, Silly, I'm far too old for you. I'll be forty in a few weeks' time, you know."

"No! No one would ever believe that. You look more like twenty-five, and you feel like – well, words can't do you justice. Come on, just once more." He slid his hands towards her thighs.

Marcella pulled away resolutely and pushed his hands away. "No, Darling. That's it for now. Well, it's hard to tell a woman's age these days isn't it. You see thirteen-year-olds who look thirty when they're all tarted up and your Lucrezia, well, she could just as easily be going on twenty-six as going on sixteen, couldn't she?

"No! She's just a child."

"Well, dress her up in a film star frock and plenty of lippy and she could easily pass for thirty."

"Never!" he exclaimed. "She's just a kid."

"Oh, really? Is that why you're devoting so much time to sorting her out?"

Marcella was just too clever by half, he thought, not for the first time.

"Has it occurred to you that things may not be quite as they seem? For instance, how do you know that palatial house you've told me about is really hers? She might be just a waif and stray spinning you a yarn."

"Well, of course it's hers. She has the key and everything. And she's no waif and stray. She's very well educated, had an English governess. Speaks English like a native."

"Maybe she *is* English."

"She says she's Italian. Does she have a foreign accent?"

"No, she has the best Italian accent, the Florence accent, like all the aristocratic families."

"There you are, then. From what she says, the family is not short of money. Brother has a new McLaren Pl. And he has that Tornado to sell."

"That could all be moonshine, couldn't it? You said the house is more like a museum. Maybe it is, and it's just closed at the moment. She could be a sort of caretaker or something, couldn't she?"

"In that case, she wouldn't be planning to rip out the kitchen, would she?"

"Well, that will be the test, won't it? If she wriggles out of that you'd better watch out, I think. I wonder if the trains are running again now."

"Rip out the kitchen, watch out, running. Call police?"

"Angel, there is no problem. Do not call the police."

"Angel," spluttered Marcella," do you have a crush on policemen?".

"Crush policemen very bad."

"Angel, you're right. I must not crush policemen,"

There was obviously no hope of further action, so Justin reluctantly detached himself from Marcella and dragged himself off to the kitchen. He glanced into the lounge and wondered if he ought to have thrown a sheet and pillow onto one of the sofas for decency's sake, but he could hear sounds coming from the kitchen. It was too late to try to disguise where he had spent the night.

Lucrezia gave him an innocent smile and proudly pointed to three mugs of tea. "Oh dear," she said suddenly, "I didn't ask if Marcella likes tea. Most Italians don't. Shall I make her some coffee?"

"Tea will be fine. I've taught her to like it," he smiled.

She was clearly not shocked by his behaviour, but then she was not a prudish stuffy English girl, was she? Italians had different ideas altogether, didn't they? But then, what would the nuns have thought? It was all beyond him.

Over breakfast on the terrace, Marcella couldn't resist asking questions about the house.

"Its very dark and gloomy, but I suppose it's interesting, as it's so very old," explained Lucrezia.

"Is it far from here?" asked Marcella.

"Just around the corner," said Justin, "so it will be easy to supervise fitting a new kitchen, if Lucrezia decides to go ahead with it."

"I don't think I have any choice, do you?" she asked, looking at Justin.

"Why don't you come and look at it before you catch your train?" asked Justin.

"Oh, yes, please do," urged Lucrezia. "It would be very helpful to have your advice."

Justin gave Marcella a quizzical look.

"Well, I suppose once the trains are running there'll be plenty of them, so another hour won't make much difference, will it?" she said.

"Well, do you see what I mean?" asked Justin. "Imagine cooking for your family in a kitchen like this."

"Oh, my!" wailed Marcella. "You're right, Lucrezia. It must be more than eighty years since this was last modernised. It can't be unreasonable to want something more up-to-date. Is there a preservation order on it?"

"The house is fifteenth century," said Justin. "So this old kitchen must be about five hundred years newer than the rest of the house. It's already an anachronism. A brand new twenty-first century kitchen can't be any more out of place than this is, can it?" Anyway, I know the Heritage Department people - had to get permission myself - so I think I could get permission quickly, while Lucrezia decides what kind of kitchen she wants."

"Well," said Lucrezia, "I think the servants might like something like this. I'd value your advice." She placed a magazine on the table, opened at a model kitchen.

"Oh, I like this! enthused Marcella. "Forget your fancy kitchen, Justin. Remember, this one has to be a sensible place where people have to get some real work done, not play the celebrity chef."

Justin pulled a face at Marcella, and bent to look at the pictures. Maybe she was right. The cupboards and drawers looked quite historic, elegant and simple.

"It's three quarters below ground, so I don't think dark woodwork would be sensible, do you? I don't want it to look like the Catacombs. And I don't want it to look institutional, all metal, either."

"No, I think this pale creamy woodwork should make the place look lighter. White or metal would look rather bleak and far too modern. Perfect. You're a clever girl, isn't she Justin?"

Justin looked again at the magazine and sighed. It was so conventional. People had been installing kitchens like that all his life. He'd been fantasising about something much more new and daring.

"It's for the servants, remember," admonished Marcella, as if she could read his thoughts. "I don't think this will ever go out of date, unlike this present one, which must have been the height of fashion once. I would definitely go for something like this, Lucrezia."

"Well, then," said Justin, "all we have to do is find it."

"I'd love to see a little of the house," said Marcella.

"Yes, of course," said Lucrezia, and they began the

'Friendly Neighbour Tour.'

"Is there a Royal Suite?" asked Marcella, after they had seen Lucrezia's lovely rooms. "There usually is in great houses like this, isn't there?"

"Well, yes," she replied slowly, frowning a little and glancing at her watch. She led them towards the grandest-looking doors at the end of the first floor walkway, then hesitated. "Would you mind waiting just a moment?" She knocked on the doors and listened. "Chez?" she called. "Cesare!"

Nothing stirred, so she opened the door a little and peeped inside. Then she went into the room cautiously.

The other two felt instinctively that they ought not to follow. They waited, exchanging questioning glances, until she returned and invited them in.

It was indeed a very grand suite, plastered and painted with country scenes in colourful Roman style. A large sitting room, richly furnished, led to a very grand bedroom, dominated by a huge four-poster bed with beautifully embroidered curtains and bedcover.

"Who does all the cleaning?" asked Marcella. "It looks very clean and shiny. Someone must be taking good care of it."

"I don't know," said Lucrezia. "I haven't lived here for five years. I spent a week here at Christmas and there were servants here then, but when I arrived on Saturday the house was completely empty. The servants seem to have deserted us, I don't know why. I shall have to ask my brother. He seems happy about refitting the kitchen. I hope I'm doing the right thing."

"I should certainly think so," Marcella assured her. "I don't think you'll find it easy to get anyone to work in your kitchen as it is, and it doesn't look very hygienic to me."

"The fridge certainly doesn't," laughed Justin. "It's obvious no one has been doing any cooking here for quite a while, so someone must be coming in just to keep the house clean. We should bump into them when we get started on the kitchen and your brother might be back by then to tell you what's going on."

"Justin says your brother has a new McLaren P1. Have you seen it yet? Where does he keep it?" Marcella asked, with a sly glance at Justin.

"I assume it must be here. Should we go look for it?"

"Yes, please!" Justin could hardly contain his excitement, but Marcella just raised her eyebrows and gave him a sceptical look.

Lucrezia led them down a short flight of stairs and opened a discreet-looking door. When she switched on the light they gasped. It was a huge flaring red and black monster of a sports car with a face like a big grinning frog with sunken triangular nostrils.

Justin whistled, and reached out to give it a tentative poke. I've had my hands on a McLaren P1, he thought. How about that! And I suppose I could actually afford one. Maybe I could get one quickly by taking this off brother Cesare's hands.

Lucrezia gave a smothered hoot of laughter. "Poor Chez! If he does take this out it will be after dark."

"Why?" spluttered the other two.

"Well, it takes a lot to embarrass Chez but I think this might do it. I'm sure he'll offload it as quick as he can. No one could be inconspicuous in a car like this."

"Well, you two," said Marcella, "I'd better leave you to play with your amazing car and your fabulous house and go join my family in Stresa. Thank you so much for saving me from a night in a refuge for the homeless, Justin. See you in September. Bye, Darling."

"The pleasure was all mine," smirked Justin, as he kissed her goodbye.

CHAPTER 7

IT'S ALL HAPPENING

"So," said Justin, after they had waved Marcella off, "do you think you're ready to make up your mind? Do you really want to refit the kitchen, and are you absolutely sure your brother is going to let you do it?"

"Let me do it!" she exclaimed. "I do hold the purse strings, you know. I asked for his opinion, not his permission. Anyway, I've a feeling he'll be home pretty soon, though I doubt he'll be interested in kitchens. If I want it he'll want me to have it. The only reason I made a fuss about the sports car was that it seemed so out of character. If he really wanted it of course I'd want him to have it, but of course he doesn't. Anyway, I'm sure we have to get a new kitchen, otherwise we can't live in the house at all, can we?"

"How does your brother manage when he's at home?"

"You may well ask!" she sighed. "I think he hardly ever stays more than a day or two and maybe lives on pizza. I suspect there may be a few girl friends begging to feed him, so he probably makes use of them, poor things."

"Why 'poor things' ?" laughed Justin.

"They're probably hoping to walk up the aisle with him someday, but that day is unlikely to dawn."

"Is he – doesn't he really like women?

"He doesn't prefer men, if that's what you mean. He complains the women are all brainless gold diggers."

"He has that problem too!" Justin found himself warming to this brother.

Since she seemed so sure what she wanted he took her to the firm that had supplied his tourist flat kitchens.

"Look!" she exclaimed. "Here's my new kitchen!"

"You'd better have a look around and make sure you don't see something you like better," he warned. Women did have a nasty habit of almost buying something, wasting the assistant's time for hours, then suddenly buying something quite different, or going into a sulk and buying nothing at all.

Lucrezia followed his advice, then returned resolutely to her first choice. "I'm sure this is the right one," she said. "Now what must I do?"

Justin was in his element, having done this so many times before. Before they left the old house he'd quickly made a sketch of the space available, marking doors, windows, alcoves and such, so that he already had ideas about what might go where.

He forced himself to be boringly sensible about the choice of electrical equipment. Everything had to be able to withstand heavy-handed servants cooking for at least a dozen people. Nothing was for show. According to Lucrezia, no one was likely to be invited to admire this new kitchen. Even her brother might not bother to inspect it, so it seemed. Strange man! Well, here's hoping the new servants would appreciate it. And maybe Lucrezia herself might try to cook something, if he did manage to teach her anything.

It had taken him ages to choose for his own projects, but Lucrezia listened carefully to everything Justin and the salesman said, asked surprisingly intelligent questions and made up her mind very quickly.

"When can your fitters start work?" asked Justin.

"In three weeks' time, sir."

"Oh dear!" said Lucrezia, "I don't think I can wait so long. Maybe another place can do the work sooner."

The salesman was very taken aback. This was a very big kitchen so there was a lot of money at stake. "Well, if it's really urgent, maybe I can find some fitters. We're usually very quiet in August, so we encourage our fitters to take their holidays now. Some of them are not going away so maybe they can be persuaded to work."

"The air conditioning is very good and there's lots of space to work in," she said. "I could give them a bonus."

"If you'll excuse me a moment, I'll make some phone calls," said the salesman.

Just then Justin's phone rang. It was Marcella. "Would you excuse me a moment?" he asked Lucrezia.

"I'll go look at the rest of the showroom," she said.

"Darling," said Marcella, "I think maybe I should have told you about the problem in Birmingham. It surfaced just after you left on Friday. Your London office were desperate to contact you, but I told them you'd gone to the Himalayas. The customer is turning quite nasty."

"The Houseman project? What's wrong with that? It was signed off some time ago, wasn't it?"

"Two weeks ago. The team reported it was working perfectly then, but apparently it's suddenly gone haywire. Housemans are getting frantic because their really busy period starts straight after the holiday. Whatever they try it just gets worse. I couldn't find anyone in Europe free to tackle it so can I pass it on to you? Since you're not away stomping around the Himalayas you might like a trip to Birmingham instead. You often say you like to get down to the coal face to see how your company is really running."

Justin groaned and swore a few minor oaths. "What about Lucrezia? You've seen her place. Surely you agree I can't turn her out to live in that mausoleum all alone, without even a working kitchen."

"You could take her with you. She'd surely add a little

lustre to the place, wouldn't she?"

"Yes, and attract a lot of attention and distract me from concentrating on the job," he grumbled.

"Well, leave her in your place. The security's good. You could ask the antique shop people to keep an eye on her. You said she can open tins and use the microwave and I know there's always plenty of food in your freezer. It wouldn't do her any harm to fend for herself for a day or two. You don't have gas, so she's unlikely to set the place on fire. Ask her not to put the grill on, just to be on the safe side. And not to throw a party for hundreds of raving teenagers! I'd better get on my train before it leaves without me, so over to you. Bye, darling."

Grumpily, Justin rejoined Lucrezia, just as the salesman returned with a big smile to announce that two of his best fitters had agreed to work the following week, especially if there was a bonus involved.

"Oh, thank you so much," enthused Lucrezia, with a smile that clearly turned the salesman's legs to jelly.

"We have to ask for quite a substantial deposit," ventured the salesman, looking embarrassed. "We have to order everything from the makers and, these days, they do demand something in advance. And our kitchen planner has to do a lot of work before the fitters start."

"But of course,"smiled Lucrezia, handing over her card.

Justin waited apprehensively for the machine to approve the card. Was she old enough to be responsible in law for payments this size? It was only a deposit, but it was a substantial amount of money.

The salesman, smiling, handed her the till receipts. The bank had honoured her card, so that was that.

On the way home they shopped in the market for salad, peaches and mangoes and big potatoes to cook in the microwave. Lucrezia was like a kid in a candy store, delighted by the produce but totally ignorant of the prices or the quantities to ask for. She was like a visitor from another planet – or another era. That convent was negligent beyond belief, he thought. But it was great fun to instruct her. It was good to feel such an expert in pretty well everything,

Next they called at the corner shop for milk, cheeses, ham, and bread straight from the oven. They looked at the pizza slices and smiled a secret smile together.

Making lunch this time was much more of a joint effort. Lucrezia proved quite expert, after a little instruction, at parting a mango from its stone. While they arranged the ham and cheeses on the plate, he explained how she could make a light meal some time by microwaving a big potato and topping the two halves with a tin of baked beans, or a tin of tuna mayonnaise.

"You know how to open tins and deal with frozen meals, and as long as you eat some salads and fruit as well you should keep the spots at bay. Maybe we should stay in this evening and do something from scratch like Spaghetti Bolognaise. We can cheat on that very easily, look." Like a conjurer he produced a tin of minced steak and a tube of tomato purée. "We can fry up an onion to make it seem more home-made and put a slurp of Martini Rosso in to make it taste more interesting. Hey presto! A good cheat's Spag Bol. We can eat some peaches and oranges if we don't want another salad."

"You are marvellous!" she laughed. "You make it seem so easy and such fun. I always imagined cooking was so difficult and so unpleasant: people up to their armpits in steam and sweating in front of roaring fires, all chopping about with huge knives and cleavers."

"That sounds positively medieval," he laughed. "But I suppose, in your old house, it might have been like that when the house was new. I think, in those days, they even slaughtered animals in the kitchens, didn't they?"

"I think they did," said Lucrezia, with a shudder.

"Roaring fires, chopping, knives, cleavers, slaughtered, I must call the Police and Fire Brigade?"

"No, Angel, do not call anyone," laughed Justin.

After lunch, Justin went into his bedroom to phone Houseman's in Birmingham. He listened with dismay to a torrent of complaints, and heard his precious system described as rubbish, a con trick, and sundry other nasty names. What on earth had gone so amazingly wrong? It was his best-selling system, should have done – in fact had been doing - a perfect job for Houseman's huge warehouses for almost two weeks before it began playing up in this very strange way.

He couldn't afford this kind of fracas. If this couldn't be fixed his whole safety-net business could be dealt a killer blow. Thank goodness he was not away in the Himalayas! There seemed no doubt that he had to get someone to Birmingham as quickly as he could.

He promised Houseman an expert would be with him the very next day, and asked for a hotel to be booked for a couple of nights near the warehouses. Next he opened up his laptop to see what his English teams were all doing at the moment. Every team was in the middle of some project, most installing the same programme that was infuriating Houseman.

He rang his Rome office and was quite surprised to get an answer - and Antonia was even more surprised to hear him. She was fielding calls from home, and confirmed that his office was shut.

"Lucky it's you, Antonia," he said. "Listen, I have to get to Birmingham tomorrow morning. I realise it wont be easy in August, but do your best. I realise I can't be too choosy – land me anywhere in mainland Britain you can, and I'll get a train or something the rest of the way. I'll get off the phone now so you can get started. Best of luck!"

CHAPTER 8

READY, STEADY, GO!

"Lucrezia, do you have many teenage friends in Rome?"

"Teenage friends?" She looked at him blankly, then furrowed her brow. "Well, you see, I've hardly spent any time here for years and so - " She shook her head sadly.

"You wouldn't throw a party if I left you alone here?"

She gave a gasp of astonishment, then laughed aloud.

"I can't see how I could possibly do that, even if I wanted to – and I don't!"

"Good!" he exclaimed, "because I'd prefer that you didn't. I've read some horror stories in the press and I don't want my flat trashed. You see, I have to go to Birmingham in England tomorrow for a day or two on business, very urgent business."

"Oh dear! she sighed. "Well, I'll go home right away."

"No, no, I don't want you to do that. I'd be grateful if you'd stay here and look after the flat for me. And I'm sure you'll be much safer here. The building is full of people. There are all the tourists in my flats; if you had some sort of emergency during the night you could knock on their doors and ask for help."

"Horror. Trashed, Urgent. Emergency. Call for help?"

"Angel, no, thank you. Shush."

"Oh, but I'm so afraid I might do something stupid and damage your lovely flat."

"Look, the antique shop people manage the tourist flats for me, so if you have problems with the electrics or drains or anything, just ring them and ask them to fix it. I'll talk to them before I go, so they'll be ready if you call."

The phone rang and he picked it up hurriedly. "Antonia? Any luck? Oh, blast! Well, keep trying, please."

"She's doing her best, poor girl, but it looks pretty hopeless. She's trying to get me on a plane to the UK. It's always the same at peak holiday times. There's always some unexpected problem. This time it's the French air traffic controllers on strike. Apparently there's a backlog of stranded people building up. I'll have to try the train. Heaven knows how long that will take,"

"Blast. Hopeless, problem, strike, call - "

"Angel, no problem, shush."

"Couldn't you try a cargo plane, or a military plane? A helicopter would take a long time and I suppose you would have to keep landing to refuel."

"Huh! What funny ideas!" Then the penny dropped. "Is that what your flying brother would do?"

"Yes. He hardly ever goes through big civilian airports. If he goes through security he sets off all the alarms. Whatever passport he presents they march him off and strip search him. He says it can be very nasty and personal. Often they question him for hours."

"Security, alarm, search, nasty - "

"Angel, shush. Why on earth do they do that? That's never happened to anyone I know!"

"He thinks it must be all the dust from the explosives. And the places he goes to often have drugs all over the place, and he can't avoid getting traces in his hair or on his clothes, and that sends the sniffer dogs crazy. And they probably think he looks like a terrorist."

"Crazy, terrorist - "

"Angel, go off duty now. How can he look like a terrorist if he looks like you?"

"He doesn't look the least bit like me," she laughed, as she went off to her bedroom.

She returned a few moments later and announced: "I've sent an email to Chez to see if he can help you."

Justin swallowed hard. Oh dear! Where was this going to end? In the bomb bay of some military plane, piloted by big gum-chewing toughs, or stuck in the cargo hold along with who knows what? Did they pressurise those things?

"Look, Lucrezia, "I could leave it till next day. I'm not going to risk life and limb to get there. Nobody's dying or anything." Not yet, anyway, he thought!

"It's a quarter to four," said Lucrezia. "The kitchen planner promised to come at four. I must go let him in."

"Hang on a moment while I make sure Antonia has my mobile number, then I'll come with you."

Next time I shall use this kitchen planner, thought Justin grimly. That celebrity designer had an ego the size of Mont Blanc. Threw a fit if Justin even tried to question his ideas. He felt as if the fabulous kitchen had been imposed on him, not designed for him. Never again!

This man, in contrast, was tactful, knowledgeable, keen to do anything possible to make Lucrezia happy. He was a problem-solver par excellence. Yes, of course it could be done, if the lady would be happy with this or that. Lucrezia readily agreed with whatever compromises were called for to get the job done as conveniently as possible. What a sensible woman she was growing up to be! The man made everything seem such plain sailing that the consultation proceeded at a great rate.

While the planner took accurate measurements, Justin called Antonia again, but the news was still bad. Warily, he checked his emails – or rather Lucrezia's emails.

'Darling Krish sorry no time pos ttqwh   ring *******
Love you, Chez'

"You have a message," he told her, with some trepidation.

"The number looks familiar. Shall I ring it for you?"

"Please," he said.

It turned out to be an air taxi company. The news there was bad as well. All their planes were already booked.

"Oh, dear! Cesare will be so disappointed if you can't help his friend. Yes, that's right, Cesare Monrosso. He tells me you've always been able to do something for him at the most difficult times. The friend's name? Justin Chase. Yes, that's right. Yes, he needs to be there early tomorrow. Yes, of course; anywhere within striking distance will be fine. Thank you so much. We'll wait to hear from you."

"How can they do anything if all their planes are booked?" argued Justin.

"You know what they say: the impossible just takes a little longer."

The impossible took only half an hour. The kitchen planner had just left when the phone rang. A seat had been found for him on a plane leaving Ciampino Airport at ten the next morning, arriving at Cotswolds Airport at about eleven thirty, British time.

Where on earth was Cotswolds Airport? Oh dear! he thought. What am I letting myself in for?

Justin stopped outside his building and took Lucrezia into the tourist shop.

"They seem to be open till nearly midnight, so if you're feeling lonely you can always come down and offer to help them in the shop." He introduced her to the shop-keepers, who were all keen to be friendly.

As Lucrezia chatted to them he spotted a lovely frock. It was white, of course. It reminded him of something.

What was it? Marilyn Monroe. It was the dress she wore when she stood over an air vent, the one that flew up to show off her lovely legs. He unhooked the hanger and took it to her.

"Oh, yes, how perfect!" cried all the shop assistants. "You must have this one: it was made for you."

"Goodness!" she exclaimed. "It's very pretty, but it's far too - well, you know, I can't imagine going anywhere where it would be the right thing to wear."

"Well, I'm sure I can. When I get back from Birmingham I shall have to think of somewhere to show you off in this. Is it your size?"

It was. Justin handed the money to the assistant. "No need to wrap it up," he said, draping it over his arm.

In the lift he held it against her so that she could see the effect in the mirror. Her expression was hard to decipher, but she didn't look exactly pleased. She really was amazing, he thought. All the other women had been determined to coax him into spending as much on them as possible, but this little madam clearly resented his attempts to spoil her. What did his sister say? 'If he thinks I'm for sale he's mistaken.' Yes, she had told one would-be suitor that, hadn't she? How was he to resolve this impasse? Needs thinking about, obviously. Best not to make a big issue of it.

He soon forgot the dress as he set to work to prepare for the fray the next day. First he loaded a number of his specialised apps onto his laptop. These were not designed for the general public. They were for professional trouble-shooters like himself, faced with malfunctioning software.

It was absolutely essential that he found a cure for this malfunction. His teams had installed this system in so many companies all over the world that he could well find his experts devoting all their time to trying to remedy problems instead of installing systems, and there was no profit in that whatsoever!

What on earth could be wrong with it? He and his brainiest staff had tested it till they were convinced it was idiot-proof. Well, they had been wrong.

It took him very little time to pack his clothes. Clothes were not his thing. He occasionally caught a glimpse of himself and winced. Maybe he ought to make more effort. Yes, he could see that this man looked somehow more impressive in his casual clothes than that one, but he was blessed if he knew why. When Marcella bullied him into buying something, her choices always did look good. If only she would marry him. Paolo always looked so cool. Probably she bought everything for him.

Next he must prepare Lucrezia for taking care of herself in his flat. He taught her how to fry onions and added a chopped up sweet red pepper to the pan.

"It doesn't belong in a classic Spag Bol," he explained, "but it certainly tastes very good. It's just as easy to use fresh minced meat, but it has less flavour than the tinned stuff. Tomato paste is much tastier than fresh tomatoes as well. And don't forget a slurp of Martini Rosso. Tins keep for years in an ordinary cupboard, so you need never run out of food. Help yourself to anything in the cupboards or the freezer."

It was their last dinner together for a few days so Justin decided to try to forget work and just enjoy her company.

"Tell me about your brother," he said. "Chezzaray. How do you spell that?"

"C-e-s-a-r-e. It means the Supreme Ruler."

"Like the Czar, or the Kaiser?"

"And Augustus Caesar, the first Emperor of Ancient Rome, Julius Caesar's adopted heir."

"When did you last see your brother?"

"In March. We went for a week to Cortina. The snow was perfect. It was quite crowded on the pistes, so Chez couldn't go very fast and got a bit bored. He asked me to ski with a pro so he could go wild skiing, but I threw a fit and insisted he took me with him. It was very bad of me, because I really couldn't cope. Not many women can.

"The chopper dropped us on top of this really hairy mountain and we had to find a way down somehow. You absolutely have to be able to jump off precipices to fly over bits where there is no snow, just rocks. My legs just aren't strong enough. I caused him real problems."

"What did you do, call the helicopter to rescue you?"

"Couldn't do that!" she shuddered. "That would have given Chez a bad name. No one would have agreed to drop him on a mountain again. We had to sort ourselves out somehow, or rather, he had to sort me out."

"So, tell me, what did he do?"

"He yelled out, 'brace yourself!' Then he came hurtling down and snatched me up and jumped. We were flying towards this huge black rock, and I just shut my eyes and waited for the impact. I was sure we were taking the quick way home. Next thing I knew we were zooming up this little slope and right into a bush. We just lay there, laughing. Our skis had come off, of course, and one of mine had slid over a precipice. In the end he threw my other ski away as well, and made me stand on his skis. That was absolute magic. He skis so much faster than I dare, of course, but with his arms around me, nothing could frighten me. I got good at balancing us with my arms and he said I was doing a good job keeping the wind off him.

"It was such fun I refused to get new skis and rode on his skis the rest of the week. Other couples tried to do it, but they couldn't. Chez said the men's legs weren't strong enough to control their skis with all the extra weight on top."

"How lucky you didn't hit that big black rock!"

"Mmmm!" she said. "Do you ski?"

"Tried it once, but there was more mud than snow; didn't seem much fun. Jumping off precipices and smashing into rocks doesn't sound like fun either - more like taking the quick way into hospital – or the mortuary."

"Yes, next stop Heaven or Hell," she laughed, as she began to clear away the debris of the meal. "Shall I make coffee, or would camomile tea make you sleep better? I expect you need to be in good form tomorrow."

While she made the tea, he checked his emails again. Another strange one from Chez. What could it mean?

'Darling Krish def ttqwh. iabud? Tue. Love you, Chez.'

"You have another email," he said, reaching for the tea.

Eagerly she took the phone, then slumped onto the sofa and swallowed hard.

"Bad news?" he asked.

She didn't appear to hear him, so he tried again. "Is there some problem? Is his trip not going to plan?"

She frowned and shrugged her shoulders. "Things seem to be coming to a head," she sighed. "I have to cross my fingers for him. If he's home tomorrow we may take a little holiday. I ought to wear something nice. That white dress you bought, may I buy it from you?"

"Pay if you must," he sighed. "It cost me next to nothing, Are you planning to wear it in Dubai?"

"However did you guess?"

"Goodness knows," he grinned. "Why Dubai? Selling the Sheik that Tornado?"

"Maybe," she said, "but he's been promising me for ages that he'll help me to jump off the Burj Khalifa."

CHAPTER 9

ORDEAL BY BLACK ARROW

By nine forty five Justin had located Universal Aviation, one of half a dozen private aircraft handling companies on the south side of Ciampino Airport. He looked in vain for the usual uniformed officials.

What now? Should he go into the office and ask for the pilot? Lucrezia had told him to wait outside. A bit too casual for his liking. And why wouldn't she ask the air taxi firm what kind of plane he'd been offered a lift on? Surely Cesare must have his limits. Would he really just accept whatever was on offer without a clue what he was letting himself in for? Pretty rash, surely.

With no uniformed flunkies to greet him, it seemed unlikely to be a flying palace. More likely a grimy cargo plane full of dead sheep or something equally noxious.

At ten to ten he heard the sound of footsteps beating a fast tempo on the echoing floor. Around the corner strode a silver fox of a man. His dark green flying suit had seen better days, but his confident stride and military bearing suggested a man of some importance.

"Mr Chase? Rob Penrose. I gather you need to get to Birmingham a.s.a.p. I can only get you to Cirencester - "

"That will do fine. I'm very grateful. It's Group Captain Penrose, I believe. I'm honoured to meet you, Sir."

He waved the compliment away. "Retired ages ago. Just call me Rob. But I've got my own little air force now - Air Force One, my one and only. And how's our friend Cesare Monrosso? What devilment is he up to now?"

"He's got a Tornado to sell," he said, hoping Penrose wouldn't ask when he had last seen Cesare. He felt a fraud, trading on the influence of a man he'd never met.

"Holy smoke! How did he get hold of that? Which air force is selling those on?"

"I've no idea where he got it, but I gather it's in good flying condition and about twenty years old."

"Really? Well, I guess it must have been from some tinpot African dictator - swapped it for a bolthole in Switzerland or something. Who's been deposed recently? Can't think of anybody. Must send Chez an email when I get a minute. Love to have a spin in that before he sells it on. He'll be in seventh heaven making sonic bangs. Great flyer! Where's he now? I've never known a man who can pop up in so many places so fast. Blink and he's gone."

"Too true," said Justin, squirming uncomfortably. "He was in Damascus yesterday, Rome this morning, and he should be in Dubai tonight."

"Typical. And how is the beautiful Lucrezia?"

"She's been staying with me while he's away," he replied rather smugly. "I'm teaching her to cook. She's on her way to Dubai now with Cesare."

"What!" exploded Penrose. "The lovely Lucrezia in a pinny! That must be a sight for sore eyes. Does Cesare know about all this? I hope you know what you're doing! Anyway, we've got to get going. Got a slot booked. If we miss it we might be stuck here for ages. Follow me." He strode off chuckling and shaking his head.

Despite his long legs, Justin had to raise a sweat to keep the man in sight. 'Mad dogs and Englishmen' came to mind. Penrose seemed oblivious to the overpowering heat as he threaded his way at the double through the ranks of gleaming white executive jets of all shapes and sizes, from obscenely large to tiny two seaters.

"Here she is, my own little Air Force One. Isn't she a beauty?"

Justin pulled up sharply and blinked. Air Force One

could not have been more out of place. Black as a lump of coal, with red triangles picking out the air intakes, she was about the size of a six seater executive jet but appeared to have only one engine – a pretty big one, judging by the exhaust hole at the rear. There were no windows in the cabin. And no roof on the cockpit.

"Have you flown one of these before?" demanded Penrose.

Justin shook his head. He swallowed hard, and scoured his mind for anything Lucrezia had said to the air taxi firm that might be appropriate.

"Every pilot's favourite, I gather," he ventured.

"Absolutely!" enthused Penrose. "Reckoned to be one of the best fighter/ground attack planes Britain ever created. Flown by the air forces of more than twenty different nations. First flew in 1951 and still in active service in at least one country. This is one of the last to be built, so she's one of the best, most highly developed of the lot, fitted up for the Swiss. They loved Hunters because they could play games with their mountains. They'd come roaring from behind like a bat out of hell, swoop and roll and disappear behind another mountain before anyone could gather their wits. They dug caverns to hide them in, next to motorways that doubled as runways. Marvellous! Let's get aboard. Follow me."

Penrose strode up the ladder and carefully threaded his tall, slim frame into the far side of the cockpit. Then he motioned Justin to follow.

Justin paused at the top of the ladder and surveyed the cockpit with disbelief. The two tiny seats were squeezed into the smallest possible space. No wonder Lucrezia had been asked his height and weight.

"Stand on the seat," said Penrose. "Only way."

Justin did as he was told, then carefully inserted his leg into the minute space between Penrose's leg and a control column, which stuck up from the bare metal floor. Breathing in and trying to shrink himself in every direction, he finally managed to lower himself into the seat with the column between his knees. Surely Penrose ought to have this control stick. He cast a glance sideways and discovered that he had one too.

"You ready to go, Mr Chase? We've already given her a good check over this morning."

"Yes, Sir," said Justin, with a forced smile. "Please call me Justin."

"Well, then, Justin, put this lot on."

This lot proved to be a padded shoulder and lap harness, all four ends slotted into the same metal boss, then a hard padded flying helmet with an oxygen mask attached. Thank God he hadn't had an English breakfast! His stomach was already tying itself in knots.

He watched, fascinated and mystified, as Penrose ran his fingers over innumerable dials, flicked dozens of switches on or off, moved plungers in and out and gave the odd gadget a light thump. Eventually he leaned over the side and called to the waiting mechanic, "Grazie mille. Andiamo."

The mechanic bent down and pulled the chocks out. Justin watched the ladder move away. There was no escape now.

"Clear behind!" shouted Penrose. He waited while the mechanic put on huge earmuffs, as the transparent canopy slid smoothly into place over the cockpit. Then he pressed the starter.

Even the padded helmet couldn't shut out the incredible whine of the huge jet engine. Conversation must surely be impossible now, but no - there must be speakers inside the helmet. He could hear Penrose muttering to himself as he set about moving the control column this way and that, clicking switches and pulling plungers, causing the engine to whistle gently one moment and then to roar right up to a scream the next.

Finally he appeared satisfied with his pre-flight checks, began talking to someone, then turned to Justin.

"Can you hear me, Justin?"

"Yes, fine."

"Now, Justin, can you fly a plane?"

"Sadly, no. I've thought about learning - " he lied. He dreaded a plane flight as much as a trip to the dentist. That unnerving feeling of being a helpless prisoner sealed into a huge tin can seven miles up in the sky -

"Don't. Quickest way to bankrupt yourself," laughed Penrose. "So, I need to tell you that this is a trainer. All the controls are duplicated, so I don't want to find myself fighting you for control of the plane if we get into a tricky situation. If I yell, 'I have control!' you must let go everything and leave it to me. Understood? Hold onto your harness to keep your hands out of harm's way. And keep your feet away from the rudder pedals and the brakes as well. Okay?"

Justin cringed away from the control column between his knees. It was no longer the heat that was making him sweat. What if he accidentally made some stupid and dangerous move? He glanced at the dashboard, crowded with switches and dials, warning lights and plungers he didn't understand, then swept his gaze to the side. There in the gloom, between his body and the bare metal side of the plane, was another array of gadgets, interspersed with pipework carrying who knows what. He pulled his arm tight against his side, in case he inadvertently caused havoc by nudging something critical.

How the hell had he got himself into this purgatory? This was not a vehicle, it was a weapon, with a brutal stink of ancient oily metal. He was trapped inside a deadly fighting machine, where he might prove to be a dangerous spanner in its works.

An unknown voice muttered something indecipherable inside his helmet and he heard Penrose reply. He gave a thumbs up to the mechanic and a goodbye wave. "Good, we've got clearance to join the queue. Andiamo. Brakes off, now a bit of throttle, and away we go."

Air Force One began to glide smoothly forward. He felt something move under his left foot as the plane swung gently round to the left. Hurriedly he transferred the weight of his feet onto his heels so that he could feel the movement of the rudder pedals without influencing them. It was both exciting and frightening to realise that he could change the direction of the plane - if he was daft enough to try.

One by one the gleaming white jets roared serenely up into the sky, and there, embedded in the queue, sat the incongruous threatening black shape of Air Force One.

The padded helmet was full of voices. They appeared to be speaking English, but nothing they said made any sense. Penrose impatiently brushed off any attempt by Justin at conversation. He was presumably listening to the voices, but he made no attempt to join in. When at last there were no more planes ahead, he heard Penrose's voice enunciating the same incomprehensible jargon, then he turned to Justin with a grin.

"Hold onto your hat. Now, Blackie, andiamo!"

He pushed a large plunger to the limit, and the plane roared ahead like a greyhound released from the traps. Justin felt the control column move towards his groin and Air Force One leapt off the tarmac and soared up into the hot blue Roman sky.

It was hard to draw breath with what felt like an elephant slumped onto his chest, crushing him back into the seat.

It was a huge relief when Penrose eased the control column slightly forward and pulled back the throttle.

"Fun, wasn't it?"

"Next stop the Moon, or at least the International Space Station," Justin laughed weakly. "She certainly feels like a thoroughbred, your lovely Air Force One. How old is she?"

"It's hard to say. She's a TMK68, completely rebuilt in 1976. Then I gave her a big overhaul when I bought her a few years ago. There's decades of life left in the old lady yet. Just a mo. Got to sign out from Ciampino." He let out another stream of jargon, from which Justin only caught something along the lines of "heading north west."

"The Frogs are back from their strike today, so we can fly direct across France. Not that it mattered much. It's not much further going over Milan and Geneva and across into Belgium but that would mean flying in over Stansted and Luton. Much better over Southampton and Bournemouth. Nice quiet pit stops if the fuel gets low."

"Is that likely, running out of fuel?" asked Justin anxiously.

"Shouldn't be, after all the modifications I've had done, but of course you know it used to be the one big bugbear with the Hunter. Hawkers designed them to carry so many cannon and bombs and ammo there was hardly any room left for fuel. About an hour was their maximum air time, but they had an incredibly fast turn around. Between sorties the whole empty weapons carriage was lowered onto a trolley and replaced by a loaded replica, while the fuel was being forced into the tanks under pressure, so she was up and away double quick. See the torpedoes under the wings?"

Justin glanced at the sinister black shapes. "You're planning to bomb the French?"

"The latest models carried Sidewinder missiles. Those things are extra fuel tanks. Most of us have those, and fuel bags in the wings, so not to worry. We can afford to waste a bit of fuel and have some fun. First we'll have to say hello to the next controllers. My flight plan's been agreed, but I still have to stay in contact and check for hazards ahead."

He pulled back the throttle a little more, cutting down the noise of the engine, and eased the control column forward. The black pointed nose was now low enough for there to be something other than sky to see out of the windscreen.

Once again Penrose swapped incomprehensible jargon with voices inside the helmet.

"Are we likely to bump into anything?" asked Justin.

"Not at this height - except for the odd private jet. We'd better keep our eyes open more than usual, though. The Frogs will have chaos to sort out – loads of airliners stuck in the wrong places. All their own fault for striking. The worst chaos should be between 32 and 38 thousand feet, where most of the airliners fly. We're at 42. The military should be either up above or way below, doing near ground stuff."

"How fast are we going? Will we see the other planes in time?"

"About 500 miles an hour. The controllers have us all on radar and should keep us informed."

Justin turned as far as the harness would allow and searched the skies anxiously in every direction. On his side there was nothing but a few wispy clouds, and the wrinkled blue sea, way, way down below. On the other side the Italian coastline stretched way ahead into the distance. It was hard to see what might be coming over the land, but Penrose must be more than capable of monitoring that. Forty two thousand feet! Eight miles up.

If only he could banish that sickening feeling that he was shut in a tiny tin can hanging by a thread over an abyss!

Voices sounded in his helmet: " - - - nine o'clock low - "

"Your side, Justin. Can you see it yet?"

"See what?"

"The plane. Coming to meet you at right angles. Small executive jet."

The sky seemed empty at first, but then, there it was, on a collision course. "It's coming to meet us. What can we do?" he shouted.

"Worry not. The controller said it's lower than us, and we have right of way, so it must alter course if necessary, and pass behind us. Keep an eye on it for me."

The plane passed quite some distance behind them, and soon disappeared from view. Once again it seemed that they had the whole of the sky to themselves.

"Well, now, I guess you're dying to have a go at flying her yourself."

Justin cringed into his minute seat in horror. "No, no," he stammered. "I wouldn't want to deprive you - - and I haven't a clue - "

"Don't worry," said Penrose cheerfully. "I've lost count of the number of novices I've taught in my time. Nice to see the young-uns finding their feet – or should I say, wings. Right, over to you. You have control."

"For God's sake don't let go of the controls," squawked Justin. "I haven't a clue!"

Penrose laughed. "Watch what happens when I let go." He took his hand off the control column. Justin expected the worst, but the plane continued roaring through the sky as if nothing had changed.

"She's properly trimmed, so until something changes, a bit of turbulence, maybe, she'll be happy as she is. Now, just take hold of the control column gently, just hold it still, and get used to the feel of it. Right, now, just ease it back towards you a tiny bit. See what happens."

Sweating with dread, Justin eased the stick cautiously towards himself. The black nose rose to block out the view of the land and sea and the wings began to roll from side to side as if the plane was waking up and stretching.

"Now," said Penrose, "We're gaining a bit of height and the wings aren't level. Very gently try moving the stick a little to level the wings and stop us gaining height."

And so began the fight. Whatever he did Justin could not make the wings stay level, but he managed to move the stick forward very slightly until there was now a wide band of land and sea visible out of the windscreen, The plane was now losing not gaining height. He eased the stick back until the view suggested that the plane was flying level.

"Well done! Now you see how things work. Just tiny movements. Now let's try a small change of course. Ease the stick a little to the left and hold it there."

Justin cringed as the left wing tilted downwards. Instinct told him he would fall out of the plane, or it would roll right over onto its back – or both!

"Gently ease the stick back to the centre position again. Hold it there. You see, we're turning just a little to the left, but the nose has gone up again. Ease it level again. Now stop the turn. Ease the stick a tiny bit to the right and then centre it again. Now get the wings straight again and the nose level. Well done. Need a rest?"

"You bet I do!" Justin gasped.

"Okay, I have control. I'll trim her now you've had a chance to see how the controls work." He fiddled about with a hidden control and the plane settled down quietly.

Maybe a conversation might deflect Penrose from making him fly the plane again. "Do you live in Rome?"

"Heavens no. I live in Cirencester and keep Blackie at the old Kemble airbase. "We don't usually stray as far as Rome, Blackie and me. but there was a big jamboree there last week. Six of us made it and did some mock dog fights for the crowds. They seemed to enjoy it. We did a show in France on the way over as well. These shows are a great way to meet loads of old pals and swap yarns. I met a few nice Frogs and Eye-ties who'd served with me in NATO. We've got two shows near home next week. You get next to nothing most of the year – maybe a bit of film work – but everybody seems to be putting on air shows in August."

"Do you have trouble finding places to land? I suppose you're not usually allowed to land in civilian airports and you need a special runway."

"No. We've as much right to use civilian airports as anybody else, if we pay the landing fee. Any normal runway will do. We risk landing on grass occasionally, if it's bone hard. Without all the heavy weapons she's much lighter. See this?" He pointed to the top of the control column and flicked up a hinged cover to reveal a button. "Line up your target and press the button. She could blow a speeding car off a motorway or shoot a bird out of the sky in her glory days. Want another turn at the controls?"

"You've given me a good idea of what's involved – but it must take months to learn to fly her properly, so I'd rather watch you."

Penrose grinned and nodded.

Thank God, thought Justin. It seemed he was off the hook. He tried to settle down and enjoy the experience. After all, it was a rare privilege to fly in a famous fighter-bomber with such a distinguished fighter pilot. And this was a fascinating glimpse into her brother's world where he called men like Penrose a friend.

"Are the Hunters usually black?" he asked.

"Well, every country decked them out in their own national insignia. Lots of British ones are painted black nowadays in honour of the famous old display team, the Black Arrows, or dark blue, like the Blue Diamonds. The Blacks still hold the world record for formation flying: twenty-two planes flying the diamond. Imagine that! Two and a half times as many as the modern Red Arrows. That was in the fabulous Sixties, when there seemed to be cartloads of money around for aviation. We had three firms all building rival warplanes. Now we have to get into a consortium with half of Europe to get a new plane off the ground. Sad, isn't it?"

"Can she break the sound barrier?"

"She's officially transonic, can fly safely almost up to the speed of sound. Neville Duke, the famous Hawker test pilot, set a world speed record with 727 miles an hour in the 1950's. Lots of people insisted they heard that Hunter make three sonic bangs then in shallow dives. Near the ground the speed of sound is about 768 miles an hour, but it's much slower way up here. We could probably make a sonic bang, but it's not a good idea. It might be the last thing she did.You have heard, of course, that two Spitfires claimed to have broken the sound barrier in the late 1940's. One of them had its propeller torn off and the other was a complete write-off."

"Grief!" exclaimed Justin. "Did the pilots survive?"

"The one who lost his propeller certainly did. He flew the plane safely back to base as if it was a glider."

"Like the man who landed the airliner on the Hudson River."

"Exactly."

"Phew!" breathed Justin. Some people must be made of superior stuff. The thought turned his stomach over.

They were heading for land. "France ahead?"

"No, that's Genoa ahead, then it's up to Turin and over the border towards Lyons, well away from Paris, I hope."

Genoa seemed to have some grudge against them. As they flew over the city the plane was tossed about like a salad shaker. "Ridem, cowboy!" Penrose laughed.

"What's causing that?" demanded Justin.

"Turbulence, that's all. Buildings absorb a lot of heat from the sun, and as the day warms up the hot air rises. Now we're over the land we may get quite a lot of that, as the weather's so hot. "Whoa, Blackie!"

"Do most pilots talk to their planes?" laughed Justin.

"If they know them very well. Blackie's my guardian angel. I'd be in a fine pickle up here without her."

"Mmm. It must be a lonely life being a fighter pilot. All alone up here for hours. So much responsibility. Beyond help if things go wrong."

"Mmm, though we rarely got to sit around for long. It was all go. Get down as fast as poss before the gas ran out; get back up quick; hunt the quarry, blast it with all you've got, then scram, before you got blown to bits. No time to be lonely - but at times like this it's good to have company."

"How did you manage to be so – you know, so downright brave?"

"Well, mainly, I suppose, by refusing to let yourself think about what could go wrong. You know the saying: a coward dies a thousand times, a brave man only once. I've seen men go to pieces and they really did seem to suffer far more than the rest of us. So, you see, letting yourself be scared is a form of masochism, isn't it?"

"Did you find a way to help the men who went to pieces?"

"Not often enough, sadly. Fear can be so contagious. One had to get them out of sight quickly, so the whole squadron didn't end up with the heebie-jeebies. I still wonder if I could have done more for them, but the rest of the men had to come first. I had to lead them into battle, not psychoanalyse them."

"I think you've got a good point there: fear as a form of masochism. Never thought of that before. It should be on YouTube or something. Are you into computers?"

"Not really. Flying's a very sedentary activity and I don't want to lose the use of my legs. Do a lot of walking. Do a bit of internet research preparing for air shows."

"I'd like to come and watch you someday. When's your next show?"

Penrose gave him a quizzical sideways grin. "Pretty soon. Now, gotta say hello to the Frogs, ask when they fancy having another extra holiday - sorry, strike."

Despite the promised chaos from the strike, the flight across France went without incident. Justin decided to man up and use any further turbulence as a chance to refuse to be afraid. The ruse worked so well that he soon felt disappointed when passing over something noteworthy had no effect on Blackie at all. When the Channel came into view he felt sure he would get a chance to demonstrate his new sang froid, but no - the sea seemed to generate no turbulence at all.

"Isle of Wight ahead. Bournemouth left – coming to the air show in a couple of weeks' time. Great jamboree. Southampton to the right. Nice civilised airports."

He exchanged incomprehensible gobbledigook with them. Apparently they had nothing to warn him about.

"I've checked the NOTAMs and there's nothing to bother us. Boscombe Down's all low and slow activities and Lyneham's now completely closed down. Better talk to Brize Norton, see if they're doing any fancy flying this morning. Might be tempted to try to join in, eh?"

Eventually, having talked to everyone he could think of,

he turned to Justin and said, "Well, we've a nice lump of quiet and unrestricted airspace ahead, so we can have a bit of fun before we get to Kemble. We've loads of fuel left, so we can have a little air show all by ourselves. Let's check you're really well strapped in. Keep your hands and feet off the controls, grip your shoulder harness and don't interfere under any circumstances."

Icy fingers squeezed at Justin's innards. What now, for pity's sake? Cowards are masochists, he thought, gritting his teeth. They suffer more than the brave. If they crashed he surely wouldn't survive. Probably wouldn't feel a thing. How can you feel anything if you're dead? To his astonishment that line of thinking seemed to have worked. He felt ridiculously calm and ready for anything.

"Keep your eyes on the windscreen. See the green fields down below and the blue sky up above? Wonder what it looks like the other up. Let's have a look."

The green fields began to swivel up like a lid on a hot serving dish. He could feel the harness pulling hard against one side of his body. The green fields reached the centre of the windscreen, then continued to blot out the entire blue sky. His whole body weight was sagging upwards into the harness, and he could feel a great rush of blood surging into his face. Then the sky began to pivot up to cover the windscreen again.

"Crikey Moses!" gasped Justin. What else could one say?

"This time watch how I do it."

Penrose moved the control column to the far right and Blackie rolled smoothly onto her back, continuing her flightpath as if nothing untoward was happening. After a short time he pushed the stick hard over again so she completed her roll back onto her front. "Easy peasy," he laughed. "Like that? Fine, now let's have fun."

As a kid, Justin had never been a fan of roller-coasters.

He could never see the point of being flung about until you screamed for mercy and had to fight to keep your last meal inside your stomach. Clearly men like Penrose must see such experiences in a totally different light.

"Come on, Blackie!" he exulted. "Show our guest what you can do!"

And by Heaven she did!

Down she dived, spinning like a top. Justin watched the ground spinning crazily nearer and nearer. Penrose must surely have lost control of his plane! At what seemed like the last minute she pulled out of her dive and swerved straight upwards like a space rocket, then began spinning again, upwards this time. Justin was seeing stars and his head was buzzing. The harness was tugging him forcefully this way and that and the elephant was back on top of him, forcing him back into his seat, making it difficult to breathe. How on earth could Penrose take this punishment and still be compos mentis enough to control the plane?

Her next trick was creating figure-of-eight shapes in the sky, tipping her passengers upside down in a fashion far more extreme than any big-dipper.

"We use coloured smoke to draw on the sky, so we have to get the shapes right. Trickier than it looks. Of course there's usually enough wind to blow the smoke around and ruin - "

"Traffic! Traffic!" yelled a voice in his helmet. "Twelve o'clock level!

"Bloody Hell!" yelled Penrose, throwing the stick hard to the right. As Blackie peeled away, a small red plane flashed past, almost close enough to touch.

"Red Arrow! What's this, a bloody war? Right, he's asked for it!" Blackie performed a very fast somersault and roared off in pursuit of the Red Arrow. "Pity I got rid of the canons. I could blast him out of the sky."

103

Justin looked at him in alarm. This surely wasn't going to be some sort of battle between a historic Black Arrow and a modern red one! The Red Arrow had turned and was heading back towards them.

"Cheeky Begger! Complete nutcase! Now what's he going to do? I'll marmalise the loony!"

To Justin's immense relief, the Red Arrow was not flying at them this time. It appeared to be intending to pass them at a safe distance to one side and well below. It began to circle, giving Penrose the chance to catch it, and he reciprocated, making a bigger circle well above.

. "Very nice. He's apologising, see?"

As the red plane circled it dipped its nose two or three times. Penrose immediately began to do the same.

"Well," he said, "he must have been just as shocked as I was. He must have been practising a stunt as well so we were both changing height and direction so much we had the controllers foxed. We should have kept a better lookout, but that's not easy when you're upside down, is it? Pity I can't talk to him. Wonder if we dare try a stunt completely dumb. Let's see if he can get the message."

He began to make a huge invisible vertical circle in the sky while the Red Arrow continued its horizontal one. Suddenly the red plane soared up through the middle of the invisible circle and headed off into the distance.

"Wayhay!" he crowed. "Very nice. Sadly, I think he's wise to leave it there. More than a little risky, trying to do stunts if you can't communicate. And the controllers are already going to have a lot to say about our near miss.

'So, Justin, hope you enjoyed your own private air show. I bet this is the only time a Red and a Black Arrow got together in a stunt. We've probably made history."

CHAPTER 10

SABOTAGE

It was early afternoon when Justin finally sat in Jeff Houseman's office, battered by a torrent of complaints.

When at last he was invited to respond, he told it calmly as it was. This system was copper-bottomed. It was very well tried and tested and had never caused any problems in its whole two years of existence, though his teams had installed it in an impressive number of enterprises in various parts of the world. This was much more than any of his competitors could claim for their comparable systems.

Yes, he admitted to himself, maybe he ought to have set up a headquarters that didn't shut up shop in August, and had staff at the ready to trouble-shoot around the world. All his competitors had them, but they needed them, didn't they? His trouble-shooters would have been twiddling their thumbs, wouldn't they? Not now, they wouldn't!

Well, that was a project for another day. Right now he personally was the only resource he had available, so he'd have to knuckle down and get started.

Jeff Houseman himself had signed this system off a fortnight before when it had been working perfectly for a week, he pointed out. Could he offer any explanation of what his staff might have done to throw it off its stride in such an extraordinary fashion?

This brought the man up short. He seemed about to burst into a rage again, then subsided like a pricked soufflé.

"Well," he said, in a conciliatory tone, "I must say I

didn't expect you to take such a personal interest in my problems and come to look into it yourself. And you seem to be right about the reliability of the system. Nobody else seems to be having trouble, according to the Internet. I suppose it could be some dope in my office, couldn't it? But I thought it was supposed to be foolproof"

"So did I," said Justin. "We challenged it every way we could, but we couldn't make it malfunction. Maybe somebody here has been trying to make it do something we didn't anticipate. Obviously, to maintain the credibility of the system, it's essential to find out how it has been corrupted and block that loophole."

"Well, I'm relieved that you're taking it so seriously. I'd appreciate it very much if you could send one of your people back to sort it out as soon as possible. There's plenty of other warehouses dying to take over my customers, and they will if we keep on making mistakes like we've been doing this last week."

"The trouble is," said Justin, "this is the busiest time of the year for us. Everybody wants to install new systems during the holiday shut-down, so all my teams are working flat out. The team that put yours in are in Gravesend now, working weekends as well on a very rushed job. I can't possibly pull them off that. It's the same with all my teams across Europe. I shall just have to look at it myself."

"Well, that's very big of you," said Houseman. "I must say, I didn't expect this level of after-sales service. I really will appreciate anything you can do. We'll do our best to make you comfortable. When can you start?"

"Right now," said Justin, "if you'll show me where I can find this ailing system."

It was the usual messy office one expects, servicing the orders in a large warehouse complex. There was an office manager and half a dozen staff, mostly women, manning the phones or dealing with mail, emailed orders, invoices and bills. While Houseman bustled about getting people to make a space where he could set up a work-station, Justin questioned the manager.

"Yes, of course we've tried restoring the system from the server, but that wipes out all our recent transactions and gives us piles of extra work trying to reconstruct them. And then, next day, it goes crazy all over again. It feels as if we've got a gremlin in the works, sitting there laughing at us."

The whole system seemed to have gone haywire, mixing up orders in a bewildering manner. Half the staff were struggling to reconstruct wiped out transactions and the rest were listening to complaints from customers, and threats to find a more reliable supplier.

"It's no laughing matter. We'll go bust if it goes on like this!" wailed Houseman."Times are hard enough as it is."

Justin steered him into his own office. "Can you think of anyone who might be trying to put you out of business?"

Houseman looked at him aghast. "Oh, Lord!" he moaned. "Any of the other warehouses, I suppose, but how are they doing it?"

"It might be an idea to think about anybody who has a relationship of any kind with one of your competitors. It's not nice to be suspicious of your staff, but it's not nice to sabotage your business either, is it? Best keep quiet about this line of enquiry for now. No need to upset people yet. First we need to find out if the sabotage is coming from outside. If it looks to be internal we'll have to risk upsetting people."

Justin's workstation was now cleared, so he plugged in his laptop and got to work. He was soon chasing the gremlins. He really had to hand it to them: they were executing some fascinating manoeuvres. If intelligent machines could have fun, they were having it now. Within a couple of hours he had a grip on the mechanisms of the malfunctions and felt sure the attacks were not coming in from outside. Things were definitely going to have to be embarrassing.

He looked around the office to find that everyone was getting ready to leave. It was coming up to five o'clock already. He could ask for everyone to be held back for questioning, but that was sure to cause problems for the women, with childcare or elderly relatives and such. And he was hit by a sudden wave of weariness. He had no stomach for it tonight. It had been quite a day! And it was already far too late to try to get back to Rome, whatever the outcome.

He asked the office manager the name of the hotel she had booked him, and requested a taxi immediately. It was lucky he did. When he went to take his leave of Houseman he walked into an ambush.

"You done for the day? Well, you must come home and meet my family. My daughter's mad keen on your games. We gave her a smart phone for passing her A Levels and she chose a few of your apps for it. I'm sure she'd love to meet you. She's a very smart kid. I'm sure you'll like her."

Justin groaned inwardly. It happened all the time. Just because he was single - had appeared on some obscure list of Britain's eligible bachelors - everybody seemed to think they could hook him for their daughters. All the daughters he had had thrust on him so far had been deadly dull, ridiculously silly or ugly as sin.

He was quite used to trotting out excuses. Incipient migraine was the first one that came to mind, and just then the taxi rolled up to the door. He was in it and away before Houseman could marshal his thoughts.

CHAPTER 11

ORDEAL BY HOTEL

Is there anywhere more calculated to depress the spirits than a run-of-the-mill business hotel? Justin sighed, dumped his bags on the bed and looked around for the wardrobe. It was just a narrow slot with four hangers, the kind with no hooks on so you're not tempted to pinch them.

Tea. My kingdom for a mug of tea! Where had they hidden the tea tray? In a dark alcove. The kettle was too big to get under the bathroom tap. He had to tip it on its side, so the water soon began running out again, but the tiny cups wouldn't need much water anyway.

Plug in the kettle. Where the Dickens was the socket? He knelt on the floor and peered into the alcove. Right at the back down in the corner. He had to twist his hand to get the plug in place.

God, it was stuffy! He struggled to get the window open a few inches, but there was another sealed window outside it. He tried the other end and at last found a way to open both layers of glass. He was rewarded by the roar of traffic gyrating merrily around the notorious Spaghetti Junction. There was no cool breeze either.

Air conditioning? Where was the controller? At last he found it on the wall, almost hidden by a picture of some weird object. Beside it was a notice: 'air conditioning does not work if the window is open'. Blast! Shut the blessed window again! The air con. was almost as noisy as the traffic. Did he really have to sleep in this torture chamber? Kettle's boiling. Tea bags? Only one? Blast! If he used that now he'd have no morning tea. He made two cups of tea out of the tea bag, then put it carefully on a saucer, wondering what kind of morning cuppa it would make. If he ate one of the two small biscuits now he would crave the other as well, then nothing for morning. Scrooges! Did they really have to pare the costs down quite so drastically? He could ring Reception for more - but he may have to hang around for ages waiting for someone to come, and he desperately needed exercise.

He took his two little cups of tea to the window and gazed at the unlovely scene outside. It was definitely no place for a walk. The only sign of green was a few stunted shrubs growing wild along the railway lines. All else was an ugly assortment of buildings no architect would be proud to lay claim to. This place must surely be short-listed for an award for the greatest number of roads packed into the smallest possible space – all of them grinding and roaring with traffic. Fresh air was the last thing he could expect to find anywhere he could see.

Did the hotel have a swimming pool, perhaps? No, said Reception. Oh. A gym? A fitness suite, they said. How was that different? Perhaps he should go have a look.

It was a small dark room in the cellar with a treadmill and two exercise bikes, one in use by a sweating, middle-aged man wearing earphones and watching a video. He didn't seem to notice Justin. Not wanting to crowd him, Justin set out for a hike on the treadmill. It was the nearest thing he was going to get to the Himalayas, he reflected, cynically.

It was no place for pleasant thoughts. Might as well use the time to think about the Houseman puzzle. It was clearly sabotage by someone with access to the system. Who could be the saboteur?

Was it sexist to rule the women out? He had never heard of a woman deliberately inventing a way to make a system malfunction. Yes, they made mistakes, but that couldn't cause this kind of havoc. In his experience, women just wanted to do the job they were paid for and go home to run their busy lives. Hackers and virus inventors were always boys or young men, with too much spare time on their hands.

The only man in the office was 'Old Bob', the retired warehouse man, now helping with telephone queries. He refused to touch a computer. That was why he didn't want to work in the warehouse any longer, now everyone had to use portable devices for stock control. He was too old to bother with all that new technology, he said.

So, who was left? Only the work experience kid. He seemed an irritating little know-all, getting under everybody's feet, the son of Houseman's golfing partner, taken on in his school holidays as a favour. They said he was a whizz with computers. Maybe he really was. Whoever had loused up that system had to be a whizz, hadn't he? Was it unfair to home in on him straight away? He seemed the best bet. He didn't have a job to lose if Houseman went bust as a result of his meddling.

Boys that age could be staggeringly irresponsible, he thought wryly. And he should know! When the police banged on their door his father had gone ballistic.

"Hacking into GCHQ? Never! He's no traitor. He's just an idiot!"

"But hacking into GCHQ shouldn't be possible, should it? They need to improve their security. I could fix it."

"You blithering xxx ! Xxxxx !"

The school told him never to darken their doors again – well, the police had impounded the school library computers.

When the police had extracted the contents of his bedroom computer, his father had taken the machine to Oxfam. He couldn't exist without a computer, so he just had to buy it back secretly and catch the next train to London, never to return.

The police soon tracked him down in Earl's Court and paid him the occasional visit, especially when he started making them mugs of tea in the middle of the night. Got quite matey.

"Have a free copy of my new computer game, 'Zombies trash GCHQ.'"

And the family forgave him eventually, once the money came rolling in.

So, it was worth a shot. If he was right, it would save upsetting anyone else with hostile questions.

Back in his room he groaned at the room service menu. It was the same old unappetising stuff he had eaten so many times before. Normally he had papers to study, maybe a conference presentation or a contract to be signed the next day. He didn't notice what he ate as he read them. Far better that way.

Tonight there was nothing to study, nothing to take his mind off the food. And it would leave its nasty smell to haunt him all night long. No, far better tonight to go down and eat the rubbish in a change of scene.

The décor in the 'Bistro' was presumably an attempt to look cheerful and modern, but succeeded only in looking cheap and very nasty. He looked for a table by a wall in a corner, but so, of course, did everyone else. It was, as usual, best to try not to notice the leathery steak, the ten times reheated oven chips and the wilting salad, but there was nothing to distract his attention except his fellow diners.

They were the standard issue: two youngsters gazing raptly into each other's eyes and an old couple munching away in companionable silence. What on earth were they doing in a soulless place like this? All the rest were in business suits. Six of them were wearing their jackets, paying rapt attention to the oldest-looking man at their table. Candidates for a job? Poor sods! thought Justin. The rest, each alone, had draped their jackets on their chair backs. They were all gazing raptly at their smart phones and trying not to notice the food.

Suddenly it occurred to Justin that he was breaking the mould. On the back of his chair hung a lightweight bomber jacket and he was wearing a T shirt and jeans. They would surely think he was a white van man, who had arrived in one of the few tradesmen's vehicles amongst the ranks of firms' cars parked outside.

Ought he to be making an effort to smarten himself up, he wondered, yet again. But wouldn't his staff be surprised? Maybe they would tease him. All his brainiest employees were equally oblivious to their clothing. Some wore the same outfit for weeks on end. One or two sometimes smelled as if they slept in it as well. But what if they were copying him, all following the low standard that he set? Now there's an uncomfortable thought.

His company was not a little maverick any more, just selling games and apps. It was growing up, making serious systems for commerce and industry. It really was time to establish some sort of head office. This current problem proved that. If he had been trekking in the Himalayas there would have been nobody to deal with this emergency. And if he'd broken his neck in the Himalayas, what then? Maybe the glib management experts ought to think again about the Kiss Principle. When does simplicity become inadequacy? Right now!

Well, time for coffee, as it was still only eight o'clock. Waiter? No one in sight. Aha, a coffee station on the far wall. He walked over and lifted the coffee pot. Empty.

"It's okay, mate. They've gone to get some more."

It was a real white van man, thinking he'd found a mate.

"You come far?" asked Justin, putting on a matey tone.

"Bermondsey" said the van man. "Got a few days' work rewiring this place for a new computer system. What's your line?"

"Computer systems," said Justin. "Got lumbered with sorting one that's gone haywire."

"Bet it's sabotage, you mark my words," said the van man, tapping the side of his nose.

Justin nodded. "My guess is a kid on work experience, real clever dick."

"Think they know it all, these kids. Just wait till they've lived a little. Where have they got to with the coffee?"

Justin glanced at the crumpled newspaper lying next to the coffee pots. "Look at that," he said. "What do you make of all this? Another clapped out old entertainer being pilloried for hugging his fans forty years ago."

Van Man peered at the lurid headlines and read the text below, mouthing the words as he read. "Poor old bloke!" he said eventually. "Done for giving the little kiddies a hug and a kiss. How's he different from Father Christmas?"

"It's going to be hard to persuade any man to play Father Christmas from now on, I guess," said Justin. "Maybe they'll have to have Mother Christmases instead."

"Then someone will say they're all lesbians or something," said the van man. "Aha, coffee at last."

They helped each other to the coffee, then headed back towards their tables. Van Man reached his first and waved towards a vacant chair at his table. Justin took it. Any diversion was better than nothing.

Van Man's phone rang. It was his boss telling him to pay his own hotel bill and claim it back afterwards. He pulled a face and switched the phone off.

"What you got there?" asked Justin, by way of conversation.

Van Man passed it over. "Only had it a couple of days. Got some of those clever 'Just in Case' apps but haven't worked out how to use them yet."

Useful consumer research, thought Justin. He explained how to use them and made a mental note of how easily the van man understood.

"Lucky I met you," said the van man. "Guess you must have got these same apps as well."

"Mmm!" said Justin Chase. If only he knew!

"Going to watch the footie tonight?" asked the van man.

"What time is it on?"

"Ten thirty. It's a recording. They're going to put it on that big screen over there. Might be a bit of fun if a few of us come down."

Justin thought about it for a moment. The man was good company, but he knew he needed a rest. It had not exactly been an easy day, and, on top of that, his body was on Italian time, so that meant the broadcast started at eleven thirty. No, let's be sensible.

He made his excuses, then headed for the door. "Enjoy the footie!" he called.

Back in his dismal room he went in search of the TV remote controller, finding it at last under a pile of leaflets in a drawer. The TV was very loath to respond to any combination of buttons, but at last it deigned to light up.

'Welcome, Mr Justin Chase'.

"Grr!" growled Justin. "Where are the programmes?"

'Pay for a sex film.'

No way. Get plenty of the real thing for free. Free? Bunch of flowers, new frock, pair of Louboutins at 1K a pop. Ought to pay for sex films instead. Far cheaper. News programmes, where were they? Ah, at last! The Americans were disclaiming responsibility for the assassination of a terrorist chieftain, but bragging about killing a dozen terrorists with a drone. The Navy Seals had killed half a dozen more at one go. What was the point of it all? Kill one and three pop up in his place. Was there nothing relaxing to watch? No there wasn't. He switched to the music channels, but they were all raucous pop.

He switched off the TV, put the two pillows against the bed head, pulled off his shoes and collapsed onto the bed. There seemed to be nothing else to do but think. That was seldom a comfortable occupation. In these surroundings it was more uncomfortable than usual.

There was something badly wrong with his life. He felt it most strongly whenever he visited his family. They seemed to do nothing special, but appeared to get so much enjoyment from little things like a new greenhouse, a holiday in France or even a barbecue with friends.

People dream of fame and fortune, of living in luxury in beautiful places, hobnobbing with glamorous people. If only they knew! The most beautiful place can be ruined by the weather or unhappiness. You soon get used to luxury and start noticing the faults. And the people? When the stardust stops dazzling your eyes, the 'beautiful people' seem so synthetic, quite commonplace, or even downright ugly. And the conversation? Trivial, brainless gossip. Celebs with no talent for anything except self-promotion.

Was this all there was to success? Was this what he had been striving for as he worked so hard to get his business off the ground? Most people work hard all their lives for pretty modest rewards, so he had been lucky. He had no cause to complain, and yet - he could understand why some people flipped, threw away all they'd gained and went bumming around the world.

You're just greedy and ungrateful, he told himself. What more could you possibly wish for? Marcella, there to be hugged every day, to tease him and laugh with him, to talk over plans with him, even to argue with him.

It was evil to wish somebody would run over Paolo. The pair of them were so obviously meant for each other. Their marriage was so strong even a little infidelity on both sides couldn't rock it. He was just making a fool of himself. He had to wean himself off Marcella.

And Lucrezia – well, now her brother was home he may never see her again, never even get to know if she really did jump off the Burj Khalifa.

Sometimes he envied his sister her quietly busy life, all so wholesome and conventional. Could he bear to spend his life as a country solicitor? No way!

He gave a sigh, heaved himself off the bed, hung up his clothes, then headed for the bathroom. Thank goodness it was bedtime at last!

CHAPTER 12

IT ALL BEGAN SO WELL

Wonder of wonders! This benighted hotel had got something right: The Full English, nicely cooked, with lots of appetising lean bacon rashers. He helped himself to a good portion of everything the food police seemed to think he should avoid, then filled a bowl with fruit to keep his conscience quiet. With such a pleasant start, maybe the day would turn out to be a good one.

As a result of that indulgence he arrived at Houseman's warehouses a little later than intended. Another night watching the traffic roar around Spaghetti Junction was too awful to contemplate, so he'd brought his bags with him, hoping for a quick exit. Even so, the work experience kid had not arrived. He had plenty of time to discuss his strategy with Houseman. The poor man looked stricken.

"His dad's my best friend. He's not in the warehouse business so why should he want to ruin me?" he wailed.

"If it is the kid, I doubt he wants to ruin you," Justin reassured him."Probably thinks he's being clever, getting one up on the oldies. Anyway, you wouldn't want to have to sack one of the women, would you? I gather they've all been with you for yonks."

"Name's Kevin," said Houseman miserably. "Shall I ring his dad?"

"Not yet. We've no proof, and I could be wrong. Let me poke around and see what comes out of the woodwork."

Why couldn't the schools teach these feckless kids to be on time? Justin grumbled as he connected his laptop to the system and brought up a selection of the mangled orders and invoices. It was more than irritating.

Kevin sauntered in, throwing cocky remarks at the youngest woman, who gave as good as she got.

Just the type, thought Justin. Thinks he's God's gift to the world and adults are as daft as Dad's Army. It would be quite satisfying to nail him. No need to feel a heel.

"Kevin!" he called, after the boy had had a few minutes to settle in, "I could do with your help. I'm sure Mr Houseman won't mind if you leave the project he set you till later. Come over and pull up a chair."

"Yea, no problem," drawled Kevin. He sauntered over, trying to look cool.

"They tell me you're quite a whiz with computers, so maybe you can give me a lesson on this. You see here, well, I order a box of Shnazzles, so what do I get? I get three boxes delivered. Right? Great! I can give my friends a few, then I'll be really popular. Do I get invoiced for one or for three? I can't quite make it out. The invoice looks like just one, so am I onto a winner? Had I better order loads more? Now, these people are ordering three boxes so they'll get nine, wont they? Bet they'll be celebrating!"

Kevin was shaking his head. "No, they'll just get one."

"One box?" said Justin. "I must be a bit thick. I can't quite follow. But what about this? This looks really clever. I order two boxes of Wombles and the system sends me a box of Flingels and a box of Teflors. Then what does it charge me for? Three boxes of Wingles? Am I right? What a joke!" he laughed.

"No, look," laughed Kevin, "you get charged for three boxes of Bingos."

"Amazing!" laughed Justin. "You really are a whiz. How did you make it do that? It must have been really tricky."

"Well, I reversed this bit of the code here, and here, and I changed this instruction just here, see - -"

"Mmmm," said Justin. "Would you excuse me?" He fetched in Houseman.

"Now, Kevin," he said, smiling, "would you explain that again so Mr Houseman can enjoy the joke? He'll be impressed to hear how you made the system mix up all the orders."

He watched in grim exasperation as Kevin's face began to flash alternately puce and white. Houseman's face was purple. Justin wondered if he would need to protect the boy from the old man's rage. It had been ridiculously easy to trick the silly kid into admitting his guilt. He had jumped straight into the trap. He'd expected to have to cross-examine him for hours. Hole in one!

The office manager had been following events from her work station. She could hear an operator struggling with an irate customer.

"What should we tell the customers, Mr Houseman?" she asked.

Houseman looked at Justin.

"Tell them we've just discovered a fault in our system and it's being fixed right now," said Justin.

"And tell them to tear up the invoices. They'll get a correct one soon and a special discount for their trouble."

"Another complaint, Mr Houseman," called an operator.

"Can we hear it on speaker phone?" asked Justin.

Now everyone could hear the torrent of complaints, the threats to change supplier. Everyone glared at Kevin.

"Nobody's complaining about getting too many. Bet they'll orders loads more." Kevin tried to brazen it out.

"What the hell do you think you're doing? Trying to put me out of business? This is going to ruin us. Our margins are so tight already we'll be supplying hordes of people at a loss with this discount. Who put you up to this? I'll have you in court. You and your dad will be in hock for ever, paying all my lost profits back."

"Look, Uncle Jeff," Kevin gasped, "It's only a joke, an April fool sort of thing. I didn't mean any harm. Don't tell my Dad. He'll murder me."

"And so he should!" yelled Houseman, "and don't 'Uncle Jeff' me. That's not going to cut any ice any more. I always thought you were a right sneaky little bastard. I should never have been daft enough to let you into my office. Well, you mucked up my new system. Unscramble it double quick or I'll call your dad to come and help. I'm going to stand over you all the way. Come on, get at it!"

Sweating visibly, Kevin stared at the computer screen, then looked frantically at Justin.

"What would you do, Mr Chase? I don't know - -"

"You don't know how to put it right?" asked Justin.

Miserably, the boy shook his head.

Justin steered Houseman back to his office. "It's no good," he said. "Yes, it would be good for him to be shown how to do it, but neither you nor I have the time for that right now. We both have businesses to run. You need to get your system sorted quickly. If you get him out of my hair I can concentrate on that. But first we need to get the silly kid to tell us exactly when he started altering the code, so we can time the restore."

Houseman sighed. "I don't know how to apologise for dragging you here and putting you through all this unpleasantness. Your system was perfect for us until that idiot got at it. I don't know how I can repay you."

"Look," said Justin. "I need to fix this system too, so I wont charge you. I'll do my best to sort it for you now."

He watched wryly as Houseman marched the kid off the premises, then settled down with a mug of tea.

Some April fool's joke! He decided to study it for a while instead of getting rid of it with a system restore. It was amazingly complex and clever. He enjoyed teasing out the intricacies of Kevin's malicious recoding and reversing them one by one. When Jeff Houseman wandered in to ask how it was going, he asked for the kid's address and phone number. The London office might want to add him to their team, if he was old enough. Once the loopholes had been closed, they could ask him to challenge the programme again to see if it was now secure. He'd enjoy that.

By lunchtime he had managed to explain Kevin's methodology to the office manager. She was very bright and picked it up quickly. He half listened, impressed, as she went around her colleagues, teaching them to spot any remaining malfunctions and deal with them. He gave her the phone numbers of his team in Gravesend. She could ring them if she got stuck after he had gone.

Now, all that was left was to find and close the loopholes. They should never have been there in the first place. If Kevin could find them, then others would eventually. That would be the afternoon's job. If he failed, then it would be back to the design team.

By afternoon tea time he felt that he had cracked it.

Houseman let his staff make personal phone calls and surf the net during that quarter of an hour, as long as the phones didn't go unanswered. It was time to phone infuriating organisations like the Gas Board or order groceries. One women was trying to get Old Bob to take an interest in computers. They were sitting together at her work station laughing themselves silly. Justin walked over with his mug of tea and looked over their shoulders - funny cats videos on YouTube. He was soon joining in the whoops of hysterical laughter and in danger of spilling his tea. He must watch these clips whenever he felt in need of a laugh.

He was talking to another operator when the words 'Burj Khalifa' caught his attention. Why were they talking about that? As he turned to look the woman let out a wail.

"Oh, no! That's absolutely awful. They shouldn't show things like this on YouTube. Don't you think it's wrong?" she asked no one in particular.

"What are you talking about? Show it again," demanded her neighbour.

Justin walked over, just in time to see the video begin.

On the screen a tall man in a dark shirt stepped out of a window onto a balcony. He turned and held out his hand. A foot appeared, clad in an elegant sparkling shoe with a very high heel. It was followed by a slender leg.

Very promising, thought Justin.Let's see the rest of this glamour puss.

Out stepped Marilyn Monroe, or at least someone wearing her famous dress. It looked strangely familiar.

The picture was indistinct, presumably shot by a mobile phone camera from an unusual angle – from behind and from somewhere just above.

The couple seemed to be looking over the balcony railing, pointing down to the riot of coloured lights gleaming beneath the black night sky. The ants crawling along bands of yellow light must be traffic on motorways. The only way to photograph those motorways from such a height must be from a helicopter or the Burj Khalifa. The girl looked down and recoiled as if afraid. The man pulled her close as if to comfort her.They had their backs to the camera but they looked an elegant couple, he with dark, collar length hair and she with lighter hair that was glamorously long and gently wavy.

Suddenly they both turned around to face the camera.

Justin gazed at the screen in amazement. The woman was Lucrezia! How amazing! What a coincidence! He was actually able to see her far away on her trip to

Dubai. Well, well, and didn't she look stunning in the dress he'd chosen for her? And those shoes! They looked like the Christian Louboutins that greedy girlfriend had tried to wheedle him into buying for her at a cost of nearly a thousand euros. My, oh my! The little convent girl had turned into a swan. What a transformation!

His amazement turned to concern. Whatever the couple had turned to see was having a disturbing effect. They dragged off their shoes and hurriedly climbed over the balcony railings. What on earth were they doing?

Astride the railings, wobbling a little, they leaned towards each other and kissed. Next moment they were standing with their heels on the outside of the railings and toes pointing out over a drop of nearly half a mile.

Suddenly an arm waved a gun from the window behind them. Simultaneously the couple launched themselves away from the railings and disappeared.

Next moment the gunman was at the balcony railing, apparently firing down at them. Then he quickly retreated the way he had come.

Justin slumped onto the nearest chair and took a gulp of his tea. He felt weak at the knees. What had he seen? Could he believe his eyes? Did he have to believe it, or could he just wish it away? It was only a video.

When did it happen? Last night, as he was grumbling about his discomfort in that dismal hotel? Was Lucrezia really leaping to her death by half mile drop?

It was long enough ago for the comments to be rolling in. The women were discussing them energetically. What would you choose, a bullet or a jump to certain death? Opinions were divided. What did Justin think?

I need to get out of here, and quick!

CHAPTER 13

HOME

Justin ran down the platform and launched himself at the narrowing gap in the nearest door, cursing the queue at the ticket office. The train was already gliding off silently as he flung himself at the nearest empty seat.

He sat for a moment, trying to gather his wits, then looked around. The first class carriage was almost full. He'd been lucky to find a seat at a table for two. Luckily the other passenger was lost in whatever was on the screen of his tablet. Relieved, Justin set up his own laptop and slumped back into his seat, breathing a sigh of relief. Thank goodness he'd managed to get away!

It hadn't been easy, but he'd managed to pull himself together enough to organise his getaway. The office manager had agreed to tell Houseman that he'd received an urgent message, asking him to go to London as quickly as possible, and that he was not to bother about charges for Justin's time. If he hadn't been feeling so shell-shocked it might have been amusing to try to guess what hourly rate he personally might be able to command, but he was past caring. Houseman could just settle the bill for that miserable hotel and call it quits.

He'd no idea what the flying taxi service or Blacky's owner was going to charge. Would have to ask Lucrezia about that. Lucrezia - ! Grief! He would never be able to ask her anything again!

He let his thoughts coast for a while, unable to get a grip. Why did he feel so shaken? Of course it was unpleasant hearing that someone you had known or admired had been killed, but this was far more than unpleasant. There must be something very special about this death. But he'd known her such a short time. How long? His mind seemed to be trying to absent itself, to avoid focusing on the situation.

Saturday evening, Sunday, Monday, and early on Tuesday morning, when they had parted at the entrance to his building. It had hurt to see how delighted she was to be going home to meet her brother.

He'd watched her sadly as she hurried away along the street, the poor little rich girl with the dress he'd chosen for her in a plastic shopping bag. She'd turned to give him a last happy smile and a wave.

And now he would never see her again.

Why was he going to London? He had no need to, no desire to. It was just a ruse to get away. Anything had seemed preferable to having to endure a long inquest into the boy's behaviour, or even worse, an evening with Houseman's family,and above all, Houseman's daughter. Yes, of course she might be a nice kid, but he had no stomach for teenage girls, especially now! And another night in that hotel? No, thank you! Finding a flight from Birmingham so late in the day seemed highly unlikely, so it seemed logical to go to London. There were surely far more flights home to Rome from there.

Could he make Heathrow in time for the usual eight pm Alitalia flight? He looked at his watch. Not a chance. What else was on offer? He reached for the laptop and keyed in evening flights. Only Air Malta? Seemed to take at least twenty-four hours. Via Antarctica? Nothing else till Thursday? Must be something, Get home to Rome or find another blasted hotel.

Home to Rome. Those words seemed wrong together. 'Home is where the heart' is felt like a sick joke. The thought of Rome, and his fabulous penthouse, turned his stomach. So where is home? The flats in Singapore and Rio didn't call to him either. He felt no more at home in them than in a really good hotel in any other city.

The little Earl's Court flat. It was ages since he'd stayed there. Couldn't take a glamorous woman to a mean little dump like that – or a business contact. Nowadays he took a suite in a smart hotel whenever he was in town. Yes, he would go home to the flat. It was about time. He'd had Lucy check it every few months to make sure no harm had come to it, so it should be usable. For years it had been his only refuge when his company was just a dream. He would go back there and relive those days, telling himself how far he had progressed, and in such a short time. Surely that would put him back together again.

Emerging from Earl's Court tube station, he was met by a barrage of familiar sounds and smells, especially the smell of curry. Yes, the same old Indian restaurant was still there. It was good to be able to order the same as usual from the same assistants who had served him long ago. Loaded with brown paper bags as well as his overnight bag, he followed the familiar route home.

There was his little basement flat. Oh, but how was he going to get in? Of course he hadn't brought the key. He threaded his way along the back alley, among the overflowing dustbins. The slab was still there. He put down his bags and lifted the corner of the greasy slab. Amazing! The spare key was still there, after all this time!

The flat smelled stale and musty, but the smell of curry soon blotted that out. He opened the dirty windows, then went in search of a spoon and fork. The tiny table against the window was thick with dust, but he unpacked the paper carriers, prised off the tops and ate the food straight from the metal cartons. Then he took the stinking empties out to the dustbins to rid the flat of the smell. Soon it would be back to stale and musty again.

He found a can of lager in the cupboard. It was warm and way out of date, but there was nothing else to drink. He didn't dare to open the fridge. It had been unused for so long its possible contents didn't bear thinking about.

The whole place was disgusting. What on earth was he doing in a dump like this? He thought of his sparkling white penthouse in Rome. Was it really the antidote to this: an attempt to get as far away from this as possible? He wished he could get away from it right now. He needed a walk. Hurriedly he locked the flat and set off.

Those evening walks in the old days had made his fortune, keeping his conscious mind quietly occupied, so that his unconscious was set free to dream, to dream up the crazy games and apps that had captured the imaginations of so many youngsters, bringing him undreamed of riches. Often these inventions seemed to leap into his conscious mind fully formed, amazing him as much as anybody else.

He no longer had to wrack his brains to think of ways to market his inventions. Now he employed teams of people to do the animation and the marketing. He was more profitably employed in dreaming up more of those money spinners.

Tonight his conscious mind refused to be put to sleep. "What's happened to the butchers?" it demanded. "Why does it look like a Polish mini-market? Why is the men's hairdressers now a nail boutique? And where did this 'Slug and Lettuce' place come from? Where's the old Irish pub?"

It was not his patch any more, no longer home. It was a grubby, noisy, smelly, alien place where he no longer belonged. Where did he belong? He hadn't a clue. He had become part of the jet set, a modern nomad. He owned flats at the far corners of the earth but belonged in none of them. He had no real home, no refuge.

He dragged himself back to the dirty flat, pulled off his shoes and flung himself onto the narrow bed against the wall. A cloud of dust rose from the shabby bedspread and from the grubby pillows he piled behind his head.

From force of habit he lit up the laptop. It was impossible to resist the temptation to touch in YouTube. The story had moved on and acquired a title: 'The Suicide Lovers.' An astonishing number of people claimed to have seen them in Dubai last night.

The Armani Hotel on the lower floors of the tower had been persuaded to reveal their names: Phillip and Elizabeth Smith of Sandringham, U.K. How did they keep their faces straight while they checked in? Hotels always demanded to handle your passport, surely. They must have had false ones. She had implied her brother had more than one.

Someone claimed to have dined at the next table in the Atmosphere Restaurant on floor 122. The waiter had brought Mrs Smith a tiny cake with a lighted candle. It must have been her birthday. They were in great spirits, laughing and joking with each other and the waiters. And they had danced in the night club as well. It was clearly impossible to avoid being noticed these days. How long before their real identities were revealed, he wondered. But did that matter, now that they were dead?

He steeled himself and played the video again. They both looked so vibrantly alive it was impossible to accept that he was watching their deaths. When they turned to face the window they looked startled, but not the least bit frightened, as he would have been at the sight of a man pointing a gun at him in deadly earnest. Again and again he watched them kiss as they climbed over the railings. They seemed to be almost smiling. How could any sane person smile at the sight of a half mile drop below?

He had never seen so many comments generated by a YouTube video. On and on they went. Who was the gunman? Why did he want to kill them? The Burj Khalifa management were insisting that his identity was unknown and there were no suspects. No, they had not secreted the bodies. No, they didn't know where the bodies had been taken to. Clothes found on the roof of the ground floor entrance lobby had been taken for forensic tests. No, there was definitely no cover up. That, of course, set off a host of conspiracy theories.

A migraine was threatening. He closed down the laptop, hauled himself off the bed and found a couple of aspirins. He had to run the water for a while before it seemed good enough to drink. As he surveyed the tiny flat, wondering what to do next, he found himself looking into the beautiful tempting eyes of Alexa Wilding, modelling the part of Lady Lilith. But the eyes that looked back at him were Lucrezia's.

No, he thought vehemently. That was too much. He lifted her roughly off the wall and walked towards the door. Into the dustbin she must go.

He opened the door and looked at the overflowing dustbins. He would have to dump lovely clean white Lucezia between the dustbins. He took her back indoors and stood for a while wondering what to do. The picture had hung on a long string. It was easy to hang it back there, face to the wall. Even that felt like sacrilege.

That really put the lid on things. This nauseating flat just had to go. First thing tomorrow he would ring Lucy at the London office and ask her to get an agent round to market it. She would need to arrange for cleaners to strip the place of all this disgusting old furniture and stuff. If the agent advised it a decorator could be called in as well – anything to get it off his hands.

He would leave Lady Lilith for the buyers. Let her fuel their fantasies.

CHAPTER 14

SURPRISE! SURPRISE!

With an expression of grim resignation, Justin watched as the imposing black doors of his penthouse flat swung open. Then he stiffened. Sounds were coming from within. Of course, it was Thursday afternoon. Anna was there, as usual, cleaning his pristine apartment. She came bustling out of the kitchen and stopped as she spotted him.

"Mr Chase, you're back, Sir. Did you have a good trip?"

"Yes, very good," he replied wearily. "And is all well with you? Family all okay?"

"Oh, yes, very well. And we've a nice surprise for you, Sir," she beamed.

Oh dear! he thought. Any more surprises I can well do without. He put on a wan smile. "Do tell me about it."

"Your friend, the Marchesa, has made you something really clever for dinner: Veal Marsala. What do you think about that?"

What did he think about that? Justin's head reeled. He didn't know any marchionesses, did he?

The 'friend' in question ended the suspense by appearing from the bedroom, carrying a mop and bucket.

His heart stopped, restarted itself with a great lurch, then began to beat as if he was running a marathon.

"Hello, Justin, welcome back!" beamed Lucrezia. "Anna says the veal will keep a few days in the fridge, so it will just need microwaving whenever you feel like eating it."

"My Lady, you should not be mopping floors," Anna wailed. "Leave that for me, please."

"Anna," said Lucrezia firmly, "I wasted so much of your time with the Veal Marsala the least I can do is try to help you catch up with your work. This marble is so beautiful it's a joy to mop it. We just have those old red tiles. You can't tell whether they're clean or dirty, so there would be no pleasure at all in mopping those. Mr Chase is very lucky to have such a beautiful home, isn't he?" She flashed him a gorgeous smile. "I mopped your bedroom first. It should be dry now, so you can unpack."

"Thank you," he said weakly. He staggered off to his bedroom and collapsed onto the end of the bed, seeing stars. Had someone thumped him between the eyes? He put his head in his hands and gave his hair a good rub. What was wrong with his head? Was he mad, or was it the rest of the world? Did he really see that video in Birmingham, or was it all a nightmare?

The sounds reaching his ears were very reassuring: pleasant house-cleaning sounds: two women chatting amiably, laughing at each other's comments. Anna's familiar voice was unmistakeable. But so was Lucrezia's. How could that be Lucrezia? Had he dreamed the YouTube video? Should he ring Houseman's office manager and ask her if they had really watched that shocking video together?

He pulled his phone out of his pocket to get her number, and out came his passport and the stub of his boarding pass. He had definitely just come back to Rome by the Alitalia midday flight. He had not been dreaming. No need to ring anybody and make a fool of yourself, Stupid, he told himself. Look at YouTube.

He powered up the laptop and rolled in YouTube. The flyer for the 'Suicide Lovers' was still there, amongst today's favourite offerings. He clicked it in and watched it yet again. It was definitely Lucrezia. And she was definitely in Dubai. There were all those people insisting they had seen her there in the Burj Khalifa on Tuesday evening, celebrating something, presumably her birthday. Once again he watched the pair of them leap off the balcony. It was a stunt. It must have been a stunt.

He scrolled through the comments, looking for revelations about how the pair had pulled it off, but nobody seemed to have twigged that yet. Everyone was still calling it suicide. The pathetic conspiracy halfwits were making up ridiculous explanations of how and why somebody had spirited the bodies away and hidden them, leaving their clothes behind.

And what a stunt it was! People as far away as Australia and the USA were sticking their oars in, trying to lay the blame on all manner of organisations and people for driving the poor lovers to self-destruction.

Phew! he thought. What a relief! And it would be great to hear the explanation. While half the world was gasping for more information, he was soon going to hear it from the horse's mouth.

He set about with enthusiasm unpacking his things and putting them in their proper places. His watch was still on English time, so he set it right by the bedside clock. That's better. Shouldn't get any jet lag from a one hour time difference. Anna had another thirty-five minutes to work, so he could fill in the time by freshening up. After a shower, some fresh clothes and a decent shave using his best razor instead of that weedy light-weight travel razor, he was feeling quite human again as he slicked down his light brown hair.

"Good night, Mr Chase," called Anna.

He went out to pay her and see her off, then went back to confront Lucrezia. She was mopping the back of the huge living room.

"So," he said, smiling conspiratorially, "how was Dubai? Did your brother help you jump off the Burj Khalifa?"

She nodded. "It was alright."

"Just alright?" he asked. "No big deal?"

"It was fantastic, of course," she said. "Did you find out what was wrong with the computers in Birmingham?"

"It was sabotage," he said. "A kid your age, doing work experience. Do you have work experience in Italy?"

"I don't know. What is it?" she asked.

"Businesses invite school kids in for a few weeks to experience the world of work. His father is the warehouse owner's best friend, so he thought he could have fun playing clever tricks on the adults. He could have bankrupt the company. Boys your age can be daft beyond belief."

She sighed and rolled her eyes. "What did you do with the boy, hand him to the police?"

"I'm suggesting to my English office that they might like to offer him a job, if he's old enough. He's got the kind of brain we need," he grinned.

She gasped and laughed. "You're amazing! So you managed to put the programme right? The poor people won't go bankrupt."

"I hope not. The kid did me a favour, really. He found a loophole where someone could get in to damage the system. I hope I've fixed it now. I'll have to contact a few of my key team leaders tomorrow to tell them how to apply the fix. Now, I'm dying to hear how you pulled off that stunt in Dubai."

"Stunt?" she said. "I don't understand - I'd better finish this floor. You can't enjoy your home until it's dry and I haven't even washed half of it yet. It looks so white and clean, doesn't it, but the water in this bucket looks quite dirty. I'll have to change it." She picked up the bucket and carried it to the cleaner's cupboard.

Justin fetched the laptop and set it up on the dining table, tuned to YouTube. When she came back with the clean water he called her.

"Come look at this, Lucrezia."

Obediently she came over to the table.

"Look at this." He watched her face as she stared at the video.

Lucrezia gasped and covered her mouth with her hands, in that universal female gesture of surprise and embarrassment. "How on earth did this get on the Net? Chez will be livid."

"Well, I can't wait to hear how you did it."

"Did what?"

"How you faked your suicide, of course."

"What?" she exclaimed.

"How you've convinced half the world that your bodies are hidden away in Dubai, while you're actually here in Rome mopping my floor."

He scrolled down the comments to show her the interest her 'suicide' had aroused. "Well, come on, I'm dying to hear how you did it."

"I must finish this floor first," she said. "And I really need to know if the veal is the way you like it. Anna said to leave mopping the kitchen till last, so could you taste it now while I finish off in here – please."

Before he could say another word she hurriedly chivvied him out of the way and began determinedly mopping around the dining table.

He opened his mouth to argue, but she clearly didn't intend to answer, just mopped with great concentration.

He sighed and took himself off to the kitchen. She was right, really. It was a good idea to get the mopping done with, so they could relax. And it would surely be a good long story; liven up the evening.

The Veal Marsala tasted very good indeed. He was

hungry, so he put it ready in one of the microwave ovens. All that tasty sauce needed something to mop it up so he put a large potato in the other microwave, then fished out a bag of frozen vegetables. Dinner would take only a few minutes to get onto the table.

"Are you hungry, Lucrezia?" he called, "or did you have a good lunch?"

"No, I only had coffee and biscuits. Yes, I suppose I am hungry. Would you like to eat my veal?"

"I can't wait. Shall we eat as soon as you've finished?"

"Yes, please. Now, there's only the kitchen left, so -"

"So, you want me out of the way. Well, I can phone my office in Rio about the fix. They'll be at work now. I'll have to try Singapore in the morning, early, then London a bit later. Enjoy your mopping."

Good. That was Rio sorted, so now for a good dinner, and Lucrezia's intriguing story. The bucket and mop had disappeared and the sound of water was coming from her suite, so she must be freshening up now for dinner. The living room floor looked dry, so he threw himself on the sofa and waited cheerfully.

She was right: the white marble floor was beautiful, every slab unique, each covered with a silvery picture of a magic snowy world, all works of art created entirely by Nature herself. Yes, the whole flat was a bit over the top, probably it was some sort of unconscious desire to expunge that horrible little flat he had somehow managed to exist in for so many years, but so what? White was a beautiful colour, fresh, clean, perfect. And split it through a prism and you had all the lovely colours of the rainbow. How nice that Lucrezia, whiteness personified, could appreciate it too!

What had led Anna to call her 'My Lady'? And before that, hadn't she said, 'Your friend, the Marchesa'? Well, well! What would his parents say if he could tell them he had a marchioness mopping his floors?

The floor by the table looked dry. He strode off to the kitchen and turned on the microwaves, took the cutlery and glasses to the dining table, then went back to choose some red wine. A nice soft merlot style would be perfect for the veal – Montepulciano? Perfect. He opened it to let it breathe and put it on the table, just as Lucrezia appeared in the pale green dress he had chosen for her.

"My Lady, Marchesa, let me show you to your table," he smirked. With a bow and a sweeping gesture he led the way across the living room and held a chair for her.

"Thank you, Sir," she said quietly, eyes downcast.

"So you really are a marchioness? Well, well. I'll have to polish up my manners, wont I."

"Oh, please," she protested. "The law says that titles mean nothing these days, but some people still like using them. I can't imagine why, can you?"

"Well, it does sound rather romantic, especially in Italian: La Markayza."

"It just sounds embarrassing to me."

"So, what is your brother, a duke?"

"No, no, he's just a marchese, a marquis, the same."

"Marquis of where? Isn't there usually some place name attached?"

"Monrosso."

"Oh, so that's why you called him Cesare Monrosso when you phoned the air taxis. I wondered why you had different surnames."

"Chez does use his title a bit. As a freelance you don't have a company behind you. If his business card just said Cesare Bordano was offering to restructure your armed forces you'd just toss it in the bin, wouldn't you. If it says 'Cesare, il Marchese di Monrosso' they might decide to offer him lunch out of curiosity. Then all he has to do is talk them into it."

"Is he good at that, talking them into things?"

"I think he could sell snow to the Eskimos."

"He sounds quite a man, your brother. I'd like to meet him. Where is he now? Have you left him at home all on his own?"

She shook her head sadly. "He's gone already. Left this morning."

For a moment he saw again the sad child with her head drooping against the window in her bedroom. Heartless brute, that brother! Those emails were clearly conventional greetings that meant nothing.

"Does he know you've been lodging with me?" he asked anxiously.

"Yes, of course. Said to thank you very much on his behalf. Would like to take you out for a meal or something some time. Oh, and he has some of your apps. He thinks they're great."

"Did he take any interest in the kitchen?"

She shook her head. "He went out and got us some pizza for breakfast."

They both laughed, but Lucrezia's laugh seemed forced. Poor Kid!

"Well, I'm so glad you came back. It was good to see your smiling face when I got home. You're nice to have around, so I hope you'll regard this as your second home." Especially as you're now sixteen, he thought, refilling her glass under cover of replenishing his own.

"You really are so very kind. I can't thank you enough," she said. "I wasn't sure if you would really want me back, but you did ask me to look after your flat and make you some meals. I've learned to mop floors and I'm going to learn to make lots of nice things like the veal, I promise."

"And it really was delicious," he enthused. "And now, pleeeese tell me about the Burj Khalifa trick. The suspense is killing me. How did you manage to survive a half mile fall without a parachute?"

"Well, of course, we didn't. How could anybody survive hitting the ground at nearly three hundred kilometres an hour, as fast as a Red Arrow train? Chez and his crazy friend rigged up a net for us to jump into."

"The video looked so real. Did you really jump off the top of the Burj."

"Yes. We asked the crazy man to let us do it against a black screen in a gym but he said the whole point of his film was to be authentic."

"It must have been terribly dangerous. Why on earth did you do it?"

"Well, Chez said the man had done him lots of favours, so he felt obliged to help him with his film. Chez has base-jumped the Khalifa a few times, so how could he refuse? And I had been begging Chez to take me down, so I couldn't refuse either, could I?"

"I thought you were going to parachute down, enjoying the view."

"So did I, but it was no fun at all."

"Angel, show the Burj Khalifa," said Justin. The wall appeared to dissolve, revealing the tallest building in the world stretching way up into the sky. "How did they fix the net? It's like a giant icicle, all sheet glass."

"Goodness only knows!" she moaned. "It was terrifying. The jumping wasn't bad. Chez said, 'Look at that gorgeous turquoise lake down there. We're going to dive in for a midnight swim. What could be more romantic?'"

"Angel, show view of lake from top of Burj Khalifa."

"Yes, I told you he could sell snow to Eskimos. After we fell into the net it all went sour. They had real trouble pulling us back into the building. Even Chez was getting rattled, and he's as hard as nails. I was terrified, looking down all that distance for so long with the net swaying, threatening to topple us out. When we managed to crawl back inside my knees were so weak I couldn't stand up."

"I hope you gave them both hell for putting you through that terrible ordeal," he said. "It was a disgusting way to treat you." The picture on his wall was giving him vertigo.

"Yes, I was so horrible to Chez he didn't hang around. Went straight off to Waziristan. Please excuse me - " The words tailed off as she put her dinner napkin to her face and pushed back her chair.

He caught her before she could blunder out of the room and pulled her face against his chest. She tried to pull away, then relaxed against him and sobbed. He stroked her lovely hair and made soothing noises, until at last the sobs died down. The extra glass of wine seemed to have made her emotional rather than relaxed.

"I'm so sorry. It was dreadful of me to embarrass you like that."

"What are friends for?" he murmured. "Now, why don't we just relax and listen to some nice music for a while. You're safe now, on terra firma - well almost. Angel, remove the pictures. I don't think I'd like this flat to be on top of the Khalifa. Five floors is high enough for me."

"Me too," she said, wiping her eyes and trying to smile.

"What's your favourite piece of music?" he asked. "Cheerful, if poss."

"Oh, there's so much that I love. Thrilling and not too sad or emotional, yes?"

"That's right. Not Elgar's Cello Concerto, say?"

"And not Mozart's Clarinet Concerto."

"Exactly. Love them both, but they make me think of funerals. Hope they'll play them for mine," he laughed.

"The Firebird!" she enthused. "Exciting and romantic - without being sentimental."

"Don't think I know it. Who wrote it?"

"Stravinsky. His first ballet, before he got so avant garde."

"Well, if you recommend it, perhaps you ought to introduce me to it. The Firebird. Tell me what it's about."

"The Firebird is the Phoenix, the magic immortal bird. When it's mortally wounded it bursts into flames, then a perfect remade bird flies out of the flames. In the ballet it helps a prince to kill an evil wizard dictator and rescue a princess. It's all very colourful and exciting."

"Angel, play The Firebird by Stravinsky, with pictures."

It was so delightful they agreed to play it again. He manoeuvred Lucrezia into sharing a sofa with him in a pretty cosy fashion. She must feel in need of a bit of human kindness, he thought ruefully, and he was the only source available. Well, he was going to make the most of this opportunity. There was so much he wanted to ask about Dubai, and if that made her cry again he could risk hugging her again, couldn't he?

"What did you think of Dubai? Did you see much?"

"We only had one evening. It's an interesting place. I think the Khalifa is magical, one of the most exquisite, romantic buildings in the world, as well as the tallest. All the space around it, the huge turquoise lake, lets you see the whole tower across the water. I loved the fountains, dancing to the music. Do you have a place there?

"Only a very small office there dealing with the whole UAE area. I go occasionally, but there are plenty of good hotels. People keep telling me property there might be a good investment, though."

"Well, I gather it's quite a safe, law-abiding place."

"But what about that gunman on the YouTube video. He wasn't really trying to kill you, was he?"

Lucrezia hesitated. "I don't know. I assumed he was part of the film. We'd have been sitting ducks in that net, wouldn't we?" She began to laugh a little hysterically.

Poor girl, he thought. Better change the subject. "Well, you looked very glamorous in your new white frock. Did your brother like it?"

"He loved it, thinks you have very good taste. He insisted on buying me the fanciest shoes he could find, covered with swarovski crystal, like your kitchen table."

"Did you wear them for your birthday party?"

She gave him a puzzled look. "My what?"

"The waiter brought you a cake with a candle, remember? It must be true, it's on YouTube."

"Oh, that," she murmured. "Yes, it was a celebration of sorts. Chez said the frock looked wrong without the shoes, so I had to."

"They certainly did look special. Next time we go to your place I'd like to see you wearing them."

"I gave them away yesterday, and the frock."

"Why on earth did you do that?"

"The girl who came to clean the house has just lost her proper job. She's entered a talent contest but can't afford an outfit. She's thrilled with the frock and the shoes are a perfect fit - isn't that amazing?"

It took his breath away. This unique little madam could give away shoes that probably cost her brother a thousand Euros, shoes that other women seemed desperate to own. Would he ever understand her?

"So, what are you going to do, now you're a grown up lady of sixteen? Are you going to tell the convent you're not coming back, or have you had enough of this scary world and want to go back to a peaceful life."

"Well, it has been a pretty scary week so far, hasn't it? And convents are nice safe quiet places, I suppose."

Her shoulders had taken on a sad droop so he gave her a friendly hug.

"Come on, cheer up. It's a bit soon to write off the world. You should give it a little longer. I expect your brother will be back soon, wont he? What has he gone to do in Waziristan, sell the Tornado?"

"Hunting again," she said, with a sigh of distress.

"Hunting? It's a long way to go for a bit of hunting. What is there so special to hunt in Waziristan?"

"Rats. Oh, no, Goodness knows. I mean yaks and yetis, you know."

Why was she so flustered?

"Rats? There's plenty of rats in Rome. What's so special about the rats in Waziristan?"

"They're evil monsters, really big and savage. The yetis are even worse. He's determined to catch a yeti."

What on earth had her brother been telling her?

"Why on earth pick Waziristan? Surely he knows it's a very dangerous place. It's crawling with terrorists and the Pakistani government is having no end of trouble trying to impose any kind of law and order. He must be crazy."

"Evil monsters, big, savage, dangerous, terrorists - "

"Angel, no problems. Shush."

"Of course he knows. He's trying to help."

"How is killing a few nasty big rats going to help? Rats must be the least of their problems. And I've never heard of Yetis doing any harm."

Lucrezia gave a deep sigh. "And it's all my fault. I was so horrid to him about Dubai he must have felt he had to do something. Poor Chez. I can't bear to think about it."

The tears began to flow again, so he hurriedly fetched

his napkin from the table and she buried her face in it.

"I'm sure you must be wrong to blame yourself. I can't believe it could possibly be your fault. But look, you might feel better if you tell him you've forgiven him for the Burj fiasco. Send him an email. Ask him to come home. Then you'll know you've done all you can."

"Do you think he'll take any notice?" she asked anxiously.

How do I know? he thought. I've never even met the man - and it sounds as if he doesn't care a fig about her feelings, but no point in telling her that. "Surely he will. Send him an email. I'm sure you'll feel better if you do."

She looked at him uncertainly for a moment, then went off to her bedroom.

"Angel, set up Rimsky-Korsakov's 'Scheherazade', he instructed. Beautiful, tuneful, soothing, just right.

When she returned he caught her hand and drew her back onto the sofa. "Now, you've sent him an email?"

She nodded. "I don't know if he'll get it. He's probably left his phone behind but he does use any computer he can find lying around in these places, so he might get the message somehow. Anyway, there's nothing more I can do, is there?" She sighed deeply, and her body slumped dejectedly again.

He slid an arm around her and drew her closer to him, until her head was resting on his shoulder. To his delight, she snuggled closer. He stroked her hair and murmured comforting things until at last she fell fast asleep.

Like the Cheshire Cat he sported a very smug smile.

CHAPTER 15

CLANG!

Lucrezia stirred. Justin opened his eyes. Was she waking up? The cool white penthouse was still filled with the seductive sounds and pictures of 'Scheherazade', the Arabian Nights romance, so he could not have been dozing for long.

She moved her head a little and her lips were now so close. He need only incline his head to reach them. The urge was irresistible. Well, she was sixteen now, so what was there to stop him?

Very gently he kissed her lovely mouth, then waited for the reaction. She smiled lazily and moved her hand up towards his shoulder. Oh joy! He kissed her again, more searchingly this time. Her hand tightened on his shoulder and her body moved a little closer. Then she gave a sigh and snuggled her face against his chest. Soon she seemed to have fallen asleep again.

So far so good, he exulted. What next? Was she willing or just too sleepy to know what she was doing? Something didn't feel quite right. Could he still be accused of taking advantage of her? How did things really stand with that brother? Cesare couldn't be naïve enough to imagine he could keep his hands off her, could he? Maybe he just didn't care, just as he couldn't care less about kitchens – or money, or McLarens. Perhaps to him she was just a nuisance. Selfish brute!

When the music came to an end she stirred. Her lips were accessible again. This time she returned the kiss. Then she murmured sleepily, "What time is it, Darling?"

"A quarter to ten, Sweetheart," he replied, delighted and surprised.

She stiffened and pulled herself upright, staring at him, wide-eyed with alarm. "Oh dear! I'm so sorry. I must have been dreaming."

"Sorry for what?" he laughed

"Oh well, you know - please excuse me." She hurriedly extricated herself from him and fled to her room.

He sighed. It was all too obvious she had thought he was somebody else. He had a rival. Was it Marcella all over again? He had come on the scene too late and she was not a snow white virgin after all. Well, Marcella was happily two-timing her husband, so maybe he should just help himself to a share of Lucrezia as well.

But maybe he had blown it. Maybe she was packing her things. What could he do to lower the temperature? Something non-threatening, something very ordinary. A walk? Why not? The temperature would still be oven-hot, but bearable by now, so the streets would be crowded. The atmosphere should be very jovial, enough to put anybody into a cheerful mood. It might be worth a try.

"Lucrezia," he called, "I'm thinking of going for a walk, maybe alongside the river. Do you fancy coming along? Get some fresh air?"

"Yes, please. Sounds good. Let me find my shoes."

Well, thank goodness for that! Normality restored.

Fresh air seemed to be in short supply in the streets below. The atmosphere felt leaden. When they turned into the next street they saw the waiter in the first restaurant taking in the glasses and cutlery, refusing a party a table outside and steering them inside.

"They don't usually close so early," Justin observed.

"They seem to think there's a storm brewing," she said. "It certainly feels very close. Maybe we shouldn't go far."

"I can't hear any thunder," Justin protested. "Let's at

least try to make the river and back."

They threaded their way amongst the tables spilling out into the street from half a dozen restaurants. Of course he let her go first, so he saw her run the gauntlet of highly personal remarks from groups of inebriated male tourists. Most were complimentary, especially from Italians, but some, particularly from the English and the Germans, were pretty suggestive and embarrassing. One comment was so obscene he felt a great surge of anger and longed to smack his fist into the leering drunken face.

Lucrezia stopped and waited for him, slipping her arm into his. "Don't take any notice," she whispered. "We don't want to get into a fight."

Once they were well clear of the scene he took stock. Even with her hair pulled back severely again she still attracted that kind of unwanted attention. *No wonder she didn't like to walk around in a Marilyn Monroe frock and f*** me heels, with that gorgeous hair on display. If she did he would need a cave-man club to keep the men at bay – and he was no cave-man!*

The sinuous curves of the Tevere (Tiber) wind through the city like a huge fat shiny snake, imprisoned by two or three storey high flood embankments, linked by romantic bridges carrying elaborate lights and statues that are all fine works of art. Here and there, amongst the floodlit buildings on its banks, stand ancient roman edifices, still defying time, the elements and the depredations of mankind after two long millennia.

Tonight the breeze that normally follows the river up from the distant sea seemed to have gone missing. The black water slid slowly along, looking thick as treacle, and strangely lifeless, despite the glowing lights reflected on its surface. The embankments in front of the Castel Sant' Angelo looked tempting as usual, dotted with stalls offering all manner of gimmicks to entice the summer tourists, but most seemed about to close for the night.

"I think we should go home, don't you?" said Lucrezia. "Or we might get very wet."

"Well, everybody else seems to think so. Anyway, it's not very pleasant, is it? Quite suffocating."

Lucrezia chose a quieter route home, trying to avoid the picturesque and trendy streets full of restaurants. They were still some way from home when the first huge spots of rain smacked down around their feet. Soon it was beating down so hard they took refuge in a doorway until the downpour eased a little.

"I think there's a lot more still to come. We'll have to make a run for it," he said.

They were thoroughly soaked by the time they reached Justin's palace. The tourist shop had called it a day and pulled down the shutters, and the antique shop had closed hours earlier, as usual. As Justin pushed open the big street door they were startled by a flash, followed a few moments later by a rumble of thunder.

They staggered into the penthouse, dripping water and making wet footprints on the gleaming marble.

"Oh, my lovely floor!" wailed Lucrezia.

"Never mind. As a special treat I could let you mop it all over again," he grinned, backing away hurriedly as she pretended to thump him. "We'd better have a shower first, then get dry. If you need a back scrubber, give me a call."

By the time he had showered, the rain was pounding on the flat roof like a million hammer drills. Barefoot, wearing only his bathrobe, and towelling his hair, Justin walked to the windows in the lounge to watch the rain. It was belting down hard onto the terrace and bouncing back half a metre into the air.

"Come look at this, Lucrezia!" he called.

She joined him, similarly attired, with a towel wrapped into a turban on her head. "Gracious!" she exclaimed, "this is a wonderful place for watching the weather. Oh! Did you see that lightning? Jupiter must be very angry, throwing all these thunderbolts around."

The terrace was a lake. Justin bent to see if the water was leaking in through the bottom of the patio doors. The ten centimetre threshold looked barely enough tonight.

Was the roof proving weatherproof? Water that seeped in usually trickled down through light fittings, he told Lucrezia. She joined him in checking all the little inset ceiling lights for drips, so they both had their backs to the window when Jupiter scored a direct hit on next door's TV aerial. The flash and bang were simultaneous and deafening.

They fled in a panic into the corridor, shocked and breathless. Instinctively they clung together, waiting for the next onslaught. The next three or four flashes came very close together, but the thunder followed a second or two later. It was no longer quite overhead. Gradually the flashes and the thunder moved further and further apart, and they breathed a cautious sigh of relief.

"Thank goodness we were not looking out of the window," breathed Lucrezia. "That flash could have blinded us. I think we shouldn't risk going into the living room again tonight. Those huge windows."

"Well, I'd better have a look to see if anything's on fire. There might be nobody home to call the fire brigade."

"Explosion, on fire, call Fire Brigade."

"Angel, wait. We'll see if we can smell burning."

She opened her bedroom window and sniffed the air while he took a cautious look through the glass doors and windows. All seemed well.

But the storm had not done with them yet. Soon the flashes and thunder drew nearer together again.

"Where is the safest place to be, here in your flat?"

"Your bedroom," he said. "It's got a good solid roof and a pretty small window facing the house next door, so the flashes shouldn't get in and blind you."

"Yes, but what about you? Your bedroom window must be dangerous: it's enormous."

"I could drag some cushions into the shower room - or you could offer me asylum for a while," he ventured.

"Well, of course. You'd be much safer in here."

Justin made a hurried trip into his bedroom and returned with an armful of pillows. "May I sit here?"

"Yes, of course. Please make yourself at home." She piled her own pillows next to his against the headboard. "Shall I make us some hot chocolate?"

"Great idea. And there are some ginger nut biscuits in the drawer. I brought them back from England. You should be safe enough in the kitchen for a few minutes, but try to keep away from the electric points. I've heard of lightning blowing them out. Angel, no. No problem."

This is what I'd call domestic bliss, he thought, biting into a ginger nut. "Do you mind if I pull your bedcover over my feet? The air conditioner's throwing cold air straight at them and they'll go blue in a minute."

"Good idea," she said. "Mine are blue already."

They got off the bed and adjusted the cover, then settled back underneath it. It was lucky they had finished their hot chocolate when the next really shocking flash and rumble startled them, or there might have been some nasty stains on the white bed cover. They dived under the cover into a protective huddle.

Oh, joy, thought Justin, hugging the cuddly thick white bathrobe with warm bare limbs poking out here and there. It seemed the most natural thing in the world to kiss her as he wormed his way into her bathrobe. Inside she was as naked as he was, a deliciously warm smooth body, not ripe and luscious like Marcella's, but not thin and bony either. She felt absolutely perfect in every way.

She offered no resistance, but she made no attempt to arouse him, as all the others had done, sometimes to the point of irritation. All his usual moves seemed somehow inappropriate, crass and vulgar. Afraid to shatter this blissful state he decided to relax and let nature take its course. And it did. Sheer bliss continued, more blissful every moment, until it was the perfect time to go for gold, - but when he pushed, the spell was suddenly shattered.

"No!" she said forcefully. "Don't do that. You're hurting me."

"It's alright, Sweetheart, Just relax. I wont hurt you. Just relax and let me in."

"No, you're hurting me. You mustn't do that, please." She wriggled and pulled herself away decisively.

He swore a few heartfelt oaths under his breath. You can't just lead me on, then push me away. It's sadistic!

But she could. And she did. There was no persuading her now. She pulled herself up and sat glowering at him.

"Isn't that how you make babies? You don't want to force me to have a baby, do you? I haven't learned to cook or run a house yet. How could I look after a baby as well?"

"Of course I don't want to force you to have a baby," he exclaimed. "You're far too young to have a baby. Surely they've put you on the pill, or something," Julia had told him that all the girls at school had been given advice on contraception. Wasn't it the same in Italy?

"No, I don't need any pills. I'm not ill."

"The contraceptive pill, I mean, of course." Why was

she being so thick?

"Contraceptives are evil. Surely you know that!"

Oh no! Those blasted nuns again! No wonder the world was over-populated and teeming with poor little teenage mothers wondering why someone up there wanted to make their poor little lives a misery!

"Well, your nuns can't tell me what to do. Just give me a minute and don't go away!"

He stormed off to his suite. There was a great flash and a bang as he opened his shower room door. "Sod off, Jupiter!" he yelled, shaking his fist at the ceiling. After a hopeless search of all the drawers and cupboards, he stomped into his bedroom, defying the storm. He slid open his banks of wardrobes and searched every pocket: trousers, jackets, even shirts. There was nothing in any of the drawers either.

"Force, hurt, unusual activity. Burglars? Call police?"

"Angel, no problems. Shush."

He slumped on the end of his bed, defeated. Idiot! Why did you let this happen? But it was ages, a year, maybe, since he had last bought any contraceptives. All his gold-diggers were on the pill, or something. He had made it very clear that he would refuse to be trapped into marriage. He was convinced that any woman he was daft enough to marry would drag him through the divorce courts within a year or two and walk off with half of everything he'd worked so hard for. And he'd whittled out all the ones he suspected had passed on a dose of something nasty, so recently there had been no need for him to bother.

He dragged himself back into her bedroom and knelt beside the bed. "I'm sorry, Sweetie," he said. "Please don't worry about it. I would hate to do anything that hurt you or spoiled your life in any way, believe me. Now, the storm seems to have gone, so I'll leave you to get some sleep. Thank you for that delicious Veal Marsala. You really are a very good cook. Tomorrow we should do something special for your birthday, go somewhere nice. See if you can think of anywhere you'd like to go. Now, good night. Sleep well."

He dragged himself back to his room, flung himself onto his huge, lonely bed, and sorted himself out as best he could, cursing himself and the nuns. Tomorrow I'm going shopping first thing, Won't miss another chance like this,

CHAPTER 16

NAUGHTY CREATURE!

Where do we go from here, thought Justin gloomily, stealing a covert glance at Lucrezia when her eyes were safely directed at her plate. Breakfast on the terrace was proving an embarrassing affair. She crept around the flat unwilling to meet his eyes – which was just as well, since he had no idea what kind of facial expression would be acceptable in the circumstances.

How had he managed to make such a hash of things last night? He'd thought he was home and dry. Everything seemed to be going swimmingly. He felt sure she was enjoying herself, then - pouff! Suddenly she was angry with him, pushing him away. He felt like a gauche teenager again. But he was a grown man with what he'd believed was a man-of-the-world way with women.

She had stopped him because he was hurting her. Yes, he knew it was supposed to hurt the first time, but how was the man supposed to deal with that? Press on regardless? How would they have faced each other this morning if he had hurt her a lot? It was embarrassing enough as things were. What exactly counted as 'date rape' - and was that a crime in Italy?

How could he have been stupid enough to imagine the nuns would put their pupils on the pill? And why had he let himself run out of johnnies? Idiot! It may well be too late to rescue the situation, but still – he should jolly well make sure he was not caught short again.

The doorbell was a welcome relief. He went to the door immediately to retrieve the post and brought a small parcel back to the table in an attempt to change the mood.

"Look at these," he said, in a hearty cheerful voice. "You'd be amazed by what these tiny dots can do."

Lucrezia looked up and smiled, clearly glad of a return to normal. "What are they?"

"Microchips. You find them in most electronics these days, but these are the newest and the tiniest. I sent for a sample to design into my next generation of products." They were so tiny it was hard to pick them up, but he managed to sprinkle a few on her hand.

"What sort of things will they do?"

"Oh, control almost anything you can think of, even blow up a tank. Your brother might be interested."

"Oh, they wont blow my hand off, will they?"

"No, nothing like that. Terrorists stick them on bombs so they can trigger them off with mobile phones. These are so tiny you could put them anywhere and nobody would spot them - ideal for spies. Angel, relax. There are no problems here now. More tea?"

In the kitchen he stuck one of his tiny microchips on the oven timer and another on his wrist, then took the tea back to the terrace.

"Listen!" he said.

"What's that?" she asked.

"The oven timer. Watch!" He turned it on and off a few times, by pressing on his wrist. "Clever, isn't it? This red one turns things on and off and the blue one goes on the apparatus you want to control."

"How clever! You should have some fun with those." She got up from the table and began clearing the breakfast things away. "I must go home this morning."

Justin's heart sank. Well, after last night - !

"It's Friday, so I have to do the accounts. May I borrow the tablet? I can't use the convent computer."

"I didn't lend it to you, I gave it to you, remember? Did

you find Wifi or Broadband in your house?"

"Oh, no, I didn't think of that. Chez doesn't need it. He has some portable military gadget to connect him to the internet. I could go to an internet cafe, as you said. I expect someone there will show me how to get online."

"You won't get much peace or privacy there will you? It's sure to be noisy and hot as hell, and I bet you some man will try to pick you up. Look, you can stay here in the cool and use this big laptop. The big screen will make the job much easier. I have to go out this morning so you can have the place to yourself. How about that?"

She sighed, then put on a smile. "You're very kind. Thank you."

There are few useful shops in the historic part of Rome - plenty of shops for the tourists, of course, and open air markets, but few specialised shops of use to the residents. There was a small general store hidden in an old house just around the corner, but it was unlikely to have what he was looking for, and anyway, imagine the embarrassment of trying to explain what he wanted. Probably his neighbours would be there and try to help.

Away from the main tourist drags, lots of shops and businesses were shut - like his own company - taking their annual holidays to get away from the heat. He was forced to tramp around sweating for quite a while before he found a pharmacy open. He bought a good stock. Yes, he was probably wasting time and money, but nil desperandum.

Disappointment engulfed him when he walked back into his penthouse. There was no one there. He gave a big sigh, but was not altogether surprised. She had not taken the laptop with her. It was still on the table with the lid open. He walked over to shut it, but saw the on light glowing. It had not been turned off. He touched the space bar and it burst into life, showing him a screenful of figures. He sat and studied them. It was a statement of an account in the Cayman Islands. The figures were so high that the currency must surely be of low value. He searched the statement carefully until he spotted the words, 'US Dollars'. Phew! This was serious money. Five million dollars had been paid into the account only yesterday. Maybe Cesare had sold his Tornado. There were no small sums on the list, so presumably this account was not used for the housekeeping.

Something moved on the terrace. It was Lucrezia, playing games with a large ginger cat. He pulled open the patio door and joined her.

"Where did you spring from?" he laughed. "I didn't see you when I got back."

"The cat came to play, so we've been chasing each other over the roofs. It's far too hot, though – the tiles burn your hands and feet - and we couldn't find any other cats to spook. There are always lots of them skipping about when it's dark, but they must be having a siesta now. They think they own the roof tops, so when they see a human up there they really freak out."

"You're crazy! You'll fall off and kill yourselves."

"Freak out, crazy, fall, kill"

"Angel, ignore those words. Shush."

"Have you ever seen a cat fall off a roof?"

"I'm not worried about the cat!"

"Have you ever seen a girl fall off a roof?" she grinned.

"I've never seen a girl *on* a roof, for that matter," he huffed. "Come in before you give me heart failure."

To his great relief she returned to her accounts.

He went into his bedroom and distributed his purchases amongst all the places he might think to look when next he had a chance to use one. Mentally crossing his fingers, he put two in his bathrobe pocket, in case one was faulty.

Must be coffee time. He got out the snazzy designer mugs that pleased her so much and approached the built-in coffee machine with trepidation. Learn to use the blessed thing, he growled to himself. You paid so much to get the blasted thing put in it's pathetic just to put the kettle on. Thank goodness his mother had brought him a kettle from England. If she hadn't he'd have to learn to use the ridiculously complicated monstrosity.

While the coffee was steeping, he puzzled over the accounts she was working on. It was not just the size of the sums of money involved that seemed strange: he was used to such large figures in his own accounts. Cesare was an arms dealer and tanks and guns cost serious money – not to mention Tornado warplanes. What was strange was the bare tidiness of the most recent entry: five million dollars – no more, no less. On the rare occasions when you negotiated a nice round figure like that something always messed it up: taxes or duties or discounts. What had one of them done to earn such a nice neat sum? Intriguing.

He poured two mugs of coffee and plonked one beside her, together with a coffee éclair from the bakers on the corner. "How are the accounts going?" he asked.

"Very well. The trades I set up last week have all done pretty well, so I've sold them and bought some more."

"Maybe you could give me some lessons in money-making in return for the cookery lessons," he grinned. "Have you made more than your brother this week?"

"Not a chance," she sighed, "But at least I know it's not my fault he's gone to Waziristan. He was asked to go."

"To do what?" he asked.

"Goodness knows," she sighed. "Did your trip go well?"

"Fine," he smirked, then had to turn away to hide his

guilty expression. "I picked up some leaflets, look. There are a few things you might like to go to in the evenings. What about this one, 'Jazz in the Park'? It starts at nine so we could have an early dinner somewhere nearby. It should be good sitting looking at the stars while we listen to the music. Do you like jazz?"

"I don't know. Maybe it's something else I need to learn."

"This band plays nice middle-of-the-road stuff, a pleasant introduction for a novice. Like to give it a go?"

"Mmm! If you're sure I won't spoil your evening."

"Look, I told you yesterday that I really enjoy having you here. I was bored rigid before I met you and you've given me lots of interesting things to think about." - and how! he smirked to himself. "Do you have much more work to do or do you want to help make the lunch soon?"

"Another ten minutes, I think, if you don't mind."

"No problem No need to rush."

Coffee mug in hand, he stared out over the rooftops. She was crazy, leaping about on the roofs. He'd seen men do that on TV, but fragile little girls! Must be Cesare again, giving her crazy ideas like jumping off the Khalifa. He thought of her terror, swinging in that net. He still couldn't imagine how anybody could fix a net to the sheer glass walls of that fabulous icicle, but she had survived somehow. It was pointless to cross-question her and bring those terrifying memories back again.

He longed to ask about her accounts, to get an idea of Cesare's business dealings. How did she find out he had been asked to go to Waziristan? Had she had an email? He checked her emails on his tablet, but found nothing new at all. Was it the five million dollars? Was that payment for the trip? What was he taking to the customers that cost such a neat round figure? And did they usually pay upfront?

Arms dealing must surely be an unpleasant business. Dealing on a large scale with governments might seem civilised, but freelancing? Who would be his customers? Small unstable states? Rebel gangs? He must have to demonstrate the killing potential of his wares. She'd said explosives dust got him detained at airports. Waziristan was crawling with terrorists from so many rival factions. Was he taking bombs and guns to them?

Was it crazy to make friends with the sister of a man like this? But he *had* made friends with her. If he tried to ditch her, surely that brother might take against him. Cesare had sent him friendly messages, according to Lucrezia, so he was now on Cesare's radar. It would surely be safer to carry on the friendship. She was not her brother's keeper – and she really was a sweetie.

"Lucrezia, did you hear that noise in your bedroom? Has that ginger tom sneaked in here, do you think?"

Lucrezia leapt to her feet and headed for her bedroom.

"Ginger! Ginger! Puss Puss, come out," she called.

Quickly, he scrolled the accounts up and down and soon found what he was looking for: two more neat round figures. Whatever Cesare was doing he had done it at least three times so far and the money had come from the same source. What sort of armaments, costing such a neat round figure, had been ordered on three separate occasions close together by the same people?

Hurriedly he tapped a few keys, then walked smartly to his bedroom.

"No cats in here," he called. "Maybe it's on the roof. Shall we start lunch in another half an hour?"

"Whatever you wish," she called.

He powered up the big wall-mounted screen in his bedroom and keyed in the link, bringing up a copy of what she was viewing on the laptop. Sneaky, yes, but he felt very uneasy. It seemed as well to know if something threatening was going on in his own home.

She closed her financial window and he watched her bring up documents in a script he didn't understand. Eventually the script turned into English, so he could work out that it was an English language version of a North Waziristan newspaper. There was a pattern to which flyers she keyed in. They were all about terrorists, skirmishes with the police or the military, or bloody conflicts between clans. There had been a bomb in a crowded market place. 35 people killed and scores injured. Evil, evil people. How could anyone justify committing such an atrocity? Would Cesare do such a thing? Or supply the bombs? What kind of report was she expecting to see? Her brother had left Rome little more than twenty-four hours ago. How long would it take him to reach his destination?

Eventually Lucrezia keyed out the Waziristan paper and began a speedy trawl of the world's major newspapers, singling out reports about the world's trouble spots: Afghanistan, the Middle East, and North and sub-Saharan Africa. Was she seeking customers for her brother? It was a sickening thought. Many reports were about refugee camps and field hospitals. How did they fit into her brother's life?

Suddenly he realised that she was spending time studying reports in languages he didn't recognise. Sometimes she found an English or French edition but more often she seemed to be managing without. How on earth many languages could she understand?

Well, she had warned him she had no interest in fashion or celebs and here was startling proof of that. Even his very clever, serious sister was no match for this strange phenomenon putting his laptop to such unaccustomed use. Was he right to feel uneasy, or was he putting two and two together and making twenty two?

And didn't he have some offbeat interests himself at

her age? His classmates seemed to think so – called him a weirdo. Well, this weirdo had not done too badly so far, had he? Probably better than any of them, so there! This weirdo was feeling hungry and he had a million euro kitchen to play with, so let's put it to good use right now.

"Ready for your cookery lesson, Lucrezia?" he called, walking breezily out of his room.

"Yes, Sir." Quickly she closed down the laptop, went to her room, and emerged in her frilly pinny.

Ridiculous, he thought. How could such a cute and dainty little creature have the mind he had just witnessed?

"Tell me something," he demanded, "how do you manage to be so useless at cooking when you're obviously as bright as a button. Surely you must find it such a disadvantage."

She looked at him with a wry smile. "You think so, do you? Do you know the second thing a man always thinks when a woman appears? Good. She can slave away in the kitchen while we men have fun. My answer to that? Well, you know that already" She laughed mischievously.

"Well, you're a very naughty creature, so no lunch for you unless you put in half the work. Is that fair?"

"Yes, that's fair," she laughed.

"And are you going to tell me what is the first thing men think about?" he asked, smirking at her sideways.

"You're a man, so I'm sure you can answer that for yourself," she murmured, with a matching smirk as she led the way into the kitchen.

Yes, and you're going to see a demonstration of that tonight, all being well, he smirked to himself.

Something seemed to have changed in her manner, he

thought to himself as he assembled the ingredients. The unworldly little convent girl seemed to be melting away. Becoming sixteen seemed to have given her a much more mature and worldly attitude to life. How strange!

"Today, we're going to do something quite tricky: Sole Veronique, a real French classic."

"Oh dear!" she moaned.

"First we'll simplify the veggies. This bag of frozen mixed veg has everything we need, even potatoes, so we sling it in the microwave and concentrate on the hard part. We'll do the sole the easy way too: just put it ready in the grill pan. The classic way is in the oven, all rolled up and drenched with white wine, but my way's much quicker and tastes better. The hard part is the roux sauce. It can go badly wrong, so we'll have to give it our full attention.

'Here we go. We melt a lump of butter slowly in this little saucepan and now we have to get a piled dessert-spoonful of plain flour to meld in with it into a smooth paste. Take it off the heat and stir and stir. Yes, a bit too much flour for the butter, so here's a little more butter. Now, here comes the really tricky bit, adding the milk. It has to go in a very little at a time, so the paste stays thick and smooth. The milk cools it down and stops it cooking, so put the pan back on the hob. Keep stirring or it will go solid and be ruined. A little drop more milk quickly: it's trying to go solid. Lift it off the heat for a few moments. Stir like crazy. That's right. Back on the hob and add more milk. Stir, stir! So far so good. Now we've got something like thick custard. We keep adding a little milk as it cooks as it keeps getting thicker for a while. Take it off the heat for a moment while we put the flavouring in. I like a fennel flavour, but don't put fennel seeds in.Everybody thinks they're fish bones and panics. A fennel flavour liqueur is best: Pernod, Pastis, Ricard, any one will do. In goes a slurp. And a squeeze of lemon. Now it looks a bit thin but it will thicken up again if we leave it on the warm hob after we turn the heat off.

"Now, put the sole under the hot grill and turn on the microwave. Keep your eye on the sauce. Keep giving it a stir so it can't form a skin or stick to the pan bottom. Put a scraping of garlic butter on each of the sole fillets, now they're hot. Now, we need a handful of green grapes, cut lengthwise. Take out the stones. Stir the sauce, and turn the fish over. Put a few half slices of lemon down the side of the plate and a frond or two of fennel or dill. Now check the fish. It's got a few light brown patches on it, so it's ready.

"And there we are. Put the fish and the veggies on the plate, pour the sauce on the fish, scatter the grapes on the sauce, Et Voilà! My quick and easy version of a real classic French special dish. Now you really are a chef, aren't you?"

"Phew!" she breathed, carrying her plate to the table. "That really was tricky. What happens if it goes wrong?"

"It ends up all ugly lumps instead of this nice smooth creamy sauce. Then, if you have guests, it's best to start all over again, or they'll think you're a rubbish cook. If you've made enough for a lot of people you could try breaking the lumps up in the blender, but the texture wont be quite right."

He passed her a glass of Spanish Rueda. "Smell this and tell me what you think."

"Smells like a bucket of fruit and flowers. It's gorgeous."

"It has to be drunk very fresh. The scent disappears as it ages. So, a toast to the chef. May you make many more delicious meals. You could cook it for your brother in your new kitchen. He'd be most impressed."

"Hmm. Can we keep it a secret?"

"Why? Why on earth would you want to do that?"

"Isn't that obvious? I don't want to get left behind in the kitchen while the men go off having adventures, do I?"

"Like roof-running and jumping off the Burj Khalifa?"

"Exactly."

"Your brother does that, does he, roof-running?"

"Yes. We used to go out most nights when everybody thought we were in bed. It's amazing what you see when nobody knows you're there. But now there are so many roof terraces like yours being built we're more likely to be spotted, especially as Chez has to keep to the ridges. He's too heavy for the sloping tiles now. When the neighbours spotted us father put a lock on the door to the roof. That was when Chez had to learn to pick locks. He can break into almost anywhere now. These new electronic locks were a problem till he found an app to deal with them – one of yours works really well."

"I don't design apps for burglars!" he exclaimed.

"He had to adapt it a little, but it works really well now."

"Grief! So your brother is a cat burglar as well as a rat catcher, is he?"

"Spose so," she laughed.

"And I thought aristocrats were so restrained and precious, so refined. You two have rocked my faith in the titled classes," he joked.

"You mean you thought we were all weak-chinned and lily-livered. Don't you know that the job of a Marquis is to guard the borders of the realm, keep out invaders and stop the savage tribes from raping and pillaging. You can't just ask them nicely – please, you savages, stop revolting, can you? You have to bash them where it hurts, show them they can't get away with things like that on your patch."

"Invaders, raping, pillaging - "

"Angel, shush. No problems. So, it's a prerequisite for

marquises to run over rooftops, jump off half-mile high towers, burgle buildings and catch rats, is it? "

"Absolutely. All that and more. We have our titles and our history to live up to, don't we? So you won't let on that I've been cooking, will you? I don't think the savage tribes would be impressed."

"Does that mean you don't want to learn any more?"

"Oh, no. I'm enjoying it. Like you, I've absolutely nothing else to do at present, marooned here in Rome – and I'm really not terribly fond of pizza."

CHAPTER 17

A WOLF SINK?

The afternoon's entertainment arrived straight after lunch: the plans for the new kitchen. Excitedly they spread them out across the table. There was a computer-generated picture giving a good impression of the finished product.

"Oh yes!" she laughed, "the staff will love this. Oh, there's only one tap over the sinks. That's no good."

"It's a mixer tap, both hot and cold in the same tap," he explained.

"Well, yes, of course, but how can they manage with only one? The kitchen maid will be preparing the vegetables in one sink and she'll be in the way when Cook needs to get to the water. Chaos. Cook will throw a fit. They must have a tap each, definitely. And maybe we should put a wolf sink near the door. Easier than having to put one in later."

"Never heard of a wolf sink. What's that when it's at home?"

"Well, Cook hated it when Chez used one of her sinks for wolf food. She tried to persuade him to use the boot room or the stables but he said that wouldn't work because the wolves are always hanging around the kitchen door. They're not stupid. They can smell the food. And visitors don't usually go to the kitchen door so they're not likely to get a fright. The wolves don't like being screamed at."

"Are you telling me your brother keeps wolves?"

"I'm not sure if 'keeps' is the right word. They just live on the estate and we feed them so they don't eat the livestock. We didn't want to make pets of them, but hunters shot their mother. They were too tiny to take care of themselves, and they were so cute we couldn't resist feeding them. Now they wont go away."

"What do your staff think about this?"

"Well, some of them get a bit nervous at times, now there are six of them. They will keep breeding. They're protected wild animals, so it's illegal to get them sterilised. We've put tranquilizer dart guns around the place and told the staff to shoot if they must. The wolves are actually useful. 'Beware of the Wolves. Trespassers may be eaten' is far more effective than 'cave canem'."

"Nervous, wild animals, guns, shoot, beware -"

"Angel, no problems. Shush. Where is this estate?"

"Near the Swiss border. We're there to stop the Swiss invading Italy. If they try we shall set the wolves on them, of course, and pour boiling oil from our ramparts. Scrub the last bit. We don't have any ramparts."

"Nor any wolves, I guess," he grinned. "You tell fantastic stories. So, being serious for a moment, you don't need a wolf sink, do you?"

"Well, Chez might fly a couple down, Raoul and Sheba, who knows? They'd be a problem because they need a lot of exercise. People might think they're just huskies, but they're not used to being on leads."

"You could take them roof-running. Nobody would spot them up there."

"They'd slither off and crash down. It would be raining smashed-up wolves, wouldn't it? They're not like cats, you know."

This conversation is sheer lunacy, thought Justin. Am I dreaming, is she crazy or is she just having fun? Can I believe anything at all she has ever told me? Her stories keep changing every day. What happened to the little convent girl? How does five years in a convent fit in with all this? It's probably all moonshine, apart from the B House – and maybe I'll get a shock on Monday when the Authorities turn up and tell me we're ripping out a famous Art Deco kitchen in a museum.

"I ought to ask the staff their views. Can we email the plans to them?"

Might as well play along, he thought. Fills a boring afternoon. He keyed in the address she gave him, fed the documents into the scanner and sent them off.

"Had you better ring and tell them to look at their emails, and explain what it's all about?" That should call her bluff, he thought cynically.

"May I use your phone?"

"Here you are. Ring your staff while I make some tea."

In the kitchen he switched on the speaker phone. Spying again - but who could blame him?

"Good afternoon. Monrosso House. Can I help you?"

"Is Mrs Lepanto available? I'd like to speak to her."

"Who shall I say is calling?"

"The Marchesa "

"Oh, My Lady, I'm so sorry I didn't recognise you. I've only been here two weeks. I'm the new parlour maid. I'll call the Housekeeper immediately."

"My Lady, how wonderful to hear you at last. I hope all is well. Can we expect you home soon? Where are you?"

"Marooned in Rome at the moment, longing to come home. How are you all? I gather we have a new parlour maid. What happened to Lily?"

"She went off with that horrid man, just as we expected. Very sad, but what can you do? Old Roberto retired last week. I'm sure you and the Master would have been pleased with the send-off we gave him."

"Oh, I'm sorry we missed that. He deserved better from us than to miss his retirement. Has he moved away?"

"No. I understand he has a life tenancy of the cottage."

"Yes, that's right, but he'd been talking of living near his daughter. I want to thank him personally and I'm sure the Master will too. And you? Is all well with you?"

"Yes, soldiering on as usual. And all's well with the estate. Fabio had to dart one of the young wolves yesterday. It was snarling at everyone and picking fights with Raoul. Poor old Raoul is getting quite battered. Sheba was howling her head off. She hates to see anything bad happen to him. I hope the Master will be home soon to sort them out."

"Snarling, fights - "

"Angel, shush," groaned Justin.

"I hope so too. I'm waiting here, trying to catch him between assignments, but he's off again so fast. While he's here he spends all his time poring over maps, deaf to the rest of the world. He might be back tomorrow so I'll try to nail his feet to the ground. Wish me luck! Anyway, what I want to tell you is that I'm having the old kitchen here in Rome refitted at last. Do I hear a cheer? I've emailed the plans to you and Enrico, so could you make it a priority to study them now. And ask Cook to look at them too, of course. I'm asking for an extra mixer tap on the main sinks like you have there. Maybe you can spot other things you're not happy about. Do you think I should put in a wolf sink?"

"My Lady, Mr. Fermi is just going past. I'll get him for you. Just a moment."

"My Lady, what a nice surprise! How are you? Shall we have the pleasure of seeing you soon?"

"Not for a week or two, sadly. I'm having the old kitchen in Rome ripped out on Monday and I've emailed you the plans so you can make sure you are all happy with it.

Do we need a wolf sink here, do you think?"

"Well, My Lady, one can never second guess the Master. He may feel he has a use for a wolf in Rome, considering the legends of the foundation of the city. The kitchen is a very big space, so there is room for a separate sink. I would find it useful myself, far preferable to my little dungeon, if you will forgive me for so describing the butler's pantry."

"Well, that settles it. If you want it you shall have it. Now, if there is anything else you can think of, please give me a ring first thing in the morning. I'm not at the B House. I'm staying with a friend across the road. Do you have pen and paper for the number? Yes, that's right. So, I wait to hear your verdict. Give my love to everyone. Goodbye."

Justin walked into the lounge somewhat chastened. It seemed that his doubts had been mistaken. There really was a country estate and even the wolves were real. And her brother was a respectable man with servants who seemed to want to see him. But why did she pretend that she didn't know what had happened to the servants when they seemed to be at Monrosso all the time? Still, maybe there had been two lots of servants in her father's day.

"Who feeds the wolves while your brother is away?" he asked.

"The stockman's assistant. If he's not available, Cook does the honours."

"Isn't she scared of them?"

Lucrezia shrieked with laughter. "Cook is not afraid of anything, and everything is terrified of Cook. If you cross her she grabs a frying pan and waves it as a weapon. The wolves run a mile! She doesn't need a dart gun."

"Terrified, weapon, wolves, gun, call police, army?"

"Angel, No. I need to reprogram you." growled Justin.

"How many servants do you have?"

"Only a skeleton staff in the house, since we're scarcely ever there and not doing any entertaining. Just the key staff: Enrico Fermi, the Butler, Maria Lepanto, the Housekeeper, plus Cook, plus a couple of general purpose maids. We can rustle up half a dozen more if we need them, the wives of the estate workers. There's the estate manager, the farm manager, stockmen, fruit and vegetable farmers - "

"It must cost the earth to have an estate like that," said Justin enviously.

"It costs nothing at all, in fact it makes a profit. The only sad part is that we've got it so well-organised it doesn't really need us. We feel rather spare. Well, the Butler wants a wolf sink for himself, so where are we going to put it?"

CHAPTER 18

SOZZLED

Justin had come to believe that Jazz sounded better when he was suitably sozzled, so he ordered a whole bottle of wine with their supper. There was no need to stay sober, as he had no intention of driving. The taxi driver helpfully pointed out that if they wanted to eat there was no need to pay for the concert. There was a cafe very close to the band stand.

The perfect table stood waiting for them, right on the perimeter, under the trees, where fireflies glowed in the damp grass by the pond. Beyond the trees, bathed in golden light, loomed proud columns, proclaiming the might, the grandeur of the glorious days when all roads led to Roma, when half the civilised world was keen to carve the letters **SPQR** – Senatus Populusque Romanus - on any construction they were proud of.

"What amazes me is how - and why on earth - did Rome, such an advanced, such a successful, such a civilised empire, just disintegrate in such a frighteningly short time?" mused Justin, as he pulled out a chair for Lucrezia.

"And Babylon and Egypt and hundreds of others, right back into the mists of time," she murmured. "Nothing lasts. Armagedon is always on the skyline, closing in. You just have to lick your wounds, move on and make the best of things."

"But what is this Armagedon?"

"Envy, jealousy. Ignorant people with no talents can't bear to see other people succeed. They destroy what they can't create and don't understand, drag everything down to their level to hide their own inadequacy."

"Well, it's good to see **SPQR** being used again these days, even if it's only on the drain covers. It always gives me a tiny little thrill," grinned Justin. "Ancient Rome has always fascinated me."

The food, the wine and the music soon worked their magic. He sprawled back in his chair, watching small black creatures swoop overhead, re-enacting the Battle of Britain. Swallows? Bats? Maybe both, who knows? The lights nearby were drowning out the stars, but he knew they were there and saluted them all the same.

He plied Lucrezia with wine but it didn't seem to do her any good. She kept stealing a glance at her watch and biting her lip. There were tight lines between her brows. She fidgeted and rubbed her face repeatedly

"Are you feeling okay?" he asked. "Is there anything I can do?"

She didn't seem to hear, so he nudged her arm and asked again. She stared at him as if he was making no sense, then shook herself and put on a forced smile.

"No, I'm fine. I like the music. So glad we came."

When the music stopped she made an effort to engage in conversation, but her exaggerated cheerfulness sounded very strained. Next time he turned towards her she had covered her face with her hands. Her whole body looked tense and rigid. Suddenly she gave a great sigh. Her hands fell limply to her sides and she sat relaxed, eyes closed. Whatever had been causing her distress seemed to have left her in peace at last.

She soon began to tap her feet and even to sing quietly along with the music. When he met her gaze she smiled her lovely smile. She was such a gorgeous creature. The urge to sweep her into his arms was so intense it was painful.

Tonight was going to be the night. She need have no worries about unwanted babies tonight. Didn't they once use alcohol to deaden the pain of surgery? Would slow and gentle be kindest, or just prolong the pain? Would it be better to be quick and firm? Perhaps he should have asked advice on the Net. He imagined trying to frame the question: then he imagined the fun the trolls would have concocting answers. Probably boys debated that kind of conundrum and shared their experiences. He'd missed out on all that somehow.

When the concert ended there seemed to be no taxis about, but they were less than three kilometres from home. His gold-diggers in their five inch heels would have mutinied, but Lucrezia was delighted to have the chance to walk. Over a patch of rough ground he took her hand to steady her - and didn't let go. Oh bliss, to wander hand in hand along the warm, quiet streets, past cafés where the last dawdling customers sat sipping their drinks, reluctant to go home on such a balmy night.

Cats came slinking out from every direction. It must be the cats' high noon. They came running and followed her a while, purring. If she moved in with him for good he'd need some kind of cat deterrent. No good thinking he'd be safe high up in his penthouse. They'd come skipping over the roof tops.

"It's such a lovely night it's a shame to go inside," she murmured, when they reached his palace at last. "Shall we sit out on the terrace and try to name the stars?"

Venus, Goddess of Beauty, had already followed the sun off to bed, but Jupiter, King of the Heavens, was holding court, brighter than any star, high up in the coal black sky. With binoculars they could even see four of his dozen moons. And that reddish star must surely be the planet of Mars, God of War. The Plough, so low in the sky, was hard to recognise, but Orion the Hunter was easy to find – even his 'dagger' was visible. It was a truly beautiful night.

He brought out the half bottle of Rueda left from lunchtime. "Can you still smell the flowers? We should finish it now before the scent disappears."

He watched with satisfaction as she toasted the stars and finished a large glassful. Was this enough to be an anaesthetic, on top of the two or three glasses she'd had for supper and the big glass with lunch?

"Oh, I feel so dizzy. I'd better go lie down," she drawled woozily.

He caught her as she swayed towards the lounge and half carried her to her room. He kissed her as he gently stripped off her clothes and laid her on the bed.

"Thank you," she murmured. "You're very kind."

He charged down the corridor to his room, tearing off his clothes as he went. Where was his bathrobe with its precious cargo? Gottit! The two johnnies were definitely still there in the pockets.

She lay sprawled on the bed, eyes closed and a soft smile on her face.

Take it easy, he told himself. No need to hurry - but he was all fingers and thumbs. Surely there must be something more slick and modern than these blasted condoms. Phew, that seemed okay now.

He lowered his body onto the bed and slid towards her, excitement mounting to a fever pitch.

"Hello," she murmured. "Everything's going round and round. Where am I? Do I know you?"

"Yes, you do, and you'll soon know me a lot better."

"Mmm?" she breathed.

"Mmm, you will, you definitely will."

Her movements were slow and sensuous and utterly seductive, driving him crazy. He was breathing hard and poised for the coup de grace.

Suddenly she stiffened. "Oh dear! I'm going to be sick.

Please help me. Where's the bathroom? I feel so sick and dizzy. Help me, please!"

"Sick, dizzy, help me, call ambulance - "

"Angel, idiot, shush! There is no sodding problem!" Cursing like a hooligan he dragged her off the bed and into her shower room.

She was as floppy as a big rag doll. She slithered out of his arms into a heap on the floor. He dragged her to the loo and held her head over the pan.

"No, no, I'll pass out and drown. Put me by the shower drain, please."

"Drown - "

He dragged her to the drain and dumped her down beside it. She struggled onto her side and made a retching noise.

"Thank you, thank you. Please go away now. I can't bear anyone to watch me being sick."

"No, I can't leave you. You might suffocate," he growled resentfully.

"Sick, suffocate - "

"No, I can't suffocate. I'm in the recovery position. Please go away."

"Call ambulance?"

"Angel, shut the f*** up. THERE IS NO PROBLEM!"

Blood'n sand! he growled to himself as he stomped back to his bedroom. What a fiasco!

But she was not too drunk to remember the recovery position!

CHAPTER 19

THE BIG RED FROG

It was aspirins all round the next morning. After a miserable night trying to sleep with a throbbing head, he staggered into the kitchen soon after sunrise. Lucrezia was already there, brewing up king-sized mugs of tea.

"Perfect!" he groaned, "just what I need, and some aspirins. I hope you don't feel as bad as I do." Marcella was right: too much alcohol did bring on a migraine far too often, and they'd drunk two bottles between them yesterday.

"Oh, terrible!" she sighed, but she looked in far better shape than he felt. Maybe getting rid of the wine by being sick had not been such a bad idea.

"Forgive me if I take this tea back to bed. Maybe the aspirins will let me sleep it off. I suggest you do the same. It's only six o'clock.

"May I take the laptop with me if you can spare it for an hour or two?"

"Of course! Keep it in your room. I have others."

Despite the headache he lit up the big screen. It seemed wise to know what she was up to.

It was not long before the Waziristan newspaper appeared on the screen – in English. Fortunately it seemed that Pashto was not one of the languages she understood. The lead story grabbed her attention.

She studied the report minutely, then trawled the paper for comments. A leading terrorist chieftain had been assassinated in Miranshah, the capital of N. Waziristan. The assassin appeared to be a local man, but all the various factions were blaming each other and asserting that he was not one of them.

The victim must have believed he was very safe in his headquarters deep inside a children's hospital, an impossible target for a rocket or even the Special Forces. Collateral damage would have caused outrage around the world. The assassin had got in by claiming to be a parent visiting his sick child. The murdered chief's bodyguard declared they had made the assassin suffer, then taken his mangled dead body to Peshawar and thrown it over the wall into the American Consulate compound. They clearly blamed the USA for the killing.

A succession of newspapers appeared on the screen, but she showed no interest in anything except the assassination. The American Consul in Peshawar insisted that no body had been found in the Consulate compound, despite a thorough search. Yes, it was true that their security cameras had recorded something apparently being thrown over their wall. No, it slipped their attention at the time. Yes, admittedly that was a serious lapse of security and the men on duty had been disciplined. Yes, an alarm should have sounded but the system had been faulty since the recent car bombs had done so much damage to the Consulate.

At last she turned off the laptop. All was quiet. He lay back on his pillows feeling sick. Could that be why she seemed so tense last night? Did she somehow guess what was happening? Was that a ridiculous assumption? It was so far away from anything that happened in his own life that he found it hard to believe that such horrific things could intrude on his safe existence. But there was no doubt that the story meant something to her, or why had she paid it so much attention? How would she respond if his far-fetched suspicions proved to be true?

Eventually he heard the water flowing in the kitchen and the thump of mugs on the sink. With a heavy heart he pulled on his bathrobe, squared his shoulders and forced himself to walk into the kitchen.

"Morning, Justin. Better now? Did the aspirins do the trick? I'm sure you'd like another mug of tea. You English seem to run on it, don't you?"

"Well, I notice you've made another for yourself as well. Your headache has obviously gone. You look as bright as a daisy."

He felt almost weak with relief. He had obviously been completely wrong in his ridiculous suspicions. He should be ashamed of having such macabre ideas. Yes, but why was she taking so much interest in such things? Goodness only knows, as she herself was so fond of saying. Goodness knows what her brother was up to in Waziristan. Selling bombs and guns to the terrorists? Who knows? Stop thinking evil thoughts. Think of something normal instead.

"We should go look at your kitchen today," he said.

"I thought the shop was shut on Saturdays."

"No, I mean your old kitchen. They're going to pull it out on Monday. You don't want them chucking lots of valuable stuff in the skip."

"I thought we needed a fresh start. Best everything goes, surely."

"But lots of things down there must be valuable antiques. The antique shop people here would probably be thrilled to get their hands on them. They're nice people. It would be good to do them a favour, surely."

"Yes, of course. I assume it's all outdated rubbish, but if it's any use to them of course they can have it. You could bring them along to choose whatever they want. I'd like to go home as soon as possible. If you have a spare hammer and a couple of big nails, I could try to nail Chez down before he rushes off again. He should be home by now. He'll be interested to meet you."

He looked at her uneasily, as the queasy feeling invaded his stomach again. He dreaded whatever was in store at the B House. Did he really want to come face to face with a man who was probably selling bombs to terrorists? Hadn't she said he was as hard as nails? And if Cesare didn't turn up, what would that signify? And how would she cope with that?

The Marchettis didn't work long hours. The antique shop was more of a hobby for them, so he was forced to wait impatiently until 10 am before he could tell them about the treats that might be waiting for them at the B House. They fussed around interminably, deciding who should man the shop, then decided to take it in turns.

"Ladies first!" insisted Bianca. "I'll be back here by eleven at the latest, then it's your turn."

"Well, happy hunting," Giuseppe called after her, envy written all over his face. Finding unexpected treasures was what made their trade so interesting.

"I've always longed to see inside this house," enthused Bianca. "It must be full of wonderful things."

"If you call really old and out-of-date things wonderful, you're in for a treat," he laughed. "The kitchen looks as if it dates from the 1930's. The bathrooms belong to the same era, but they still look very glamorous. Lurezia thinks they still work well, so it would be a shame to rip them out. We're sure that the kitchen's not worth preserving, though. It just has to go. "

Lucrezia had left the wicket door open. He stood in the courtyard and called her name, but there was no reply.

"Well," he said, "she asked me to show you the kitchen so we'd better go ahead. Maybe she's just slipped out for a moment." He led Bianca down the hidden staircase.

"My, oh my! This is like stepping out of a time machine, "enthused Bianca."It must be over eighty years old." She stared around her in delight and wonderment. "I don't know where to start."

"Well, there's no hurry. Just take your time. I'll go see if I can find Lucrezia."

She was not below stairs, nor in any of the ground floor rooms. Maybe she'd gone up to her old suite on the first floor. No, she was not in there either. He stood on the corridor and looked around. The door to the Royal Suite was open. He walked towards it tentatively, listening for voices. All was silent, but it seemed only polite to knock.

"Hello?" called Lucrezia.

"It's me, Justin. Am I disturbing you?"

"No, come in. Are the Marchettis interested? Did you bring them along?"

"Very interested, quite excited. Bianca is down in the kitchen now, marvelling at it all. Would you prefer me to stay and supervise her."

"I can't see what harm she's likely to do, can you? She can have anything that takes her fancy."

"So," he said, his heart beating a little faster than usual, "Has your brother arrived? Are you going to introduce me." Might as well face up to the encounter. Better than spending ages dreading it.

She shook her head. "I can't find him. He must be here somewhere. Maybe he's gone out to get something to eat. I didn't get here till just after eight. I should have come earlier before he could get away. I've been waiting here for nearly two hours. He should surely have found something to eat by now. If I come down to say hello to Bianca he could come back and go out again and I'll miss him again."

"You could leave him a note," he suggested.

"Good idea." She hurried across to the writing desk and wrote in large letters: 'Welcome home, Darling.

Please don't go till we've had a chance to talk. I'm down in the kitchen.' She looked at it for a moment, then wrote a copy. "I'm not sure where to put these. He might not look at the desk. Food. Always homes in on food - bad as the wolves."

She strode across the sitting room and opened a hidden door in the panelling. To his amazement she had revealed a kitchenette. She put the note on top of the fridge, then moved it to the drainer. "What do you think? Where would he be most likely to see it?"

"There on the drainer. You didn't tell me you had another kitchen. This looks quite modern. Now I see why your brother never goes down to the old kitchen. He has a very nice flat up here. Do you have a kitchenette in your sitting room?"

"Me? I don't cook, remember?"

"If I were your brother I'd insist you did your share." He wagged a finger at her and she laughed.

"If I had the right equipment I might deign to cook you a nice hedgehog and a few pigeons, but I'd probably get arrested, wouldn't I?"

"Yeuch! And what, pray, would be the right equipment?"

"A hot camp fire with a few flat stones around it and some nice soft mud."

"Whatever do you want with the mud?" he demanded.

"You cover the bodies with a thick layer of mud, then, when they're cooked, you bash off the mud and off come the prickles and the feathers, of course."

"I can just imagine you squatting over a camp fire knocking spines off hedgehogs!" he jeered.

"Well, I did offer, and you turned it down. Too humble a meal for you, eh? You are obviously a man who has never gone hungry. Let's go see Bianca."

Bianca was having a wonderful time. She rushed

towards Lucrezia and grasped her hand.

"My Lady, it's so kind of you to let me see your kitchen. Such a thrill. Are you really going to have it taken out? What a shame!"

"If you'd been here last Christmas you would understand. It caused a riot. Cook was waving her frying pan and threatening to bash that weird old coffee machine to bits. The Butler had to physically restrain her. All the old equipment had seized up and refused to work. We had to fly our engineer down to get the essentials working. Nobody in Rome was prepared to try to repair it. So, if we want to use the house at all we have to fix this kitchen. If it's any use to you, please help yourself. Please excuse me."

Justin followed her up the stairs to the Royal Suite.

She gave a sigh. "Where is he? He surely can't have gone away again so soon."

"Maybe his plane has been delayed. What time did you expect him?"

"About eight."

"If you got here just after eight he would hardly have had time to unpack. Where's his suitcase? I think his plane has been delayed, surely."

"He doesn't do suitcases."

"Rucksack then."

"Doesn't do luggage." she frowned.

"He must have lots of things to carry around. What about the information about his products to show his customers? And a change of clothes, surely."

She shook her head. "Whatever can have happened to him?"

Bianca called from the courtyard. It was time to change guard with her husband. They went downstairs to see her off. When Bianca had gone, Justin persuaded

Lucrezia she should search the drawers and cupboards and put anything useful into one of the pantries. He soon found himself alone. She had slipped back upstairs to look for her brother. With a sigh, he began to do the job for her.

Good job he did, he thought. Beside the sinks he found a drawer full of very fine, expensive knives. Why buy new ones that might be inferior? Enthused by this find, he searched out tea towels to wrap things in and trays to pile them up on. There was enough shelf space in the various sculleries to hold all the useful things he could find, and there were plenty of them.

Eventually he paused for reflection when the well ran dry. Just how many lies had she told him? That was surely the same cook who frightened the wolves at Monrosso. Maybe the servants had not resigned in disgust at the old kitchen: they had just paid it a flying visit for Christmas. Or was that conversation with the staff at Monrosso some kind of hoax? He couldn't imagine how she could have pulled it off. What on earth was she up to? She'd been making a fool of him all along. Maybe he should tell her to stay home and keep out of his life. He trudged up to the courtyard.

Lucrezia was still pacing the corridor outside the Royal Suite. So, that brother still had not appeared. Maybe the sniffer dogs at the airport had singled him out again. If they detained him he could be hours late getting home. Surely she was used to that. But hadn't she said he rarely travelled on normal passenger planes? He may have landed miles away from Rome.

Why was she so convinced he'd arrive at eight this morning? He must have sent an email. He keyed in Lucrezia's number and password, expecting to find a few new messages between them, but there was only her last message to him: "Good luck, Darling. Come home soon." What gave her the idea he was coming today?

Giuseppe's arrival provided another diversion and Justin played host to him too. He was interesting to talk to, so it was no penance. It was amazing to hear that almost everything in the old kitchen had some value to somebody, even the ancient broken machinery. At this rate there would be little left to throw in the skip.

Giuseppe identified some weird gadgets such as levers and hooks on long stems for lifting manhole covers and pulling down dampers in the fireplaces. Justin asked him to label them, then put them together in a pantry. If they went in the skip perhaps they would be sorely missed.

Lucrezia at last came down to help. She made an effort to be nice to Giuseppe, but her whole body seemed to droop with misery. He felt a strong urge to hug her, tell her her brother would turn up very soon. She was so intriguing and so gorgeous. Did it matter if she was inventing a make-believe world? It was surely more fun than boring reality.

Finally, conveniently at lunchtime, there seemed to be no treasures left to find. She gave Giuseppe a brief tour of the house – not easy, as he tried his best to linger and drink in all its splendours so he could describe it to Bianca.

"She can come on Monday when the workmen are here, and you can show her around," said Lucrezia. "They plan to start at eight o'clock, so you'll have time before you open your shop, wont you?"

When they reached the corner shop Justin suggested they gave in to temptation and bought pizza slices.

The pizza slices were hot, so they laid them in their wrappers on the famous Swarovski crystal kitchen table, then demolished them without plates or cutlery before they could cool down. It felt a deliciously inappropriate way to treat such a fabulous work of art, and they giggled like school kids doing something wicked.

"This table really is quite beautiful," she said. "How much did it cost?"

"About thirty thousand euros," he said with a wry grin. "Yes, okay, I must have been out of my mind. I admit it."

She seemed to have put her worries aside as she made the coffee. He passed her the fruit bowl and watched her little white teeth bite into a peach. He pictured the flat without her, and his heart sank into his sandals. Who cared if she was making a fool of him. He was enjoying every minute of it.

He ought to think of something absorbing to help keep her mind off her brother. He was running out of ideas for passing the time, shut up in his penthouse. Cooking had never been his favourite occupation and now she had admitted her ignorance was a deliberate sham he felt a fool for wasting his time trying to teach her. Anyone who could cook hedgehogs and pigeons in mud on a camp fire had surely enough nouse to use a frying pan if she wanted to. Perhaps they should brave the heat, go out somewhere - but where?

"Would you fancy a trip to Tivoli, to Villa D'Este, this afternoon? I'm developing shack fever, shut in here every day, aren't you? This leaflet says there's a light and music show synchronised with the fountains every Saturday. That should be worth seeing."

"Well, It's a lovely thing to see, but last time I went we had to park a long way away and the traffic was chaotic. There were so many people in the garden you could hardly move. Ostia Antica never seems to get crowded."

"Ostia Antica?" He had been meaning to go there ever since he arrived in Rome but had never done so. "This leaflet says it's as good as Pompeii, and it's very easy to get to; there's a train stop right at the site. You've been there, have you? What do you think?

"Mmm. I've seen it in the spring. Gorgeous! Wild

flowers everywhere, but a man with a strimmer was mowing them all down. I felt so sad about the flowers I stopped enjoying the site. Yes, I'd love to go see what it's like in the summer. There's lots of open space so it should be cooler there."

"I'll look up the train times." He picked up a tablet.

"Would you mind if we went round to my house on the way? I'd like to see if our cars are okay first. Shall we go now, as soon as we're ready?"

At the B House she ran up the stairs to the Royal Suite and came back with two large sun hats, then she led the way down into the garage and pressed a button. The wide garage door rolled up, letting in harsh sunlight to illuminate the huge red sports car in all its brutal glory. She took a controller out of her bag and pressed it. The car doors opened like a bird stretching its wings.

"This looks fun," she grinned. "Do get in." She climbed in and patted the passenger seat.

He hurried towards her anxiously. "Look, Lucrezia - - "

"There's plenty of parking space at Ostia Antica." With a wicked grin she started the engine.

"If you prefer to go by car let's use the Mercedes."

"I think the key is in the car. We could go in convoy, if you like. Or see who gets there first."

"Lucrezia! Come on, now. What would your brother say if he knew you were thinking of driving his car."

"Is it fun to drive or shall I sell it on without bothering to try it. Jump in - or are you scared of women drivers? We have a far better record than the men, you know."

"Move over, then, and let me drive. You're surely not old enough to be on a public road."

His words were drowned by the roar of the engine as she manoeuvred the car out into the street and gunned the accelerator. He hurried out and scrambled in beside her, fuming with annoyance and anxiety as the doors came down to imprison him.

The back street was so narrow that both wing mirrors were in danger of scraping the house walls. They could not get out to change seats if they wanted to – and Lucrezia clearly didn't! He winced at the sight of a tight corner ahead, but she sang to herself as she confidently eased the car betweeen the huge stone blocks of the ancient walls with barely a centimetre to spare.

"Pull in as soon as there's space and let me drive," he ordered, but she sang even louder to drown him out.

As soon as the road widened she began struggling to find her seat belt, driving with one hand or momentarily with no hands at all.

"Belt up, Justin! You're breaking the law!" she chortled, grinning, when he tried to remonstrate.

Oh, Hell! That notorious three lane roundabout loomed ahead. He cringed into his seat as she accelerated straight into it, roared around it and out the other side, still singing merrily.

"Look, there's a bus stop. Pull in and let me drive."

"Wonder how you work this dashboard computer. You're a computer freak, Justin. Could you get this screen to show something useful? At least let's have the speedo on view. Wonder if there's an ejector seat. We are on the right road, aren't we? Can you be the navigator so I can keep my eyes on the road?"

He gave a great sigh of frustration and resignation. Anything he tried to do to stop her would just endanger them both. A large and complicated sign board was looming up and he teased out the route as instructed. "Far left lane!" he instructed. "This is going to be tricky."

"Where on earth are the indicators?" she complained, poking around the steering wheel. "Ah, got 'em! Give way, people! Make way for the Big Red Frog!" Nonchalantly she nosed her way smoothly leftwards from lane to lane, forcing the traffic to let her in, then giving them a wave of thanks.

Reluctantly he began to relax. Amazing as it seemed, she appeared to know what she was doing. Had the convent that had failed to teach her to cook taught her to drive instead? But surely the minimum driving age in Italy was 18. And wasn't there a rule about powerful cars? An extra three years older? Holy Moly!

At last the road opened onto a motorway and she gave a whoop of delight. "Come on, Froggie, have fun!" She gunned the engine, startling everyone around, roared up to the speed limit, then settled into the traffic stream.

"Wonder if there's a test track anywhere near here? It would be fun to see what the Froggy can do, wouldn't it? Can you find the radio? At least we can try that out. Have you found the handbook in the locker? You could try to find out how I'm supposed to drive this thing, couldn't you? I expect I'm doing it all wrong."

"It's a bit late for that now, isn't it, but you seem to be doing okay to me," he said grudgingly.

"We have company," she announced calmly.

Moments later a police car drew level. Lucrezia smiled and waved to the occupants. They didn't wave back.

The police turned on their flashers, accelerated past, then swerved in front of them. Calmly Lucrezia pulled into the side of the road behind them. She lowered the side window and waited, smiling, as the policeman got out and walked menacingly towards them.

"This your car, Madam?" he growled,

Lucrezia nodded.

"May I see your driving licence?"

Oh, God! thought Justin. Now we're for it. What will

they charge us with? Under-age driving, no licence, no insurance. In England they'd impound the car and crush it, all million euros' worth of it. Do they do that here? Will they get me for aiding and abetting an unlicenced minor? Grief! We'll be in the papers. Will I ever live it down? We'll be mobbed by paparazzi. The trolls will have a field day about Lucrezia living in my flat. They'll put a nasty slant on it for sure.

Lucrezia opened her bag and handed him a card.

The policeman studied it carefully, looked hard at Lucrezia, then handed it back. "Interesting car you have here, My Lady Marchesa. I don't think I've seen one before. Do you mind if I ask what it is?"

"A McLaren, the P1, their latest model. Very new. First time on the road. It's an English car."

"You don't fancy one of ours, a Ferrari, Lamborghini?"

"How can you be sure you have the best if you don't try the rest? This is fun for a change, but I'm sure we'll soon be pining for one of our own more stylish models. Maybe a Huracan like yours." She flashed him a conspiratorial smile.

"You do have insurance, My Lady?"

She reached into her bag again and pulled out a folded sheet of paper. The policeman studied it carefully, looked at the car's number plate, then solemnly handed it back.

"All in order?" she smiled.

"All in order, My Lady. May I say, My Lord Marquis, how I admire your gallantry in offering your lady the inaugural drive. I hope you have many pleasant drives in your very interesting new car." Solemnly he touched his hat, gave a little bow and walked slowly back to his car.

They waited silently until he was well out of earshot, back inside his patrol car, then Justin let out a deep sigh of relief.

"Thank goodness you brought your documents! That could have been pretty nasty."

"Now you know why we don't like flashy cars. We'll probably be stopped by every patrol car that spots us. This car is so rare and so eye-catching they'll be dying to know what it is. And when we park it at Ostia Antica some wag might score the paintwork with graffiti. Some jealous people just love doing that. It might cost thousands to get it fixed. And how do you like being a Marquis for a day?"

"Well, remembering the prerequisites for the job, I think I'd better resign right away."

CHAPTER 20

OSTIA ANTICA

The fate of Ostia Antica was very different from that of Pompeii. As everybody knows, disaster struck Pompeii so fast that many people suffocated in the downpour of blazing volcanic ash before they could run away. Their agonised bodies are on show for all to see.

If there are any bodies in Ancient Ostia they must be lying peacefully where their relatives buried them a thousand or two years ago. Their town lay buried too, for a thousand years, until modern archaeologists dug it up. A few hours there is a pleasant, relaxed experience and a fascinating glimpse of life in an ancient Roman seaport.

They strolled along the ancient main street towards the harbour. Mosaic pictures on the pavings identified the ruined shops on either side. The white mosaic of the huge bathing pool of the public baths shimmered in the sunshine, decorated with boys riding sky blue sea monsters. Life in the ancient town must have been luxurious and elegant.

Eventually the road simply stopped at a level expanse of yellow parched grass, stretching as far as the eye could see. Once this was the Mediterranean Sea, busy with ships bringing grain from Roman North Africa to Rome's most important port. Transferred to barges, it was taken up canals to feed Rome. By 440 AD the Vandals had conquered North Africa, cut off the supply of grain, and deprived Ostia of its main source of income, employment and cheap food. The people gave up the fight to stop the Tiber from silting up the harbour and the river mouth. Now the sea shore is many miles away.

The Vandals starved out Rome as well. The emperors had paid for bread made of this cheap grain to give free to the poor every day. Now grain was scarce and very expensive, so taxes were imposed to feed the poor. The rich fled Rome to escape the taxes: the poor because they were starving. Plagues wiped out half the population and Rome could no longer defend its empire. Barbarians forced their way in from every direction, longing to become Romans but unwilling to accept Roman authority. The Goths had finished off the Roman Empire by the end of the 5th Century A.D. Ostia staggered on for another four hundred years, until pirate raids frightened away the last inhabitants in the 900s. Then the wind buried it slowly with sand.

They walked back to the town centre, then up and down the side streets lined with houses, two and three storey warehouses and hotels, some looking little worse than Justin's derelict palace had once done. Entranced, he stood there, dreaming of getting in the builders, turning them into flats and offices, bringing life back to the town again. It was such a lovely site, slumbering under the bright sunlight.

The buildings looked quite similar to those of any old Mediterranean town, but there were striking exceptions. The public loos were very public indeed. Inside an enclosure, a long stone bench had about twenty big holes, embarrassingly close together. Water once ran in a channel below to flush the deposits out into the drains. In front was another small channel to dip a sponge in to wipe yourself clean – in full view of everyone. No wonder the Romans had a ribald sense of humour!

On many street corners there were cafés or bars with slabs at counter height with similar sized holes, some with large earthenware jugs still stuck in them, which once held wine or foodstuffs.

Everywhere drains, water pipes and central heating

were visible. Such things disappeared for more than a thousand years after the memories of Roman life melted away. Even concrete was forgotten until reinvented in about 1900 AD. Far too much modern concrete has already started crumbling, but the huge concrete dome of the Roman Pantheon has lasted two thousand years already, and its concrete is not even reinforced.

"It's frightening that such an advanced civilisation could melt away, and technology just go backwards," mused Justin. "Roman technology seems easy to understand, but their conquerors couldn't make it work, could they? Imagine trying to recreate our modern technology if our civilisation was destroyed!"

"People nowadays are so useless at basic survival skills they wouldn't survive long enough to try," said Lucrezia.

"Well, on that happy note I need a big mug of tea," said Justin. "Shall we go back to the café?"

"Look, there's a concert in the theatre here tonight" said Justin, pointing to the poster on the window of the café. "Should we get tickets? Kill an hour or two in the café?"

"Well, we usually find lots to talk about," she said.

The café didn't have a lot to offer, but the heat didn't encourage an appetite.

"No alcohol for me," warned Lucrezia. "I'm sure to be stopped on the way home. Then we would be in trouble."

"I think you should let me drive. We were very lucky not to get arrested on the way here. I assume your papers are forgeries. They may be rumbled next time."

She raised her eyebrows, then looked steadily at her plate. "The insurance only covers Chez and me. You can't just add anybody to the cover for a powerful car like that. They want to know everything about your driving history."

"Let me look at your driving licence," he demanded.

"Cheeky!"

"Well, if it's genuine you must be at least 21."

She smiled and shrugged.

"So how old are you?"

"You should never ask a lady her age."

He looked at her in silence, seething with resentment. She had surely been deceiving him from the start.

"Look, Justin," she said earnestly, "tell me this: if a strange man comes up to a girl in the street and asks her lots of very personal questions, does she have a duty, legal or moral, to tell him all her private affairs?"

He caught his breath and took stock. Then he sighed.

"You're right. I had no right to try to pry into your private affairs. You had the right to fob me off with any lies you could think of. I'm sorry."

"Thank you," she said, treating him to her knee-weakening smile. It was impossible not to smile back.

"Well, now," he ventured cautiously, "am I still just a strange man in the street?"

"What would you like to be?"

"A friend. What would you like me to be?"

"Sounds good. Yes, let's be friends."

"Friends ought to be able to trust each other, though, don't you think?"

"Does that mean you can't trust me if you don't know how old I am?"

"Well, don't you feel a bit - sort of adrift - if you don't even know what generation the person is you're friends with? You can expect an older person to have more experience and knowledge of the world than a sixteen year old, surely."

She sighed. "I don't want to have to keep things from

you, Justin. You've been a very good friend to me when I badly needed one. I don't know what I would have done without you - maybe tried to get a convent to take me in. I was thinking about that when you tried to chat me up."

"Not that convent you'd just run away from!"

She burst out laughing. "I made that up as well as the aunt."

"Are you telling me you didn't spend the last five years in a convent?"

She shook her head, smiling ruefully.

"So, had you been in Rome all the time?"

"No, no, I arrived that morning. I hadn't been to Rome for ages, apart from that one Christmas week."

"Did you really not know how to switch the lights on?"

She shook her head. "I've hardly ever been in the house on my own. I'd forgotten how lonely and scary it feels."

"So, are you going to put me straight and tell me which generation you belong to? Then at least I'll know how to treat you properly?"

She gave a big sigh and made a helpless gesture with her hands. "I don't want to mislead you Justin, if it means so much to you, but honestly, I can't tell you because I really don't know. How old would you like me to be?"

"What a daft question!" he exploded. "How can you not know? Have you got amnesia or something?"

"Amnesia? Yes, I've got amnesia. How old are you?"

"29"

"Is it good being 29?"

He nodded.

"Well, then, can I be 29 like you?"

"No!" he exploded. "Dont be idiotic. Anyway, I can't believe you're as old as me," he finished lamely.

"22 is what it says on my papers," she offered, "so are you happy with that?"

"Are you just playing games with me?" he growled.

She handed him her driving licence, and, sure enough, 22 was her age.

"You're a very good actress," he sulked. "You really had me fooled."

"Well, you treated me like a silly school kid, so I just did what you expected. I was so exhausted and miserable it was a relief to be bossed around and not have to think for myself. It was perfect therapy. I can't thank you enough."

"So where were you before you came to Rome last Saturday - and why were you feeling so bad?"

She took a breath as if to speak, then frowned and shook her head. "Amnesia," she muttered. "Amnesia. That's it," She looked at him and smiled. "It must have been really bad, and a nasty thump on the head. All I can remember is feeling half dead and very sorry for myself. I feel so much better now, thanks to you, and my memory is creeping back, little by little."

"It sounds as if you had concussion. I wish you'd told me. I would have got you medical help. We should get a doctor to look at you on Monday."

The concert was a disappointment: a pop group with little appeal to either of them. They soon got tired of covering their ears against the din of the huge array of speakers cluttering up the ancient Roman stage. In the dark it was hard to see much difference between this huge stone indestructible theatre two thousand years old and a modern pop concert. A Roman arena with tens of thousands of spectators must have been as noisy as any modern football stadium, but amplifiers hadn't been invented then. Lucky Romans! thought Justin. One of modern man's worst inventions. They left at the interval.

"Sorry. I shouldn't have suggested that," said Justin, as they walked to the car park marked 'Staff Only'.

"It was a good idea," she smiled. "but a bad concert."

Bribing the staff for a space in their car park had proved very wise. She had parked the Red Frog alongside a shed with its nose to the fence. Its other two sides were now well boxed in. Its tyres were still inflated and they could see no graffiti on the paintwork. They lifted two crush barriers out of the way and they were free.

Within a quarter of an hour the first Panther flagged them down. The young policeman was so entranced by Lucrezia and her car that he scarcely looked at her documents, but ten minutes later the next patrol was a very different kettle of fish. He scowled at her as he photographed her documents and sent them off to headquarters. Justin's stomach tied itself in knots. They could well be forgeries; she could be rumbled now. The more she tried to charm the cop the nastier he got. Male chauvinist pig, thought Justin. He's longing to get his hands on the McLaren and cart us off to a cell. Oh grief!

It seemed the answer had arrived. The scowler raised his eyebrows, then handed her documents back with a very sulky look. She turned on her knee-weakening smile, and the policeman visibly squirmed. Those documents had somehow passed the test.

CHAPTER 21

PHANTOM SUPERCAR

Only another ten kilometres to go. Beside the motorway, the industrial estates were merging into the shabbier fringes of the Eternal City. Soup and a glass of wine for supper would be nice, thought Justin.

Oh, no! Another Panther, pootling along in the slow lane, suddenly woke up and smelt something interesting: something red and black and gleaming, with a shape out of science fiction. What the blazes? Don't let it get away!

"Oh damn! Not again!" sighed Lucrezia. "Ridiculous! Surely three times is more than enough."

"You could lodge a complaint. It's surely harassment."

"A bit mean. They love cars. They only want a look. We could give them a bit of fun instead. Tighten your seatbelt, Justin. You're on, Panther!"

"Lucrezia, don't do anything stupid. We're nearly home."

"Me, stupid? Watch this!"

She indicated right and braked hard. The sky blue and white Alfa Romeo, hazard lights winking, coasted past and pulled onto the verge ahead of them. At the last minute Lucrezia floored the gas pedal. The McLaren P1 roared its approval, flung Justin hard against his seat back and took off like a rocket, demonstrating its legendary acceleration. Shrinking rapidly in their rear view mirrors, the startled Panther turned on its flashers.

"Stoppit, Lucrezia, they'll get you for speeding; impound the car!"

"Me, speeding?" She pointed to the speedo: it was just shy of 120 kph. "Did you time us? Should be 0 to 100 in two point eight seconds."

But, of course, within the legal limit of only 120 kph, the Alfa had no problem catching them up. The flashing police car crept closer and closer. It was coming alongside now and winking right, instructing her to pull onto the verge. Suddenly she flicked the indicator right and slewed off the motorway so fast Justin was flung against the door.

"Bye bye, Panther," she murmured.

"Lucrezia, are you crazy?" he yelled.

"You're distracting me, Justin. Why not do something useful? Tell me what the Panther's doing."

What could he do? Any interference from him could kill them both. From the top of the run-off he could see the police car reversing. It would be up the exit in no time.

"It's reversing. It's not giving up."

"Catch me if you can," she chuckled. "Call the Huracan: then we can really have fun."

"Are you stark raving bonkers!" wailed Justin.

"Flattery will get you nowhere. Hang on."

Once again she flung the car into a last minute turn, plunging into a maze of narrow ancient streets, once homes but now just shabby workshops and storage, fortunately empty of people and parked cars on this late Saturday evening. Now and then he caught a glimpse of the Panther crossing a junction. Were the cops enjoying this game of hide and seek, he wondered.

Suddenly the Frog tried a somersault – but it failed, and dropped its rear wheels back onto the road with a thump. The road ahead was blocked with tables and throngs of merry-makers. Thank Heavens for good brakes! Where was the Panther? Oho! Here it came.

Lucrezia reversed quickly, and the chase resumed.

"Oh my God, you've had it now!" wailed Justin. Another Panther had joined in the fun, this time a car with a shape that sent tingles down his spine: huge slanting fairings that even the sky blue livery couldn't soften, a wolf bursting out of sheep's clothing. Surely a tiger, not a panther. No, a shark, with vampire fangs and evil slanty shark's eyes. "You asked for the Huracan and you've got it." This stunning new present from the Lamborghini company is the pride and joy of Rome's traffic police.

All over! There were panthers coming towards them from two directions. He held his breath. She turned sharply again, charged straight into a black void and turned the car lights off. It felt like a steep bumpy slope heading down from the road into oblivion. He strained his eyes to make sense of the huge black shapes looming up on every side. Soon she was using them as slalom posts. How on earth could she see where she was going? When his eyes got used to the darkness he realised they were trucks. It was a big unlit derelict site being used as a lorry park.

Suddenly the site was raked by two sets of very bright headlamps. The Panthers knew their city. They could play cat and mouse with her now, and there were two of them, one a rival for the McLaren.

Lucrezia roared one way, then the other, the tyres squealing, gripping the ground like crampons. The Panthers' lights showed clouds of dust billowing up from three sets of shrieking wheels. She was proving a confusing quarry, only visible when caught in the Panthers' headlights, and hurtling off in unpredictable directions, but surely it was only a matter of time before they trapped her.

There was a squeal of brakes. The two squad cars had stopped - nose to nose.

"Oh, no!" squealed Lucrezia. "They haven't smashed the Huracan!" She raced towards them, then circled them to have a closer look.

"Idiot!" yelled Justin. "Go home now, while you've got the chance."

"They look okay, thank Goodness!"

They looked more than okay, both reversing fast.

"Time to go," she said, spinning the steering wheel. The tyres squealed as the wheels spun, flinging up pebbles like gunshot. She was off, roaring up the bumpy slope and out into the narrow streets again.

"Go home now!" Justin yelled."Head for the main road."

"Just when I'm enjoying myself? Hello, Panthers!"

She swung left, and led the panthers on a crazy chase through the shabby deserted streets again.

"Hee! Hee! Hee! You can't catch me."

She was taking the corners so fast now even the McLaren couldn't keep all four wheels on the ground. If there were any neighbours to hear the din, Heaven knows what they thought was going on! The panthers had one car too many, jamming on the brakes far too often to avoid running into each other. They must be cursing her – and each other - to high Heaven.

"Another course in tactics wouldn't come amiss," she murmured.

She used one of their contretemps to put a few seconds of distance behind her. Once again she hurtled down into the lorry park, lights off, and this time put a wall of lorries behind her. Suddenly she clapped on the brakes, skidded a quarter turn to a halt, then cut off the petrol engine.

The car crept forward silently, straight towards a wall of gargantuan ancient stone blocks, thick with creepers. Justin cringed. The wind-screen went totally black, there was a swishing sound, then they bumped ahead for ages. At first he could see nothing at all, then something began to take shape, lit by a strange light too dim even for sidelights. They were creeping along a narrow tunnel, lined with monstrous slabs of stone.

"Where the Hell are we?" he asked shakily.

"Cloaca Maxima. Well and truly down the drain."

"No! Stop right now. It's far too narrow."

"Pliny says you can drive a piled-up hay cart along it."

"Two thousand years ago, maybe, but everybody knows it's full of rubble and filthy water and the roof's caving in."

"Oh, really?" she said. The ancient sewer curved away to the right. Carefully she nursed the big squat supercar around the bend, and just in time. Way behind them, back around the bend, the tunnel was suddenly lit. She stopped the car silently.

"They're following us."

"I doubt it," she said. "They're just having a look at the entrance, wondering if we're daft enough, and listening for the engine. They wont risk the Lamborghini. They think they know where we'll come out if we have gone in, so they'll go and wait for us there."

The light went out. Claustrophobia replaced it. "Do you have a clue where you're going? Any minute the roof might cave in and we'll be buried."

"You think so? Oh dear!" said Lucrezia. Still using the electric motor, she began to crawl ahead. The car bumped over some impediment, water splashed, and the stench of sewage filled the car.

"You're wrecking a beautiful car," wailed Justin.

As nightmares go, this had to be up with the worst. They were stuck. She had now managed, by lots of tiny manoeuvres, to wedge the car into a junction, each wing tight against a rough stone wall.

"Could we get out of the roof?" He should try to be positive, swallow the panic twisting his guts. Here they were – where? In a drain somewhere under the city, a long way from the entrance, a drain said to be impassable, full of rubble falling from the roof. What if it rained? No, please!

"Mmm?" She was knitting her brows and making movements with her hands, rehearsing a plan of action.

"The roof. Could we get out?"

"What? It's solid rock."

"No, the car roof. We can't get out of the doors: they're too close to the walls."

"We really must get this corner sliced off."

Many people over the last two thousand years must have thought the same thing, judging by the deep scratches on the orange-brown rock. Pity nobody had actually bothered to do it.

Well, they wont need to bury us, he thought, and we've a fabulous million pound coffin, all bright and shiny – well it *was* before she covered it with dust and filthy water.

"While we're stopped you could look for tiny cameras and stuff. The archeologists are doing a survey of these mines. They might be watching us."

They might rescue us, thought Justin. Give them a ring, He pulled out his phone. Come on, show willing! 'No service provider,' it said.

"There's about ten metres of rock above us here."

"That's nice to know," he said.

He looked around. There seemed to be tunnels going in every direction, lined with rough hewn alcoves and columns. Mushrooms? Racks of shelves, all sprouting mushrooms. There was a stack of empty boxes piled against one wall. A mushroom farm down here in Hades? Pluto would pop up next and start picking them. Something moved. A figure, dressed in something hard to see, was lurking in the shadows.

"Somebody over there, look!"

The figure dodged behind a column, then ran off down a passageway.

"Cat burglar, probably," she said. "Great escape route. Lots of interesting things go on down here. There don't seem to be any homeless people around at the moment. It's dry most of the time and not a bad temperature. It must be nicer to sleep in the park in this heat."

"What happens when it rains? These sewers must be death traps."

"They're not sewers, they're Roman mine workings."

Justin studied the rough hewn, yellow and brown walls. No glint of metal or anything sparkly, as far as he could see. "What were they mining? Copper, tin, gold?"

"Concrete. The concrete that rebuilt Rome, after the great fire in 64 AD. Nero ordered it for all public buildings and apartment blocks so the new Rome could withstand fire and earthquakes. He had the right idea, didn't he?"

Justin exploded with mocking laughter. "Concrete! How could they mine concrete? It's not a rock, its a man-made mixture. They manufacture it at the building site. Haven't you seen them doing it?"

"This is the special volcanic rock, the magic ingredient that makes Roman concrete the best the world has ever seen. Modern concretes just can't compare. Experts are researching it now, trying to learn to make it again. The Pantheon is still the biggest non-reinforced concrete dome in the world, still intact after nearly two thousand years. They used to turn this rock into rubble and mix it with lime, With half lime and half this special rock it will set under water to make docks and bridges. Some are still in perfect condition after two thousand years of use. The Romans knew what they were doing, but thank goodness the authorities have banned any more mining here. The rock under this city is like Gorgonzola cheese."

Was that a rat? Rats! Rats, and yet more rats, scuttling around, tiny eyes gleaming in the dark. Nothing else seemed to be moving now, and they weren't going anywhere either, trapped in this huge red frog.

."Well, Goodbye. It's been interesting knowing you."

"You're off then? Where to? Have you got a torch? Can you remember the way?"

"What was it you said the other day: next stop Heaven or Hell? Carbon Monoxide from the exhaust should do us in pretty soon. They say it's such an easy death you don't even notice till it's far too late."

"I didn't know electric motors made Carbon Monoxide. Ah, well, then, better get going. My arms needed a rest."

Once again she patiently manoeuvred, a few centimetres forward, a few back. Justin cringed, waiting for the scrunch of scraping metal, but maybe his ears weren't working.

"Goody good! Here we go," she said at last.

They soon met another cross roads, and she hesitated.

"Go straight ahead. Don't get stuck again."

"That leads into the river; it's normally under water."

"So, how much farther to where the police are waiting?"

"Oh, that exit's way back in the Cloaca, only a little way from where we first came in. Everybody thinks that's the only bit that's passable. They don't realise there's a way through into these ancient mines."

"Do you mean we could have got out ages ago? Why in Heaven's name have we come so far?

"The man said go home. I'm sure that's what he said."

"Are you trying to tell me this is the way home?"

"Ask the Frog. Everyone knows horses can find their way home and the Frog has nine hundred horses under its bonnet."

"Ha! Ha!" moaned Justin. "At this moment, I'd like to strangle you."

"You'll spend the rest of your life right here if you do."

"Yes, that has occurred to me. Look, that tunnel ahead looks wider."

"It's certainly more exciting. The roof has collapsed and a whole house has fallen right down through it. Wonder if anyone's living in it now."

At the next junction she made the usual multipoint turn, then began to drive into one of the tunnels.

"No, Lucrezia, not this way. Can't you see it's been bricked up!" he protested. "Blood'n sand!"

As usual she took not a blind bit of notice. The light died away. Blackness enveloped them completely. She stopped the car. He felt her wriggling. Was she trying to slide her slender body out of the car door?

"What are you doing, Lucrezia?" he demanded, reaching towards her in the blackness, but she had made her escape. He was alone. He groped around for the door control, but his door opened only a few centimetres before it banged against the wall. No way out his side. From what he remembered of the Frog's interior it would be hard to drag himself into the driver's seat, and he may be too big to squeeze out of her door.

Somewhere nearby he heard the faint whirr of an electric motor; then she came struggling back into her seat. He felt the car move forward again. It stopped, and she climbed out again. What on earth was going on? Suddenly his door opened and he felt her hand grasp his shoulder.

"Come out," she said. "We're home now." She steered him forward, stumbling in the darkness. Light at last! It was a great relief to walk out of a small door into a narrow back street. Ahead, a garage door was swinging open. She walked across the street and pressed a button on the garage wall. Behind him he heard another garage door swing up - and there it was: the McLaren.

"Clever, hey?"she smirked as she walked back to the car, "And don't you dare tell anyone about it, or else - "

"Or else what?" he growled.

"I'll set my big brother onto you, of course," she smiled.

As she drove the McLaren across the street into its home he stared at its huge, red froggie face. It was definitely grinning.

"How long before the police come knocking on the door?" he asked wearily.

"They didn't ask your name and address, did they, and the neighbours will tell them nobody's lived in my house for years. And what could they put on their charge sheets? Their famous Huracan, plus a souped-up Alfa Romeo, couldn't catch a fluffy girl driving an English car? She didn't even break the speed limit. Half the time she was barely visible, then she just - melted away. Explain that to your superiors. We chased a phantom supercar. What was it? Goodness knows! They'd never live it down."

"What about that bad-tempered pig who stopped you earlier on? He sent headquarters a copy of your licence. They'll surely put two and two together."

"Well, good luck to them, then," she laughed and tossed her head.

"You seem to think you can get away with murder, that the laws don't apply to you," he scowled reprovingly.

"You know what they say: 'rules are for the guidance of wise men and for the obedience of fools.'"

"Well, you're neither a man nor a fool - "

"So, you're right. The laws don't apply to me. Perhaps I'll try a little murder next."

With the Red Frog safely back in her garage, Lucrezia

ran up the stairs to the Royal Suite. It seemed presumptuous to follow, but he doubted he had the energy in any case. He sat on the wooden staircase and checked her emails.

She had sent two messages: "Where? What?" and some time later, "Where? What?" again. There were no replies.

Lucrezia came slowly down the stairs, shoulders drooping sadly.

Maybe there was no need to worry about that dangerous big brother any more.

CHAPTER 22

OOPS, OH DEAR!

Lucrezia was unusually quiet as they walked the short distance to his penthouse. There was a frown between her eyes and her shoulders drooped.

As soon as she reached her bedroom she lit up the laptop. He hurried to his bedroom and switched on the big screen. Predictably she was viewing her emails. Nothing but the usual advertising rubbish that seems to get through every known filter. There was still no answer to her pleas for information from her brother.

She began her familiar trawl of the Waziristan papers. Suddenly she stopped at a bizarre story of an explosion. Two local men had got into a confrontation. One grabbed the other, pushed him around a corner into a quiet side street, then jostled and hugged him until he literally exploded, breaking several windows and causing a few minor injuries to bystanders. There was little left of the men, but one of them had been wearing a bomb vest.

Justin gave a silent cheer. Hug a bomber! Hope it starts a new craze. Be a real hero. Get the monsters before they kill loads of innocent bystanders. Well done, man, whoever you are – were! Did he realise what he was doing, or had he been as surprised as everyone else when the bomber exploded? All this senseless carnage. Would it never end?

Lucrezia followed the story around the world for a while, then closed down the laptop. "Justin!" she called. "Would you like some hot chocolate and a ginger nut? She came in grinning like the McLaren.

Her mood swings were bewildering, he thought, as he sipped the hot chocolate. She seemed so worried about her brother last night at the Jazz concert and today when he'd not arrived home. Maybe the rats had got the better of the Pied Piper this time, and if he had been batting for both sides and selling bombs to terrorists he'd surely got his just deserts. She must have some idea what he was doing, but she seemed to hero-worship him, so why was she now so cheerful? Maybe she'd really been afraid of him; maybe dreading his arrival.

Well, whatever. Maybe he could stop worrying about getting on the wrong side of that brother. And there was definitely no need to treat her like an innocent child any longer. She'd made him feel an idiot for the last few hours, telling him so many lies his head was reeling, then driving like The Stig on speed and scaring the pants off him. Maybe he should tell her to go home. Yes, he could do without all this agro. Life would be -

Imagine telling his staff what he'd been up to. Trekking in the Himalayas? Tramping about in the rain all day, then eating weird food in a steamy tent reeking of sweaty socks? No way! He'd been co-pilot for a famous fighter, looping the loop in a deadly war plane, seconds away from demolishing a Red Arrow mid air. And imagine being chased by the police in the Huracan, leaving them standing and finding your way home through the sewers and the mines. They'd think he was making it up.

And it was all because of Lucrezia. You great Wuss! Man up, stop whining. You've nothing better to do, so toughen up. Jump in with both feet and give her a run for her money. Time to redress the balance, show her who's the boss. Time to play some of *my* games. Why wait for Sophia ? Never liked her in the first place. Shouldn't be too difficult. I'm a great deal stronger than Lucrezia.

Once they were both in bed, he got out again and knocked on her bedroom door. "I've got you a rather belated birthday present, Lucrezia. May I come in?"

"Yes, of course," she called, and sat up in bed.

"What do you think of these?" He handed her two broad silver bracelets.

She examined the intricate patterns chased on the outsides. "They're lovely. Are they really for me?"

"Of course, and I'm sure they'll fit. Hold out your arms." He snapped them onto her wrists.

"They really are lovely. Thank you so much."

"Hold your arms up so I can see them properly."

Dutifully she held up her arms. With speedy movements he had practised for days, he clipped both her wrists to the bedposts.

"Oops!" said Lucrezia. "Oh dear!"

"Slave bracelets" he said calmly. "Now you are my slave. You said it was good therapy to be told what to do, so now you can have lots more of it. Maybe it will cure your amnesia."

She pursed her lips and looked him in the eyes, then turned her head to examine each bracelet carefully. With her hands chained well apart it seemed obvious there was no way she could free herself.

"Oh, Master," she intoned playfully, "What would you have me do?"

"You don't need to do anything at all, My Sweet. Just uncross your legs and relax." He whipped off the bedcover to reveal her lovely naked body.

She did neither. Instead she tried to engage him in a serious discussion about civilisation in general and the Romans and slavery in particular. He felt his ardour diminishing a little. Did she think she could put him off with boring intellectual discourse? He determined to develop cloth ears and just watch her lovely lips moving as she tried to calm him down. She succeeded a little but not enough. He'd been longing for this moment for too long, and she was such a tempting sight.

He made no attempt to hide what he was doing as he pulled on a condom.

She watched him solemnly. "Whatever is that?" she asked, with big round eyes.

"Just uncross your legs and I'll show you," he smirked. There was no need to rush. He took his time to deploy himself over her helpless body. "You look so delicious I think I'll eat you. Which bit shall I eat up first? He nuzzled her pert breasts and her gently rounded tum. Finally he settled on the lovely mouth that was still trying gamely to bore him into losing the ability to do his worst.

He had better get on with things before she succeeded and made a fool of him again. He bent one knee and aimed it at her thighs, trying to prise her legs apart. Her legs were much stronger than he expected. If he pushed much harder she would be black and blue. While he was wondering how to solve the problem she suddenly bent her own leg and kneed him in the groin.

"Auwww!" he yelled. You little viper! That's not cricket."

"Is this how you play that game in England? I thought it was supposed to be deadly dull," she spluttered.

"Part your legs or you're going to get hurt," he growled angrily. "Serve you right, kneeing me like that. Play the game properly."

"Game? I've had enough of this game. Please take off these bracelets," she said quietly.

"Slaves have to buy their freedom; you surely know that. Part your legs and pay the price."

"But you haven't bought me yet. Slaves don't come free, do they? How much do you think I might cost?"

He found himself trying to calculate some value for her in a slave market. She had caught him again. Maths did nothing for the libido.

He kissed her again very firmly to keep her quiet and

tried again to prise her legs apart.

She managed to turn her head away and shrieked into his ear, "Fire! Fire!"

"Call the fire brigade?" asked Angel.

"Yes, you do that," muttered Lucrezia.

The fire alarm in the hallway was making one hell of a racket. He determined to make one last desperate effort to get his way before the fire got too serious, but it was useless. With Lucrezia screaming in one ear, Angel in the other and the alarm assaulting them both his ardour died away and he was forced to admit defeat.

"I'm sorry you don't seem to like my little game," he said lamely, as he released her from the bedposts. "I hoped it might cure your amnesia - shock therapy."

She gave him a withering look and began to pull on a dress. There was nothing for it but to hurry along to his bedroom and throw on some clothes. Then he rushed frantically around the penthouse stuffing things into shopping bags and his briefcase.

From the corner of his eyes he saw Lucrezia slip out of the patio doors.

"Don't open the doors, Lucrezia!" he yelled. "You'll create an updraft and make the fire ten times worse!"

She pretended not to hear him, and walked around the terrace having a very good look over the edges. Then she came back inside irritatingly slowly. "There are three ways out," she announced authoritatively. "You could try climbing over the roofs, but they're pretty steep and slippery, and you're heavy enough to crack the tiles and fall right through. You could walk the prop that keeps these old houses from toppling onto each other, but it's only ten centimetres wide. I know it will take my weight, but I doubt it would take yours and it's five floors up. Or you could use the lift, as usual."

"You can't use the lift in a fire. It could stop between floors and you'd cook to death. Come down the fire stairs." He grasped the handle of the fire door and pulled. It refused to budge. Idiot! He yelled silently. Why didn't you get that locksmith to come back and fit a fire lock? He'd only done the tourist flats to placate the fire inspector. There was a keyhole but he'd never been able to locate the key. How stupid can you get?

Lucrezia had called the lift. "Are you coming, or shall I go without you?"

"We'll get cooked or suffocated," he wailed.

"Fire, death, suffocated, call Fire Brigade, Police, ambulance - - - ?"

"Good idea, Angel. Call them all," she laughed.

She grabbed him by the shirt front, gave a tug and he toppled into the lift. After what seemed an excruciatingly long time he staggered out again on the ground floor, to be met by a bedlam of overexcited people. People in various stages of undress were moaning and grumbling in an assortment of languages; firemen from at least three fire engines were bustling about doing who knows what, and the neighbours were providing an interested audience in the background.

Somebody pointed out Justin, and suddenly everybody was harassing him. The foreigners, presumably from his holiday flats, were demanding to know what was going on and when they could get back to bed. What could he say? He had no idea what on earth was happening.

"Are you the owner of this building?" a voice boomed in his ear, over the shriek of the alarm. "Where is the fire?" It was an important-looking fire officer.

"You tell me," said Justin helplessly. "I've no idea."

"Well then, who rang the alarm?"

"I'm sorry, I really don't know."

"Well, I can't smell any smoke, so it can't be much of a fire, so will you turn off the alarm," asked the fireman. "We're here now, so it's not doing any good, is it?"

There followed one of the most embarrassing ten minutes of his life. It had never occurred to him to make a mental note of where the fire alarm control box had been sited. With the alarm screeching deafeningly, upsetting half of Rome, the firemen spread out through the building, trying to find the control box. At last the noise was cut off with a shock like a beheading.

The firemen then set out to find the alarm that was still winking. They found it finally in his penthouse. Everyone looked accusingly at him.

"You know that setting off a fire alarm without justification is an offence, Sir?" said the fire chief.

"Is it?" he asked wearily. "Well, yes, of course, it should be, shouldn't it? And I assure you I would never dream of doing such a thing. It must be faulty. I'd be glad if your fire inspector could visit me to help identify the fault."

"Do you have any youngsters in your home, Sir?"

"No, no, just myself and this lady. The very last thing we would want to do is cause a disturbance like this in the middle of the night. It's most embarrassing."

The fire officer moved closer, presumably to see if he could smell alcohol. Then he spotted the fire door.

"Yes, officer, that door needs a fire lock. I'm shocked to realise the locksmith missed it. I travel a lot so I don't spend much time in this flat. I only realised tonight that the job hadn't been done."

Feeling thoroughly shell-shocked, Justin watched the three fire engines drive away. Then the watching crowd slowly melted into the night.

CHAPTER 23

WHERE ARE YOU, CESARE?

The fire alarm was screaming; firemen rushed around madly, axing his precious penthouse to pieces. Foreigners crowded round him, pointing at him, demanding something, and jabbering away in languages he couldn't understand.

He struggled woozily into a sitting position and rubbed his eyes. The only sound was the church bells ringing out a reminder of the Sunday morning services. He breathed a great sigh of relief. What a night! He had jumped off the top of the Burj Khalifa into a Hawker Hunter and fired a rocket smack into a hospital, releasing a torrent of great slavering rats. They made straight for him, gnashing their huge pointed teeth, and dragged him into a cave full of gigantic mushrooms where waves of sewage came roaring towards him. He was sweating profusely and in need of a shower.

As he dried himself off he reflected that those nightmares may not be so far from real life for that rat-catcher brother. Why on earth would a marquis, with a nice cushy life, swanning about a fine country estate pretending to keep the Swiss from invading Italy, choose to spend his time and energies in such horrible places? Lucrezia said the estate was making money, so why did he need to sell weapons? He must be a demented sadomasochist of the first order. Well, he had not turned up as expected, and the evidence that had fascinated Lucrezia seemed to hint that he may have killed his last rat, or whatever it was he liked hunting. She may have to wait in vain for him forever.

Lucrezia! Oh dear! Last night's events in her bedroom came flooding back. Playing sex slaves didn't seem much fun if the slave wouldn't play the game properly. She seemed to have cottoned on perfectly well at first. Then it all went wrong. Maybe it was a bit premature to try things like that. He should have tried it out on Sophia first, as she was the one who suggested it. Maybe she was still a virgin, but if she was really twenty two that seemed unlikely, especially as she had not been shut up in a convent. Maybe he should be much more masterful, make her do what he wanted. After all, she was so much weaker than he was, and who was going to stop him, if that dangerous brother really had turned up his toes?

He dragged himself out of bed and into the kitchen. It was clinically tidy as usual. The kettle was still warm, but she hadn't made a mug of tea for him. Small wonder, he thought sheepishly.

Her bedroom door was open, her bed was neatly made and the laptop was closed on the dressing table.

He went out onto the terrace and scanned the rooftops.

"Miaauw!" said the big ginger tom curled up on one of the chairs. He sighed and stroked the cat for comfort. It purred and rubbed its head against his arm. Maybe a cat might be a less complicated friend than all those scheming women. "Puss! Pusswuss!" he called, as he walked back into the flat. It followed him into the kitchen and watched with avid interest as he opened a tin of minced steak.

As the cat demolished the meat, he glanced at the kitchen clock. 7.45. She must have gone to the B House for 8.0 am again. What was so special about 8.0 am? What time had she arrived that Saturday a week ago? It might be interesting to ask. Had she come on a plane and if so, where from? Did she really have amnesia, or was that just another lie? After all, she'd remembered that she *hadn't* spent five years in a convent, so why couldn't she remember where she *had* been? Marcella didn't trust her, did she? And it seemed Marcella was right, at least about her age. Those car documents could well be good forgeries - their passports certainly were: Phillip and Elizabeth Smith of Sandringham! So, how old was she? Certainly older than sixteen, he decided.

He carried the remains of the meat outside and the cat obediently followed. Much more co-operative than those tricky women. He stroked it to show he had no wish to hurt its feelings, then closed the window and shut it out.

Hurriedly he finished dressing, grabbed a few biscuits, and set off for the B House, eager to know what might be going to happen next.

Lucrezia didn't seem to notice him as she locked the wicket door. It was only ten past eight so she had waited only minutes. How strange! Although the heat was not yet oppressive, she trudged slowly along the street, then stopped at a junction as if wondering which way to go. She looked so bewildered and woebegone he longed to go and hug her, but after last night - well, he'd better wait until he had some idea how she might react.

At last she set off along one of the streets towards a shabby old church, its bells mercifully silent. To his surprise she climbed the steps and disappeared inside. He followed her quietly at a safe distance. It was so dark he could see no sign of her at first. The windows were huge, but the pictures on the glass were so heavily coloured and dirty that hardly any light penetrated the cavernous interior. As he peered into the gloom, a candle flame began to move. Lucrezia was pushing the base of the candle into a stand in one of the side chapels far ahead along the nave. He heard the wooden seat creak as she sat down.

He crept quietly along the deserted nave and propped himself against a pillar out of her sight. She was staring at the candle as though mesmerised. He shifted from foot to foot as time slipped slowly by. Was she going to watch this blessed candle until it burned right down?

At last relief arrived. A man came in and the door slammed shut behind him, with a bang that echoed around the empty building. She got up and began to walk towards the exit. Silently Justin slipped out and waited till she emerged, blinking in the sunlight.

"Are you alright, Lucrezia?" he asked. "You don't look very well."

She shook herself and put on an unconvincing smile.

"Hello, Justin. You're out early."

"There's a café round the corner, opens early on Sundays for people who've been to an early service. Do you fancy a danish and a cup of tea?"

"Good idea. Where is it?" she replied.

Breathing a great sigh of relief, he steered her along the street to a table under a big umbrella.

As they munched the danish pastries he tried lamely to put things right, mentally crossing his fingers and toes.

"Sorry about last night. My silly game got a bit out of hand. You can hit me with a rolling pin if you like."

"What's a rolling pin?" she asked. They both laughed.

Thank goodness for that! he breathed. She really was an incredibly good sport. It was such a shame she had this obsession with her brother, but maybe soon, with the risks that he seemed to be taking, fate may set her free. But how would she cope with the idea that she may never see him again? This uncertainty must be very stressful. Maybe it would be good to help her come to terms with things.

"Lucrezia" he said, looking her steadily in the eyes, "are you going to spend the rest of your life waiting for your brother? Why do you need to see him so badly?"

She gave a big sigh and a helpless gesture. "I just want to persuade him to stop going to horrible places like Waziristan. Wouldn't you, if he were your brother?"

"You bet!" he agreed. "He must be crazy."

She nodded and sighed once again.

"You must be worried that something bad might happen to him there."

"Of course!" she exploded. "I can't bear to think what he's letting himself in for. It's absolutely nauseating. It gives me nightmares."

I know what you mean, he thought.

"How will you cope if he doesn't come back?"

She gave the helpless gesture again. "I'll have to stay here for a week or two, till the house is habitable. Then, I suppose, I'll go to Monrosso for space to think. No point in going looking for him. He could be anywhere. All I can do is wait until he gets in touch again."

"I don't know how these things work in Italy, but in England a Marquis usually has an heir who takes over the title and the estates as well. Is there a chance you might lose Monrosso?" He braced himself for shock and tears. He must do his best to comfort her.

She shrugged. "The heir is a sheep farmer in New Zealand. He wont leave New Zealand so he'd let me run the estate. No problem. Nothing need change."

He stared at her aghast. One minute she was worried sick about a brother she appeared to idolise, the next she was counting the spoils in cold blood. Would he ever understand her? Was she quite right in the head?

To calm his own nerves, he turned to more mundane topics. "Tomorrow morning they're coming to rip out your kitchen. We ought to have a last look to see if we've forgotten anything, before it's gone forever. Demolition men can be incredibly quick."

What next, he wondered, when they locked up the door. Lucrezia had flown up the stairs to the Royal Suite again but there were still no answers to her messages.

So she still couldn't believe the worst had happened.

Well, until there was some official confirmation of her brother's demise the heir couldn't turn her out, could he? Monrosso sounded the next best thing to Paradise. It would be great if he could persuade her to take him there. If he hadn't bullied her into refitting the kitchen they could have gone there straight away. Well, the refit should be finished soon, so maybe he would be lucky.

And now, how to pass another suffocatingly hot afternoon? She was clearly not in the mood for dancing. And after yesterday he'd be an idiot to suggest braving the heat with an excursion. She would surely seize any excuse to drive the Big Red Frog again. She didn't seem afraid of being thought a timid wimp, did she? He could imagine her, singing merrily, challenging the police to another duel – while he cringed in the passenger seat, begging her to slow down. Maybe next time they'd call up their Gallardo as well as the Huracan. She was a bit of a menace, wasn't she? He could imagine her causing mayhem in a convent. They needed something mundane and time-consuming to take her mind off her brother. Cooking again? What else?

"I think we'll make some minestrone today. We had nothing healthy yesterday and we can put loads of vegetables into it. Let's go shopping."

The food markets, including the one in the Campo Dei Fiori, were officially closed on Sundays. It was flea market day. But there was always an out-of-hours fruit and vegetable stall operating on some part of the famous square. They found enough fresh vegetables to make a half-decent minestrone, and by the time they got home it was time to start making the lunch.

The fabulous kitchen was the perfect place to play the cocktail barman. With a flourish he put together two perfect pre-lunch Mojitos, with big sprigs of apple mint from a shady corner of the terrace.

She took the tall glass and sipped it cautiously.

"Ooh! I love this," she purred. "Never tasted this before. Yum yum!"

On a fairly empty stomach, with only a few nuts and crisps to soak up the strong dose of white rum, it had a pretty intoxicating effect, which, as usual, encouraged her to throw caution to the winds.

"I didn't realise you were religious," he said, once they had got to work with their knives and chopping boards. It was a lengthy mundane task that didn't need much concentration, as long as you only chopped the veggies and not your fingers. He had long ago stopped worrying about Lucrezia's fingers. She seemed to have a very healthy respect for knives and considerable fine skill in wielding them. "So, you could tell me about Heaven and Hell – and Purgatory and all that, since it's Sunday. I've never been able to get my head around things like that."

"Can't help you there. I've never met anyone who's been to any of those places, have you?" she replied, skilfully slicing the strings off the green beans.

"But you believe in eternal life, in the immortality of the soul?" He put a handful of sliced carrots into the pan.

"What's a soul? Can you give me a scientific analysis of a soul? I've never come across one. Do you want me to string all the beans? There's quite a lot. You could argue that plants have souls. Their seeds survive death, but they are future living things, not past ones, so I suppose they dont count as souls in the religious sense."

"You don't believe in immortality then? Yes, we'll put the spares in the fridge. So, what happens after death?"

"I don't recall saying I didn't believe in immortality. As for what happens to humans after you're dead, I shouldn't worry about it. Your brain will give up working, so you won't register anything that's happening. It will be like a very deep anaesthetic, no dreams, nothing."

"You're contradicting yourself. I think you just implied you did believe in immortality, yet our brains will have stopped working and we won't know anything about it. Funny kind of immortality. Makes no sense to me."

"Humans are not immortal, are they? Oh I do love this Mojito. Could I have another, do you think?"

"You might be sorry. You could get very drunk."

"Just one without as much alcohol, then, pleeese."

Giving her a reproving look, he refilled her glass with a much weaker mixture, but it still smelled pretty good.

Over the rim of the glass she gave him a smile that did strange things to his inside. She may be eccentric but she was certainly seductive, especially when tipsy with Mojito. But after last night's fiasco, he must surely be on a sort of probation, so he ought to try to be a gentleman - at least today. It was Sunday. Intellectual discussion was a good passion killer, as she had tried to demonstrate last night, so back to immortal life.

"So, if humans can't be immortal, then, what can?"

"I can't see any scientific reason why all living things shouldn't be immortal. We all make telomerase to repair our telomeres, but as things stand at present, most land creatures just dont make enough of it so their telomeres wear out and they die. So far they've discovered only a few immortal worms and some ciliates, single cell creatures that can repair themselves indefinitely. Lots of sea creatures seem immortal. Turtles and jellyfish seem ageless and some extremophiles, things living near blazing hot volcanic vents deep in the oceans or in the Antarctic ice. And Tardigrades, of course."

"Tardigrades? Where would I find one of those?"

"Everywhere, if you have a microscope. Little uggly

bugglies with eight stubby legs. Lucky they're no bigger or we'd be in trouble – they've got a nasty bite. And you can't get your own back by killing the little beasties. They've survived a ride in space stuck to the outside of a rocket. They can be dried into powder, but cover them in water and they're walking within twenty minutes."

"Weird," said Justin. "But what about insects? They seem to have the kind of second life that humans dream of. In their first life they slither around on their stomachs eating, then they grow their own coffin and die in it. Then comes their resurrection: the coffin bursts open and out comes a fabulous creature with long legs and huge eyes. It unfolds its wings and flies up into the heavens like an angel. If you hadn't seen it happen you wouldn't believe it, would you?"

"Absolutely," agreed Lucrezia. "And lots of plants could count as immortal - the ones that grow from cuttings like Japanese Knotweed. They tried chopping it into tiny bits to get rid of it, but all the bits sprouted in no time. Now it's coming up through floorboards like the Triffids."

"If that's true, why hasn't it taken over the world by now? Has it just dropped in recently from Outer Space?"

"Apparently it was struggling to grow on the slopes of Mount Fugi; then some plant hunter took cuttings to Kew. Away from volcanic fumes it grows like wild fire. Maybe it *will* take over the world, now it's been given the chance."

"Lucky humans don't sprout if you mince them into bits, so we wont find ourselves knee deep in humans."

"Thank goodness for that!" she laughed. "But they're over-populating the world in their own way, aren't they?"

"What if Hitler and Genghis Khan had been immortal? There'd be no way of ever getting rid of them, would there? If humans could sprout from little blown up bits we could be knee deep in Hitlers - and have Genghis Khans coming up through the floorboards! Imagine that!

Yeuch!" he laughed. "Immortality? No thanks!"

A lazy afternoon, dozing and reading the Sunday papers, was followed by an evening watching TV, all very cosy and domestic. She seemed to have forgotten about being chained to the bedpost. Amnesia? Maybe a girl friend with amnesia had something to recommend it.

When he was ready for bed he checked the TV had been switched off in the living room, then put out the lights. Her door was not quite closed and her light was flickering strangely. He padded along quietly to take a peek.

It was a candle, flickering in a vase on the dressing table. She was sitting on the end of the bed staring at it between her fingers.

"Where are you, Cesare?" she whispered. "Tell me, please, where are you? Where are you?"

CHAPTER 24

STRIPPERS

Momentous Monday morning got off to a roaring start. Even before they turned the corner to the B House, the throaty growl and the rattle of chains told them that the rubbish skip was already being delivered.

"Sign here," barked the driver, thrusting a clip board under Justin's nose.

"It's your kitchen," he smirked, passing it to Lucrezia.

It was going to be interesting to see how much notice the workmen would take of their girlish employer.

He had applied liberal amounts of WD40 to the ancient locks and hinges so she could now open the doors easily. He helped her to prop the huge wooden street doors wide open. Almost immediately a small white open truck drove into the courtyard.

"We're looking for a kitchen that needs destroying," grinned the driver. "Have we got the right address? We pulled the wrong one out a week or two ago. You should have heard the fuss."

"You've got the right one this time," laughed Justin. Good to meet somebody who obviously enjoyed his work. "Yes, you can park in here."

The two men in khaki overalls climbed out of the truck and looked around. They rubbed their hands together and flexed their muscles.

"We need your signature before we can wreck the place," grinned the smaller, jokier one. "Right here, please."

"Such a shame," said Bianca, who had just walked in wheeling a push chair.

"Shush!" said Giuseppe, pushing an antique pram. "Lots of people are going to enjoy buying the bits and pieces, aren't they?"

Justin had noticed some of those bits and pieces already displayed in their windows. They had pushed those same wheels on the same journey two or three times already, so all that was left was either wired in or screwed to the wall. He turned to hand the form to Lucrezia but, surprise, surprise, she was running up the stairs as usual.

How long was she going to keep up this ridiculous charade? Why on earth did she think he would arrive today? He hadn't phoned or sent any emails. It must be some kind of irrational fixation. Maybe he should try to persuade her to see a psychiatrist. If the man hadn't popped his clogs he might surely be having a nice break with some new girl-friend or something. Surely he didn't need to inform his sister of every move he made.

"Could you show them to the kitchen, Giuseppe, while I go and get the Marchesa to sign this."

With a sigh, he trudged up the stairs towards the Royal Suite, then nearly cannoned into her as she came back out almost immediately.

There was no need to ask if there was any sign of her brother. Her forehead was furrowed and her eyes were brimming with tears.

"Lucrezia," he said firmly, "you don't look very well. Why don't we sit down here for a minute so you can tell me what's the matter?" He pulled her firmly down onto the steps and sat beside her.

"I don't know. I don't understand it. I don't know where he is. He seems to have disappeared off the face of the earth. He's even shut me out of his mind. He only does that if things are really, really bad. He doesn't seem to understand that frightens me more than anything."

"Look, Lucrezia, do you think we should call a halt to this kitchen refit if you feel in such a state, and with your brother missing?"

"I can't do that. I promised the staff they wouldn't have to spend another Christmas like the last one."

He pursed his lips and censored what he felt like saying. She had definitely lied to him. The servants hadn't walked out in disgust: they'd paid it a flying visit and gone back to Monrosso. She'd been planning to refit the kitchen all along. She'd seized the chance to use his expertise to do the job. And what on earth was she playing at now?

"Is there a chance you might be spending all this money for a New Zealand sheep farmer?" he demanded.

"What?" Her face was a picture of bewilderment.

She had to be made to face facts, for her own good. "If your brother doesn't come back, will the sheep farmer take over this house?"

"No, definitely not. This house is not part of the Monrosso estate. We owned it for hundreds of years before we got Monrosso and the titles. We own it jointly. It's either ours or mine, but it certainly wont belong to the sheep farmer. I have to get rid of the kitchen. We should never have put in anything so useless and showy in the first place. I loathe it more than the rest of the house."

"Well, then, you need to sign here so they can start ripping it out."

Down in the kitchen the strippers had already made progress. The steps up to the back street entrance were now a wooden slope, where a small mechanised fork lift truck was advancing steadily.

"Right," said the spokesman, taking the form from Justin, "now we can start. Where's the switchboard and the shut-off valves for the gas and the water."

"Only bottled gas here," said Justin. "Sorry I can't help you with the others. It's not my house." He felt himself redden as the memories of Saturday night's hunt for the fire alarm switchboard came flooding back.

"Whose house is it then?"

"The Marchesa's, but she's only just inherited it so I'd be amazed if she has any idea where the services are. Sorry."

He was not the least bit sorry. He was delighted that nobody could blame him this time. He could just be an interested spectator.

"Here we go again," sighed the small stripper. "Always the same with these really old houses. Once we found the wiring was linked up to next door. The neighbours had been paying the bills for both houses. You can imagine the blazing row when we discovered that."

After half an hour's frustrating search around the basement it had become obvious that the routes of the power lines and water pipes were unfathomable. There seemed to be no way to cut off supplies to the kitchen.

"Does that mean we can't change the kitchen?" asked Lucrezia.

"Oh, no. This just calls for emergency procedures."

This should be fun, thought Justin. Might pick up some useful tips. He watched, impressed, as they sprayed foam onto pipes to freeze them, then quickly cut them open and plumbed in new stop taps. Easy when you know how!

It was less comfortable to watch them tackle the wiring - from a safe distance. This time they put on big rubber boots and gloves, and with shears with thick rubber covers on the handles, took deep breaths - then cut the live wires in two. Justin's stomach clenched as they blithely taped over the live cut ends with red tape, and finally stuck on labels reading "live - beware."

Booby traps, thought Justin. Could that be legal?

"You need to tell the electrician about these wires this afternoon. Very important."

"You bet," breathed Justin, as they traipsed back into the kitchen.

"Now," said the smaller stripper. "I declare this kitchen a dangerous work zone. Everybody out, so we can start."

"Oh, but you said we should keep an eye on the things we want, so they don't get damaged," protested Bianca.

"I'll get you some stickers to put on them, and I'm sure these gentlemen will take care of them, wont you?" Lucrezia smiled at the strippers.

"We'd rather take care of you," grinned the spokesman.

"How sweet!" smiled Lucrezia. "I'll bring you down a beer for that."

"Actually, I think we're right out of beer," she said, when they all went up to the courtyard.

"We can't give them builders' tea - they're not English," said Justin. "Just lend me your pushchair for ten minutes, Bianca, and I'll go stock up on beer and biscuits. I'll get alcohol-free beer. Workmen here seem to prefer it."

As he set off with the pushchair he heard an almighty crash, accompanied by a few expletives and a burst of laughter. Those strippers certainly enjoyed their work.

Well before lunchtime it was all over. The Marchettis had wheeled off their spoils and the strippers were sweeping up and carrying out their tools.

Lucrezia pulled a face at the sight of the bare, bedraggled room that had, only a couple of hours before, been a stylish but useless Art Deco masterpiece. The walls of huge stone blocks were patched with bricks of various colours and vintages. Here and there, pockmarked plaster suggested it had been painted many different colours over the five centuries of its existence. There seemed to be traces of a picture on one wall.

"Looks like a country scene. Is that a sheep?"

"There was a vogue for country scenes in the fifteen hundreds," she said.

"I wonder where they used to slaughter the animals," mused Justin.

"In this scullery here, next to the back street door. They hung them over that drain there until the blood stopped flowing, then butchered them in the scullery next door."

"Yeuch!" exclaimed Justin. "You'd think it would turn them into vegetarians. I wonder how the kiddies reacted to it."

"They got upset, had nightmares for a year or two, but they just had to get used to it. Death was part of normal life in the old days. People had big families, and lots of them died in childhood. If you survived till you were forty you were a freak. Most people today have never seen anyone die and can't get their heads around the idea."

"Imagine if we had a time machine, could whizz back through the last five hundred years - see what happened here. I bet this house has some exciting tales to tell."

Lucrezia drew a deep breath and exhaled slowly. "You could be right," she breathed.

"Well, we can't leave the house till the electrician arrives, so one of us had better get some pizza again."

"I'll go," said Lucrezia. "You know more about electric wiring than I do."

She passed the painter on the stairs, carrying in his roller and a big tub of milk white paint. His instructions were to paint the ceiling and the upper parts of the walls while the electrician fixed the new electric sockets. The kitchen shop had co-ordinated everything so brilliantly. Full marks to them, thought Justin.

Below stairs was no place to sit and eat the pizza, so Lucrezia suggested they should eat it in the Royal Suite.

She seemed to know exactly where to find everything they needed in the secret kitchenette. She must have known it was there all along. She could have moved into her house and lived in her brother's suite quite comfortably. She'd been making a fool of him here as well. But he might be doing her an injustice. She had spent more than two hours in these rooms a few days previously - long enough to explore the kitchenette.

The electrician just nodded and gave the usual Italian shrug when Justin pointed out the booby trap wiring. It was obvious he'd seen that kind of thing before. When Justin showed him the numerous apologies for control boxes, and the tangle of wires going who knows where, he said exactly what Justin expected.

"I'll have to give the kitchen an entirely new circuit. Have to bring a new fusebox tomorrow. Anyway, that wont stop me putting in all the new sockets, will it? "

As the electrician was working alone, Justin offered himself as electrician's mate. It was a good chance to improve his own do-it-yourself skills. After lending a hand as often as he could on his own project he could talk the talk well enough to gain the respect of any tradesman. It also gave him the chance to double-check the new sockets against the plans to satisfy himself they were being installed in exactly the right places. At 6 o'clock the man declared that everything was finished. When Justin had found a socket missing, the man had driven off. The kitchen shop had closed, but he left a message about the missing socket, just in case he somehow missed the electrician the next day.

Lucrezia, meanwhile, had watched the first socket being installed, then lost interest and disappeared. He could hear her laughing as he walked up the stairs to the first floor. Had the rat-catcher arrived at last?

He found her in her suite with a woman from next door, doing something with a voluminous dress from the costume museum downstairs.

"Hello. What are you two up to?" he asked.

"Oh dear!" exclaimed Lucrezia, looking down at the dress in alarm.

"It's alright, My Lady, I've finished. It's quite alright for anyone to look at it now."

Lucrezia gave a sigh of relief, then smiled at Justin. "Well, how do you like my favourite dress? Suzanna has persuaded me to donate it to the Vatican Museum. They've wanted it for ages, but I couldn't bear to part with it. Suzanna is going to make me a replica, and it wont be fragile like this, so I'll be able to wear it without worrying."

"It looks familiar. Where have I seen it before?" he mused. It was a truly beautiful frock, of dark green silk, patterned with roses in gold and silver thread. The square neck of the tight bodice was edged with cream-coloured lace. From the shoulders, lace formed a distinctive vee shape, pointing to the tiny waist.

"Do you have the hat, My Lady?"

"No, I threw it away ages ago. It looked so terribly un-flattering. I suppose that was a stupid thing to do."

"Well, I suppose I could make a replica for the museum. It looks fairly simple in the picture, doesn't it?" She pointed to a long poster in a frame on the wall.

Justin walked across to look at it. Sure enough, there stood a girl wearing a dress identical to the one Lucrezia was wearing. "I agree about the hat," he laughed. "It looks like a kind of turban. I don't think it would suit you at all. This girl had an awful lot of titles: Princess of this,

Duchess of – one, two, four different places, Lady of here, there and everywhere. I wonder how you had to address her."

Lucrezia shrugged and smiled. "Well, I suppose I'd better say a fond farewell to this dress now and let you take it, Suzanna. You can tell the museum they can take the rest of the costumes in the morning. Could you go for a walk, Justin, while Suzanna gets me out of this dress?"

"I'll give you a hand as well," he laughed.

"Men not allowed. Ladies only," said Susanna firmly.

"No, don't take it off yet. Such a shame. It looks as if it was made for you. If this is your last chance to wear it, why not keep it on just for this evening? It would be great to sit and gaze at you across the dinner table."

"I can come around and take it off for you later," said Suzanna. "I'm not going out tonight."

"We could come round to your house. Then we wouldn't need to fix a time, would we?" said Lucrezia.

"Why do you need Suzanna to take it off? I can surely undo any buttons on the back, if you can't reach them."

The two women laughed. "It's not as simple as that, believe me," said Suzanna. "I'll be in all evening, so any time will do, My Lady. Shall I go now, if you don't need me? I'll take as many costumes as I can carry."

CHAPTER 25

THE RED ROOM

It had not occurred to Justin that walking the short distance home with Lucrezia in her historic dress would attract so much attention. One group of tourists seemed very excited, jabbering away and rushing about trying to photograph each other walking next to her. Lucrezia laughed and paused to let them get their selfies, but he hurried around the corner out of their sight.

"Vatican! Papal Apartments!" cried one of the tourists. "Look! It's her, I'm sure! Lucrezia! Lucrezia!"

That was quite enough for Lucrezia. She picked up her skirts and ran. Once she was inside his palace, Justin closed the street doors firmly on the excited mob. He grabbed her hand and pulled her to the penthouse lift.

"What on earth was that about?" he demanded, once the lift began to move. "How did they know your name?"

"You may well ask!" she exclaimed breathlessly. "Well, it was your idea, wasn't it? Don't blame me. I just hope I haven't damaged this dress."

Justin flung himself onto the soft white sofa.

"Well," he said, "what an eventful day! You've got rid of your horrible old kitchen at last, and the electrics are done. Tomorrow the plans will come to life. Happy?"

She lowered herself carefully onto a straight-backed dining chair and arranged her skirts. "Well, I'm sure the staff will be delighted."

"You don't look very comfortable on that chair. Come sit on the sofa."

"This is as comfortable as it gets in a dress like this. If I don't sit up straight I can't breathe. This gold and silver wire is scratchy. I hope you appreciate how much I'm suffering to amuse you tonight." She smiled demurely.

"Oh, shame!" he exclaimed. "Well, then, the least I can do is make you a special dinner. What do you want to do while I make it? Listen to music?"

"Do you have any Renaissance music to match the dress?"

It took Angel some time to find, but, at last, the unfamiliar sounds of early Sixteenth Century music floated around his starkly modern penthouse.

She smiled, and, to his surprise, she began to sing, quietly, gently, in a language he couldn't recognise.

"What are you singing?"

"Petrarch. One of his sonnets. Lots were set to music."

"Latin?"

She shook her head. "Italian, as it sounded when this dress was made."

He watched her from the kitchen as he waited for the microwave to thaw out one of his special dishes. There could be no occasion more worthy of it, surely.

He turned the lights down to a low romantic setting, put two large candelabra on the dining table and his best glasses and cutlery. He opened a bottle of good wine, but sadly she tried to refuse to let him pour her anything at all. He poured her a glass in case she changed her mind, and when she didn't, he couldn't let it go to waste.

"Not even water!" he exclaimed. "Why ever not?"

She smiled primly. "In this dress it's impossible to carry out any - you know, bodily functions. I'll have to wait till Suzanna lets me out of it after dinner."

"I can help you get out of it. Just tell me what to do."

"I don't know," she insisted. "Suzanna's family were our ladies' maids for centuries. They're sworn to secrecy, so only they know how to take off frocks like this."

"That's crazy! Why make frocks you can't get out of?"

"They were designed for young heiresses, so no one could steal their virginity and lower their marriage value. It has a built-in chastity belt, so the parents could be sure they would come to no harm if they lost sight of them during a ball. In those days there were lots of balls. Everybody loved to dance. It wasn't wise to go out walking in the evenings for exercise. Every man carried a big long sword and a dagger to defend himself. Well-born women never went out without an armed escort."

"The Renaissance era looks so elegant and glamorous on films, doesn't it. I never realised it was so dangerous."

"How many brawls with swords did Shakespeare write into 'Romeo and Juliet'? And I think, in almost every one of them, somebody was killed."

"Swords, daggers, defend, armed, brawls, killed - -"

"Angel, shush. There is no problem. Anyway, let's not think about depressing things like that. You say the dress is meant for dancing, so now we've finished dinner, why don't we do just that? Just a minute while I find some dance music."

"I don't think modern dance music would be right for this dress. The music we're listening to now is a pavane. It's a nice slow dance so you could do it easily."

"Angel, show us video of people dancing a pavane."

Lucrezia was right: it was easy to pick up, even though he was a little muddle-headed, thanks to a whole bottle of strong wine all to himself. After very little practice he could devote all his attention to Lucrezia and her thrilling dress. She looked quite stunning. If the girl on the poster was half as attractive, every man within sight would be trying to lower her marriage value. He longed to pull her close, but the pavane kept them prudishly apart.

"They're dancing a galliard now, look. Can you manage this? It's pretty energetic. The man has to pick the lady up and swing her around like an ice-dancer, see?"

Great! Just what I feel like, thought Justin. He was soon staggering crazily around the room and whisking her up into the air like a toddler. Those Renaissance people knew how to have fun on a dance floor.

When the video ended they crashed together onto a sofa, breathing hard.

Her neckline was so near to his nose. His nose seemed to have developed a mind of its own, and buried itself into the valley between her breasts.

"Stoppit!" she laughed breathlessly.

"Why? Why?" he laughed. "You're good enough to eat and I just have to eat you up right now." He smothered every bit of bare flesh with kisses, but most of her body was all too well covered. He had to get into this dress.

The bodice was way too tight for his hands as well as her body. He tried to slide it off her shoulders, but the long sleeves were as tight as sausage skins. He slid his hands around her waist, but there was no gap between the bodice and the skirt. He caressed her enticing legs through the silk of the skirt, surreptitiously drawing the skirt up away from her feet until he found the hem at last. Bare legs? No. They were still covered in silk, plain silk, not embroidered with metal thread, but it covered her gorgeous legs just as well.

"Stoppit, Justin!" she spluttered. "You're wasting your time. Stoppit, will you!"

"No," he growled. "You're just too gorgeous to resist. You've been playing silly games with me all week but you wont put me off tonight." After all, he thought triumphantly, that dangerous brother seemed to have overplayed his hand at last, so who was there left to deter him? A sheep farmer in New Zealand? Ha! Ha!

As his hands reached the tops of her thighs she wriggled and tried hard to pull away from him, but he pinned her firmly to the sofa with his body.

She was utterly delicious; she was driving him crazy. These silk leggings must end somewhere. Frantically his hands explored her legs and body, searching for a way to drag them off, as his passion grew stronger and stronger.

"Don't stain the dress. It's famous. Be careful!"

"Blood'n sand!" he yelled, "take the blasted thing off!"

"I can't take it off! I told you, didn't I? Now, stoppit, Justin, please!

"Well I can take it off!" He heaved himself drunkenly off the sofa and headed for the kitchen. There were several kinds of scissors in the drawer. He chose the biggest pair. They should be equal to anything, even metal wire.

He stormed out of the kitchen to grapple with Lucrezia, and caught sight of her fleeing into her bedroom. No problem, he thought. There was no lock on the door.

Locks? Ha! Ha! He staggered along the hallway and rummaged in the hall table drawer. With a smirk he unlocked the door of the former cloaks cupboard. Hmmm. It was about time he tried out his new equipment, wasn't it? No need to wait till he could get hold of Sophia. With all these forms of restraint, it wasn't necessary for the other player to know how to act the victim, was it? He must get her feet chained up so she couldn't knee him where it hurt.

Lucrezia fought a losing battle to prevent him from opening her door, then jumped up onto the bed and bounced around, trying to evade him. Even without that voluminous dress she wouldn't have stood a chance.

"Angel, call the cavalry," she shrieked with laughter.

"Angel only takes orders from me,"

"Dangerous madman on the loose. Murder, mayhem!" laughed Lucrezia.

"Dangerous madman, murder, must call the police."

"Angel, cancel that. Shush. Go off duty." He hurried into his bedroom and switched off the power to the machine. This digital assistant needed to go back to the design team for modification. It was more trouble than it was worth. And he should strip off now, get ready for the fun. He tossed his clothes onto his bed..

He cornered Lucrezia, grabbed her around the waist and carried her like a wriggling sack along the hallway to his new red gloomy den. He stood her on her feet and reached out for a manacle.

"Goodness!" laughed Lucrezia. "What an amazing room! I've never seen anything like this before. It looks like some kind of machine. What is it called? What does it do? Do explain it to me." She clasped her hands behind her back and tucked them into the folds of the dress.

"Just give me your hand and I'll show you," he grinned.

"These must be meant for feet." She bent down quickly and twisted around so he was too late to grab her arms. "They're awfully small. Are you supposed to put your great big feet in here? You'd never manage that. You got the wrong size, didn't you?"

"What do you mean, the wrong size? Of course I got the right size. Do you think I'm some kind of ignoramus?"

"Then why is this contraption only big enough to fit a very small person? Is this a game for midgets?"

"It's not for midgets. It's big enough for anyone."

"Never! Whoever sold you this was just taking you for a ride, palmed you off with stuff they couldn't sell, and you fell for it like an idiot, didn't you?"

"Nonsense!" he yelled. "I'm not an idiot. I haven't bought a load of reject stock."

"Well, no man could get into that, could he? Unless he was a midget."

"Of course he could!"

"Never. Not in a month of Sundays. They saw you coming, didn't they, and just took you for a ride."

"Look!" he yelled. "I'll prove it to you. If it's big enough for me it's bound to fit most men. You can't call me a midget, can you." It was tricky to get his foot into the contraption but he managed it.

"Where does the other foot go? Oh, I see. You have to push it in here. But this is definitely too narrow for a man. No, you'd have to push hard. Go on, then, push."

She straightened up and surveyed him. "You know, I think you may be right. Let's try the hands. Look, the hands are just right as well." She clicked the bracelets into place. "Yes, it certainly seems to be man-sized. You certainly don't look like a midget, and it seems a good fit for you. So, what are you meant to do with this weird contraption now?"

He reached out towards the scissors on the cabinet by the door, but his hand couldn't reach them. She had chained his hand to the wall. And his other hand. And his feet. How on earth had she managed to do that?

"Four fails and a gotcha!" she murmured.

"What's that, Lucrezia?"

"For sure it fits you."

"Okay, Lucrezia, you've proved yourself wrong. You have to admit I was right. It's definitely man-sized, isn't it? You can undo me now and I'll make some coffee."

"How do I do that?" She inspected one of the bracelets carefully from a safe distance. "There seems to be a keyhole. Where can I find the key?"

Where the hell had he put the keys? He hadn't even realised they had keyholes, had he? Well, he would surely have put them close by, wouldn't he? In the same drawer as the room key. "In the drawer, just there."

She rummaged around in the drawer, then made a helpless gesture. "No keys here."

"They must be there somewhere. Have another look."

Obediently she poked about inside the drawer, then shook her head sadly. "Shall I call a locksmith?"

"At this time of night? And me with nothing on? Don't be ridiculous! You'll have to find a way to get me free."

She stared at him with a look of bewildered innocence, her hands in a helpless gesture. "I can't think what to do. I've never seen a machine like this before. What is it for?"

What is it for? How on earth could he answer that?

He didn't get the chance to work out any kind of answer.

There was a frighteningly loud noise of something very heavy battering his front doors. Then a voice yelled out.

"Open this door. Open this door, NOW!"

Lucrezia set off towards the doors.

"Don't open the door, Lucrezia. I can't talk to visitors all chained up, without a stitch on, can I?"

She turned and looked at him with big round eyes, then walked slowly up to the doors.

"LUCREZIA, - DON'T OPEN THE DOOR!!

"If I don't he'll break it down," she said. Calmly she stretched out her hand towards the door frame.

Then she turned to look at him and smiled as the doors began to open.

CHAPTER 26

RETRIBUTION

The shiny black doors of his penthouse flat swung open silently as Justin tensed himself for the onslaught. Burglars? Police? Firemen? Mafiosi? Customs? Drugs Police? Any of them seemed equally likely or unlikely. Had somebody tried to frame him, or was it some sort of protection racket? He shivered in his birthday suit.

Despite all the noise, there seemed to be only one man standing motionless in the fashionably dim light of the lift vestibule – one very big, bulky man. After a moment's pause, the man stepped forward into the hallway and slowly turned his head this way and that to survey the scene. As his eyes came to rest on Justin he raised one black eye-brow. Finally he reached out for Lucrezia's hand and bent his head to kiss it. They stood, smiling into each other's eyes, for what seemed to Justin an unreasonably long time.

"So," said the big man in a rich bass voice, "What are we doing this evening? Perverts' fancy dress party? When does it start?"

"Well," said Lucrezia, "you make a very fine Himalayan bandit, but aren't you rather hot in all that gear? You could ditch that nasty thick blanket, couldn't you?"

"You wouldn't call it nasty if you'd been sleeping out in the cold with me." He swept off the huge heavy blanket and slung it into the corner of the hall, revealing grubby loose grey pyjamas and a rough brown waistcoat. His flat round cap went flying in the same direction like a discus.

"That's better," he said, running his grubby fingers through his long, greasy, rat-tailed hair. It was hard to guess his age as his weather-beaten face was covered by a big black bushy beard.

"Sweetheart, this outfit is amazing. You look perfectly authentic and utterly revolting - and you smell like a charnel house. It's these clothes, isn't it? Anyone would think you stole them from a rotting corpse."

"Right first guess."

"Aaagh!" wailed Lucrezia, "do you really have to stoop as low as that?"

"Look, how far do you think I'd get if I went around dressed like James Bond and smelling like a whore's boudoir? Wouldn't last two minutes. And afterwards I can't go around in the buff, can I?"

"You forgot your brown contact lenses. You must have stood out a mile, surely."

"No, I didn't. Lost them after the first rat, of course. But lots of Pashtuns have blue eyes, so I looked like a different person. Worked very well."

"Something went wrong this time, didn't it? Somebody else got to your rat first."

"No. What gave you that idea?"

"You don't usually use a knife."

"Didn't have a choice. The great scaredy cat was always lurking inside a big bunch of heavies. The nearest I could get was about here."

He backed towards the entrance, then fixed his eyes on Justin.

FLASH! THUD! A knife was quivering right beside Justin's ear. It had appeared in the bandit's hand, then left it so fast he couldn't believe it had really happened – until he turned his head. He felt suddenly sick.

"You missed!" said Lucrezia, "and you wouldn't get a second chance, would you?"

"Oh, you wanted me to hit him? Where exactly? Pick

your spot." The look of contempt he bestowed on Justin was chilling, as he dragged the knife out of the red padded wall behind him.

Lucrezia pursed her lips and scanned Justin's naked body painfully slowly, She raised her hand as if to indicate the chosen spot, while the bandit took up his throwing stance again, swinging the knife by its point.

Frantically Justin searched his mind for something that might dissuade her, or appease the smelly monster, but his mouth was so dry he could barely croak.

At last Lucrezia held out her hand.

"Gimme!" she said. "He's not a rat."

"Not a rat? Are you sure?" The bandit's expression reminded Justin of a kid deprived of his toy, but he tamely handed the knife to Lucrezia and she put it in the drawer. As soon as she turned her back, the bandit took it out, gave Justin a hint of a grin, then secreted it back into his clothes again.

"How did you get home? You obviously didn't come the quick way. I expected you days ago. I was afraid they'd locked you up somewhere. What went wrong?"

"Goodness knows. Seem to have developed a homing instinct for those dustbins. In the end the Yanks gave me a lift to the NATO base at Aviano, just to get rid of me. Got sick of finding me there."

"In the Consulate compound in Peshawar?"

"Mmm." he nodded. "Then managed to beg a lift to our base at Practica. Came the last few kilometres in a truck full of cabbages. I was picking our lock when I thought you were sending a distress signal. What's the problem? You seem to have things well under control, as always."

"Well, about ten minutes ago I was afraid I was losing the set. I didn't mean to drag you here. You must be longing for a good soak in the bath. Sorry."

"So, this creepy pervert was winning, was he? What kind of game are you playing? Can anybody join in?"

"Sabrina Fair."

"Sabrina Fair! With a sado-masochist! Phew! That's what I'd call an extreme sport. So, what's the score?"

"Five nil. Four fails and a gotcha! The bigger the risk the bigger the buzz."

He laughed and shook his head, then fixed Justin with his startlingly blue eyes.

" 'Tis chastity, my brother, chastity. She that has that is clad in complete steel, and a thousand liveried angels lacky her.' Strange poem, Milton's 'Comus'. 'Spect you know it. A thousand guardian angels! Overwhelming odds against you, I'd say. So, that's why you're wearing the dress, Krish. How many more rounds do you intend to play?"

"None. I've had enough."

"Well, this looks like a gotcha! and a half, so quit while you're winning. What do you want done with this disgusting specimen? They enjoy being tortured, so I'm told."

"I think they prefer torturing other people, especially women," she said. "It's usually because they're impotent, can't get up any interest in sex without torturing somebody first. But lots of them seem to think it's just a silly game."

"Oh, really? You think torture is just a silly game, do you, you nauseating creep? Maybe you need a little education. I see you've still got your finger nails. Do you know where he keeps the pliers? Could you lay your hands on them?"

The bandit walked over to Justin and looked down at his feet, then inspected his hands, gripping the end of the little finger nail and giving it a tug.

No, Justin screamed inwardly. Not my poor fingers! This is supposed to be worse than having your teeth drilled without anaesthetics. What made this foul smelling beast tick he had not the slightest idea, and could think of nothing to say that might deflect him from his plans. Anything might just annoy him even more.

"Bags I do the hands," called Lucrezia, rattling around in the tool box. "You can do the smelly feet."

This must be a nightmare. Please God it's just a nightmare. Justin's flesh was trying to creep away and hide.

"Have you ever smelt gonads frying? Your own, I mean?" The bandit revealed his stained teeth in an evil grin. "There's a socket down here, so all we need is a length of flex with a plug on. Floor polishers usually have long flexes. Why don't you take these great big scissors, Krish, and cut a good length of wire off? Bare live wires should get them cooking in no time."

"Lucrezia!" Justin called to her desperately, but she just went off with the scissors. Whatever had he done to deserve this? Whatever his crime, this was surely a hideous over-reaction.

"Krisha, is there anything flammable lying around? We could teach him what it feels like to be burned at stake, smelling your own legs roasting. And we could disembowel him first." He whipped out the knife.

Justin fought to suppress a scream, but the wail came from Lucrezia instead.

"Stoppit, Cesare! Stoppit! Stoppit!" She was growing more hysterical by the second.

"Sorry! Sorry!" He wrapped his arms around her and rocked her to and fro like a baby. "Shush! Shush! Poor little Love! It's alright. They gave up doing that centuries ago, didn't they?" I'm sorry, - sorry."

Lucrezia soon calmed down and dabbed her eyes with her sleeve.

"Is there anything to eat in this place?" asked the bandit,

"You're as bad as the wolves." She pulled a hanky from her bosom, suppressed a sob, and blew her nose. "There's some nice chocolate cake."

"Where? Where? Lead me to it."

To Justin's immense relief, they went off to the kitchen and he heard them raiding the fridge. Hope it chokes them, poisons them, anything to get them out of his life.

"It's a long time since I had the chance to strip you out of this frock." The bandit was almost purring. "Stand still."

"No, stoppit. Wait till we get home."

"There must be a bed here somewhere, or does he sleep hanging up like a bat? Hey, look at this table! Looks like a sacrificial altar. Come on, lie down. We've never tried it on anything as fancy as this."

"Do you men think of nothing else but sex?"

"Food. I dream about food as well. You know, home cooking, not the disgusting stuff I usually get. But I've been dreaming about you for months and months, so come here, stop wriggling away."

"No! No! No!" exclaimed Lucrezia firmly.

"Oh! So. Do you want me to promise never to touch you again?

"No! No! No!" she laughed.

"Explain yourself, Lady," he demanded.

"No, not now; no, not here; and no, not while you smell like a rotting corpse."

"Well then, state your terms."

"Yes, in our own home. Yes, in our own bed, and yes, please, when you smell like the man I love."

"Fair enough. Now my terms: Yes, we go home this very minute, no delays accepted. Yes, you scrub my back. Can't think of a third. Can I add that later?"

"I don't promise to agree if it's not in the original treaty. But I'll be happy to scrub every tiny little bit of you if you like. Oh, you greedy pig! You've eaten all his chocolate cake."

"Well, if that's the worst thing that's happened to him today he's got off lightly, hasn't he? Now, come on. No delays. You've agreed a treaty."

They bounced out of the kitchen hand in hand and swept past him without a glance. As the doors began to close behind them, Lucrezia turned to look at him. "What about Justin?" she said.

"No delays. We agreed a treaty, remember?"

As the doors closed she gave him an apologetic wave.

CHAPTER 27

HELP!

Justin strained his ears to hear the faint sounds of the lift door closing. Then came the whir of the lift machinery. Then silence. Would they change their minds and come back? He stared at his toe nails and cringed. Please God they wont come back!

At last he breathed a sigh of relief. Of course they wouldn't come back. That great murderous brute had other things on his mind, hadn't he? His own sister. Disgusting, wasn't it? No, she didn't look the least bit like him, did she? And he looked old enough to be her father – even her grandfather! What on earth made her fancy the obnoxious creature? Even a thorough scrub with a Brillo Pad would surely not make him remotely presentable, would it? She was definitely unhinged.

And she'd really set him up this time, hadn't she? The nasty little viper! He moved his hand to scratch his nose, but it jerked to a halt half way. It was chained to the wall. He checked each hand and foot carefully. Yes, they were all on rather short chains. If he could just move one hand far enough to touch the other he could find a way to unfasten them. He wriggled his body into one distorted position after another, but nothing seemed to work. They would just have to come back and release him.

He imagined the two of them cavorting around in the Royal Suite, Lucrezia scrubbing every little bit of him in that glamorous Art Deco bathroom. How long would they spend in that great four poster bed? All night, probably. And in the morning, imagine the pillow talk.

"What on earth made you move in with that disgusting sado-masochist?"

"Well, I just fancied living in a nice light modern penthouse instead of this dark, gloomy palace, didn't I?"

How on earth had she bamboozled him into taking her in? He reran their first encounter. What had she done to persuade him to take her home? Try as he might he could pinpoint nothing. She'd taken a lot of persuading, hadn't she? He'd had to push her every little step. She wasn't keen to let him tour her empty house, tried to hide the fact that there were no servants there to guard her. He'd told her no hotel would take her in, no restaurant give her a table for one. It was join him for dinner or go hungry. He'd done all the bamboozling, hadn't he?

Why? Why had he insisted on taking her in? There was no shortage of women in his life. Why did he want a fifteen year old virgin? Why? What had she got that Marcella and Sophia and all the rest didn't have?

She was innocent. She was helpless. She wasn't using him as a cash cow – or getting even with her cheating husband. The boot was on the other foot: he had the upper hand. This time she was the victim. He could practise spicing up his sex life on a girl too inexperienced to realise what a blundering dope he really was.

"First he got me drunk and tried to rape me -"

"The Blaggard!"

"Then he chained me up to the bedpost - "

Oh, come on, that wasn't rape! I just wanted to initiate you into the joys of grown-up sex. You'd have loved it. All the gold diggers can't get enough of it, can they? Anyway she's over sixteen, isn't she, so nobody can call me a paedophile.

Rapist? Well, maybe that's different, maybe age doesn't come into that. Will he insist she goes to the police? Oh grief! Definitely be in all the papers. Prison? Whatever will that be like? Maybe end up sharing a cell with those clapped-out old entertainers. But I'm not like that!

Honestly, I didn't mean any harm!

"Then he chased me round the flat and tried to chain me up in his weird little red padded room so he could cut up my fabulous Renaissance dress and - -"

"I'll murder the rat! I'll tear him limb from limb!"

For pity's sake, Lucrezia, don't tell him till morning! Just give me time to get out of this idiotic contraption and catch a plane to - well, Rio or Singapore first stop, while I see how the land lies.

He was sweating profusely now. That should help to lubricate his feet. He tried twisting his feet this way and that and pulling them up hard against the anklets. Damn and blast it! Just grit your teeth and give them each a real hard tug and pull the chains out of the wall.

He yanked and tugged until the pain was too much to bear. A stain was spreading across his beautiful white marble floor. You can't get blood stains out of marble. Maybe the whole floor would have to be replaced.

He had no memory of any keys being discussed or handed over, so maybe the bracelets worked like the ones he'd used on the bedposts. There were little flush catches on those. You just had to press them to open the bracelets. He curled his fingers as far round as he could, trying to feel the edges of the bracelets, but he could only reach a very small section of each of them.

Yank them off the wall, you great wuss! That's what these he-men did in films. Looked so easy. He took a deep breath and yanked and yanked till the blood began to run down his arms and drip onto the bloody mess beneath his feet. It was slippery down there. This blood must be a good lubricant, surely. He scrunched his fingers hard together trying to make his hands as narrow as possible, but it was self-defeating. The punishment he'd been meeting out to them was making them swell and throb. The fingers looked like bright pink sausages.

They were not going to slide out of the bracelets now.

It was hopeless! He had no option. He would just have to wait for someone to get him out of this nightmare. They would be back in the morning, surely.

But why, unless they brought the police to arrest him? She'd been nice and friendly to him all week, hadn't she? And she seemed to have made light of the slave bracelet episode, so maybe she wasn't going to be vindictive.

The kitchen fitters would arrive at eight. Surely they'd need his advice to fit it properly, and come and fetch him.

But Lucrezia had known what she wanted. She and the kitchen planner had done all the choosing and deciding, while he was wishing they'd put in something more exciting. And surely, now he was home, that brother would want to put his oar in. They'd be so bound up in the kitchen that they probably wouldn't give him another thought. Well, that was a mixed blessing. At least they may not bother to set the police onto him.

Crash! Thud! What on earth was that? Flames were flickering. He could see the dining table reflected in the mirrored wall of the entrance hall. On the floor near the table the stub of a candle was flickering. It must have somehow managed to topple out of the candelabra, roll along the table and drop to the floor. Grief! Was it going to burn the place down? Was he really going to smell his own gonads frying? Or his own legs roasting like a medieval victim of the terrifying religious fanatics?

"Angel, fire! Fire! Fire! Call the fire brigade. Angel, wake up! Call the fire brigade!"

But no matter how loud he shouted there was no response. And then he remembered: he had switched his digital assistant off.

His teeth chattered as he watched the flame flare, then die away, leaving just a wisp of smoke and a nasty brown stain on his lovely white floor. Phew! But will the other candles topple down as well? The low lights seemed steady now. It seemed the other candles had already burned right out. Calm down. Relax!

So, who could he expect to get him out of this contraption? He ran through everybody he could think of - but they all thought he was stomping about in the Himalayas, didn't they. If only he hadn't lost patience and shut off Angel! She would have got the fire brigade in in no time. Panic was setting in. The sweat was dripping off his chin and tickling his legs.

Anna! Anna would be coming on Thursday afternoon. An awful long time to wait. It was only Monday evening. What condition would he be in by then? Certainly past caring how ridiculous a figure he was cutting, hanging there starkers. You couldn't starve in three days, but he'd heard that death from dehydration didn't take long. And he was loosing blood as well, how much he couldn't tell, as the puddle on the floor seemed mostly behind him.

He could try shouting for help, but the flat was so well insulated that probably nobody would hear him.

Something was tugging at his memory: Lucrezia and Anna, talking about mopping the floor, Lucrezia offering to do it while Anna was on holiday. When was Anna going on holiday? He checked over dates in his mind. Sunday 10th. Yesterday. Would Lucrezia turn up to mop his floor? After the way he'd treated her, it seemed highly unlikely. So what would Anna find when she let herself in in two weeks time? A rotting corpse?

"Help! Angel, help! He yelled till he was hoarse.

There were weird red shapes dancing in front of his eyes and a strange buzzing in his ears. The buzzing grew louder and louder till it sounded like the engine of the Hawker Hunter jet - - -

CHAPTER 28

A SURFEIT OF DOCTORS

Help! He was drowning! Water was flooding into his mouth and nose. He coughed and spluttered, struggling violently to turn his face out of the torrent.

There was a large foot right beside his nose. He wasn't a contortionist, so it couldn't be his. Besides, there was black hair sprouting from the lightly tanned leg above it.

"Don't drown me, I'll talk, I'll talk!" he wailed.

"Give me the shower. He thinks you're water-boarding him," Lucrezia was laughing. "It's alright, Justin, we're just trying to clean you up. Look, you hold him up while I wash him down. Can't you get his head up? You can drown in two inches of water, you know."

Extremely strong hands grabbed him by the hair and yanked him into a sitting position.

"Aoww!" squawked Justin, clutching at his hair.

"Just look at his wrists!" she exclaimed. "We shouldn't have left him so long, should we?"

"We should have left him for good. Who needs sado-masochists? It was only a few hours, and anyway, what possessed the idiot to string himself up like that? What was the plan? Were you supposed to brand him with hot irons or something? We could string him back up, now we know he's alive, and torture him a bit. You'd like that, wouldn't you?" He pulled Justin's hair back, forcing his face to tilt upwards.

A man of about his own age was glowering down at him, a man with thick black wavy hair and a fashionably neat trimmed beard. He was dressed in shorts and a singlet and looked as if he spent a lot of time in the gym.

He might be good-looking if he would just stop scowling.

"Why are you being so horrible to poor Justin? What harm has he done you?"

"Huh! You give me the best soporific known to man, then, when I'm enjoying the first sleep in a comfortable bed in ages - bang! I'm on the floor - with you kicking me awake, yelling at me to get dressed and rescue this noxious creep."

"Oh, poor Darling! Never mind. Once we've got him patched up we can go straight home to bed. So, now, could we have a little professionalism, please? We've a casualty here, bleeding from multiple wounds. Let's demonstrate the famous bedside manner, shall we?"

The man gave a sigh, let go Justin's hair and wedged a strong knee against his back as a support.

"So, superficial injuries to both wrists and ankles, caused by repeated violent contact with metal cuffs. Anything else amiss, Sir?"

"Mmmm?" said Justin.

"Wake up, Sir, pay attention." He gave Justin a shove with his knee. Lucrezia gave him a reproving look. "Do you suspect you may have other injuries not immediately obvious to your doctors?"

"Don't know. Don't think so," muttered Justin. His teeth were chattering so much he could hardly speak.

Lucrezia bent down beside him. "He's shivering. I'll get you some of your big sports towels, Justin, to warm you up. He'd hate getting blood on that white bathrobe. Do you think he's going into shock? Perhaps we ought to call an ambulance."

"No, no, don't do that!" squawked Justin. Anything was preferable to having to explain his injuries to the Casualty Department. And somebody might spot him and put him on YouTube. "There's a doctor staying in flat

6, one floor down. You could ask him to come up"

It was a great relief to feel the big sports towel around him. He had felt so vulnerable – and so embarrassed - slumped there stark naked, dripping blood and water.

"What kind of doctor?"

"Retired doctor."

"Why do you want another doctor? You've got two experienced trauma specialists already."

"What do you mean? Where?"

"You know Lucrezia, neurologist and trauma surgeon. I'm the other Dr Bordano, cardiologist and trauma surgeon. She does the brains and I do the hearts."

"You're making this up. I don't believe a word of it!"

"Look, you joker, I'd much rather be in bed. If you - "

"Cesare, come on, let's get him fixed up. Justin, if you don't co-operate we'll call the ambulance. Okay? Now, why don't we put him in that black recliner in the living room so he can bleed as much as he likes without messing up the white furniture? While you do that I'll see what First Aid stuff I can find in the kitchen. I'll put the kettle on in case we need to sterilise anything."

"Why not make some tea while you're at it? Put plenty of sugar in his. He must be pretty dehydrated. We'd better treat that first of all." He yanked Justin up out of the shower as if he was almost weightless, strode into the living room and dropped him none too gently into the chair. "Stay!" he ordered, as if he was talking to a dog.

Lucrezia came back with the First Aid box under one arm and a steaming glass in her hand. "Sip this a little at a time and see how you get on with it," she ordered. "If you feel worse or sick stop drinking it at once." She arranged another dark-coloured towel around the chair.

"What is it?"

"We can't fix you up with a drip, because we don't have

the equipment, so this is the next best thing, warm water with a bit of salt and sugar. We need to get your blood pressure up just a little or you might go into shock. Then we'd have to get you to a hospital where they have resuscitation equipment."

Meanwhile, Cesare had done a quick trawl through the cupboards in the shower rooms.

"So, we've no anaesthetics, no antibiotics, no antiseptics, no drips, no drugs, no scalpels, no sutures, no steri-strips- "

"Situation normal then," shrugged Lucrezia, and they both laughed. "I saw some superglue in the tool box."

"Great!" said Cesare. "That, plus some sticking plasters, should deal with this lot. And this is the cleanest operating theatre I've seen in ages. Did you have time to make the tea? I'm half asleep."

"First things first," grinned Lucrezia. She went back into the kitchen and came back with three steaming mugs. "No, Justin. We have to see how you get on with that rehydrating liquid first. The rule is nil by mouth for shock victims, so we need to be a bit cautious. Quite a balancing act. Now, Doctor Bordano, let's scrub up. That running kit should be clean enough for minor surgery, shouldn't it? Or do you fancy doing a heart transplant?"

Perhaps it was the thought of the tea that made Justin determined to get the rehydrator down, and when they reappeared they seemed quite pleased with him.

"Right," said Cesare, and pushed the recliner down flat. "No signs of shock now. Ready to operate, Dr Bordano?"

"Ready when you are, Dr Bordano," she smiled.

"The blood's washing the cuts clean, but these grazes look a bit of a mess. Has he got any hand sanitiser? I could only find an empty bottle."

"No, I need to get some more," said Justin.

"Oh!" said the trauma surgeons simultaneously. "The casualty's conscious."

"Highly irregular," said Lucrezia. "Somebody shot the anaesthetist?"

"Kidnapped, I gather. Pity. Nice girl."

"You can vouch for that, I guess."

"Gather ye rosebuds while ye may."

"He's got some honey."

"And plenty of money. Wouldn't be Manuka, would it?"

She went into the kitchen and came back waving it in triumph. "Just what the doctors ordered."

"What are you going to do with that?" asked Justin.

"I'm not sure I can handle this" said Lucrezia. "I'm not used to being cross-questioned by patients on my operating table. If you distract me I might excise the wrong bit of your brain."

"I could stun him if you like, since we have no anaesthetics." He gave Justin a diabolical grin and raised his hand in a threatening gesture.

Justin closed his eyes and held his breath.

"I think he's dead now. We can finish the job in peace," said Cesare.

"Oh, good," she said.

Justin played dead to the best of his ability, and the two surgeons pressed on cheerfully, teasing each other amiably. He even managed to keep mum when the honey stung the grazes and one of them kept a painful pressure on the wound leaking the most blood.

"Right," said Cesare. "That should do." He put his ear to Justin's chest for a moment, then tipped the chair up into a sitting position and checked the pulse in his wrist. "I guess you'll live. We've cleaned the wounds as best we can with water and the honey, but you'd better keep an eye out for any sign of blood poisoning, any dark red streaks coming away from any of the wounds. If you see that you must go to Casualty immediately and get some antibiotics, or you could be in real trouble."

"Otherwise," said Lucrezia, "You'd be advised to avoid anything too energetic for a day or two so you don't risk opening up the wounds. Remember, you've only plasters and superglue holding them together."

"Would you object if I offered your patient a little advice, Dr Bodano?"

"I should be glad to have the benefit of your expertise, Dr Bordano."

Cesare leaned forward and looked Justin sternly in the eyes. "Mr Justincase, as one of your doctors, may I offer you a little advice. Get rid of that infernal machinery and see a psychiatrist. Next time you may not be rescued in time."

"Thank you for the advice," Justin mumbled, unable to meet his gaze. "I've decided. It's going, double quick."

"Good man," said Cesare, patting him on the shoulder. "I'm sure you wont regret it. Your tea's still warm. I think you've no reason to worry about shock setting in any more, so enjoy it. Look, you need the sugar. It'll help you replace the blood you've dripped all over the floor."

"I'm sure you can guess how grateful I am. I probably owe you my life," he mumbled shamefacedly. "I wish there was some way I could make it up to you."

"Well, you've done that already. You've done so much for me I can't thank you enough," enthused Lucrezia.

Both men looked at her in astonishment. "What do you mean?" they asked simultaneously.

"When I got home ten days ago I felt so bad I didn't know what to do with myself. I was thinking of asking a convent to take me in for a while. Then you picked me up and gave me just the treatment that I needed. After a few days with you I felt so much better. Then you started playing that fun adult game, Sabrina Fair. You are so good at it you forced me to up my game till it got really exciting. I feel tons better now."

"Then why on earth did you let me torture him?" exclaimed Cesare. "I thought you were egging me on."

Yes, why? Answer me that, thought Justin.

"You didn't hurt him. You never even touched him."

"Psychological torture can be nearly as bad for one's health as physical injuries. You should know that, Copper Nob Neurologist."

"When will you get it into your thick black head that neurologists are not the same as psychologists."

"You're so easy to wind up, aren't you?" he grinned. "But you surely can't condone that nauseating red room? He must be really twisted to enjoy that."

Justin cringed and looked away. Did they have to discuss him like this?

"Well, it's strange. It doesn't seem the kind of thing that would appeal to him really. He seems perfectly nice and rational. But I thought he deserved a kick in the pants just for owning it, so I didn't try to stop you. I knew you wouldn't hurt a helpless man you knew nothing about."

"It's going back tomorrow," Justin muttered.

"Good!" said the two Doctors, grinning at each other.

"Well, let's clear up and go back home to bed," said Cesare, putting the spare plasters back in the First Aid box. He followed Lucrezia into the kitchen. They whispered at first, but soon forgot he could hear them.

"Why did you feel so bad last week, Krish? Why didn't you tell me all about it in Dubai."

"I didn't want to spoil everything. We've had so little

time together for months. I just wanted to enjoy being with you, but it all went wrong. We were home almost before we got there. And then you had no time for me at all, just wrapped up in maps, maps and more maps."

"Please, tell me what happened. What upset you so?"

"There were four of them, so I didn't stand a chance. I don't think I can talk about it," she said in a strangled voice. "Not yet. But they sent me home the quick way, when they'd had enough."

"Who did this? Do you know their names? Where can I find them?" There was a nasty harsh edge to his voice.

"Sweetheart, you can't find them. A shell hit their headquarters. Saw it in the papers last Wednesday. Nothing but rubble. All dead."

"Well, they got off lightly," he snarled. "Lucky for them!"

"I shouldn't wallow in self-pity. It happens to women all the time. I just have to put it behind me and come up smiling. So, can we drop the subject now? Talking about it brings it all back. Life has to go on, and on, and on -" Her voice took on a hysterical edge.

"I should have been there for you, poor little love. I'm sorry, sorry. Please don't go back. Surely you deserve a break and a bit of TLC. Surely we've earned some time together, after all these months."

"I can't go back to Fallujah, can I? Everybody's either dead or disappeared."

"So, what do you plan to do? Find another field hospital in some other place?"

"I just don't know. I'm not sure I can psyche myself up to it again – not just yet." Her voice was strangled as if she could hardly speak. "When are you going back?"

"Dunno. Run out of options. Came home quick so many times I can't think of anywhere left to go. And I can't make sense of it any more. One minute you're comrades, fighting side by side, the next they're cutting your head off. Sometimes wish I could crawl into a hole and stay in there forever."

"What a lovely idea! Is there room in your hole for me?"

"It won't do for me if there isn't. Now, can we go home and crawl back into that gorgeous bed? I think your friend the pervert will survive. Hey, do you think he can hear us? Maybe we said too much when I first arrived. Stupid, wasn't it? Somehow I didn't see him as a sane human being, strung up in that ridiculous contraption."

"I shouldn't worry. Look at these pictures. I took them before we took his chains off. If we need to keep him quiet these should do the trick, don't you think?"

"Clever! You're not just a pretty face, are you? Jeeze, just look at this! Oh, yuk!" he laughed. "Who's going to believe a word he says about us if they've seen these? We should make copies and put some in the bank, then we don't need to care a fig what he's heard, unless he suddenly decides he'd like to be a laughing stock right around the world. We can say he's crazy and talking nonsense. We are respected doctors, after all."

"Well, even before all this he seemed just as keen as we are not to be noticed."

"As long as he stays that way he's no problem, then. But if he starts talking about us, well - that might be - inconvenient - and rather unwise of him."

CHAPTER 29

FIRE! FIRE!

Those Bordano doctors may have slept well in their grand four-poster bed, but Justin certainly didn't sleep that night. His wrists and ankles gave him hell, aching and throbbing and smarting till he felt forced to take a big dose of aspirin. Surely it ought to be a criminal offence to sell gadgets that could so easily condemn people to a lingering death! Somebody should complain to the authorities. But who would have the face to do that? Certainly he wouldn't.

He leapt out of bed - ouch!! - ouch!! - as soon as it was light and began a frantic search for the bill for his diabolical room. As his battered limbs complained he grew more and more angry, angry with the makers, angry with the installers and furious with Sophia. It was all her fault, telling him he was boring in bed! Telling him sado-masochists had exciting sophisticated adult fun. Pain increased sexual pleasure - my foot! Maybe she'd never experienced much pain. He wished she could feel his ankles at this moment. They were certainly doing nothing for his libido!

At last he found the bill and telephoned the installers. No reply. He looked at the clock. It was only 6.30am. Idiot! Maybe he really did need that psychiatrist. Calm down, Idiot! He had to get control of himself. It was certainly time for a rational reappraisal of his life. Thank goodness everybody would be back at work in his Rome office in less than three weeks' time! Work would put some structure back into his life so the Devil couldn't make work for his idle hands. The fire lock. That needed doing too. He located the address of the locksmith and sent him an email to come as soon as poss. What else?

He walked around his flat to see if anything needed doing. Crikey Moses! It looked like a battle zone! The black recliner was draped with bloodied towels, and brown stains marked the routes to and from his shower room - dried blood soaked into the marble. Oh, grief! His beautiful floor! The shower room was easy to rectify. He grabbed a mop from the cleaner's cupboard and soon removed the congealed blood from the little mosaic tiles. So, no problems there.

Come on, face up to it! Tense and grimacing, he opened the door to the Red Room. It was even worse than he had feared. He'd expected blood, but this was a sewer. He had not been able to free himself, but all the mobile contents of his body had managed it. Aaaagh!!! He shut the door and made himself a king-sized mug of tea. He couldn't call the de-installers with the place in this disgusting state. He hadn't the face to call in contract cleaners, either.

Cleaning was not one of his skills, but he approached the problem very cautiously, realising how much worse he could make the mess if he let it spread around. Just in time, he thought about blood poisoning. If any of the filth got near his wounds he could be in trouble. He wound several layers of cling-film tightly around all four wounded areas and found some rubber gloves and wellies. After a long time, and a lot of careful trial and error, it was as clean as it was going to get, until a marble specialist had tackled the hideous soaked-in stains. Then he phoned the S&M installers.

"I want rid of it today," he demanded. "If you take it out you can have it back for free."

"I'm afraid there'll be a charge to take it out, Sir."

"In that case I'll take it out myself and sell it on E-Bay. Would you rather I did that?"

If they'd called his bluff he'd have had no end of trouble trying to find some way of ridding himself of it. He certainly wouldn't have had the face to try to sell it on E-Bay. Imagine driving around, trying to find somewhere secret to dump it, and getting stopped by the police!!!

Thank Heavens it didn't take them long to change their minds! An hour later they were on site, unscrewing it all with power screwdrivers.

Justin sneakily collected up the gadgets and hid them.

"You can have the lot when the walls are bare," he said grimly. It was all very different from the time they had installed it. He'd been amused by their ribald innuendoes and nudge nudge, wink wink. Now he couldn't believe what must have been going on in his head. They clearly resented having to strip out the red velvet wall boards which were unlikely to be reusable, but Justin was feeling vindictive. He waited until they had carried the wall boards down to their van before he let them have the manacles and chains, whips and other nasty paraphernalia.

As they left, the locksmith arrived. Justin made him a coffee and asked if he knew anything about fire alarms. The man climbed up Justin's ladder and poked about.

"Looks fine to me," he insisted.

Something fluttered down to the floor. It was a blue microchip.

"You little - ! Well, could he blame her? After all, he had chained her up to the bedposts. Grief! Whatever had he been thinking off? He'd chained up a brain surgeon, a saint working in a field hospital under fire in Iraq ---! And a marchioness at that. Why hadn't she shopped him to her brother? His blood ran cold at the memory of Cesare snarling at her account of the men who had done something - goodness knows what, but obviously pretty nasty - to her. It sounded as if he might have taken great pleasure in murdering them slowly if they weren't already dead. What if she did tell her brother what he'd tried to do to her? Holy Moly! But she was not just a good sport, she was a saint!

The marble specialist couldn't spare any time till next week, and advised him strongly not to try anything himself. It would be sure to make matters worse. Just mop the floors with clean water as usual. He longed to mop the whole flat, to wipe out everything to do with yesterday, but he'd already done far more than he should, at the risk of opening up the smarting cuts, so it would have to wait.

He sat down at his desk with a mug of tea. There was a pile of unopened mail. It seemed he must have put his life on hold, totally consumed by this obsession with Lucrezia. He needed to force himself to cut her out of his mind, and pick up the threads of his normal life again. The chance of any future relationship with her must be nil. It was obvious the pair regarded him as a disgusting and pathetic weirdo, and no wonder! How could he look them in the eye after what they had seen last night? Yeuch! Yeuch! Yeuch!!

Late that afternoon, when the worst of the heat had abated, he set out to find a tube of plaster filler. He still had no idea what he could use the Red Room for, but to rewrite the excruciating memories it needed to look completely different. The screw holes reminded him of the weird and nauseating gadgets that had been screwed there so they had to go right now. He could even see the dent made by Cesare's knife. Auch!

It took him ages to find the plaster paste, but at last he headed home clutching a good big tube. The B House was almost on the way, and drew him like a magnet. Had the electrician put in that missing socket – and the new fusebox? Had the fitters arrived, and the cupboards. Had they put everything in the right places? They were fitting his new kitchen, behind his back, without his help. While the doctors cracked jokes with the workmen he was out in the street, unwanted, persona non grata. Loneliness turned his feet to lead. Another relationship soured; another new friend turned into a bully bent on tormenting him. Why did things always go wrong?

Walking past the B House was pointless, since he wouldn't dare to ring the bell, but maybe, just maybe Lucrezia might be at the door, and might invite him in. She had aways been such a good sport. He plodded on until traffic blocked his way. Traffic jams happened occasionally, when tourists stupidly tried to go the wrong way along one-way streets, or drive along streets too narrow for traffic. He edged past two blocked cars, then suddenly scented the smoke. There was a plume ahead, rising up into the hot blue sky.

He hurriedly squeezed past the large motor caravan with it's cargo of quarrelling children, then came to a halt with a sharp intake of breath. The big street doors of the B House were ablaze. Three big gas bottles stood in the courtyard near the open doors, waiting for the gas company to collect them. They must have discovered a third one somewhere and that was far from empty. It had done something he had never heard of – catch alight. It had turned itself into a blow torch, with a wide-angled roaring flame playing on the great wooden staircase and the open doors. That ancient woodwork had had five hundred years of summers to dry out, and it was crackling and blazing merrily. If they had tried to fireproof the wood it had not been in the least effective.

Somebody should call the fire brigade. He pulled out his phone, but before he could dial, he heard the wail of a fire truck, then another. Those fire engines needed to hurry up. All those ancient beams, brocade curtains and tapestries would soon be roaring with flames. The occupants of the caravan were jumping up and down and wailing now, as well they might, but there was nothing they could do. The road ahead was far too narrow and there were at least two cars behind them, now frantically signalling to the fire engine to back up and let them back out. It was the only thing to do, but the delay was excruciating.

Anxiously Justin peered into the courtyard. The flames were making serious headway now, licking along the covered walkways that provided access to the rooms on the first floor. Suddenly Lucrezia appeared at the door of the Royal Suite. She looked around, but the blazing staircase was the only way down, She began to run along the burning walkway.

"No, Lucrezia!" he shouted. "The staircase is on fire!"

She almost certainly didn't hear him, but she soon saw that for herself. She looked around frantically, but there was no way down. The staircase was an inferno and the walkway behind her was blazing now. She dragged open the door to the front room, slipped inside and closed it behind her. She may be relatively safe for the moment, but for how long? Even if the flames couldn't reach her the smoke was sure to find a way into the room. He could see her at the window now, trying to open it. With a ladder they could surely get her out.

He ran frantically up and down the street, banging on the street doors, yelling,"Help, fire! A ladder! Somebody find a ladder!" But not a soul came out of the nearby houses, despite the commotion. The occupants must all be away.

He almost cannoned into Doctor Bordano, who came hurrying towards his blazing home, carrying a bulging shopping bag.

"Lucrezia!" yelled Justin. "Look! Look! She can't open the window." He pointed to the window frantically.

The doctor breathed a few choice oaths, dropped the

shopping bag and ran across the open entrance to assess the situation.

"I can't find a ladder! There's nobody at home," yelled Justin.

The doctor ran back to the opposite wall and began taking very deep breaths. Suddenly he hurled himself forward across the street and leapt right over the blazing gas bottle.

"Crikey Moses! Oh my God!" wailed Justin. He ran towards the entrance, but the roaring heat hit him with a shock that knocked him back. He caught a glimpse of the doctor leaping up the blazing staircase, his weight making it sway like a ship in a gale. It seemed a miracle that he managed to reach the top. As he leapt onto the walkway, the staircase buckled and swayed right away from its moorings. Shrieking and creaking, it began to disintegrate as it crashed down into the courtyard, sending up sheets of flames and clouds of glittering sparks.

It was a relief to see the doctor shut the front room door behind him.

Justin heard the fire engine roar into place behind him. Thank Heavens! Now, all they needed was a ladder –

"A ladder! Look! People up there trapped! Get a ladder up there now, now, please! Look!" he yelled at the firemen.

But Lucrezia had disappeared.

He ran to the entrance and tried to peer in through the smoke. A great roaring explosion of flames and sparks drove him back. Now the first floor corridor was dropping down towards the courtyard, pulling the beams supporting the front room floor. Eerily slowly they sagged, then came crashing down, bringing the room wall along with them.

There was a gaping hole where the front room used to be. Everything, just everything that had been in that room must have fallen down along with the floorboards.

The courtyard was a funeral pyre. Nothing could have survived that inferno.

Justin ran up and down frantically, peering into the flames and smoke, hoping by some miracle they'd managed to escape.

"Move along, Sir. You're in the way." The fireman grabbed his shoulder and steered him away.

"There are people in there - " he gibbered.

"If there are we'll get them out. Now, please move out of the way, Sir. You're hampering our work."

He watched for a while from a distance, unable to tear himself away. Two men in white overalls were talking to a fire chief. Must be the kitchen fitters. "They are both out," they were saying. "The Marquis has gone to the market and the Marchesa has gone to the bank."

"No, no," cried Justin. "They were both in there. Behind that window, trying to get out. I saw them."

"They are out. We definitely saw them both go," said the taller fitter.

"Now, please move along, Sir. You're impeding our work. And please take your shopping. It's in the way."

He opened his mouth to protest, but the fireman hooked the doctor's shopping bag onto his arm and steered him forcibly away from the B House.

Frantically, Justin walked up and down the nearby streets, listening to the distant hubbub. If only there was something he could do. Maybe he ought to go to the police station and tell them what he'd seen. But how was that going to help? Maybe the sheep farmer might get his inheritance a little quicker. But he'd heard some chilling stories about how foreigners, innocently reporting crimes, trying to be helpful, had ended up being charged with the crime themselves, as the police had no one else in their sights. Better just shut up and let things take their natural course.

There was nothing he could do for the doctors now, was there?

Nothing anyone could do.

CHAPTER 30

MORE SURPRISES

The smell of wood smoke had replaced the noxious smell of sewage when he reached his flat at last, but it was not an improvement. It reminded him constantly of the doctors. They had left a life of luxury behind to help people in the most unpleasant and dangerous of places. Yet disaster had felled them in the most unlikely place of all: the 'safety' of their own home. They had hit that big black rock this time, "Taking the quick way home. Next stop Heaven or Hell," as she put it.

What a waste! The world wouldn't miss people like me, he thought sadly. What have I done for humanity? Invented a few silly games and frivolous apps. Yes, the computer systems may be worth something to the world, but there were plenty of other systems on the market.

It was surprisingly painful to think he could never meet them again - even though he'd be too embarrassed to look them in the eye. They were the most interesting people he'd ever encountered. He longed to know more about them - even though that was only researching obituaries.

He got out his phone and swiped through the messages the pair had sent to each other, planning to delete them, but he couldn't bring himself to do it yet. 'Pos ttqwh.' And again 'def ttqwh.' Possibly taking the quick way home? It fitted, but he was coming home, not dying, surely. It must be a sort of joke. The letters may represent something different altogether. Who knows?

He Googled 'Doctor Bordano', but found only the bare details of their qualifications on the Medical Register.

Yes, she really was a brain surgeon and he was a cardiologist. He'd studied at Kings College, Cambridge and The Royal Brompton Hospital, and she at Oxford and The National Hospital for Neurology. So that's why they both spoke such excellent English - and he could even quote English poetry. There were no dates of birth, only dates when they achieved their qualifications. How odd! So he still didn't know how old she was!

'Monrosso' was very little more informative: 'Estate of the Marquis of Monrosso, near Lugano, created in the late 17th century to guard the border against the famous and much feared Swiss mercenaries. Present house built in 1745, not open to visitors.' That was it. No pictures, no personal details, nothing. They really did keep a low profile. However did they manage to do it?

'Marquis of Monrosso' had a few bald details of a pair at society functions in the 1930's. There was an indistinct black and white photograph of about a dozen people in party gear. Two of them slightly resembled the doctors. Their great grandparents? But there was no mention of any more recent holders of the title. How odd!

He gave up the search and switched on the TV, just in time for Rome's evening news. "Fire destroys the Borgia House." The what!! There were lots of pictures: of before, when the house was intact, and now, still blazing.

"One of Rome's most important historic houses, built by Rodrigo Borgia in 1492 for his extended family when he arrived from Spain to become Pope." Holy Moly! Grief! The Borgia House! He should have guessed, shouldn't he? The neighbours could have told him the truth if he'd thought to ask.

Lucrezia Borgia? Never! It was obvious why she might want to change that name, wasn't it? She'd have paparazzi buzzing round her like flies, and tourists going crazy to get her into their selfies. Her parents must have been idiots or sadists to name her Lucrezia. But it was, perhaps, better to change the notorious surname. Even 'Anna Borgia' would arouse interest, wouldn't it? Well, it had worked, hadn't it? 'Bordano' had kept them both under the radar. But was there really a connection? Were they really Borgias?

Could he find a link? He opened a search engine again. There may be nothing about the Bordanos or Monrosso, but there was certainly plenty about the Borgias. The famous Lucrezia, born in 1480, daughter of Rodrigo Borgia (Pope Alexander the Sixth), held many titles, including ruling Duchess of Ferrara. She died aged 39, shortly after giving birth to her eighth child. Apparently she was an able ruler, admired as firm but fair.

The same was said of her older brother Cesare, who ruled Valentinos and Romagna for a while. He was a much admired army commander, praised by Machiavelli, and employed Leonardo da Vinci to design new weapons. He was killed in battle in Spain, aged 31.

The famous Borgias lived in a violent age when peace and order were rare. Powerful Italian families schemed and fought to gain the papacy. The Spanish cardinal, Rodrigo Borgia, was popular, tough and determined and had four clever, determined children to help him exercise power. His Italian rivals accused him and his family of all kinds of skulduggery to try to weaken his authority. Probably the Borgias were no worse than any powerful Italian family of the time.

So, the famous Lucrezia had plenty of descendants, but what about Cesare? Born in 1475, he married a princess and they had only one daughter. He had at least 11 illegitimate children too, so his bloodline might still be around. Phew! Interesting. Had he really had two genuine Borgias in his flat? Would it be possible to prove it? That would be something to amuse him while he had nothing else to do. Could he find out more about the very secretive Bordanos? And the Monrossos? Or were they all three the same thing?

There were only a few paintings of the famous Cesare Borgia himself. The most credible one had Dr Bordano's black hair and beard, but the face was thinner and less good-looking, maybe painted when he was in very poor health in 1503. But he was famed for his good looks, and reputedly the model for the 'White' images of Jesus Christ promoted by his father. Earlier eras had painted Christ with much darker, less European features.

There were lots of paintings said to be Lucrezia. Some were a joke, plump-faced and dark-haired, more like the Mona Lisa, but some startled him - dainty little creatures with pale skin and a mass of coppery fair hair. There was even a description of her: 'charming and beautiful, with eyes that constantly change colour.'

The pictures brought a lump to his throat. Why hadn't he taken her photo? He'd had so many opportunities. He printed out the pictures from the websites, the ones that really did look like "his" Lucrezia, and stuck them to the wall opposite his bed. That turban didn't suit her at all. She was only 13 when she wore that green dress with the pointed lace, soon to be married off to a much older man for the first of three dynastic unions – poor little kid! In his mind he heard Cesare's rich bass voice: "Poor little love!" He was reputed to have been very fond of his little sister. "Some men are not very kind to women," she had said. Apparently that husband had not treated her kindly. He sighed with shame.

Well, maybe he could seek out the city archives to help him through the next few empty weeks. Better research them than mope around pining.

CHAPTER 31

AND A SHOCK

Wednesday was one of those mixed-up and miserable days when he really didn't know what to do with himself. He awoke with a headache - no wonder, after a night of tossing and turning and rewriting history ad nauseam.

He watched the early morning news, expecting more about the fire, and there it was. A spokesman from the Ministry of Antiquities was pontificating about the negligence of the owners, who should have installed a sprinkler system, employed a caretaker, or donated it to the city. A curator of the Vatican Museum said that the owners had already donated all the contents that his museum had been prepared to accept.

The owner, the Marquis of Monrosso, was unavailable for comment, but his lawyer insisted that the Ministry had rejected his offer to donate it to the City and suggested he open it as a private museum at his own expense. Running a museum was surely the last thing that adventurous pair would want to do! And no wonder he was unavailable for comment, he thought bitterly. How long before they deduced that the pair of them had been cremated in that very fire they were all arguing about?

He shut off the TV, unable to stomach any more. He needed to shift this headache. Aspirin? He set off towards his shower room and stopped. That big ginger cat was pawing at the patio door to the terrace. What was it up to, scratching at the glass like that? He opened the window and it shot in like a rocket, straight into the spare room and up to the wardrobe door.

"Hey, stop scratching the door!" he shouted.

The cat paused for a moment and gazed at him, then

scratched even harder.

What on earth did it want? Mystified, he opened the wardrobe door. The cat ran inside, stopped as if puzzled, then sniffed the hems of the dresses.

Oh, dear! thought Justin. I'll have to get rid of those. He lifted out the white shift dress. The cat came out of the wardrobe and circled his legs repeatedly, staring up at him as if trying to communicate. He took the dress into the kitchen and the cat followed him eagerly. He opened a tin of steak. It gobbled up the meat with one eye on the dress the whole time. He picked up the food and walked towards the window, but the cat didn't follow. It just sat there staring at the dress. So, even food took second place. He put the dress back in the wardrobe and tried to shut the door before the cat could get inside, but it was far too fast for him.

"Come out!" he demanded, stretching his bandaged wrist into the wardrobe. The hiss and snarl warned him to withdraw pretty fast - quickly enough to avoid its slashing claws. A cat scratch or a bite might carry enough germs to give him the dreaded blood poisoning.

His family were dog people, so cats were a bit of a mystery. It seemed he had a lot to learn about cats. Well, it wasn't doing any harm in there, as far as he could tell, so maybe he should just leave it to come out in its own good time. He'd heard people say cats did exactly as they pleased and could turn nasty if thwarted, and that seemed to be true. He left it to its own devices.

Maybe he'd been taking too many aspirins recently. Maybe a bit of exercise would shift the headache. He'd been neglecting his exercise regime as well as everything else. He couldn't face the gym and the jokey banter, so he put on his running togs and set off on a jog that soon deteriorated into a walk in the heat, which seemed even more oppressive than ever.

Inevitably he found himself passing what was left of the Borgia House. They had put crush barriers across the entrance to the courtyard. There were no doors left to close, only the badly charred frames, still warm to the touch. The window where he had last seen Lucrezia was a gaping soot-blackened hole.

It made him feel queasy and weak at the knees to look at the mess, especially just inside the doorway. There was very little left of the room that had been their last refuge. The floor had disappeared – he had watched it fall. There was so little left where that raging bonfire had been that the chance of finding a bone - even a skull – must be remote.

The courtyard was full of debris, most of it still smoking and steaming. Here and there little flames leapt up and died as he watched. Those huge dark beams and the hunky Spanish furniture could probably smoulder on for days. Might the sparks set nearby buildings alight? Could it burn down half of Rome? The Great Fire of London had been stoked by a strong, gusty wind. Thank goodness the air was so still that the wisps of smoke were rising harmlessly! The few sparks didn't even make it to the tops of the blackened stone walls.

It was now in a far worse state than his own palace had been before he rebuilt it. It would be easier to convert it into flats with only the outer walls still standing – if the authorities could be persuaded to allow it. He pitied that sheep farmer who might be going to inherit it. What a millstone! Would they demand he restore it to its original condition? Thank heavens it's not mine, he thought.

When he reached his building he saw Giuseppe opening up the door of the antique shop.

"Do you know anything about a big ginger tom that prowls around here?" he asked. "Do you know who owns it?"

"Do you mean the Marchesa's cat?"

"I thought maybe it was a stray. Didn't know it was hers."

"Well, it is and it isn't. It seems to be a feral cat, born without a home, but the Marchesa saw it trapped up on a chimney pot when it was a tiny kitten - bitten off more than it could chew. While everyone else was trying to get the Authorities to come and rescue it, she just climbed across the roofs and came down with it wrapped around her neck. She even took it to Oxford with her when she was doing her medical degree. Took it to lectures in a basket. Best educated cat in Rome. But she couldn't take it to the hospital while she did her clinical practice, could she? She kept finding it new homes, but it was back here in no time, so in the end we all promised to feed it whenever it asked. We always know when she or the Marquis is coming home. It seems to have second sight - gets very excited."

"Oh, Justin, isn't it terrible about the Borgia House?" said Bianca. "All that history gone up in smoke."

"Well, we saved what we could," joked Giuseppe, pointing to some of the spoils in his window.

"Giuseppe!" She gave him a reproving look. "But I'm not sure if they will be glad or sorry. I know they wanted it off their hands, so - - "

Justin stopped himself just in time. He'd decided to say nothing about the doctors. Who knows, somebody might try to blame him for the hideous fiasco. After all, he'd bullied her into refitting the kitchen, hadn't he, so maybe it was partly his fault. But blaming him wasn't going to bring them back to life, was it?

"Do you know the Marchesa well?" he asked.

"Not really. They're both nice and friendly, but we've only seen them occasionally over the last ten years we've lived around here. They went to the States to do lots of trauma courses when they'd done their medical studies in England. Apparently the Americans know more about treating violent injuries. Then they worked in a U.S. field hospital in Afghanistan to get experience. Since then they seem to have been to every dangerous horrible place you can think of."

"I wouldn't let my wife work in horrible dangerous places like that, would you?" asked Giuseppe.

"The Marchesa - she's not his wife, is she?"

"Well, if she isn't, she shouldn't be using that title, should she?"

"But, I thought she had the title in her own right --"

"Well, she's certainly not a dowager Marchesa, is she, not at her age? She surely can't be his mother, can she?

Justin went up to his flat in a daze. It just got worse and worse, didn't it? How many more crimes was fate going to lay at his door?

That evening another thunder storm broke out, every bit as exciting as the last one. He took refuge on the bed in the spare room, tormenting himself with memories of that first time he had managed to get into her bed. She had felt so perfect, so enticing. Could any man really blame him for wanting her so much?

There was a blinding flash of lightning and a deafening crack of thunder.

Blood'n sand! What on earth was that? Something heavy had landed on the bed. Hurriedly he put on the light, expecting to see a hole in the ceiling.

"Miaaaw!," said the big ginger cat, wiping its nose on his cheek and purring loudly. He made a half-hearted attempt to push it away, but it refused to be deterred. He gave in and stroked it. It felt so comforting.

CHAPTER 32

LOOK WHAT THE CAT FOUND

Thursday was a big improvement. The early morning air felt so fresh it was a pleasure to go out onto the terrace. The cat thought so too, and shot past him as soon as he opened the door. He watched it scuttle up onto the roof like a squirrel, and run along the ridge tiles. How she would have loved to chase it!

He decided not to raise a sweat by jogging. A nice fast walk felt much more civilised. It was great to have the newly-washed streets to himself and he realised it felt good to be alive. How terrible that they couldn't feel that too, ever again. Stop thinking like that, he told himself. It did no good to anybody. Life must go on - for the living.

He didn't even try to resist turning along the street leading to the Borgia House. Somebody had erected a hoarding across the entrance with 'DANGER KEEP OUT' on it. He couldn't see their crematorium now.

The ginger tom came galloping along the street and pushed its head into the gap at one end of the hoarding. It slid its body quickly through the gap. What was it up to? If it was trying to find Lucrezia it was going to have even less luck than it had in the wardrobe. He peeped through the gap and saw it frantically digging a hole. It was easy to squeeze through the gap, then he stood for a few moments taking in the scene.

The rain had made a few changes. It had swamped the glowing embers out completely. There were no more flames or wisps of smoke. The ruins were now stone cold. Here and there, water dripped intermittently from beams still anchored in the heavy stone outer walls, but now drooping down towards the courtyard.

There was little more than ash near the wide street entrance, ash now hammered down to look like concrete by the downpour of the previous night, and topped off by a few bits of badly charred debris. He picked his way down the centre of the courtyard where the debris lay thinner and located the cat very close to the back corner. It was digging furiously, but why had it chosen that spot? Clearly the fire had not been quite so fierce here in the corner. There was much more heavy debris strewn about, heaped up nearly two metres high.

A rattle of tiles slid off the remains of the roof and crashed onto the debris below, narrowly missing the cat. The ginger tom beat a frantic retreat. Then it turned, surveyed the rest of the threatening roof, then crawled on its belly back to its digging site with its ears pinned down. Justin didn't know much about cats, but he could recognise fear when he saw it. Yet, despite its fear, the cat resumed its frantic digging. How odd was that?

As he scanned the debris he had a strange sensation that it was not quite still. Was he hallucinating? He staggered back onto a patch of level paving and stared in disbelief. The debris was moving, moving like a huge animal breathing. A lump of charred wood reared up slowly and slid down the side of the heap.

And then he saw the hand.

It was grey white and chalky, like a statue in a museum. And it was moving. It seemed to be exploring the space around it. The shock hit his stomach and he could feel the hair standing up on the back of his neck.

"Miaaw!" The cat's cry seemed urgent. What did it think it had found: more hands? Crikey Moses! Grief!

He should get help immediately, get this seen to. He turned to face the entrance, but swung back immediately. That was a cough. And another. That was not a moving statue, it was living person..

"Hello!" he called shakily. "Is there anybody there?"

"Hello!" a voice answered. It was hoarse but familiar. "Justin, is that you?" She broke into a fit of coughing.

"Lucrezia. Oh my God, Lucrezia!"

"It's Justin. Oh, thank Goodness!

"Are you alright?" he squeaked hoarsely.

"No" they answered in unison. "Would you be alright in our shoes?"

"Don't worry, I'll go get help. Hang on, don't go away."

Both of them succumbed to great fits of coughing.

"Don't make us laugh with mouths full of dust," spluttered Doctor Bordano. "Now listen, Justin, don't go anywhere. Did you hear that? We don't need anybody to come and interfere. If you're prepared to help we'd be grateful: if not, just leave us in peace and don't tell anybody. Do you understand?"

"No, I don't understand. You need help. You can't possibly get yourselves out from under all this debris."

"Don't you believe it. We've been in worse pickles than this."

"Please, Chez, be nice to him. I've had more than enough of this." She coughed and coughed.

"Well, then, tell me the best way to help. Where are you exactly? I can only see a hand."

"In bed," coughed Lucrezia.

"What? In bed? Which way is your head?"

"Towards the wall, as usual."

The tops of two charred bedposts projected from the rubble against the back wall. This must be the Great Four Poster in the Royal Suite. The whole suite had fallen into the courtyard and the next floor had tumbled down on top. The roof was sagging threateningly. If that fell he would be buried too. Best not to look at that.

He surveyed the huge heap of charred and mangled debris. They needed bulldozers, surely, but then, how do you get two fragile humans out of this with a bulldozer without finishing them off? He'd seen casualties being dug out of earthquakes on TV. He'd seen no machinery, only rescuers and their sniffer dogs. The ginger tom was still digging frantically. He'd better follow suit.

He chose each piece of debris carefully, terrified he might release other big pieces to come sliding down on top of them, to injure them or even to finish them off. He wasn't used to heavy work like this. He couldn't keep this up much longer. The protective bandages on his wrists and ankles were filthy and the wounds were giving him hell. At last Cesare intervened.

"Feels much lighter now. Might be able to free my legs. Stand back while I give it a try."

The strength in those legs must be inhuman. Debris went flying. The next moment Cesare was squirming down out of the hole he'd created and struggling upright.

"Thanks. You're a real pal. I'm out, Krish. Have you out in no time. Move over, Ginger!"

The cat scampered up onto a good vantage point on top of the debris. Charred wood and tiles flew in every direction and Justin backed off quickly to save his own skin. Cesare lifted her out gently, carried her to a clear patch of paving and sat down to comfort her.

"Poor little Love! All over now. You're safe now." He rocked her like a baby.

She put her arms around him and coughed and coughed and coughed.

Feeling rather spare and somewhat embarrassed, Justin stared down at the pair. They looked like museum statues, the same stony look. They seemed to be coated with ash. They were stark naked, but looked so perfect it would be wrong to cover them up, like putting bathrobes on Michelangelo's David and Botticelli's Venus.

He looked around the courtyard. The place was a total wreck. What were they going to do? Lucrezia had said she had no relatives and there was no one she could stay with while her kitchen was being gutted. If that was true where could they go? And they couldn't go anywhere in that state of undress, lovely though they looked. They wouldn't be incognito for long if they tried streaking to the nearest hotel. And what hotel would take them in all covered with ash and bleeding scratches. On closer inspection, they looked even worse than he must have looked three days before. The cuts and scratches were everywhere, all over their bodies. Obviously they had been trying very hard to fight their way out of the debris, and they could have internal injuries of some sort as well. They should surely be in hospital.

"No way, Jose!" they said vehemently.

"Well, if you have no better ideas, I'd better go get you some clothes. You can't leave here dressed like this, can you? Birthday suits are out of fashion."

There was a tourist shop just around the corner - there always is in the historic centre of Rome. The proprietor was busy hanging up T shirts on the frame outside the door. She was surprised to see a customer so early in the morning. It was barely 9.0am.

He quickly chose a dress for Lucrezia - he knew her size. Then he found a rail of beach shorts for men. How big was Cesare? How big was Michelangelo's David? More than five metres tall. Well, Cesare was nowhere near five metres tall, so calm down and stop messing about! His hands were trembling and his heart was beating far too fast. Take a deep breath and concentrate on the job in hand. He chose a fairly large size and the least offensive T shirt he could see. Shoes? He had no idea what size. Flip-flops seemed the best idea, big for Cesare and small for dainty Lucrezia.

They were trying to clean themselves up, shaking the ash out of each other's hair and trying to brush it off each other's bodies, but it was making little difference. They still looked like marble statues come to life - marble statues leaking blood from innumerable places. What a mess! He couldn't take them anywhere – except home.

"Unless you have any better ideas, you'd better come home with me."

They looked up at him forlornly and shook their heads.

Even Cesare needed a hand up. Struggling out of the debris seemed to have worn him out. Lucrezia tried to walk, but her knees buckled and she sank to the ground. Cesare tried to carry her but was barely able to support himself. Remembering how he had felt on Monday night, when they had rescued him, he could sympathise.

He gave Lucrezia a piggy-back. It seemed the least embarrassing way to carry her, and they all put on forced smiles and waved when a group of Chinese tourists went by laughing and pointing at them. Yes, we're having fun.

There were two bodies on the floor of his shower this time, and it was Justin who was watering them. They seemed so exhausted that he shampooed both their heads for them. What lovely thick hair they had! And Cesare's beard had grown astonishingly long in only two days. Afraid of hurting their cuts and grazes, he hardly dared to touch their bodies at first, but they didn't seem to notice, so he gave them a good scrub with a loofah to get the ash out of the wounds.

Lucky he had washed the sports towels. He wrapped up Lucrezia, carried her into the spare room, and laid her on the bed. "You two need a rest. I'll wake you at lunchtime. How about that?"

"You're very kind. We really do appreciate all you're doing for us," she murmured, then coughed and coughed.

He dragged Cesare up onto his feet, wishing he had the strength to lift him bodily the way Cesare had lifted him, but Cesare seemed in no condition to give a repeat performance. He collapsed onto the bed beside Lucrezia with a very deep sigh. "Thanks, Pal. We'll make it up to you as soon as we've got our act together."

"You're very welcome any time," grinned Justin. It felt sweet to have the upper hand for a change.

He made himself the best breakfast he'd had in ages, and when he'd finished that he took his second mug of tea into the lounge. He sat there turning the events of the morning over and over in his mind as he put clean bandages on his wrists and ankles. Rest the injuries, she'd told him. Fat chance he'd had to do that! The last few days had been some of the most strenuous in his life. Compared with them, the Himalayas might have been a doddle!

Nothing made sense, did it? Why weren't they dead? He had as good as watched them die. But maybe there was another way out of that room and they had got out before the heat and smoke killed them. They had opened hidden doors in the panelling and gone through from room to room until they reached the Royal Suite. Yes, that explained everything. Then the far end of the building collapsed as well and trapped them.

He reran that scenario in his mind. Yes, it fitted. Or did it? It fitted if you took away Tuesday night, the whole of Wednesday and right through till Thursday morning. Where did they spend all those hours? Not in the ruins of the Royal Suite, for sure. He had seen it smouldering on Wednesday, bursting into little flames. It would have cooked them to a frazzle. So where on earth did they spend Wednesday and then how did they get trapped in the middle of the ruins of the Royal Suite? Surely they didn't climb into the bed after the rain had cooled it down on Wednesday night and then the floor above fell on top of them? Surely the floor above had already fallen by Wednesday morning. Maybe he was wrong. He must be. There was no doubt they were alive. He had scrubbed them all over, so he should know.

The cat was dancing around outside the window. When he let it in it ran straight into their bedroom. He peeped through the partly open door and watched it burrow into a space between them. They looked to be sound asleep.

He awoke on the sofa at lunch time. Well, he must have needed a good sleep after all those disturbed nights. They were still asleep so he had plenty of time to cook. As they seemed so low, maybe invalid food would be best, something easy to digest. He made them mixed root vegetable mash and hake with a sweet-ginger flavoured sauce, all easy on the digestion. They could have any fruit they liked as well. Doctor Bordano's shopping bag had been full of gorgeous fruit, so he could help to eat it now.

The doctors did their best to do justice to his efforts, but they didn't seem well at all, both struggling to breathe and clearly exhausted.

"Look, Justin," said Cesare, "be honest with us, please. How inconvenient is it for you to be lumbered with us like this? We'll clear off out of your hair as soon as we can. What about your holiday flats? Any chance of renting one of those?"

I've had this conversation before, thought Justin.

"Look, Lucrezia stayed with me for a week and she will tell you that I really enjoy having some company and something interesting to think about. If you can share the spare room with your wife you won't take up any more space, will you? If you want a space to yourself you can have that little room in the hallway. There's absolutely nothing in there now, and I've just redecorated it."

"Good man!" said the doctor, with a weary grin.

Glad I got that sorted, thought Justin. Now I should have a clean slate. After all, nobody got hurt except me.

"Do you have to see anybody in authority about the house," he asked.

"Well, I suppose we'll have to," he replied wearily. "That house has been a pain for years. The Authorities throw spanners in the works of everything we try to do. They've even banned us from selling it to anyone except the city council, but they can't afford to buy it just yet. We offered to donate it, but they can't afford to take it on. I bet they'll order us to rebuild it exactly as was."

"Then we should emigrate to New Zealand again," coughed Lucrezia.

They both laughed, which brought on a long spate of coughing.

"Don't you think you two ought to see a doctor about those coughs?"

"Well, I'll consult Dr Bordano and you can consult Doctor Bordano. Are you happy with that, Justin?"

"As long as one of them can fix that cough. I gather you two are Oxbridge medical graduates. And the Ginger Tom is too. What did he get, a two-one."

"A first in Mouseology and a blue in roof-running."

"So, if you were only 17 when you started your medical degree, that's at least 24 when you've got all your qualifications, then how long working in field hospitals?"

"Five or six. I've lost count."

"So, you must be as old as me. You're not 22, are you?"

"If you say so," she shrugged, then coughed again. "You wouldn't let me be 29, would you? I did offer."

"You can't just pick a number. When were you born?"

"No idea. Can't remember anything about being born, can you?"

"Does he always ask personal questions like this?" asked Cesare.

"Fraid so. But it's no good trying to answer. Whatever you say he wont believe it, will you?" she grinned.

"Well, you must admit you've told me a lot of fibs."

"Ask me no questions and I'll tell you no lies. You agreed I didn't have to tell the truth to nosy strangers."

"So, I'm still just a nosy stranger."

"No, of course not. Ask me some questions and I'll do my best to answer them."

"So, how old are you really?"

She looked at her husband helplessly. "What can I say? Why does it matter so much? Justin, I can't answer because I honestly don't know."

"You must have some idea. 29, 30, 35. No, never 35."

"35, 135, 535, haven't a clue."

"12,035?" Cesare was laughing. "He just won't stop, will he? If he never believes what you say anyway, you can tell him we've been around since the Stone Age. That'll give him something to think about."

"I just feel sort of adrift if I can't, well, --"

"If you can't pigeon-hole people. I see what you mean," said Cesare. "Well, what puzzles you most about us? Let's have it out on the table."

Lucrezia raised her eyebrows and stared at Cesare.

He grinned. "You put those photos in the bank on Tuesday morning, didn't you? Why are you worrying about what he knows about us. He's not going to sell it to the newspapers, is he? You're not going to go around dishing the dirt about us, are you?" He fixed Justin with a fierce stare. "We would hate to have to do the same to you. Mutual blackmail, you might call it, or just tit for tat. What's in a name?"

"No need for threats, is there? Can't we all be friends?" asked Justin uneasily.

"I thought we'd already decided we are friends," said Lucrezia. "And you're being a very good friend to us. We really do appreciate it, don't we, Chez?"

"So, ask some questions." Cesare challenged.

"Alright," said Justin, taking a deep breath, "What are you really, a doctor or an arms dealer?"

"Both. No problem with that, is there? Anything to do with soldiering has always been the family business, and if you can heal your men when they get wounded, they have even more reason to be loyal to you. In a war zone every side wants to be friends with the arms dealers. You've a virtual permit to go anywhere you choose."

"Until you get kidnapped and held to ransom."

"Who's going to pay a ransom for me? I've no company or government behind me, and how can I get weapons for you if you've got me chained up?"

"So, you sell bombs to blow people to bits today, and then you stitch them back together again tomorrow."

"No! I draw the line at bombs, and those disgusting land-mines. You can't control who they're going to maim. But think about this: you see some poor woman hiding in a bombed-out building, trying to protect her kiddies and her ancient parents, and a gang of terrorists are trying to beat down her door to chop off all their heads, so what do you do? The least you can do is throw her a few guns and give her a sporting chance. Or sell her side a helicopter gunship to put a rocket up the terrorists."

"And the profits help finance the field hospitals, pay for the essentials the charities never seem to think of, like swabs and plasters and sutures, and disinfectants and drips and light bulbs and generators, and waste bags and buckets and mozzie killers and nets and, well, all the things that are too boring to make good copy in their magazines," said Lucrezia. "They send us out-of-date drugs for conditions we never see and fancy apparatus we can't use in a tent - -"

"Mmm!" mused Justin, "food for thought. But how do you know which side are the goodies? The Middle East, now --"

"You're absolutely right. A few years ago it seemed obvious who were wearing the white hats and who were the villains, but now - well, it's total chaos. Millions of humans seem caught in a vortex, desperate to slaughter each other while they spin down madly into Hell. Nothing and nobody can stop them. Once we believed they were growing more civilised as time went by, but now it seems hopeless. I've decided to stop interfering. Maybe it just has to be. The wrong species has come out on top. Humans have morphed into something so evil they're about to self-destruct. Or with a bit of luck some big asteroid will hit us. Let's hope whatever evolves next will deserve to live on this wonderful planet."

"You think the end of the World is nigh?" asked Justin.

"No, no, the World is good for about another 7 billion years before it gets sucked into the sun. By about 4 billion years from now it will probably have managed to rid itself of all forms of life. In the meantime there should be plenty of time for a few new kinds of sentient beings to evolve. Maybe they'll be more amenable to reason, and take better care of each other and the planet. We can only hope."

"Indeed!" said Justin. "But sadly we won't be here to see them. Now, tell me, how on earth do you fasten a net to the outside of the Burj Khalifa?"

"Why do you want to do that? I think you'd find it nigh on impossible."

"Well, you and your mad friend certainly found it difficult last week didn't you? I've been telling Justin how scared we both were hanging in that safety net, waiting to be rescued. I still get nightmares about it. And it's so embarrassing, seeing ourselves on YouTube, jumping off the balcony. Have you seen it?"

Cesare shook his head. "No - but it was a nightmare, certainly, so take our advice and don't try it."

"And one more question. Who's your personal trainer? Which gym do you use? How did you get that body? "

"Fighting. Training my men. Wouldn't recognise a gym if I saw one."

CHAPTER 33

HOLY SMOKE!

Their morning's sleep seemed to have done the refugees little good. It was obvious they were finding conversation increasingly painful.

"You two should be in hospital. Your coughs are even worse. What's the matter? Do you know?"

"Just the ash and the dust, very caustic. It does the lungs no good at all. Don't worry: it's not catching," said Cesare.

"We're sorry to be such a nuisance, but we'll probably be as fit as lops tomorrow, so please don't worry about us. We'll go to our room and leave you in peace."

"No need to do that. I've got work to do," he lied. "If you'll excuse me I'll spend an hour or two in my room. You two just relax on the sofas and see if that helps."

In his bedroom he switched on the wall screen and the intercom system. Yes, it was sneaky, but their blackmail threat was unnerving. It implied they had something serious to hide, something as damaging to their reputations as the pictures she had shot of him, hanging in that disgusting S&M contraption, inches deep in excrement.

It must be Cesare's activities in Waziristan. Probably he wouldn't want the media to get a window into that, would he? What exactly had he been up to? Something worth exactly five million dollars a time, maybe even - - Well, he could certainly throw a knife, put it exactly where he wanted, couldn't he? Where had he learned to do that? In a circus?

Surveillance was nothing like the spy films. All they talked about was their predicament, how to sort out their affairs. They couldn't even go home to Monrosso without the price of the fare, and there were lots of things that had to be dealt with first in Rome. First they would go to the bank to fix up new cash cards. That may take days, with no documents to show to prove their identities, and how could they get cash in the meantime for essentials like phones and food and something to wear. Once they had a smart-phone they could talk to their lawyer and accountant - if they could find their numbers - and ask them to contact the authorities and the insurers, and to act as a postal address in Rome. Problem after problem after problem. Poor things! Having your home burned down created problems he'd never even dreamed of. Maybe he should prepare things now in case anything like this ever happened to him. Well, unlike them he had his offices; he should get himself personal safes and put copies of all the documents he might need in them.

Eventually all went quiet except for the coughing. Lucrezia seemed to be in a really bad way. Maybe a quiet afternoon would help.

Lucrezia was too ill to eat dinner, and Cesare hadn't much appetite either. They put her to bed, then Justin went back to his bedroom to gain more experience as a bogus MI5 agent. Their conversation scared him.

"It hurts so much to breathe. I think my ribs must have punctured my lungs. I don't know how long --"

"Poor little love! Think how good you'll feel tomorrow. Just keep thinking that."

"But what state will the house be in tomorrow? The top floor looked so unstable. It might have crashed down already. I'll be buried again." She was coughing quite hysterically now, and he was coughing too. "Look, now you're coughing up blood as well. Don't deny it. What if you get stuck in Peshawar again, behind the dustbins?

It took you days to get home last time. There must be something we can do."

"I'll go round now and stabilise the place, then we'll have nothing to worry about. You'll have to be brave and hang on till Justin goes to bed. Imagine the fuss if --"

"Please take him with you. I don't have the strength to deal with him. I'm sure he'll call an ambulance the moment you're out of the way."

Justin heard the spare room door close, hurriedly switched off his gear and tensed himself for the onslaught. It seemed he was going somewhere. Where and why?

"Justin, you've done so much for us already I hate to have to ask for more."

"It's been a pleasure, so, go on, ask for more."

"I guess you must be quite fond of Krish - "

"Well, she livened up my dull life very nicely last week," What might this be leading to: accusations? he thought warily.

"Well, you can see all's not well with Krish."

"She looks like death. It can't be just the dust: she's coughing blood. She should be in hospital. Why the delay? I think it's criminal." Must be pride, he thought: I'm a marvellous doctor, better than any hospital.

It was.

"Look, we're both doctors. Lungs as well as hearts are my field. There is absolutely nothing any hospital can do for Krish, except cause us a lot of trouble. You have to believe me. Krish means more to me than anything. Why on earth do you think anyone else would look after her better? But you and I can do a lot to help her, if you care enough to make the effort. Do you?"

He squirmed uncomfortably. Damned if you do, and damned if you don't. He shouldn't be too effusive or that might get him into trouble. "Just tell me what you want. Stop beating about the bush."

"We need to go sort things out in the Borgia House right now. Are you game?"

"We can't leave Lucrezia in this state. And it's black dark. Surely it can wait till morning. Then you can get workmen in to do any sorting out that's really urgent. Surely a few hours won't make any difference. The fire's gone out completely now, so it's no danger to anyone."

Cesare sighed. "I'm afraid that's where you're wrong. That lump of the top floor that hasn't fallen yet looks very precarious. It could topple any minute, right on top of our bed, you know, the Great Four Poster."

"Well, you'll just have to keep well away from that bed then, wont you?"

Cesare looked at him with wrinkled brows. "I wish it were so easy, but the truth is that if it falls down before about nine tomorrow morning we'll be in dead schtuck, far worse than this morning, so I have to sort it now."

"That's ridiculous," growled Justin. "What a lot of fuss for a mashed up ancient bed. Can't you get a replica made - if it's worth the bother? You ought to give all your attention to Lucrezia, and I still think it's criminal not to take her to hospital. She seems in a really bad way."

"Well, come and ask her yourself. Surely she knows what's good for her. Come on, ask her."

He was right. Lucrezia, between coughs, begged him to help her husband 'fix things' in the Borgia House.

"Okay, defeated two to one," he sulked. "Let's go."

"Good man," said the doctor, between coughs. He sounded as if he should be in hospital as well. "Have you got some scruffy old clothes. We'll have to get dirty again. And some gloves to protect your hands. The moon's nice and bright, but we might need a torch."

"All my clothes are scruffy. Take your pick." Mystified, he watched as Cesare shoved shorts and T shirt into a shopping bag, then came out of the spare room stuffing one of her dresses in there too, and her flip-flops.

"Try these," he said, passing him his largest pair of flip flops.

"Thanks. You're a real pal. Now, let's go." He slipped into her room to give his wife a kiss. "Hasta mañana," he said. "Chin up!" Then he headed briskly for the door.

As they stood in the moonlight assessing the situation, a large tile slid off the sagging roof and crashed down onto the remains of the bed where he had discovered them that morning.

"She was right, wasn't she? That could have killed her. We have to bring all this lot down. It's certainly not safe. Best you take a breather at a safe distance. Don't want you injured. Could you find somewhere to put this bag? Somewhere obvious where we'll spot it in the morning."

Justin backed off and went looking for a place to put the bag of clothes. Now what?

Cesare took several deep breaths, ran a few steps and leapt into the air. The man was an ape! Or a gold standard acrobat. He swung and scrambled and pulled himself all the way up to the sagging roof, sat there for a few moments, presumably catching his breath, then staggered to his feet and charged up and down the tiles, leaping gaps, jumping down hard onto the roof, using his own weight to try to bring it down. Slates crashed down like hailstones. At last the whole structure began to creak and sag, writhing and warping and tearing itself up as it fell. Cesare rode it down like a surfer, leapt clear and hit the ground hard, then staggered forward and rolled himself up into a ball.

He was breathing hard and coughing his lungs out

when Justin joined him. Sitting on a blackened beam, they watched as the mess writhed and slithered, rattled and scraped, and clouds of dust rose high into the air.

"Try not to breath it in," warned Cesare. "Imagine lying underneath all that."

Justin just whistled. It was too hideous to contemplate.

It took a while for the air to clear, but it gave Cesare a rest. The roof had brought down what was left of the top storey as well, so there were massive amounts of debris.

Cesare groaned and put his head in his hands. "Give me strength," he muttered. "We've got to move all that by dawn."

"Why on earth--?" Justin gasped furiously. "That's just ridiculous. We could surely get a demolition firm to clear it in the morning with proper machinery. We should go see if Lucrezia is okay. She looked half dead to me."

"Krish tells me you never believe anything she says, but listen to this – but don't go broadcasting it or you know what else will hit the press, and we'll deny everything and say you're crazy --"

"What on earth are you talking about?" demanded Justin. "We should go see to Lucrezia. Surely we've done what she wanted."

"We've barely started. Look, you berk, tomorrow Krish will be underneath all that lot. How would you like to be in there with her?" If I end up under there as well we could be there for years and years, while they argue about what to do with the ruin. If I end up in Peshawar instead they might lock me up for years, and all the time poor Krish would be trapped under all this lot. I have to clear all this away if it kills me. And it probably will," he added under his breath.

"You're the one that's crazy," cried Justin. "You're talking like a lunatic. Nothing you say makes any sense. Why on earth should any of us be under this lot? And we've not a hope of clearing it by morning. Count me out."

"Have you forgotten where you found us this morning?"

"No, and I can't think how the hell you got there. It makes no sense. How did you do it, and why on earth?"

"I wish I knew. It was great when we always woke up in bed. We just thought, 'thank Heavens for that', but now, well, it's a nightmare - -. But I'm just wasting precious time. Poor Krish."

He was astonished to see tears in the eyes of this great big he-man, before he turned away and began to limp toward the daunting pile of debris He watched as Cesare took deep breaths again and began to drag a huge beam out of the pile. Why would he put himself through this if he didn't believe it was vital for Lucrezia? And if this crazy nightmare was true and Lucrezia really did end up under the rubble again, could he forgive himself if he had stood back and watched Cesare struggling alone?

He picked his way over to the site of the submerged bed and said gruffly, "Look, I don't understand what on earth is going on, but if it means such a lot to Lucrezia and to you, I'll do my best. You know what's needed so just use me as a labourer."

"Thanks, Pal," said the doctor. "Could you grab that end of this beam?"

It was only two-thirty, long before dawn, when Cesare at last seemed satisfied with their progress. They slumped, exhausted, onto the cleared space that marked the position of the Great Four-Poster Bed. Cesare gave it a brush with a scratched and bleeding hand. He hadn't bothered with gloves, had he?

"She'll be fine here now, wont she?"

He's completely bonkers, thought Justin. "Now what?"

he asked. He was utterly exhausted, and hoped from the bottom of his heart that Cesare had no other crazy ideas for wearing them both out.

"You've been great," said Cesare, "made all the difference. I doubt I could have lasted long enough to do it on my own. You'd better go home and get some sleep. Could you put up with us for breakfast? Then we can go to the bank and stop sponging off you. Can we take you out to dinner or something tomorrow?"

"That would be great," he said. In fact it all looked highly unlikely. Cesare looked utterly exhausted and his cough was now as bad as Lucrezia's. "But I'm sure you both need emergency treatment of some sort. Are you sure there isn't anything that can be done?"

"Nothing, but you can stop worrying about us now. Thanks to you, she'll be fine. Look, can you do just one more thing for us - something very easy this time?"

"Well, say," said Justin.

"Just promise me you wont disturb Krish. Don't open her door – and for pity's sake don't call in anyone to look at her. It's vitally important that she's not disturbed. If you don't feel you can agree I'll have to try to drag myself back there to protect her."

"So, what are you thinking of doing, then, if you don't come back with me?"

"I'll stay here and wait for Krish. It's a lovely night for star gazing. And I'm heading for a very good sleep - the best."

Justin trudged home through the silent streets, too exhausted to do more than put one foot in front of the other. What would have happened if he had decided to stay with Cesare? He had toyed with the idea of pretending to go, then hiding among the rubble to see what happened. But what could possibly happen? For some lunatic reason Cesare seemed to believe that Lucrezia would be in a fit state to visit the ruin after dawn, and lie on what was left of the four-poster bed. What on earth for? They must be members of some weird religion. He'd said the kitchen table looked like an altar and invited her to lie on it, hadn't he? And what did all that crazy talk about Peshawar mean? And being trapped for years under piles of rubble? Had he misheard or misinterpreted? Could Cesare really have said all that, or was this just another nightmare, or a fit of insanity, either his or Cesare's?

When he'd showered off the dirt he walked to the spare room door and listened. Lucrezia was not coughing any more. Carefully he turned the handle, opened it a little and listened. All was eerily quiet. He listened for the noise of her breathing, but there was not a sound. Had some one called an ambulance to take her away? He didn't dare to face the more likely explanation.

He eased the door open a little more and peeped cautiously inside. In the moonlight he could make out a large body, far too big for Lucrezia's. What on earth had happened to her?

Smoke, golden coloured smoke, was spiralling up from the body. As he watched, it began to float towards him like sparkling cigarette smoke. Hurriedly he backed out of the way, and watched it floating past him out of the door and along the corridor towards the lobby. There it turned downwards, flattened itself and streamed out of his flat under the entrance doors.

Something in the room must be on fire. Hit the fire alarm? He cringed at the memory of the time Lucrezia set it off. Did he really have to face all that again? Perhaps he'd better pull himself together, find the source of the fire and see if he could deal with it himself.

He reached towards the light switch, but something froze his hand. Did he really want to investigate the bed? Something told him it may be a disturbing sight. Cesare had told him very firmly not to investigate, so he must be expecting something strange to happen. Should he call the Fire Brigade to help him tackle it?

But there was no heat, no smoky smell or sign of flames, nothing for a fire brigade to tackle. There was only this strangely glowing, golden, scented smoke, flowing steadily up from the bed, out of the guest room and out of his flat under the doors. His stomach lurched, the hairs stirred on the back of his neck and he tensed himself to run. Run where? He was trapped. All he could do was back into a corner and watch. Get a grip, he told himself shakily. It was weird, it was scary, but it seemed to be doing no harm. Maybe he should do as Cesare had said, keep away and pretend he'd kept his promise to leave her door unopened.

But he had let the smoke out. Was that a disaster? He closed the door and waited, hardly daring to breathe. He gave a great sigh of relief as the smoke began to creep out under the door and resumed its route out of his flat. It was going to find its way out, with or without his help.

He staggered into his bedroom on shaky legs and closed the door firmly. Maybe he was so exhausted he was hallucinating. He was just too weary to deal with any more crazy things tonight. He grabbed a bath towel, rolled it up and laid it along the bottom of his door. Whatever you are, you're not coming in here, he vowed silently. Then he collapsed into bed and pulled the sheet over his head.

CHAPTER 34

TOO MANY QUESTIONS

It was not the dawning sun that woke Justin on Friday morning. What woke him was the terrifying sight of Cesare, surfing off the roof straight down towards him, riding a huge roof tile.

"Look out!" he yelled, flinging himself sideways out of the line of fire.

Woumph! All was still. Cautiously he opened his eyes and looked around. It made no sense. White marble and white plaster, lit by brilliant sunlight. He lay sprawling on the floor beside his bed. Blood'n sand! He rubbed his head and inspected himself for damage. Apart from the sweat bands disguising his wounded wrists and ankles, nothing was amiss. He pulled one off to inspect the healing process. Fine. Another day might be enough.

It was a huge effort to drag himself up from the floor. Every muscle ached. Was this how it felt to be old? He sat on the edge of the bed taking stock. Who was where? Had Cesare managed to limp back here? And what about poor Lucrezia? He leapt off the bed as quickly as his aching muscles would allow and struggled into a bathrobe. The door was jammed at the bottom with a rolled up towel. He had sleepwalked through that other crazy nightmare as well. Scared of a bit of smoke? Never!

The guest room door was closed, as he had left it, and there was no sign of any smoke. Obviously that was just another nightmare. He took a deep breath and tentatively opened the door. Thank goodness there was no huge smoking body! But where was Lucrezia? The room was empty. He limped anxiously around the flat, searching every place a human could get into. That ginger tom would find her. He dragged open the terrace door and scanned the rooftops. No cat. And no Lucrezia.

He went back to inspect the guest room properly. This was the first time she had left without making the bed. The sheet lay very wrinkled, not perfectly smooth as she would have left it. Had Cesare come back and taken her away? But surely he would have heard them go.

The waste bin beside the bed was filled to the brim with crumpled sheets of kitchen roll he had given her to cough the blood into. The sight of all that blood had made him furious with Cesare for refusing to call an ambulance. But now there was not a spot of blood on any of the sheets: they were crumpled, but clean as a whistle. How could anyone pull off such a conjuring trick? He looked in the big bin in the kitchen, and the one in the lobby, but the bloodied sheets were not there. But who could have wrinkled up a bin full of clean ones? And why?

Was this another nightmare? Every night these days seemed to be blighted by nightmares, and real life seemed just as scary and confusing. How on earth could he be sure what was real and what was only a nasty dream? Was he losing his marbles? Was this how it felt to be insane?

Tea, that's what he needed. He was running low on tea. A nice big mug would set the world to rights. He put the kettle on, and the radio as well, to bring an air of sanity and normality to his life.

"Bewitched, bothered and bewildered am I," sang the crooner.

"You can say that again!" Justin exploded. So the crooner did.

So, what now? Should he hang around waiting? Waiting for what? Goodness knows where they'd taken Lucrezia. Was Cesare with her, or still hors de combat in the ruin? Perhaps he should go and look there first. Anyway, it was a good time for a jog - well, maybe a walk – or a limp, before it got too hot, and he could go via the Borgia House.

How many times had Lucrezia hurried around there with the ridiculous, inexplicable hope that Cesare would be there in the Royal Suite at 8.0am? But he never was. Well, he'd said he would be waiting there this time, so, had she somehow managed to drag herself around there? What on earth were they hoping to achieve if they did meet there? Perform some weird religious rites?

He gulped down the tea as he pulled on his running togs, then grabbed a handful of biscuits and headed out into the warm and empty streets.

At the Borgia House he slid through the gap in the hoarding and surveyed the scene, so different from the eerie ruin of the night before. There was no longer a piece of sagging top floor threatening to bury the remains of the Royal Suite and the crushed four-poster bed. The level space they had cleared the night before was out of sight, hidden by the blackened timbers they had heaped up near the centre of the courtyard. Right on top of the pile sat the cat, serenely washing itself.

"Miauw!" it said solemnly.

"Miauw to you too," said Justin, carefully picking his way over the debris.The sunlight dazzling his eyes made it hard to see the charred beams and unstable rubble and he almost lost his footing more than once. Sunlight? Since when did sunlight shine upwards from the ground?

Well, they had definitely achieved their rendezvous this time. There they were, lying perfectly still, side by side, like effigies in a medieval church, lighting up the far corner of the blackened ash-filled ruin. They were the wrong colour for an ancient church, a sort of glowing sandy gold instead of the usual greyish stone. It was hard to focus on them: their golden glow dazzled his eyes. He narrowed his eyes and forced himself to stare. Their outlines looked far too big, strangely blurred, misty and swollen,

The hair on the back of his neck was bristling. He stopped in his tracks, not daring to go any nearer. Should he go get help? Something seriously weird was going on. But who do you call to deal with something weird like this? Police? Fire Brigade? What could they do? There was no fire or flood, no riot to quell. The media would be here, quick as a flash, fighting each other to get a scoup like this, catch the first aliens to visit the Earth. No, thank you: media interest was the last thing he wanted. Goodness only knows what Cesare would do to him if he exposed the two of them. He'd issued plenty of warnings, hadn't he?

Calm down; don't do anything rash; just keep out of their sight and watch what they are going to do, he told himself. After all, even if they were aliens, they'd been perfectly civilised house guests and done him no harm whatsoever.

He spotted the bag of clothes that Cesare had brought last night and crept quietly through the ruins to retrieve it. They looked as if they might be needing them.

Once he had the bag in his hand he steeled himself to look at them again. The glow must be fading: it no longer hurt his eyes. He could focus on them better now. They seemed to be shrinking and their outlines were becoming steadily clearer. Heart thumping loudly, he forced himself to climb over more rubble to get a better view. Close to, they looked creepily unreal, lying there totally immobile like waxworks, not even breathing.

He looked around him fearfully. Were members of some alien gang, or some strange religious sect secreted somewhere? Might they try to turn him into an exhibit for Madame Tussauds? Should he try to call the police? If they heard him speak maybe they would come creeping out of their hiding places and grab him before help arrived. He should get the hell out of this place. But that was easier said than done: he had put a lot of debris between himself and the entrance. Why did he go poking his stupid nose into things he didn't understand?

The church clocks began to strike. It was eight o'clock: that magic hour that had obsessed Lucrezia. She looked so perfect lying there, the gorgeous hair flowing over her lovely creamy-white shoulders. He couldn't resist moving a little closer, and closer. And Cesare too. He could push David off his pedestal and climb up there to replace him. Surely few would maintain it was not a fair exchange - except for the big bushy beard. But they were just too perfect, their skin evenly coloured, without a single blemish. That was what always gave waxworks away, wasn't it? They looked far too perfect. How different his hands looked from the scratched and bleeding mess they were in last night. Last night? It was only - how long? Less than six hours ago. Had he grown that huge beard in only six hours? He had trimmed his beard only yesterday afternoon. Crazy. But what were these figures? Had someone copied them in wax, or, more horrifically, covered them with wax and smothered them? Was he watching the end of a process?

Suddenly he almost fell over backwards. Was he imagining things, or had the waxworks started moving? Weak at the knees, he scrambled to the nearest lump of rubble he could sit on, and watched, transfixed.

The waxworks were definitely moving now, breathing almost imperceptibly at first, then more and more deeply.

Cesare took a deep breath and opened his eyes. Then he turned his head and smiled at Lucrezia.

"Wake up, Sleeping Beauty, wake up!"

"Isn't the Prince supposed to kiss her first?" she

murmured, turning her face towards him.

"Well, I think that could be arranged," he grinned, rolled over and pulled her into his arms.

Justin cringed with embarrassment and looked away. He ought not to be watching a married couple in the nuddie, hugging each other like this. Fortunately for him the cat chose that moment to jump right on top of them and snuggle in between them, but anyway they seemed to have less embarrassing things on their minds.

"So, here we go again, my love," she said. "Pity we can't find some way of keeping our clothes on. Could we grow nice thick fur like Ginger?" She gave the cat a hug.

"And end up in a zoo – if they didn't shoot us dead. Wonder what they'd label us. Humanoid black panther? Pale-faced orang utan?"

"We could grow white fur, be abominable snowmen," she suggested. "No, not in Rome in August, I suppose."

Cesare sat up and surveyed the blackened ruins of his home. "Nowhere to shelter and nowhere to go - -."

He had the most beautiful singing voice, but what didn't the lucky man have? And he had Lucrezia as well.

"Well, we can't leave here nudo come un verme, can we?" She sat up and looked around. "What are we going to do? Creep out tonight and raid people's washing lines? How will you manage a whole day with nothing to eat? We need to find somewhere to hide. Maybe part of the basement might be habitable. We could live down there like rats and go out raiding the dustbins in the moonlight."

"You can't get into the big street dustbins nowadays. They're all sealed up like bank vaults. Poor old rats haven't a chance."

"Poor old rats? Aren't you the rats' worst enemy."

"Not the little furry ones. Got a very soft spot for them.

When you're chained up in a dungeon they make nice pets. But you've no need to worry about clothes. Justin's put a bagful somewhere around here. There's a frock for you, and some running kit for me. So, first stop the bank. Then we can get something to eat."

"How are we going to prove who we are? Oh, we said we'd phone Medici's, ask them to contact the bank and try to fix things for us, but it might take days. And how are we going to get a phone? Should we ask the Marchettis for a loan? I gave them lots of stuff for their shop so they surely shouldn't mind. Then we can go to the flea market and get a few essentials. Which of the flea markets open on Thursdays? Can you remember?"

"Via Sannio? Must be open on a Thursday. You know, next to San Giovanni."

"Pity it's Friday, then." Justin found his voice at last.

"Friday? No, it's Thursday. Hello, Justin. You've not been here all night, have you?"

Both of them stared at him with expressions of alarm.

"No, I went home for some sleep, as you suggested. Just got here."

They stared at him, then at each other, then visibly relaxed.

"He was great last night, Krish. Worked his socks off getting the bed clear. Look at that huge pile of rubble. We moved the lot last night."

"Justin, you really are a sweety. Come here for a hug."

How could he refuse? Embarrassment made his flesh crawl as he hugged her lovely naked body with her husband looking on in obvious amusement.

"I'll get you your clothes," he mumbled, and hurriedly produced the bag. Ridiculous, wasn't it? He'd spent days trying to get her clothes off, and now he couldn't wait to get them back on. "It really is Friday," he insisted. "What did you do on Wednesday?"

"Are you sure?" They looked to be genuinely puzzled.

"Absolutely. Tuesday afternoon was the fire. Yes?"

They nodded hesitantly.

"Then yesterday, Wednesday, you dug us out. Thanks again, Justin," said Cesare. "We promise you won't have to do that again – "

"No! Correction! On Thursday I dug you out. If I'd tried that on Wednesday I'd have been roasted alive. This place was hot as hell, flickering and smouldering like billyho. It was hot enough to roast an ox. So where were you two on Wednesday?" And what the f*** is going on today, he was dying to ask, but just one million dollar question at a time.

They looked at each other in silence, with furrowed brows. Lucrezia must be wracking her brains, trying out the most plausible lies. It would surely be a lie, wouldn't it? It always was with Lucrezia. Why bother to ask her? Why not make up some ridiculous scenario of his own?

They were looking at each other wide-eyed. They looked genuinely amazed and mystified. Simultaneously they gave the familiar Italian shrug of helplessness and looked him forlornly in the eye.

"Haven't a clue. Did you spot us anywhere?"

"No, I jolly well didn't. And how the hell did you get out of that death trap front room and end up under the rubble at the opposite end of the house? Was there a secret door? And another and another right to the Royal Suite?"

They stared at each other again. Then she rallied a little and nodded. "Yes, lots of secret doors. They always have them in really old houses, don't they?"

"And why are you two as fit as a fiddle? I thought you were not long for this world last night. You were coughing your bleeding lungs out and covered in cuts and scratches, but just look at you now: perfect as waxworks. How the hell did you work that trick? And how do you grow a beard like Methusalah in less than six hours? And what was all this stuff this morning, lying around glowing like fires and looking as dead as door nails? You've got a lot of explaining to do."

They stared at him silently, then looked sadly at each other and sighed.

"Cesare, do you have to? He's been so kind and helpful to me when I really needed a friend – and he dug us out as well and moved all this debris. And he took us in yesterday and cleaned us up and -- What would we have done without him? Can't we think of some other way out of this?"

Was she pleading for his life?!

"Hey, hang on a minute," gasped Justin, tensing himself ready to run for it. But he hadn't a chance, had he? Cesare would grab him in seconds, and have his guts for garters, wouldn't he? Oh Grief! Why hadn't he kept his big mouth shut? They could easily dispose of a body in this huge blackened ruin.

"What did you do with those photos, Krish?" asked Cesare, fixing him with cold blue eyes. He had brought his hands together, slowly tapping the edge of the right hand down into the left palm. Hadn't she said he didn't normally use a knife? It seemed he didn't need one. "Are you sure they're safe in the bank?"

"Well, some in the bank and some with Medici's. I posted them off on Tuesday morning. And some to Vetriano's as well. We're well covered. No need to worry, surely? Justin has no more desire to be plastered all over the media than we have, have you, Justin?"

"Are you threatening me?" Justin's voice was hoarse.

"Depends," said Cesare. "Are you threatening us? We can't afford to get ourselves plastered all over the media either. You can surely understand that now. So what are you - what *were* you thinking of doing about us?"

"*Doing* about you? Well, what could I - ? I've got no plans - have you?" he stuttered.

"We need to think about it."

Justin took a deep breath and decided to show a bit of spirit - it might be the last thing he ever did..

"Look, just for my own satisfaction, whatever you decide you must do, just tell me what you two have done that makes you so keen not to be outed?"

They looked at him in silence for a while, wide-eyed, then at each other. Finally it was Lucrezia who spoke.

"It's not so much what we've done, it's what we *are*. You've just told us you've seen all that for yourself."

"So, what *are* you?" he whispered hoarsely. "Aliens?"

They both took deep breaths and hesitated, then gave that familiar Italian gesture of helplessness.

"Goodness knows!" they said in unison.

"We didn't arrive with labels round our necks," said Cesare.

"And we've never found anyone to ask," said Lucrezia. "But we're pretty sure that if Big Pharma ever get their hands on us, we'll be chained up in cages forever in secret laboratories. They'll try murdering us in every possible way, trying to find out what makes us tick, so – you see - "

"What price immortality?" asked Cesare.

****

Did Justin survive?

Read Book 2

BOOK 2:

GOODNESS KNOWS HOW!

Cesare, Marquis of Monrosso, and his 'unusual' family struggle to save their idyllic stately home on Lake Como from bankruptcy. Justin Chase's nefarious computer-hacking skills prove vital, and he gamely lends a hand with their amusing money-making schemes, hampered by their mischievous free-range farm animals - and a pack of wolves.

In desperation, Lucrezia returns to Fallujah, and proves even deadlier than Cesare. Finally her twin, Kerallyn, Justin's new girlfriend, disappears, to surface as a gruesome new exhibit in Rome's Modern Art Museum.

****

Can they rescue Kerallyn – without giving their deadly secret away? Read:

BOOK 3:

BOOK 3

GOODNESS KNOWS WHERE!

Justin Chase's computer-hacking skills prove useful once again, enticing out 'Survivors' lying low in some of the World's most fascinating places. Can he form them into a mutual help society, or are they too dangerous to handle?

The 'Survivors' at Monrosso find thrilling new ways to make their idyllic country estate pay its way, despite the protected wolves. And they must now rebuild their palace in Rome as a tourist attraction.

But first, superhuman methods are needed to rescue poor Kerallyn from her perspex coffin in Rome's Modern Art Museum – without giving the game away.

BOOKS 4, 5 AND 6

Books 4, 5 and 6 bring in more 'survivors' unearthed by Justin Chase, not all of them welcome additions to the family. And how do you get rid of a 'survivor' if he proves to be a threat to all mankind?